Shifting Calder
Wind

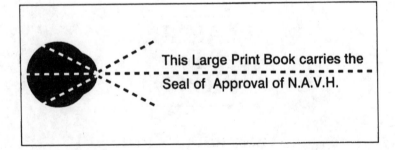

Shifting Calder Wind

JANET DAILEY

Waterville, Maine

Published in 2004 by arrangement with
Kensington Books, an imprint of Kensington Publishing Corp.

The text of this Large Print edition is unabridged.
Other aspects of the book may vary from the original edition.

Set in 16 pt. Plantin by Ramona Watson.

Printed in the United States on permanent paper.

The Library of Congress has cataloged the Thorndike Press® edition as follows:

Dailey, Janet.
    Shifting Calder wind / Janet Dailey.
      p. cm.
    ISBN 0-7862-5652-4 (lg. print : hc : alk. paper)
    ISBN 1-59413-019-1 (lg. print : sc : alk. paper)
    1. Calder family (Fictitious characters) — Fiction.
2. Ranch life — Fiction.   3. Montana — Fiction.   4. Large
type books. I. Title.
PS3554.A29S47 2003
  813′.54—dc21   2003053317

Shifting Calder Wind

PART ONE

A shifting wind,
It calls to him,
As a Calder fades
And his mind grows dim.

Chapter One

A blackness roared around him. He struggled to surface from it, somehow knowing that if he didn't, he would die. Sounds reached him as if coming from a great distance — a shout, the scrape of shoes on pavement, the metallic slam of a car door and the sharp clap of a gunshot.

Someone was trying to kill him.

He had to get out of there. The instant he tried to move the blackness swept over him with dizzying force. He heard the revving rumble of a car engine starting up. Unable to rise, he rolled away from the sound as spinning tires burned rubber and another shot rang out.

Lights flashed in a bright glare. There was danger in them, he knew. He had to reach the shadows. Fighting the weakness that swam through his limbs, he crawled away from the light.

He felt dirt beneath his hand and dug his fingers into it. His strength sapped, he lay there a moment, trying to orient himself, and to determine the location of the man trying to kill him. But the searing pain in his head made it hard to think logically. He reached up and felt the warm wetness on his face. That's when he knew he had been shot. Briefly his fingers touched the deep crease the bullet had ripped along the side of his head. Pain instantly washed over him in black waves.

Aware that he could lose consciousness at any second, either from the head wound or the blood loss, he summoned the last vestiges of his strength and threw himself deeper into the darkness. With blood blurring his vision, he made out the shadowy outlines of a post and railing. It looked to be a corral of some sort. He pushed himself toward it, wanting any kind of barrier, no matter how flimsy, between himself and his pursuer.

There was a whisper of movement just to his left. Alarm shot through him, but he couldn't seem to make his muscles react. He was too damned weak. He knew it even as he listed sideways and saw the low-crouching man in a cowboy hat with a pistol in his hand.

Instead of shooting, the cowboy grabbed for him with his free arm. "Come on. Let's get outa here, old man," the cowboy whispered with urgency. "He's up on the catwalk working himself into a better position."

He latched onto the cowboy's arm and staggered drunkenly to his feet, his mind still trying to wrap itself around that phrase "old man." Leaning heavily on his rescuer, he stumbled forward, battling the woodenness of his legs.

After an eternity of seconds, the cowboy pushed him into the cab of a pickup and closed the door. He sagged against the seat and closed his eyes, unable to summon another ounce of strength. Dimly he was aware of the cowboy slipping behind the wheel and the engine starting up. It was followed by the vibrations of movement.

Through slitted eyes, he glanced in the side mirror but saw nothing to indicate they were being followed. They were out of danger now. Unbidden came the warning that it was only temporary; whoever had tried to kill him would try again.

Who had it been? And why? He searched for the answers and failed to come up with any.

Thinking required too much effort. Choosing to conserve the remnants of his strength, he glanced out the window at the unfamiliar buildings that flanked the street.

"Where are we?" His voice had a throaty rasp to it.

"According to the signs, there should be a hospital somewhere ahead of us," the cowboy replied. "I'll drop you off close to the emergency entrance."

"No." It was a purely instinctual reply.

"Mister, that head wound needs tending. You've lost a bunch of blood —"

"No." He started to shake his head in emphasis, but at the first movement, the world started spinning.

The pickup's speed slowed perceptibly. "Don't tell me you're wanted by the law?" The cowboy turned a sharp, speculating glance on him.

Was he? For the second time, he came up against a wall of blankness. It was another answer he didn't know, so he avoided the question.

"He's bound to know I was hit, so he'll expect me to get medical attention. The nearest hospital will be the first place he would check."

"You're probably right about that," the cowboy agreed. "So where do you want to go?"

Where? Where? Where? The question hammered at him. But it was impossible to answer because he didn't know what the

12

hell town they were in. That discovery brought a wave of panic, one that intensified when he realized he didn't know his own name.

He clamped down tightly on the panic and said, "I don't know yet. Let me think."

He closed his eyes and strained to dredge up some scrap of a memory. But he was empty of any. Who was he? What was he? Where was he? Every question bounced around in the void. His head pounded anew. He felt himself slipping deeper into the blackness and lacked the strength to fight against it.

He simultaneously became conscious of a bright light pressing against his eyes and the chirping of a bird. Groggily he opened his eyes and saw filtered sunlight coming through the curtained window. It was daylight, and his last conscious memory had been of riding in a truck through night-darkened streets.

Instantly alert, he shot a searching glance around the room. The curtains at the window and the rose-patterned paper on the walls confirmed what his nose had already told him: he wasn't in a hospital. He was in a bedroom, one that was strange to him.

His glance stopped on the cowboy slumped in an old wicker rocking chair in the corner, his hat tipped over the top of his face, his chest rising and falling in an even rhythm. Surmising the man was his rescuer from the night before, he studied the cleanly chiseled line of the man's jaw and the nut brown color of his hair, details he hadn't noticed during the previous night's darkness and confusion. The man's yoked-front shirt looked new, but the jeans and the boots both showed signs of wear.

He threw back the bedcovers and started to rise. Pain slammed him back onto the pillow and ripped a groan from him. In a reflexive action, he lifted a hand to his head and felt the gauze strips that swaddled it.

In a flash the cowboy rolled to his feet and crossed to the bed. "Just lay back and be still. You won't be going anywhere for a while, old man."

He bristled in response. "That's the second time you've called me an old man."

After a pulse beat of silence, the cowboy replied in droll apology, "I didn't mean any offense by it, but you aren't exactly a young fella."

Unable to recall who he was, let alone how old he was, he grunted a nonanswer.

"Where am I, anyway? Your place?"

"It belongs to some kinfolk on my mother's side," the cowboy answered.

He studied the cowboy's blue eyes and easy smile. There was a trace of boyish good looks behind the stubble of a night's beard growth and the sun-hardened features. A visual search found no sign of the pistol the cowboy had been carrying last night.

"Who are you?" His eyes narrowed on the cowboy.

There was a fractional pause, a coolness suddenly shuttering the cowboy's blue eyes. "I think a better question is who are you?"

"Maybe it is," he stalled, hoping a name might come to him, but none did. "But I'd like to know the name of the man who quite likely saved my life last night so I can thank him properly."

"You dodged that question about as deftly as a politician." Blue eyes glinted in quiet speculation. "But I don't think that's what you are. You strike me as a man used to asking the questions rather than answering them."

"Now you're the one dodging the question."

"My friends call me Laredo. What do your friends call you?"

His head pounded with the strain of trying to recall. Automatically he touched the bandages again.

Observing the action and the continued silence, the cowboy called Laredo guessed, "You can't remember, can you?"

"I — don't you know who I am?"

"Nope. But I'll tell you what I do know — the material in that suit you were wearing wasn't cheap, and those were custom-made boots on your feet. It took money to buy them, which leads me to think you aren't a poor man. There's no Texas drawl in your voice, which tells me you aren't from around here, at least not originally."

"We're in Texas?" he repeated for confirmation. "Where?"

"Southwest of Fort Worth."

"Fort Worth." It sounded familiar to him, but he didn't know why. "Is that where we were last night?" he asked, recalling the city streets they had driven through.

"Yeah. In Old Downtown, next to the stockyards."

"There's an old cemetery not far from there," he said with a strange feeling of certainty.

"You couldn't prove it by me," Laredo said with an idle shrug of his broad shoulders.

He fired a quick glance at the cowboy. "You aren't from around here?"

"No. I'm just passing through. Now that it looks like you're going to live, I'll be leaving soon."

"Not yet." He reached out to stop him with a suddenness that sent the room spinning again. Subsiding weakly against the pillow, he swallowed back the rising nausea.

"I told you to lie still," Laredo reminded him. "That bullet gouged a deep path. It wouldn't surprise me if it grazed your skull."

He fought through the swirling pain, insisting, "Before you go, I have to know about last night. The man who shot me — did you see him?"

"I guess if you don't know who you are, you don't know who he is either, do you?" Laredo guessed. "I'm afraid I can't help you much. All I saw was the figure of a man with a scoped rifle. I couldn't tell you if he was old or young, tall or short, just that he didn't look fat."

"Tell me what you saw." He closed his eyes, hoping something would trigger a memory.

After a slight pause, Laredo began, "I'm not sure what it was that first caught my eye. Maybe it was the car door being open and all the interior light flooding from it while the rest of the parking lot was so dark. You were standing next to it facing another man. His back was to me so I didn't get a look at him. It took me a second to realize you were being robbed. He did a good job of it, too. You don't have a lick of identification on you — no wallet, no watch, no ring. Nothing. He even took your spare change. Right now you don't have a cent to your name."

"But this robber wasn't the man who shot me." He recalled Laredo mentioning a man with a scoped rifle. He couldn't imagine a common thief carrying one.

"No, he wasn't. The shot came from behind you. The second I heard I knew it didn't come from any handgun. You dropped like a rock. Your robber jumped in the car and hightailed it out of there."

"I half remember hearing a vehicle peel out. Somebody yelled. Was that you?"

"Yup. I wanted your sniper to know somebody else was in the area. About the same time I saw you moving so I knew you weren't dead. He snapped off a shot in my direction. I saw the muzzle flash and fired back."

"Do you usually carry a gun?"

18

Amusement tugged at the corner of his mouth. "Like I said, we're in Texas, and the definition of gun control here is a steady aim."

He managed a brief smile at Laredo's small joke. "What time was this?"

"Late. Somewhere between eleven and midnight."

He wondered what he was doing there at that hour. "Aren't there some bars in the area?"

"A bunch of them."

From somewhere outside came the familiar lowing of cattle. "Are we in the country?"

Laredo nodded. "The Ludlow ranch. It's a small spread, not much more than a hundred acres. It hardly deserves to be called a ranch."

"Why did you bring me here?"

"I didn't have many choices. I probably should have taken you to a hospital like I first planned. But with you being unconscious, I couldn't just drop you off at the door. Taking you inside meant fielding a lot of questions I didn't want to answer. So I brought you here." He allowed a small smile to show. "I figured if you died, I could always bury you in the back forty with no one the wiser."

"Except the Ludlows."

"I wasn't worried about Hattie talking."

"Who is Hattie?" The hot pounding in his head increased, making it difficult to string more than two thoughts together.

"Since Ed died, she owns the place." After a slight pause, Laredo observed, "Your head's bothering you, isn't it?"

"Some." He was reluctant to admit to more than that.

"No need in overdoing it. Why don't you get some rest? We can talk more later if you want. In the meantime, I'll see if I can rustle you up something to eat."

"Did you say you were leaving soon?"

"I did. But I won't be going just yet." Moving away from the bed, Laredo crossed to the window and lowered the shade, darkening the room.

He closed his eyes against the pain, but it wasn't so easy to shut out the blankness of his memory. Who the hell was he? Why couldn't he remember?

He slept but fitfully, waking often to hear the occasional stirrings of activity in other parts of the house. The instant he heard the snick of the bedroom door latch, he opened his eyes, coming fully alert.

He focused on the woman who filled the doorway, a tray balanced in her hand. She

20

was tall, easily close to six feet, with strong, handsome features that showed the leathering of long hours spent in the sun. She wore boots and jeans and a plaid blouse tucked in at the waist, revealing the firmly packed figure of a mature and active woman.

"You're awake. That's good." Her voice had a no-nonsense ring to it, kind but firm. "I brought you some soup. I thought it would be best to keep you to a liquid diet at first."

"You must be Hattie," he guessed as she approached the bed.

"That's right. I assume you still don't know who you are so I won't ask your name." She set the food tray on the nightstand next to the bed. "Do you think you can manage to sit up or do you want some help?"

"I can manage." Breathing in the broth's rich beefy aroma, he felt the first rumblings of hunger. With slow care, he levered himself into a sitting position. Once he was sitting upright, Hattie slipped a pair of pillows behind him for a backrest. "Thanks. The soup smells good."

"It's homemade." She set the tray on his lap. "Is there anything else you need?"

"My clothes."

"Sorry, Duke, but I'm afraid they are pretty well ruined. I have your shirt soaking, trying to get the blood out of it. Maybe a professional cleaner can get the stains out of your suit, but —"

"Why did you call me that?" He stared at her curiously.

"What?" She gave him a blank look.

"Just now you called me Duke."

"I did?" She seemed almost embarrassed, then shrugged it off. "I guess it's because you remind me of him."

"Who?" he persisted, determined to know who it was he resembled, aware it might mean nothing — or everything.

She looked him square in the eyes. "John Wayne. The Duke. You do know who he is?"

"The movie actor." He dipped the spoon into the soup.

"That's right."

"And you think I look like him." It started him wondering about the face that would look back at him from a mirror.

"It's not so much that you look like him, but you remind me of him," she replied, then explained: "You're both big-shouldered and broad-chested with craggy features. A take-charge type who isn't afraid of rough-and-tumble." She cocked her head to one side. "Does that help?"

"Not really," he answered, more annoyed than disappointed.

"I wouldn't worry about it too much." She studied him thoughtfully. "Amnesia caused by a head trauma is usually temporary. Most of the time, memory comes back in bits and snatches, but in rare instances, it can return full-blown."

He caught the professional phrases she used. "You sound like you know something about it."

"Before I switched careers to become a lady rancher, I was a registered nurse."

"So that's why Laredo brought me here last night." It made sense now.

Hattie smiled in a dismissive way. "He knows I have a weakness for taking in wounded animals and strays."

"Where is Laredo?"

"He went to town to get some clothes for you."

"I got the impression that he might have had some trouble with the law. Has he?"

Her mouth curved in a smile that didn't match the cool, measuring look of her eyes. "Laredo said you asked a lot more questions than you answered." She was taking her time, sizing him up. He had the feeling this was one woman who made few mistakes in judgment. "If" — she stressed the word — "Laredo has ever had any trouble with the law, it happened on the other side of the border. One of those cases of being at the wrong place at the wrong time with the wrong people, I suppose. If he wants you to know more than that, he can tell you himself. But I think you have already discovered that he's the kind of man you want at your side when there's trouble."

"We both know I wouldn't be alive today if it weren't for him." He stated it as a fact, without any show of emotion.

"I hope you remember that." She started to turn away then swung back. "As soon as Laredo gets back with a set of clothes for you, I'll bring them in. They probably won't be the quality you are used to wearing. Just jeans, shirts, and some underclothes —"

"They will be fine," he cut across her words, a little irritated that she seemed to think he believed he was above wearing ordinary work clothes. "I'll pay you back as soon —" He broke off the sentence, recalling that Laredo had told him he didn't have a cent to his name. It grated to think he was dependent on someone else.

"Don't worry about the money right now. Just eat your soup." Hattie pointed to the bowl in an admonishing gesture. "And don't try to get up by yourself. With all the blood you've lost, you're likely to be as wobbly as a newborn calf. I'll come back later to pick up the tray."

The first few spoons of soup took the edge off his hunger, but he ate every bit of it, determined to regain his strength. Yet the effort tired him. Eyes closed, he relaxed against the supporting pillows.

All the unanswered questions came swirling back. It took some effort, but he managed to ignore them and concentrated instead on the few facts he knew about himself, searching for something that felt familiar and right.

A pickup rattled into the ranch yard. He listened to the creak of its door opening and closing, followed by the sound of footsteps approaching the house. Already they had a familiar sound to them, and he guessed they belonged to Laredo.

Within minutes the cowboy walked into the bedroom, toting a big sack. Laredo's eyes were quick to notice the empty soup bowl.

"Good to the last drop, I see," Laredo observed.

"It filled the empty places," he replied and glanced at the sack. "Hattie said you were going to pick up some clothes for me.

Do you have some pants in there?"

"Sure do." Laredo tossed the sack on the bed and lifted off the food tray. "I'll get this out of the way first."

He knew better than to make any sudden movements that might start his head spinning again, and pushed himself off the pillows with care. The paper sack rustled as Laredo dug into it and pulled out a pair of Levi's. He swung his bare legs out of the bed and reached for the jeans.

"I'll give you a hand getting into these," Laredo said. "I don't want you taking a nosedive onto the floor. In case you don't know it, Duke, you're a load to pick up."

"That's what Hattie called me," he remembered.

"Until you can remember your own name, Duke is as good as any." Laredo worked the pants legs over his feet and kept a steadying hand on him when he stood to pull them the rest of the way up. "And you didn't take it too kindly when I called you an old man."

He saw the mischievous glint in the cowboy's blue eyes and took no offense. "No man likes to be called old. You'll find that out . . . " he paused and swept an assessing glance over Laredo. It was difficult to pinpoint the cowboy's age, but he thought he

26

was on the long side of thirty. "And it won't be too many more years before you do."

"I'm afraid you're right about that," Laredo conceded with a rueful grin.

The movement had started his head pounding in earnest again. Gritting his teeth against it, he looked around. "Is there a bathroom close by?"

"Just down the hall. I'd better walk with you, though. The house is old and the floor is uneven," Laredo warned.

Unsteady on his legs, he had to rely on Laredo's support more than he liked as they crossed the bedroom and entered the short, narrow hall. When Laredo pushed open a door on the left, he waved off any further assistance and entered the bathroom alone.

After relieving himself, he shifted to the sink and inspected the face in the tall mirror above it. It was rugged and raw-boned with age lines carved deep around the mouth and eyes. Layers of gauze were wrapped around his head like a turban. The dark brown hair below it showed a heavy salting of gray. He studied every detail, but the brown eyes looking back at him belonged to a stranger.

"Old man," Laredo had called him. The

gray hair and age lines seemed to bear that out, but there was plenty of muscle tone in his broad chest and shoulders, indicating he still had ample strength and vitality. He examined the variety of scars on his torso. Most of them were old and faded, with a straightness to them that suggested surgical incisions. But one, along the side of his ribs, had a fresh look to it that suggested it wasn't much more than a year old.

But he had no memory of how he had gotten any of them.

His own mind bombarded him with questions that had no answers. Who was he? Where did he live? What did he do? Did he have a wife? A family? Was anyone looking for him?

There was a light rap on the door. "Are you all right, Duke?"

He turned away from the mirror and kept a steadying hand on the wall as he moved to the door. "I'm fine."

Laredo ran a sharp eye over him when he opened the door. "What took you so long?"

"I was trying to get used to that face in the mirror."

"It must be hell not being able to remember who you are," Laredo said, more as a statement of fact than an expression of sympathy. "I'll give you a hand back to bed."

"I'm going to sit up for a while."

"Are you sure?" There was skepticism in the side glance Laredo sent him. "You're still pretty weak."

"I won't get any stronger laying in that bed."

"That's true enough."

"If Hattie has any coffee made, I could use a cup."

"I'll check." Once Laredo had him settled in the corner rocking chair, he went to see about the coffee. He returned with two mugs, handed one to the man he called Duke and lifted the other. "I thought I'd join you, if that's okay."

"Have a seat." He motioned toward the bed. Laredo sat sideways on the mattress, his body angled toward the corner.

"So what are your plans?" Laredo raised the mug and took a cautious sip of the steaming coffee.

"Does it matter? You'll be leaving soon."

"You are definitely good at dodging questions. Maybe you are a politician," Laredo said with a grin.

"Why be one when you can buy one?" The words were barely out of his mouth when he knew he was echoing a sentiment he had heard before. He could almost hear the man's voice.

"That has the ring of experience talking," Laredo observed. "And judging from that suit you were wearing, you probably have the bucks to buy a half dozen politicians."

"If that's the case, then somebody should be wondering where I am. They may already be trying to track me down."

"You mean someone other than the guy who tried to kill you," Laredo inserted dryly.

"Yes, he's the wild card in the deck," he murmured thoughtfully.

"Something tells me he's doing a little sweating about now, wondering whether you are dead or alive. It's bound to be driving him crazy that you haven't turned up anywhere yet."

"He could have cut and run."

"It's possible, but not likely."

It was the certainty in Laredo's voice that prompted him to challenge him. "Why not?"

"Because he isn't sure yet how scared he should run. He knows you were hit, and so far you haven't surfaced, which has to make him think you died. If I were him, I would hang around just long enough to find out."

"It takes a man with cool nerve to do that." And, he reflected, it said a lot about Laredo that he thought that way.

"I think he already established the coolness of his nerve when he laid in wait for you. It was pure luck on your part that he didn't succeed." Laredo idly swirled the coffee in his mug. "It strikes me that you have two options. You can either stick close to the ranch and wait for your memory to come back —"

"That could take days, weeks — even months," he broke in, his voice sharp with impatience.

"I had a feeling that's the way you would react." A small smile edged the corners of Laredo's mouth. "At the same time, if you show up around the old Stockyards, asking questions and trying to find somebody who might recognize you, you would be tipping your hand — maybe even giving him another chance at you."

"I know," he acknowledged grimly, aware he was between that proverbial rock and a hard place.

"There's another alternative," Laredo said.

"What's that?" He studied the cowboy with a watchful eye.

"I could do the asking."

"I thought you were supposed to be leaving soon. That's what you said."

Laredo moved his shoulders in an indifferent shrug. "If I'm a few days late crossing the border, my friends won't worry about me."

"I see." Common sense told him that Laredo's suggestion was a sound one, yet it grated on him that he would have no active part in it.

"I know you hate the idea of sitting here and waiting, but it's the most practical solution. By now others will have noticed you are missing and started asking questions. It wouldn't arouse anybody's suspicions if I nosed around, too."

"No, it wouldn't," he agreed. "But I can't help wondering why you want to involve yourself in my problem."

"Curiosity, pure and simple," Laredo replied. "I can't help wondering who you are. Besides," he added in jest, "I saved your life. The way I figure it that makes me responsible for you."

Hattie walked into the bedroom, saw Laredo sitting on the bed, and made a sharp pivot toward Duke. "What are you doing out of bed?"

"Drinking coffee."

"You can finish that in bed." She plucked the mug from his hand and set it on the dresser top before he could raise an objection.

"I've laid in it long enough," he protested.

"I'll be the judge of that," Hattie informed him. "And I say this afternoon you rest. Tonight you can have supper at the table with us."

"Not me, Hattie," Laredo inserted. "I won't be here for supper."

"You're leaving, then?" Her expression became shuttered to conceal her disappointment at the news.

"Not permanently," Laredo replied. "I'm going into Fort Worth and see if I can find anybody who remembers Duke."

"You'll be careful, won't you?" she asked in all seriousness.

"I always am." He matched her tone and look.

Chapter Two

Lightning raced in jagged streaks from the black clouds. On the heels of it, thunder boomed and rolled across the plains of eastern Montana as the rain fell in sheets, driven by a whipping wind.

The patrol car's windshield wipers worked at high speed, their rapid rhythm adding to the tension. Acting Sheriff Logan Echohawk gripped the steering wheel with both hands as the headlight beams struggled to penetrate the curtain of rain and the premature darkness beyond it. The high, hard slash of his cheekbones and the pitch-black color of his hair spoke to his Sioux ancestry, but it was the gray of his eyes and the expression in them that always drew a second look, usually a wary one.

Just in time he spotted the intersecting side road and slowed the patrol car to make the turn into the east entrance of the Calder ranch. A brilliant flash of lightning briefly illuminated the sign that hung over the road. Logan had only a glimpse of the letters that spelled out the name CALDER CATTLE COMPANY before he passed under it. It was an unprepossessing entrance for a ranch that encompassed nearly six hundred square miles within its boundaries, making it roughly the size of Rhode Island. From the east-gate entrance, it was a forty-mile drive to the ranch headquarters.

And Logan knew the drive would never seem longer than tonight. He wasn't eager to get there, not with the news he had to bring them. It was a close-knit group that inhabited the Triple C Ranch, as it was better known. Most of the hands were descendants of cowboys who had worked for the ranch's founder, Chase Benteen Calder, who had staked a claim to the land well over a hundred years ago.

The history of the ranch was long and legendary. Although relatively new to the area, Logan knew much of it. Over three years ago he had married Cat Calder, daughter to Chase Calder, a grandson and namesake of the ranch's founder.

This last year had been a rough one for everyone on the ranch, but especially the family, who were still mourning the loss of the son and heir, Ty Calder. His death had been tragic and violent, and the motive for it was one that still made no sense to Logan. But the twisted logic of a killer rarely stood up to scrutiny.

Ty's death had been a crushing blow to Chase; no man ever expected to outlive his children. But the heavier burden had fallen to Ty's widow, Jessy. Not only did she have the difficult task of raising their three-year-old twins, Trey and Laura, by herself, but also the responsibility of running the Triple C would ultimately pass to her. No one doubted, however, that Jessy had the makings of an able leader. Born and raised on the Triple C, she could ride and rope with the best of them. Under Chase's tutelage, she was rapidly learning to handle men as easily as she did cattle.

Lightning forked from the clouds in blinding tongues of light, briefly illuminating the vast expanse of treeless plains. A crash of thunder shook the air. Logan kept his eyes on the dirt road ahead of him. As violent as the storm was, he knew it was nothing like the one that was about to break over the Triple C. The news he was bringing was likely to shake the ranch to its very foundation.

At the Triple C headquarters, light blazed from the windows of the barns, sheds, commissary, and cottages that housed the hired help. More light pooled around the towering yard lights, its brightness dimmed by the slanted sheets of rain. In the darkness of the storm, the gleam from the multitude of ranch buildings gave the headquarters the appearance of a small town.

Dominating it all was The Homestead, an imposing two-story house, fronted by towering columns, that stood on a high knoll. Built on the site of the ranch's original homestead, resulting in its name, the Calder family home had long been the heart of the ranch. From it, the ranch business was conducted just as it had been for over one hundred years.

Guests were few and far between in this empty corner of Montana where the nearest city was hundreds of miles away. But those who did drop by were always welcomed. Tonight was no exception.

Another booming clap of thunder rattled the windows in the den. Steeped in the ranch's storied history, the room had become the traditional place to entertain guests.

John Montgomery Markham, brother to the Earl of Stanfield, stood at a front window, watching the jagged lightning bolts that streaked out of the dark clouds. Idly he took a sip of the iceless bourbon and water in his glass. Tall and athletically trim, he turned from the window with an easy grace.

His smile reached across the room to Jessy, who stood near the massive stone fireplace. "A fascinating display. I have heard a great deal about the ferocity of your summer thunderstorms. It far exceeds anything we get in England."

"You'll get used to them now that you have taken up residence in our part of the country," Jessy replied, referring to his purchase of the Gilmore ranch four months ago, which made him the Triple C's newest neighbor.

"I expect I will," he conceded. "Still, it's lucky I arrived when I did. I should hate to be driving in that."

"It can definitely be dangerous, but these storms tend to be fast travelers. Fortunately the worst should be over soon."

John Montgomery Markham, who preferred to be called Monte, was quick to catch her choice of adverbs. "Why 'fortunately'?"

"Because we lose more cattle to lightning strikes than any other cause. In flat country like this, they stand out like lightning rods."

"I hadn't considered that possibility," he admitted with typical frankness. "It seems each time I visit the Triple C I learn something new about raising cattle in the American West."

His openness to new methods or ideas was just one of the many things Jessy had come to admire about their new neighbor. Another was his failure to adopt western attire since moving to Montana. No blue jeans, cowboy boots, or Stetson hat for him. Instead he opted for English riding boots, jodhpurs, and an Aussie hat. Monte Markham was English through and through, and proud of it.

Jessy ran her glance over his aquiline features, thinking, not for the first time, that they reminded her of a poet or a scholar. His brown hair had a touch of red in it, and his hazel eyes occasionally held the glint of his dry British wit. Like herself he was barely forty and single, in his case the result of a divorce several years ago.

It had been almost two years since Ty was killed, and the pain of that was just as strong. Ty had been her first love. There were times, especially at night, when she ached to feel the touch of his hand and the strength of his arms around her. She also knew it was natural that she would. She was a woman with the needs of a woman. What with the ranch to run and two children to raise, most of the time she successfully pushed them aside. Yet at odd moments they surfaced.

"There is always something to learn in the cattle business," Jessy said.

"Indeed." Monte lifted his drink in acknowledgment of the fact as another sharp clap of thunder shook the glass in the window frames.

"Mommy, tell the storm to be quiet. It's being too noisy." Three-year-old Laura sat with her legs folded under her in the big leather desk chair as she worked diligently at coloring the picture in her activity book, red crayon in hand.

"I'm afraid it won't listen to me." Jessy smiled at the little girl behind the desk, fair like her mother, but with more golden lights in her hair than were held by Jessy's tawny shade.

Laura paused long enough in her coloring to release a dramatic sigh. "I wish Grampa was here. He'd tell those cowboys to chase the cattle away."

"What cattle is that?" Monte switched his indulgent smile from Laura to Jessy. "I believe I missed something."

"Chase told them that the cattle up in

heaven stampeded and they were hearing the thunder of their hooves," Jessy explained.

"And the lightning is their hooves on rocks," Laura was quick to insert, then cocked her head to one side, gazing at him with her deep brown eyes. "Didn't you know that?"

"I confess I was totally ignorant of the cause," Monte declared in mock regret.

Laura's eyebrows furrowed together in a perplexed frown. "What does ig'rant mean?"

"The word is ignorant," Jessy corrected, enunciating it carefully. "And it means he doesn't know."

"Oh." Satisfied, she bent her head over the coloring book. "Grampa can tell you about it when he gets back."

"I shall make a point to ask him," Monte replied with a slight bow in the child's direction. A series of whoops, clumps, and vocalized *bang-bangs* came from the living room. Monte arched an eyebrow. "I do believe a shootout is in progress."

Jessy paused to listen. Long ago she had learned a mother's trick of blocking out sounds of boisterous play, allowing only cries of pain or panic to filter through. "Trey and Quint," she said, needlessly identifying her son and nephew. "I think the posse finally caught up with the out-laws."

His mouth curved in an amused smile. "And who is the outlaw?"

"Trey, of course. Being a sheriff would be much too tame for him."

Monte laughed as he was meant to do, ending with a mild shake of his head. "I don't think you quite realize how very much I enjoy spending time here. I suspect I miss my own family. My brother and his wife have three very rowdy youngsters — older than yours, of course, and all boys, full of pranks and rough-and-tumble play. I find myself looking for an excuse to come here. I fear that I will ultimately wear my welcome thin."

"I wouldn't worry about that," Jessy said, dismissing the suggestion. "You will always be welcome at the Triple C."

"And I promise that I will do my best not to take your hospitality for granted."

His air of formality had a tongue-in-cheek quality to it that made it easier for Jessy to tolerate. She had always been a down-to-earth person, frequently speaking with a man's bluntness.

She did so now. "To be honest, when I first met you, I assumed that if there was anyone in Montana you would want to spend time with it would be Tara."

He feigned a shudder of distaste. "Please," he dragged out the word in emphasis, "don't tell me I made that poor of a first impression."

It was so dryly said, with so many undertones of criticism of Tara that Jessy laughed warmly and richly. If nothing else, the fact that Monte shared her dislike of her late husband's first wife was enough to endear him to her.

"It wasn't anything you said or did," Jessy assured him. "It was merely an assumption on my part."

"Frankly, I don't know if Tara is fascinated by my brother's title or hopeful that I might introduce her to the current Earl of Stanfield."

Laura sat back on her heels, bright-eyed with excitement. "Is Aunt Tara coming tonight?"

"No. She's off on a trip somewhere." *Thankfully,* Jessy added to herself.

"Is she in Texas with Grampa?"

"I don't know where she went this time, honey," Jessy replied, despairing that her daughter would ever get over her idolization of Ty's first wife.

The corners of Laura's mouth turned downward. "I want a red dress like this one." She referred to the picture she was coloring. "If Aunt Tara was here, she'd get me one."

"I don't want to hear you asking Tara for one, Laura," Jessy warned, mollified that maybe it was only the presents Tara showered on the twins that attracted Laura to the woman.

Suppressing a smile, Monte inquired, "How old did you say she is?"

"She will be four."

"Ah, that explains it. She is nearly a woman grown."

"And very particular about what she wears. Everything has to match." Even worse, she loved dresses. Jessy blamed Tara for that. As a child, Jessy had been too much of a tomboy to ever want to wear a dress. Her daughter's desire for anything and everything feminine was totally alien to her.

"Good news." Cat sailed into the den, carrying a serving plate crowded with appetizers. "Sally says dinner will be ready in fifteen minutes. With any luck, Logan will be here by then, but with this storm I wouldn't be surprised if he gets called away to an accident scene."

She offered the assortment of appetizers first to Monte, then to Jessy. Standing side by side, the two women were a study in contrasts. Cat, with her glistening black hair and green eyes, was petite and strikingly beautiful, gifted with a tremendous capacity for emotion, which she rarely concealed. On the other hand, the fair-haired and hazel-eyed Jessy was tall and boy-slim, projecting a steady calm and innate strength. It was rare that she ever revealed what was going on inside her head, whereas Cat was an open book.

"The two of you do understand that I am accepting this dinner invitation only on the condition that you come to my ranch on Sunday." After a scant pause, Monte added, "Chase will be back by then, won't he?"

Jessy nodded. "When I spoke to him yesterday, he said he planned to fly home on Friday."

"Good." He nodded decisively. "I am eager for him to see my new arrivals."

"What new arrivals?" Cat asked.

"Your cattle arrived, then?" Jessy used the lift of her voice to turn the statement into a question.

"They did," he confirmed.

"You imported some cattle," Cat guessed and helped herself to a cracker mounded with crab salad.

"Not just any cattle," Monte asserted with a hint of pride. "These are registered Highland cattle."

"Highland," Cat repeated. "Aren't those the ones that have shaggy hair hanging around their horns, making them look like they have bangs?"

"Their appearance is quite distinctive," Monte agreed with his typical flair for understatement. "But their attributes are many and valuable. Once the American public learns of them, the demand for Highland beef will soar."

"What makes Highland beef better than any other beef?" Cat showed her skepticism.

"In my opinion, it tastes better, and the Queen agrees with me. But more than that, it is a naturally lean beef with lower amounts of cholesterol. In short, it is the ideal product for consumers who love beef but have to watch their cholesterol intake for health reasons."

"Is that true?" Cat frowned and glanced at Jessy. "Is he pulling my leg?"

"Delightful as that exercise might be, I assure you that everything I said is absolutely true." His mouth curved in a smile of understanding. "But please don't take my word for it. Read up on the breed yourself."

"Don't Highland cattle have long horns?" Cat's frown deepened in an effort to recall more about the breed.

"Yes, but nothing as impressive as those." Monte gestured to the set mounted above the fireplace mantel.

Impressive they were. Taken from a longhorn steer named Captain, the horns were long and twisted, the span of them measuring more than five feet across. The brindle steer had led the first herd of Calder cattle north from Texas to Montana and each subsequent drive thereafter. When the longhorn had died of old age, Benteen Calder had kept his horns and mounted them above the mantel in the steer's honor, making him forever a part of the family lore.

"Few modern-day longhorns grow sets like that pair of old mossy horns," Jessy remarked.

In the living room, Cat's nine-year-old son, Quint, let out a shout, and the big house echoed with the rapid thud of feet running across the hardwood floor. Quint dashed by the doorway toward the foyer. Trey raced after him, skinny arms pumping, his expression grim with determination to catch up with his older cousin.

"Hey, Dad!" Quint's happy greeting

reached all the way back to the den.

"Logan must be here," Cat realized, throwing a glance at the rain-lashed windows. "I didn't hear him drive in."

"With all the lightning and thunder, that's hardly surprising," Jessy said.

Quint's voice came from the foyer. "It must be really raining hard out there. The rug's all wet where you're standing."

"Howdy, Sheriff." The smaller voice belonged to Trey, who insisted on calling Logan by his official title rather than uncle. "Did ya catch any bad guys today?"

" 'Fraid not," was Logan's low reply.

"Maybe tomorrow ya will," Trey suggested, optimistic as always.

"Maybe," Logan agreed, then asked Quint, "Where's your mom?"

"In the den with Aunt Jessy and Mr. Markham."

Three sets of footsteps of varying weight approached the den. Flanked by two boys, one the spitting image of himself, Logan walked into the room, minus his hat and raincoat, with his face still wet from the rain.

Seeing him, Laura grabbed up her coloring book and bounded off the chair. She ran up to him. "See the red dress I colored, Uncle Logan."

Gray eyes skimmed the three adults standing near the fireplace before he bent his head to look at the picture. "Good job, Laura." The comment had a perfunctory ring. Turning, he laid a hand on Quint's shoulder. "Take the twins in the other room, Quint, and keep them occupied for a while."

Alerted by something in his father's tone, Quint tipped his head back and inspected his father's face. When Quint was barely out of the toddler stage, the Triple C cowboys had dubbed him "little man" for his quietness and adultlike seriousness. His basic nature had changed little during the intervening years. As a result, Quint was quick to pick up subtleties that most nine-year-olds would have missed. His father's somber expression made him uneasy.

"Is something wrong, Dad?"

Logan replied with a slow nod. "I'll tell you about it later. Take the twins to the living room for me."

Quint knew something bad had happened. As much as he wanted to stay and find out, he understood that he had been given the responsibility of the twins, and he had been taught that a man shouldered his responsibility; he didn't protest or try to wiggle out of it.

Without another word, Quint herded the twins out of the den and into the hall. A short distance from the doorway, curiosity got the better of him. He steered the twins over to the wall and raised a finger to his mouth to shush them. Trey was quick to obey, certain it was the start of some new game. Laura twirled about, making the skirt of her sundress flare out.

"Are we gonna sneak up on somebody?" Trey asked in a stage whisper, causing Quint to miss the question his mother asked.

"Sssh," he admonished and cocked his head to listen, grateful that his father hadn't closed the doors to the den.

The low timbre of his father's voice responded in answer. "About an hour ago, I received a phone call from the Fort Worth police. The news isn't good."

"Daddy." There was fear in his mother's voice. "Something happened to him."

"There was an accident . . ."

The instant he heard the words, Quint felt all sick and scared inside. It was his grandfather, that big, tall man who had always seemed so rock-solid and strong. He had been hurt.

"He's all right, isn't he?" his mother rushed the words, then never gave his father a chance to answer. "We'd better call and have the plane fueled so we can take off as soon as the storm lifts."

"Cat." The name was spoken with firm command, and something died inside Quint. He didn't even notice Trey making like a monster, teeth bared and fingers curled in menace as he stalked his pirouetting sister. "It's no use. He was killed on impact."

Not wanting to hear any more, Quint swung blindly away from the den. It felt like there was a hand at his throat, choking off his air while not letting a single sound escape. In a kind of trance he moved toward the living room, barely aware of Trey racing to get there ahead of him while Laura skipped alongside him, blond curls bouncing.

He threw himself onto the sofa, slumping in a heap, conscious of the tears welling in his eyes and the awful pain in his chest. Trey clambered onto the cushion beside him and bounced on his knees.

"Come on, Quint. Let's play," Trey urged with growing impatience.

"No." His voice sounded strangled to his own ears.

Trey pushed his face close to Quint's and peered intently at him. "Are you crying?" he said in disbelief.

Laura tipped her head to one side. "Did you hurt yourself?"

"No." Quint worked to recover his speech. "It's Grandpa. He died."

Laura immediately propped her hands on her hips and declared with exaggerated scorn, "He's not dead. He's in Texas."

Looking at the twins, he forgot his own pain and struggled to find a way to make them understand. "You're right, Laura. He went to Texas. But he had an accident while he was there, and he died. Now he's in heaven with your daddy."

Her brown eyes grew big and dark, the brightness leaving them. "But Grampa said he'd come back."

"When he told you that, he didn't know he'd be in an accident," Quint explained.

"He died and went to heaven like my daddy." Laura spoke the words slowly as if trying to grasp the exact significance of them. "Does that mean he's only gonna be a picture for me and Trey to look at?"

"That's right." But the thought that he would never see his grandfather again, never ride on roundups with him, never hear him tell the stories about the cattle drives, was beyond Quint's imagination. His grandfather had always been there for him. Always.

"No!" Trey's denial was instant and explosive. His mouth took on a mutinous set. "My grampa is not dead."

"He is so, Trey," Laura declared with great importance. "He's up in heaven with Daddy."

"He is not!"

"Is too!"

"Is not!"

As he listened to their war of wills, his own feelings of grief washed over him. Suddenly Quint didn't know how to stop this battle of tempers. When his father appeared in the living room, he looked up with gratitude

"All right, that's enough shouting." Logan broke up the pair.

Trey glared up at him, chin quivering in a mixture of rage and hurt. "I don't care what she says — my grampa's not dead!" With that, he raced for the stairs.

Logan threw a sharp, probing glance at Quint. Quint ducked his head, admitting, "I listened at the door."

"I see." Logan sat down at the sofa's edge next to him and cupped his hand over the boy's knee in silent comfort. "I'm sorry, Quint. I know how close you were to him and how much you are going to miss him. Anybody who knew him will — including me."

The tears came in earnest. Quint tried to sniffle them back. "Why, Dad?" he murmured brokenly.

Logan curled a hand around the boy's neck and pulled the nine-year-old into his arms. "I wish I knew." He slid his fingers into the boy's raven black hair, unconsciously ruffling it. "Your mother and I are going to fly down to Fort Worth in the morning." He continued to talk in a calm, even voice while Quint sobbed against his shoulder. "We need to make arrangements to have his remains brought home for burial. While we're gone, Jessy would like you to stay here and help her look after the twins. Can you do that?"

"I guess."

Logan smiled at the mumbled answer. "I wish we could stay here with you. But from now on we all have to pitch in and help Jessy for a while. It's what your grandfather would want."

Pulling away, his head still down, Quint wiped away the tears with the back of his hand. "Does that mean we'll move here?"

"No." He combed some of the dark hair off Quint's forehead with his fingers. "Jessy is in charge here. She'll do fine."

But that didn't mean she would have an easy time of it, and Logan knew it. Distracted by the sound of light feet running down the stairs, he looked up to see Laura. When she reached the bottom, she made a beeline for Logan.

"Trey is in Grampa's room. I told him to get out, but he wouldn't listen." Her dark eyes snapped with temper.

He had only to look at the anguish in his own son's face to know that all three of these children were too young to endure this kind of grief. The twins hadn't been old enough to understand when Ty was killed, but that wasn't true anymore. He glanced in the direction of the second-floor bedroom.

"It's all right if Trey stays in your grandpa's bedroom for a while," Logan told her.

Dissatisfied with his answer, Laura turned away. "I'm going to tell Mommy." Off she went.

Chapter Three

With dusk purpling the sky over Fort Worth, the streetlights flickered on. The mix of neon and backlit signs stood out above the storefronts. But the sweltering afternoon temperatures had yet to wane.

The air conditioner in Laredo's pickup worked mightily to cool the cab's interior. It brought only modest relief as he cruised down Main Street, a troubled frown creasing his forehead.

This detective business had turned out to be a bit more difficult than he thought it would. So far he had hit every saloon, bar, and restaurant in the Stockyards District, certain the man he called Duke had to have been at one of them on the previous night. Every time he had dragged out his carefully rehearsed spiel that he was supposed to meet a man there but had lost his business card and couldn't recall his name, then offered his description of him. Each time he had struck out.

That troubled him. Duke was the kind of

man who stood out in a crowd, even at his age. Yet no one remembered anyone matching his description. It was always possible that he hadn't asked the right person. If necessary he would make the rounds again, but later.

Right now his focus was on hotels. Judging from the expensive cut of the suit Duke had been wearing, Laredo had decided to check out the more upscale hotels first. He pulled into the lot of the next one on his list and parked the pickup in an empty space.

Inside the foyer, he located the registration desk but paused before approaching it. At the two other hotels, he had learned that hotel clerks were stingy with information about possible guests, something their patrons probably appreciated, but it didn't help him. Laredo glanced around and noticed that the bell desk was manned by a Mexican-American. He veered toward him.

"*Buenas noches, amigo,*" he greeted the man, making use of his fluency in Border Spanish.

"*Buenas noches, señor.* How can I help you?" the man asked in thickly accented English.

Laredo didn't make the switch back to

his own native tongue. Instead he continued to converse in Spanish, trotting out his customary spiel but giving it a few new wrinkles. Specifically he pleaded hard times, claiming he desperately needed the job the man had offered him.

The bellman repeated Laredo's description of the man they had dubbed Duke and added a few more details in the form of a question. Laredo brightened immediately.

"*Sí*, he is one *mucho hombre*."

"Ah, *señor*." The bellman looked at him with abject regret. "The man you seek ees *Señor* Chase Calder. Eet grieves me to tell you, but ees dead."

Startled, Laredo repeated in disbelief, "Dead? Are you sure?"

"*Sí*. The police, they come here thees afternoon. I hear them talking to the manager. They say his car, eet crashed last night and he ees dead."

"*Gracias*." His mind raced with a dozen possibilities. He started to turn away, then stopped. "*Señor Calder*, where was he from? Maybe this is the wrong man."

The bellman lifted his shoulders in a shrug of uncertainty. "Some place up north, I theenk. Maybe Montana. I cannot say for sure."

"Gracias." Laredo tapped a hand on the desk in finality and walked out of the hotel.

He climbed back into his pickup and drove out of the lot. This unexpected turn of events meant there was only one place he might get additional information. The next stop was the police station.

The desk sergeant glanced up with disinterest when Laredo walked in, but the glance made a practiced, sweeping appraisal of him just the same.

"What can I do for you?" The question was a half challenge.

"A man by the name of Chase Calder was killed in an auto accident sometime late last night. The family called and asked if I would come down and identify the body and spare them that ordeal. Could you direct me to the morgue?" Laredo counted on the fact that no one else had stepped forward as yet.

"Do they know you're coming?"

"No."

"What was the guy's name again?"

"Calder. Chase Calder."

"What's your name?"

"Richard Hanson." That was the name on the driver's license in his billfold.

"Just a minute." The sergeant called

someone on the phone, repeated the gist of Laredo's request, then nodded at the response he received. "Right," he said and hung up. "Detective Stabler will be right out, Mr. Hanson."

"Thanks." Laredo moved away to cool his heels in the waiting area.

It was closer to five minutes before Detective Stabler made an appearance. A heavyset man in shirtsleeves and a tie, he walked up to Laredo and extended a hand.

"Hanson, isn't it?"

"That's right." Laredo briefly shook hands with him. "You must be Detective Stabler."

The man nodded in confirmation. "You wouldn't be any relation to the Hansons of Hanson Oil, would you?"

"I wish." Laredo smiled smoothly.

"Don't we all," he agreed. "But I thought I should ask. It seems Mr. Calder was an important man."

"Yes," Laredo replied, playing along, then repeated his previous request to identify the body on behalf of the family.

The detective gave him a sideways look. "You do realize that would be pointless."

"Why?" Laredo asked in wary question.

"I guess you didn't hear. But it appears the car's fuel tank ruptured on impact and the whole thing went up in flames. By the time the responding fire units were able to put the fire out, the body was burned beyond recognition."

"Then how were you able to determine it was Mr. Calder?"

The detective began to tick off the reasons, some Laredo had already surmised. "First, the car was a rental. When we checked the agency's records, the car was signed out to one Chase Benteen Calder, Montana driver's license. Among the personal effects that were recovered was a badly charred wallet, but the driver's license was still readable. It was issued to Chase Calder. A hotel key was also found, which we were able to trace to the hotel where he was staying." He stopped, his eyes narrowing on Laredo with a hint of suspicion. "Why would you think it wouldn't be Mr. Calder?"

"No reason. I guess it was just the shock of hearing about the fire. It threw me for a minute."

Satisfied, at least temporarily, with the explanation, the detective nodded. "I understand. Some of the family will be flying in tomorrow to claim the body." It was one of those exploratory remarks to see how much Laredo knew and how close he really was to this family.

"That's right. They are eager to finalize arrangements to have the body shipped home to Montana. I don't know if they plan on flying it back on their plane or not." He added the last to bolster his credibility in the detective's eyes. "Thank you for your time, Detective. I'm sorry I took up so much of it for nothing."

"No problem, Mr. Hanson."

A blaze of sunlight through the window heralded the arrival of morning. The man called Duke sat up on the edge of the bed, relieved to discover the room didn't spin even though his head continued to pound unmercifully. He donned the thrift-shop jeans and shirt and ventured out of the bedroom, following the smell of coffee.

He was still a little on the weak side, but definitely stronger and more sure of his step than he had been the day before. But that was the only improvement. His memory was just as blank as it had been.

When he crossed the threshold into the kitchen, Hattie Ludlow walked in the back door. Her gaze made a quick inspection of him. "I didn't expect you up so early. Feeling better, are you?"

"Some," he confirmed and looked out the window. There was no sign of the pickup. "Where's Laredo? I never heard him come back last night."

"It was close to midnight when he rolled in. He hollered at me just a few minutes ago and said he was going into town but he would come right back. Have a seat and I'll pour you a cup of coffee." She motioned to one of the chairs at the kitchen table.

He sat down at the chrome table. "What did he find out yesterday? Anything?"

"I don't know. I only heard him come home. I didn't get up." Steam rose from the cup she set before him. "Are you hungry enough for some bacon and eggs?"

"Sure."

"How would you like your eggs? Over easy, sunny side up, or scrambled?"

"Over easy, I guess," he replied, irritated to find he didn't even know how he liked his eggs fixed.

Soon bacon sizzled in its own grease, filling the kitchen with its distinctive aroma. Like so many things, the smell was familiar, but it triggered no memory, only more questions that probed for one.

He watched as Hattie broke two eggs in a bowl and deftly slipped them into a hot skillet. With a pair of tongs, she lifted the bacon strips from another iron skillet and laid them on a paper towel to drain. She checked the eggs again, then glanced his way, catching him looking at her.

"I'm not used to people watching me so closely when I cook," she remarked with a touch of amusement. "Are you that hungry, or haven't you ever seen anyone fix breakfast before?"

"Everything you have done is familiar to me. I must have watched a woman cook before, but I don't know who she was."

"It could have been your mother or your wife." Hattie scooped up the eggs with a spatula and slipped them onto a plate. She carried it and the platter of bacon to the table, setting both in front of him.

"What makes you so sure I'm married?" He didn't feel married. Laredo and the mirror had said he was up in years. But he wasn't so old that he didn't find a woman like Hattie attractive.

"I can't imagine some woman letting you get away," she informed him with a dry smile. "Although I doubt any woman married to you would have an easy time of it."

"Why do you say that?" he asked, not sure what she meant by it.

"For one thing, you're too used to being the one in command," Hattie replied. She hesitated, measuring him with a long glance. "And I suspect you keep your own counsel. If there is a problem, you don't talk about it until you have a solution. Most women prefer to be a part of that decision process since it will affect their lives as well. It can be very irritating to be informed of the problem and the solution after the fact."

"I suppose it would." He reached for a piece of toast.

"Out of curiosity, Duke," Hattie poured herself a cup of coffee and sat down at the table opposite him, "how do you plan on finding out who you are?"

"I'm not sure." He broke the egg yolk with his fork and dipped a corner of the toast into it.

"You must have a few ideas." She spooned some jam onto a piece of toast.

"A few. It will depend on what Laredo was able to find out last night, if anything." An instant later, he realized her game and sent her an amused glance. "Are you happy that I proved your point and refused to discuss my problem?"

"You were slower to catch on than I thought you would be. Your head must be hurting."

"Not as bad as yesterday."

"I'm sorry, but I don't have anything stronger than aspirin for it.

"I'll survive." He took another bite of eggs and chewed. "What kind of operation do you run here?"

"What do you mean?" Hattie frowned.

"Laredo said you have a small ranch. Is it a cow-and-calf outfit?"

"Do you know something about a cow-calf operation?" She studied him closely, her dark eyes bright with interest.

He thought about that a minute. "I guess I do."

"Those cowboy boots aren't just for show, then," Hattie observed before answering his original question. "In my position, I can't really afford the financial risk that goes with ranching. I need an income that is a bit more reliable. I worked a deal with a local rancher to run his cattle on my place. He pays me rent for the pasture and labor costs for looking after his stock as well as reimburses me for any hay or feed."

"It's not an uncommon arrangement. I understand quite a few small ranchers are opting for deals like that. It's a bit like sharecropping in the old days," he heard himself say. He didn't understand how he could have knowledge of such things yet no recollection of his personal identity.

"It keeps the wolves away from the door," Hattie replied.

"The financial kind, anyway," he said with a knowing smile.

"Why, Duke, I do believe you are flirting with me." Hattie mocked, but it didn't mask the pleased look in her eyes, a look that hinted at her interest in him.

A dog barked outside, sounding an alarm as a vehicle approached. Rising from her chair, Hattie glanced out the window. The barking turned to excited yelps.

"Laredo is back," she announced.

A new tension gripped him, heightening his senses. Each sound from outside came sharply to him — the crunch of tires on gravel, the sputter of a dying engine, the slam of the cab door, and the approach of footsteps to the rear door. Unwilling to betray his eagerness to hear the results of Laredo's investigation, he didn't look up when the cowboy walked into the kitchen.

"You're up. That's means I won't have to wake you." Laredo crossed to the table, tossed a newspaper on top of it, pulled out a chair, swung it around, and straddled it.

"Did you have any luck?" He pushed his plate away and leaned back in his chair, reaching for his coffee cup.

"You could say that." Steady blue eyes

67

held his gaze. "I located a bellman who remembered you, said your name was Chase Calder. Unfortunately, according to the morning paper" — Laredo gave it a push toward him — "you're dead, killed in a car crash the night before last."

He picked up the paper, but the type was blurred. He extended his arm, trying to bring it into focus.

"Need some reading glasses, do you," Hattie guessed, rising from her chair. "I'll get you a pair of mine. They might be the right strength."

Questions buzzed in his head, but he held his silence until he read the article. Hattie's glasses worked well enough to allow him to see the print. The write-up was a small one, between two and three inches long. Its length was mostly due to the identity of the victim in this particular traffic accident. Even then there were few facts to glean from it, merely that the deceased was Chase Calder, owner of the Triple C Ranch in eastern Montana.

"Chase Calder." He spoke the name, but it had no more meaning to him than if he had said John Doe. He set the paper aside and laid the glasses on top of it. Hattie picked up both.

"Do you remember anything at all about

the man who robbed you?" Laredo studied him thoughtfully.

"No. I only remember you telling me that you saw a man holding me up. My memory starts with the slam of a car door, gunshots, and a vehicle peeling out."

"That was your holdup man, making his getaway as fast as he could," Laredo stated, "taking with him your wallet with its identification and driving the car you rented. He even managed to wind up with the key to your hotel room."

"It's also possible the victim was Chase Calder."

"It's possible," Laredo conceded. "But I don't believe it. That article in the paper omits one important detail — following the crash, the car burst into flames. The body was burned beyond recognition. Granted, I didn't get a good look at your robber, but to the best of my recollection, he was about your height and build. He could have even been about your age. We may never know, unless the family requests an autopsy. At this point, the authorities definitely haven't ordered one. Why should they when they are convinced they know both the man's identity and the cause of his death?"

"But there's someone who knows the

dead man isn't Chase Calder," he murmured, thinking out loud.

"That's right," Laredo said with a decisive nod. "The man who tried to kill you. It's possible that he might not know that the thief took off in your rental car, but not likely."

"He won't know for sure unless I come forward — assuming I really am Chase Calder."

"The newspaper archives might have a photo of Chase Calder," Laredo told him. "That's one way you could find out. Of course, there is another way."

"What's that?"

"Someone from your family is flying in this morning to arrange to have the body shipped home for burial. I have the name of the mortuary they'll be using on the Fort Worth end. All you would have to do is show up there and wait to see if you are recognized."

"I could." But doing so would only answer whether or not he was Chase Calder. It wouldn't solve anything else. If anything, his situation might be worse. His killer would know he was alive, but he wouldn't know who that man was.

"You could, but you won't," Laredo guessed.

"No, I don't think so."

Hattie looked up from the article, the reading glasses perched on the end of her nose. "Why not? Think what your family is going through right now," she protested.

He experienced a twinge of guilt, but it didn't change his decision. "I regret that, but —"

"You regret it! That is the most heartless thing I have ever heard." She glared her disapproval.

"Maybe it seems that way, but I think it's best for now," he replied calmly.

Hattie stared at him long and hard, her lips pressed tightly together. "And as long as you think it's best, that is all that matters, isn't it?"

"This isn't the time to come forward." It was a gut decision. Right now his instincts were the only thing he could trust.

"It could take months for your memory to return," Hattie warned.

"And in the meantime," Laredo spoke, "there's a man out there who wants him dead. For all he knows it could be a member of his own family."

That possibility had clearly never occurred to Hattie. It showed in the sudden doubt that flickered in her expression. "Still," she began, "you must be curious about your family. Don't you want to know if you have a wife? Children?"

"Of course I do." Impatience riddled his voice, but it was born of his inability to remember for himself.

"I can find out the answers to those questions." Laredo pushed off the chair and stood up. "Hopefully without raising too much suspicion."

Gratitude tinged the look he gave Laredo. He was fully aware of how much he already owed this man. But, in addition to that, there was a connection between them that he couldn't fully explain. Perhaps it was the sense of mutual regard.

The irony of it wasn't lost on him. He was a man with no memory, seeking his identity. Laredo, on the other hand, sought to conceal his identity under an assumed name.

"I don't know where you plan on going," Hattie said, "but you aren't leaving this house until you've had breakfast."

"I wondered how long it would take before you offered me some of those bacon and eggs you served him." Laredo walked over to the counter and helped himself to some coffee.

By midday the temperature had climbed to well over ninety degrees, and it felt even hotter than that on the concrete streets and sidewalks of Fort Worth, signaling the onset of another scorching Texas summer.

Inside the hotel lobby, the air was cool. Comfortably ensconced in a leather chair facing the hotel entrance, Laredo pretended to peruse the newspaper he held open while keeping one eye on the front door. He was playing the odds that the arriving family members would stay at the same hotel Calder had used. An early morning trip to the newspaper archives had turned up a photo of Chase Calder. There was no more doubt they were one and the same man.

As busy as the lobby was, with people coming and going and meeting, no one took any notice of his presence even though Laredo had been sitting there close to an hour. He figured he had another hour before someone from hotel security came around to "talk" to him.

A man and woman came through the front door, followed by a porter with their luggage. The man was tall and lean, with jet black hair partially covered by a black Stetson. His gaze made a thorough sweep of the lobby, noting people and details with the watchful alertness Laredo had usually observed in those in law enforcement.

Laredo lifted the newspaper a little higher and shifted his attention to the petite woman at the man's side. She had a face and figure that any male would notice. Laredo had an odd longing to see her smile, but her face was expressionless, almost stony and lifeless. At first he wondered if the two had had a fight. Then another possibility occurred to him.

After folding up the newspaper, Laredo stood up and drifted closer to the registration desk to covertly observe the pair. The woman stood to one side, staring sightlessly at the floor, while the man arranged for their hotel room. She looked up once, straight in Laredo's direction, yet she didn't appear to be looking at anything.

Her eyes were green, and full of more pain than he had ever seen in a woman's eyes.

Intent on the couple, Laredo didn't notice the woman who entered the hotel. His first awareness of her was when she glided into his vision.

"Cat, darling, I am so sorry." She reached out to the petite brunette to clasp her hands. "I just heard about Chase. How horrible for you."

Chase. Laredo hid a smile at the name. His instincts about the pair had been right;

they were part of the Calder family.

"Tara." Surprise registered briefly in the woman's face before her expression dulled again. "How did you know we would be here?"

"After Brownsmith called me with the news, I phoned the ranch," the woman called Tara explained. "Sally told me that you and Logan had left this morning and planned to stay here. As soon as I learned you hadn't checked in yet, I came right down. It's foolish of you to spend the night in a hotel when I have that big old house with all those empty guest rooms. Let me take you to my place. You shouldn't be staying in a cold, impersonal hotel, not at a time like this."

"I —" The Calder woman didn't appear to be too thrilled with the invitation.

"I insist, Cat." The other woman used her most persuasive tone. "No one knows better than I the agony you are going through right now. It hasn't been that long ago that I lost my own father. Believe me, I know how deeply you are hurting."

This woman called Cat was the daughter, Laredo realized, and made a closer study of her so he could describe her later to Duke. Correction, Chase Calder.

When the man joined the two women,

the daughter turned to him. "Tara wants us to stay at her place."

"Too late. We are already registered, and our luggage is on its way up. But we do appreciate the invitation, Tara." His refusal was warmly polite but firm.

The Tara woman took it better than Laredo had expected. She made a small moue of regret and looked at Cat with genuine empathy. "As much as I would like to argue against your decision, I won't. This isn't the time for family to be squabbling."

So Tara was some sort of relation to Calder as well, Laredo filed away that piece of information.

"Good," Cat stated. "Because I simply don't have the strength to argue."

Tears welled in her green eyes, and her lower lip quivered with the strain of holding her emotions in check, but she kept her chin high. Maybe she didn't resemble her father in looks, but she had clearly inherited some of his grit.

To Laredo's surprise, a delicate teardrop slipped down Tara's cheek. Gracefully she wiped it away, showing him a flash of her discreetly manicured nails.

Smiling in a forced show of composure, Tara asked, "Have you been to the funeral home yet?"

"No," the man answered. "We came straight to the hotel from the airport."

"In that case, I have my car here. Let me take you." When she saw their joint hesitation, she rushed, "Please. I would like to help in some way. You and Ty were here for me when my father died. Let me return the kindness you showed me."

"Of course." The woman named Cat seemed to regret her initial hesitation in accepting the offer. "It will be much more convenient that relying on taxis."

"I'll have the valet bring my car around."

The man stopped her. "Not just yet," he said. "First Cat and I need to go to our room and freshen up a bit. It was a long flight. We'll meet you down here in, say, forty-five minutes to an hour."

"Of course. I'll wait for you in the bar," Tara replied, then hesitated, a look of grief sweeping over her expression. "Oh, Cat. I just can't believe Chase is gone."

Briefly the two women embraced in a moment of shared pain and loss. The wetness of tears glistened on the cheeks of both women. With his arm circled around her, the man led Cat to the elevator bank. Tara watched them for a moment, then pivoted in a graceful turn and headed toward the hotel bar.

After allowing a span of seconds to pass, Laredo followed her. Tara sat on a tall stool at the bar, managing to project a certain aura of innate elegance. At this hour there were few customers. Laredo picked a seat a few stools away, closer to the bartender.

In a low voice intended for the bartender's hearing only, Laredo said, "I'll pay for the lady's drink. I'll have a beer, whatever is on tap." He withdrew a twenty-dollar bill from his wallet and laid it on the counter.

The bartender glanced at the money and nodded. When the man set a glass of chilled white wine in front of Tara, she said, "How much do I owe you?"

"The gentleman paid for it already, ma'am." He nodded in Laredo's direction.

She stiffened, throwing him a cool look of suspicion. Laredo lifted his beer glass in a salute to her. "My sympathies, ma'am."

His remark dissolved her coolness in an instant, leaving her puzzled and uncertain. "I'm sorry. Do I know you?"

"No, ma'am. But I happened to see you out in the lobby a minute ago with some of the Calder family."

"Do you know the Calders?" she wondered with the beginnings of curiosity.

"Only Chase Calder," Laredo answered truthfully. "The news of his death was a real shock."

"To everyone," she agreed and sighed deeply.

"Are you related to them?" He injected an idle note into the question.

"I was married to his son." She lifted the wineglass and took a dainty sip.

He caught her use of the past tense and guessed that at some point they had gotten a divorce. "To tell you the truth, I half expected the son would be the one who came to claim the body."

"Don't you know?" Anguish deepened the velvety darkness of her eyes. "Ty was killed nearly two years ago."

"Killed?" He made no attempt to mask his surprise. "How?"

"He was murdered." Her voice trembled with a tightly controlled anger tinged with bitterness.

He thought immediately of the attempt on Chase's life. "Did they ever catch his killer?"

"Yes."

Her clipped, one-word response served only to feed his suspicions. "Was any motive established at the killer's trial?"

"There was no trial. Ballard was killed

by Buck when he tried to stab Chase."

"Who is Buck?" Laredo was determined to gather as much information as possible to help Chase fill in some of the blanks and possibly trigger the return of his memory. And if that didn't work, he would at least know some of the players in his life.

"Buck Haskell. He works for me."

He arched an eyebrow in confusion. "Don't you live here in Fort Worth?"

"Yes, but I also have a summer home on the Triple C. Buck looks after it for me when I'm not there." She seemed to realize the incongruity of her statement. "I know it must seem strange that I would keep a home there after our divorce, but I still regard the Calders as my family. Cat is like a little sister to me. And there are the twins. They are as precious to me as if they were my own."

"The twins," he repeated, not sure if these were more of Chase's children.

"Yes. They are Ty's by his second marriage. A boy and a beautiful little girl."

"Chase's grandchildren." Laredo nodded as if remembering them only at that moment. "What are their names again?"

"The little girl is Laura and the boy is Trey. Actually, Trey is named Chase

Benteen Calder, after his grandfather. But Chase referred to him as his little 'trey spot' almost from the moment he came home from the hospital. And the name Trey stuck." She swirled the wine in her glass. "It's probably just as well that it did. It would have become confusing to have two people called Chase in the house, especially for the child."

"It certainly would." He took advantage of her willingness to speak about the family, recognizing that people found it easier to open up to a stranger. "I don't mean to sound nosy, but I can't help wondering why you seem so sure that this man Ballard killed Chase's son when he never came to trial. I know it's logical to think that, since he made an attempt on Chase's life, but . . ." He let the sentence hang with a question mark.

"Because Ballard admitted it to Jessy before he died." Something in her expression told him that Ty's death was a subject she found particularly painful. Was she still in love with the man, or was there another reason for it?

"Who is Jessy?" he asked, shifting the focus.

"Ty's second wife." Her voice had an edge to it. Clearly Jessy was not popular with her, but few ex-wives did like the women who supplanted them in their husband's affections.

"I guess the Calder ranch will pass into the daughter's hands," Laredo remarked, seeking information without asking for it.

"As I understand, Jessy will be in charge." The dislike in her voice thickened.

"Really?" He arched an eyebrow, suspicion sharpening. "Whose idea was that?"

"Actually, it's what Chase wanted." She took a big swallow of wine as if washing down a bad taste.

"Really," Laredo murmured, much less skeptically. "I guess he would know whether she was qualified to run it or not."

"Oh, she has the qualifications," Tara agreed with an undertone of sarcasm. "She was born and raised on the ranch, just like her father and his father before that."

"Sounds like a clannish bunch." His comment evoked only silence from her, which served as a kind of confirmation. Laredo wondered how welcome Tara had felt coming there as a new bride. And he also wondered how tolerant this elegant woman had been of the ranch hands. No doubt she was more at home in Fort Worth society than a ranch setting. "When will the funeral be? Have they said?"

"It's tentatively planned for Tuesday." She ran her glance over his face, curious and measuring. "Do you plan to attend?"

"I was thinking about it. What's the closest airport?"

"Commercially? That would be Miles City."

"Do you usually fly into there?"

"No. My company has a landing strip at Blue Moon. I use it," she explained. "It's much closer to the ranch. I imagine most people will make use of the airstrip at the Triple C."

"I forgot. The ranch has its own landing strip, doesn't it," he guessed.

"Yes." Idly she held the wineglass by its stem and swept a skimming glance over his boots, jeans, and hat. "What business are you in? Cattle or oil?"

"In Fort Worth, it's usually one or the other, isn't it?" He smiled, deflecting the question. "Wasn't it Amon Carter who said: 'Fort Worth is where the West begins. Dallas is where the East peters out.'"

"Something like that," Tara agreed with a clear lack of interest. "So which is it? Cattle?"

"Yup," he lied. "I met Chase several years ago at a function of the cattlemen's association." He downed a quick swallow of beer and pushed off the stool. "I'd best be going or I'll be late for my appointment. It's been nice talking to you. Pass on my sympathies to the family. Maybe I'll see you again at the funeral."

He left the hotel bar before she could ask his name, a plan of action beginning to take shape in his mind.

The windmill's long blades went round and round, pushed by a strong south breeze. Each rotation was punctuated by a grinding squeak, a sure sign it needed oiling.

Too restless to remain in the house and too weak to venture very far, Chase sat in an old high-backed wooden rocker on the front porch. The steady breeze kept the afternoon heat from becoming too unbearable and brought the familiar smells of the land to him. His gaze wandered over the Texas landscape with its high, rolling hills covered with sun-seared grass. Trees were few, confined mainly to watercourses.

Idly he studied the cattle grazing in the fenced pastures. For the most part they were crossbreeds, a mix of Brangus and Black Baldies. None were branded, only ear-tagged. The observation prompted him to glance again at the old branding iron hanging on a porch post as decoration of sorts.

On impulse, he pushed out of the rocker and wandered over to the post, lifted the branding iron off its nail, and turned it upside down. C- was the brand. He had the odd feeling it should mean something to him, although he didn't know why a Texas brand should be familiar to him, not when he was supposed to be from Montana.

He decided it was the letter C. Maybe he really was Chase Calder, even though the name sounded as alien to him as Duke. He sighed, frustrated by the damnedable blankness of his mind.

Off to his left, Hattie elbowed the screen door open and walked onto the porch carrying two tall tumblers. "I thought you might like a glass of lemonade."

"Sounds good." He hooked the branding iron back on its nail. "Where did you find the old iron?"

"In an old shed — and I mean *old* — that used to sit where the barn is." Hattie paused beside the post and gazed at the branding iron in a remembering way. "When we were hauling stuff out of it prior to bulldozing it down, I grabbed up a stack of old feed sacks that I thought I might use for something, and the branding iron was sandwiched among them." Turning, she flashed him a wry smile. "I ended up throwing the feed sacks away and keeping it."

"It's been well used."

"Yes. If only it could talk, I'll bet it would have a lot of stories it could tell about the old days."

He knew he must have stories of his own to tell, but he couldn't remember them. He downed a long swallow of the tartly sweet lemonade, his glance running to the dirt lane, seemingly on its own accord.

Lowering the tumbler, he pondered aloud, "I wonder when Laredo will be back."

"You know what they say about a watched pot." Hattie eyed him with a knowing look.

"Point taken." He eased himself back into the rocking chair, conscious of the faint trembling in his leg muscles.

"Still weak, aren't you," Hattie observed.

"A little." It went against the grain to admit it, but there was no hiding it from this woman.

"It will take your body some time to build back up its blood supply. You prob-ably should have had a transfusion. As soon as you finish your lemonade, I'll change the bandage and see how it's healing."

"Maybe this time you can bandage it in something smaller than this turban." He raised a hand to the gauze strips that circled much of his head.

"I probably could if I shaved your head, but I don't think you would look good bald," Hattie replied, a mischievous glint in her dark eyes.

His mouth crooked in an answering smile. "I'll keep my hair, thank you."

"I thought you would."

At the top of the porch steps, the yellow dog lifted its head to stare down the lane, ears pricking at some distant sound. A growl started deep in its throat then escalated to an eager whine as his wagging tail thumped the wooden floorboards.

"Laredo must be coming," Hattie guessed, her own gaze shifting to the ranch lane.

When the pickup pulled into view, the dog bounded off the porch and raced to meet it, barking a welcome. He ran alongside of it until it stopped close to the house, then danced impatiently by the driver's door waiting for Laredo to step out. Laredo obligingly rumpled the dog's ears and walked up the cracked concrete sidewalk to the front porch.

"What did you find out?" Chase asked as Laredo mounted the steps.

"I know your funeral is scheduled for Tuesday." Joining them on the porch, Laredo hooked a hip on the rail, his body angled toward Chase, and tipped his hat to the back of his head.

His mouth quirked briefly at the wry humor in Laredo's remark. "Back in Montana, I assume."

Laredo nodded. "The services will be held at your ranch. The closest town is a place called Blue Moon. Does that ring a bell?"

"No. What else did you learn?"

"I saw your daughter. Fortunately she doesn't look anything like you. She's slim and petite with black hair and green eyes, somewhere in her late twenties to early thirties. They call her Cat." But there was nothing in Chase's expression that suggested to Laredo he remembered any of this. He went on to describe the son-in-law and former daughter-in-law Tara, then explained about the death of the son Ty, the wife and twins he left behind, and the assumption that Ty's widow would take over the ranch's operation. When he finished, he paused a beat then shrugged. "That's about it, I guess."

"You never mentioned Calder's wife." He still found it difficult to think of himself as Chase Calder.

"No one else mentioned her either, and I couldn't think of a way to ask about her when I claimed to know you. But I think it's safe to say that she probably died some years ago. But if your daughter looks anything like her, she must have been a beauty."

The names whirled through his head — Ty, Cat, Jessy, Trey, Laura, Tara — every one of them meaningless. He threw a challenging look at Laredo. "You still think I'm this Chase Calder?"

"I didn't hear anything to cause me to change my mind," he replied evenly.

"You mentioned that my son was killed. Do you think there is any connection between his death and the attempt on my life?"

"There doesn't appear to be," Laredo answered. "But you are the only one who can say for sure about that."

"And I don't remember." The frustration of that was galling.

"I think you have answered all the questions that you can from here," Laredo stated. "If you want to learn anything more, you'll need to go to Montana."

"I agree." He also knew it was the only way to find out whether he was really Chase Calder. But how would he get there — without tipping his hand — when he was flat broke.

"That pickup has some high mileage on it, but I think it will make it to Montana." Laredo eyed him with quiet interest.

"You aren't suggesting that Duke try to drive there in his condition, are you?" Hattie looked at him aghast.

"No." Laredo didn't blink an eye. "Actually I was thinking along the lines of driving him there myself. What are the chances of you getting someone to do your chores for you, Hattie? I would feel a lot better if you came along with us. I know Duke is on the mend, but . . ." He let the word trail off.

His proposal caught her off guard, but nothing ever threw Hattie for long. Her dark gaze made a critical appraisal of her patient.

"That wound will need to be watched closely for infection these next few days," she murmured, half to herself. With the matter settled in her mind, she made an abrupt pivot and strode to the door. "I'll call McFarland. I did his chores while he and Joy Ann went to their son's wedding in Phoenix. He owes me."

For a long moment Chase simply looked at Laredo. Finally he said, "You don't have to do this."

"I know." A slow smile spread across his mouth while the look in his blue eyes remained serious. "But it's the only way that I'll find out how the story ends."

"I can't pay you yet," Chase said, thinking of the ready cash that would be needed to pay for gas, meals, and lodging.

"I have the feeling you are good for it." Laredo straightened away from the railing, coming erect. "We might as well start throwing some things in a suitcase. The road to Montana is a long one. The sooner we leave, the sooner we'll get there."

PART TWO

A shifting wind,
It hides his face,
But no one can take
A Calder's place.

Chapter Four

The morning breeze ruffled the black bunting that draped the front of The Homestead. The movement of the fabric created a sound that was like a sighing moan. It matched the pall that hung over the entire Triple C Ranch.

Jessy felt the heaviness of it as she climbed the veranda steps. Her glance touched on the black wreath that hung on the front door, signaling a house in mourning. She paused at the top of the steps and turned to sweep her gaze over the sprawling Triple C headquarters.

Everywhere there was a stirring of activity as the ranch hands carried out their routine morning chores. But the black armbands they wore took away any semblance of normalcy. The shock and the grief went deep — as deep as the emptiness.

Not a single one had questioned her right to assume control. They recognized she was in charge now and accepted it. But things weren't the same. And nothing would be the same until the reins were once again in the hands of one who was Calder by blood. Even Jessy felt it. She had been entrusted with the responsibility of holding the ranch together so it could pass intact to her son.

Already the subtle job of grooming Trey had begun. A dozen times in the last three days Jessy had noticed the special attention the older hands now gave Trey — not in a way that would spoil him, but one that would train him in the ways of a Calder and the codes he would be expected to follow. Jessy felt a mix of pride and gratitude toward these men, and those feelings buoyed her, despite the long and difficult day that lay ahead — for all of them.

She turned her gaze to the private cemetery located a short distance back from the river. A blue canopy had been erected over the opened grave that soon would become the final resting place of Chase Benteen Calder.

Currently the closed casket that held his remains sat in the den where a space had been cleared for it. From the moment it had been set in place, someone had sat with it day and night. The ranch hands had started it, partly Jessy suspected as a way to make his death seem more real, something the closed casket had made difficult for a great many.

The *snick* of a latch alerted her to the opening of the front door. Turning, she saw Monte Markham when he stepped out of the house, a pajama-clad Trey riding on his shoulders.

"Mind your head, now," he warned Trey in his distinctive British accent, then noticed Jessy standing at the top of the steps. "Ah, there is your mum. Isn't that good luck? We found her straight away."

"Good morning." Jessy's glance touched on the Englishman's aesthetically fine features before it shifted to the dark scowl on her son's face. It troubled her the way Trey had changed from a wild rapscallion to a somber, almost angry little boy since learning of his grandfather's death. "Looking for me, were you?" She reached up and lifted him off Monte's shoulders. As always, Trey reminded her of a spindly colt, all arms and legs. "What's the problem?"

Trey clamped his mouth shut in mutinous silence and fixed his gaze on the shoulder seam of her chambray shirt.

Monte quietly supplied the answer. "He is a bit reluctant about attending the funeral."

The explanation earned him a glare from Trey. "My grampa's not dead."

The topic was one Jessy had discussed with Trey at length. She didn't choose to go into it with him again. "If you'd rather not, you don't have to go," she replied with an easy calm, well aware that his absence would be a disappointment to the ranch hands, who wanted a Calder to be made of sterner stuff. "I'm sure Quint will understand."

His dark gaze bored into her. "Quint's going?"

"Yes." Jessy was careful to say no more than that. Trey might not be four years old yet, but he was intelligent, and quick to recognize when he was being manipulated.

"Maybe I'll go," he said cautiously.

"That's up to you." She remained very matter-of-fact. "But right now I think you should go upstairs and get some clothes on." Setting him down, Jessy pointed him toward the front door and gave him a light swat on the rump. "Scoot."

He ran to the door, his bare feet slapping across the veranda's wooden floor. He grabbed hold of the handle and gave the heavy door a mighty tug, pulling it open, then disappeared inside. When the door closed behind him, Jessy let her attention come back to Monte.

His look was soft with compassion. "Death is always difficult for a small child to accept."

She nodded. "The closed casket just makes it that much harder."

"Yes. It eliminates one of those final rites that provide us with a sense of closure," Monte agreed thoughtfully.

"Funerals have always been for the living." Almost automatically she thought of Ty and the void his death had created in her life. But she had become adept at shifting the focus of her thoughts. "When I left the house this morning, I noticed your Range Rover. I realized then that you must have volunteered to take the dawn shift sitting vigil. That was very kind of you, Monte."

"Believe me, I wish there was more I could do," he said with utmost sincerity. "But it would be futile for me to suggest that you call me if you need help with something. I am certain countless others with considerably more knowledge and experience than I possess have already offered their services. Truthfully, I have never met a woman who appeared to be more capable of running an operation of this magnitude than you. Quite likely it is I who will be coming to you for advice." His smile was warm with a rueful amusement.

She widened the curve of her mouth in response. "Anytime, Monte. You know that."

"Thank you." He inclined his head. "And I would hope that if you ever should want some undemanding company for dinner or an evening of idle chatter, you will feel free to call me."

"I'll do that," Jessy assured him.

"You say that easily, but I hope you mean it." Despite the slight twinkle in his eyes, he studied her with a thoughtful regard. "This is hardly the proper time to be speaking of such things, but with the press of people who will be attending the funeral today, I doubt I will have another chance to speak privately with you. This new role you have assumed brings with it considerable responsibilities and obligations, of which I am certain you are aware. Perhaps you also know that it will place you apart from those around you. There will be occasions when you will wish to be an ordinary mortal. I know it is a desire my brother, the Earl of Stanfield, has expressed to me more than once. At such times, I ask that you remember my offer. There," he concluded, his smile taking on a winsome quality, "I have made my little speech — and no doubt bored you dreadfully."

She laughed low in her throat. "You are never boring, Monte."

"I am relieved to hear that. Since coming here, I have overheard more than one local remark that I sound stuffy and a bit pompous. I suspect it is this accent of mine that gives that impression."

"They clearly don't know you very well," Jessy replied.

"I am glad you feel that way," he said, then paused. "I don't quite know why, but from the very first, I have always felt comfortable with you. If I said such a thing to most women, they would be insulted, but I think you know that I mean it as a compliment."

"I do." Thinking back over the last three days, Jessy realized that Monte had spent considerable time at The Homestead, a quiet presence somewhere in the background, never asserting himself, never seeming to be in the way, turning his hand to anything useful whether it was answering the telephone or accepting delivery of a telegram. Even the night when Logan had brought them the news of Chase's death, it hadn't seemed intrusive for Monte to be there. In those first few moments afterward, she remembered the touch of his hand on her arm, the sensation of it as a kind of steadying force. And the look in his eyes had been one of recognition for the change in status Chase's death meant for her. At the time she had given it little thought.

"I find it easy to be with you, Monte," Jessy admitted freely.

"Gracious," he dryly arched an eyebrow over twinkling eyes, "we sound like members of some mutual admiration society. Why does it feel so awkward to express honest emotions?"

"I don't know." With typical unconcern, she shrugged away the question. Such things had never troubled her. "You can drive yourself crazy trying to analyze the reason. Even if you figure it out, what does it change?"

Monte threw back his head and laughed. "What does it change, indeed," he declared. "You are a marvel, Jessy, always so straight and direct, yet somehow so difficult to fathom."

"I'm not a well," she said dryly, finding such talk ridiculously fanciful.

Monte just smiled. "If you were, you would likely be a bottomless one. But," he paused and seemed to gather himself, "I have kept you long enough. I merely wanted to make certain that you knew I understood the unique position you now hold, and that I am available if you ever want company."

"Thank you."

He didn't press for a more definite answer. "I'll see you later at the funeral." He brushed a hand over her arm in farewell and moved down the steps toward his Range Rover.

Jessy didn't linger to watch him leave. She had a dozen different tasks to accomplish before the hour of the funeral arrived. She didn't bother to dwell on the offer he had made, not even to wonder if the day would come when she would want such company and, if it did, whether she would call Monte.

A huge throng of mourners crowded the small cemetery by the river that had long been the repository for the ranch's dead. It was a notable group who gathered to pay their last respects to Chase Calder, numbering among them the governor as well as senators and congressmen at both the state and national level.

Strains of the old hymn "Shall We Gather at the River" filled the silence, sung by a local church choir. On Jessy's left, Laura sang along, la-la-la-ing the numerous words she didn't know. Trey was slumped in the chair on her right, swinging his legs back and forth, thumping them against the chair in a discordant tempo to the music. A quiet and solemn Quint sat next to him, his hands folded in his lap, his gray eyes fixed on the flower-draped casket. Beyond him were Logan and Cat, who was dry-eyed and pale, her hand spread across the Bible she held.

A sniffling sound drew Jessy's glance to Sally Brogan, the former proprietor of Blue Moon's lone restaurant and bar and current housekeeper at The Homestead. Her snow-white head was bowed in grief as she blotted at the tears on her cheek with a lace-edged handkerchief. With the recent loss of her own husband, Jessy well understood the pain of Sally's grief. For years Sally had nurtured a quiet love for Chase. There was a time when Jessy had thought the two might marry, but that hadn't come to pass. Now he was gone. And any hopes Sally might have had of one day becoming his wife were gone with him.

Jessy let her gaze wander over the solemn faces of the assembled mourners. She knew just about everyone there. She couldn't recall the names of a few of the out-of-state ranchers, but their faces were familiar.

Then her roaming glance touched on a stranger standing a few rows back from the gravesite. He was tall and broad-shouldered, dressed in a tieless white shirt and brown sport coat. A cowboy hat was pulled low to shade his eyes from the bright morning sun. But it didn't prevent Jessy from getting a good look at his strong, clean-cut features. His face had a youthful freshness about it that was belied by the deep etching of character lines. Jessy guessed his age at somewhere in his late thirties or early forties — a contemporary of herself. Which only made her more curious about who he was.

She checked out the people on either side of him, thinking the stranger might be kin to one of them. But she knew both families. If he was related to either of them, it had to be a shirttail connection.

Her curiosity waning, Jessy started to pull her glance away. At that moment he made eye contact with her, and she found herself gazing into a pair of steady blue eyes. Ever so slightly, he dipped his head in acknowledgement of the exchange. She felt a flicker of something. With a trace of self-consciousness, she broke the contact and reached over to still Trey's swinging legs.

Beside her Laura sang out the hymn's closing word with confidence, "Ah-men."

In the hush that followed, the portly Reverend Pattersby stepped forward, his voice lifting to intone, "Let us bow our heads in prayer."

There was a stirring of movement throughout the crowd as the men removed their hats and ran quick, combing fingers through their hair. Jessy threw a fast look at the stranger, catching a glimpse of sun-streaked brown hair, before she, too, bowed her head in an attitude of prayer.

After the service, food and refreshments were served at the huge timbered barn located not far from the cemetery. Laredo joined the throng inside where a lavish spread awaited them, a series of strategically placed buffet tables groaning with food.

Laredo sampled a few items and drifted among the guests, eavesdropping on conversations as people swapped stories about Chase Calder. He deliberately steered clear of the family, although he was careful to keep track of their whereabouts, especially the son's widow.

He hadn't figured out what to make of

this tall, slender woman. He covertly studied her again from a distance, taking in the classic purity of her strong, clean jawline and the prominent ridging of her cheekbones. Her long hair, the color of spun-dark caramel, was pulled back from her face, secured at the nape with a tortoise-shell clasp. She exuded a calm confidence and quiet strength that seemed a match for the job before her.

But Laredo remained a little wary. With control of the ranch passing to her, she was the obvious one who stood to gain the most from Chase's death. Yet from the snippets of information he had managed to glean, Chase had been grooming her for the position ever since his son's death. Which would seem to indicate she had his full trust.

Someone jostled him from behind. Laredo glanced back as a man said, "I'm dreadfully sorry."

The man's distinctly British accent briefly caught Laredo's interest, out of place as it was among the western drawls around him. He encountered the dismissing flick of the man's glance before he continued past him, providing Laredo with no more than a glimpse of a finely sculpted aquiline profile.

Laredo nudged a cowboy in a black armband standing next to him. "Who's the Englishman?" he asked curiously.

The cowboy threw a glance at the man's back. "That's Markham. He bought the old Gilmore ranch last spring. His brother's a baron or duke or something over in England."

Laredo nodded his thanks for the information and filed it away, not sure what it meant, if anything.

Tired of the crush of people and convinced there would be little to gain by hanging around longer, Laredo slowly made his way to a rear exit.

Emerging from the barn, he automatically glanced in the direction of the cemetery. Something white moved among the headstones not far from the blue canopy. He focused on the small dark-haired boy dressed in a white shirt and black dress pants, and recognized him at once as Chase's grandson.

A scan of the area revealed no adult in the vicinity. Unsure if the boy's ultimate destination was the cemetery or the river just beyond it, Laredo hesitated only a split second before striking out for the cemetery. As he approached the grave site, he slowed his pace to a leisurely stroll.

The boy stood beside the granite stone that marked the adjoining grave, the one inscribed MAGGIE — BELOVED WIFE AND MOTHER. Below that her full name was listed: MARY FRANCES ELIZABETH O'ROURKE CALDER followed by the dates of her birth and death.

"Hello there." Laredo pretended to just notice the boy. "I didn't realize anyone else was here."

The boy looked at him with suspicion. "Who are you?"

He was a gangling kid, a little tall for his age. Despite the babyish softness of his face, he had the beginnings of Chase's hard, square jaw and the snapping darkness of his eyes.

"My friends call me Laredo." He pushed his hat to the back of his head and crouched down to the boy's level.

" 'Redo is a funny name."

"I suppose it is," he conceded. "What's your name?"

"Trey."

"Pleased to meet you, Trey." Laredo reached out to shake hands with him, adult to adult. The boy accepted the gesture with suitable gravity. "Trey is a good name."

"My grampa gave it to me."

Laredo slid a glance at the gleaming coffin. "I imagine you miss him a lot."

Anger flared in his eyes. "My grampa's not dead. He's in Texas."

"How do you know that?" Laredo asked, curious as to the source of this knowledge.

"I just know." It was an emphatic statement, but one made without any clear basis in fact.

"I see." Laredo nodded, careful not to inadvertently start an argument.

Satisfied that his statement wasn't being challenged, Trey pointed to the casket. "Quint says they're gonna put that in the hole and cover it with dirt."

"Yes, but not for a while yet. Who's Quint?" Laredo wondered idly.

Trey frowned over the question. "He's Quint." Which clearly settled the matter in his mind.

Dipping his head, Laredo hid a smile and nodded again. "Of course he is."

"When my birthday comes, I'm gonna get a horse of my own just like Quint."

"Quint has a horse, does he?"

Trey bobbed his head in affirmation. "Her name's Molly. Quint lets me ride her sometimes. She's kinda slow though."

"What color is Molly?"

"Brown," he replied then cocked his

head to the side. "Are brown horses always slow?"

"Not always. What color horse do you want?"

Trey lifted his shoulders high to his neck in an uncaring shrug. "Red — or maybe yellow like Dandy. My grampa said he'd find me a good one."

"Is that why he went to Texas?"

Brightening visibly at the question, Trey gave him a wide-eyed look of new anticipation. "Maybe."

A searching call came from the barn area, the wind carrying it away from them. Laredo looked up and saw the widow poised in a stance of alertness. "Does your mom know where you are?"

"No," Trey replied with a glimmer of defiance.

"I think she's looking for you." Straightening, he cupped his hands to his mouth and shouted, "He's over here!" He waved his hat over his head until she started toward the cemetery. When he glanced at the boy, he noticed the glumness that pulled down the corners of his mouth. "Mothers worry a lot, don't they?"

"Yeah," Trey agreed without enthusiasm. "I guess that's their job."

"I guess," Trey sighed the words and

threw a glance over his shoulder to observe his mother's approach.

Laredo pretended not to notice the sharp study of her gaze when she joined them. At the last minute she glanced down to Trey. "I wondered where you went."

"I'm okay," he muttered in response.

"I didn't know that, though." She lifted her gaze to Laredo, a look of unspoken demand in her eyes. "I don't believe we have met," she challenged.

"His name's 'Redo," Trey inserted, puffing up a little that he knew something she didn't.

"Laredo Smith." Supplying the rest of it, Laredo touched a finger to his hat brim. "I guess I have the advantage because I know you're Jessy Calder."

She didn't respond in kind to his lazy smile. Neither was she cold or hostile, but rather regarded him with a steady calm. "How do you do." She extended a hand with a forthrightness that had a hint of masculine ease in it.

Her grip was firm and sure and brief, but the warm sensation of it lingered in his palm. "Trey was just telling me about the horse his grampa is going to buy for him."

An indulgent smile touched her wide lips

when she glanced at her son. "Yes, he's crazy about horses."

"I'm gonna be a cowboy," Trey asserted importantly. "I got a lasso and everything. And I'm real good at catchin' stuff with it. Aren't I, Mom?"

"You are definitely getting better."

"Can I go get my rope?" he asked hopefully, then made a slight face. "I don't want'a go back in the barn."

"You can if you want, but you have to stay close to the barn," she said and he took off at a run. "And don't try to rope any of the horses in the corral," she called in warning.

"I imagine boys can be a handful at that age," Laredo remarked when she turned back to him.

"He's easily bored," she admitted.

"I saw him down here by himself. With the river being so close by, I thought someone should keep an eye on him."

She seemed to appreciate the gesture. "That was kind of you, but O'Rourke is somewhere among the cottonwoods. He would have made sure Trey didn't fall in the river."

Startled, Laredo made a quick scan of the tree-lined bank, observing the silhouette of a horse and rider that he had previously overlooked. "Who's O'Rourke? One of your ranch hands?" His first thought was that she had someone standing guard.

"No. He's Maggie's brother." She tipped her head toward the gravestone of Chase's late wife. "Whenever Cat is out and about, you can count on O'Rourke being somewhere close by — Laredo, isn't it?"

"Yes."

"Are you from Texas?"

"I've spent some time there," he replied, deliberately noncommittal. "This is my first time in Montana. It's a big, wide country. It reminds me a bit of Texas the way it rolls into forever. I can understand why everybody says the Triple C is prime cattle country."

"It is good land." Automatically she let her glance sweep over the vast expanse of grass that stretched away from the river. Her expression softened with a mixture of pride and deep affection.

"You love this land, don't you," Laredo observed.

"It's been my home my whole life. There isn't an inch of it I haven't ridden."

He found himself admiring this woman with her unusual combination of strength and easy calm. "I understand you are in charge of the Triple C now. A place this size, that has to be a bit daunting."

She looked him in the eye with a man's directness. "You simply take each day as it comes and keep an eye on tomorrow. As long as you take care of the land, it will take care of you."

The statement had a profound ring to it. "Did Chase teach you that?" Laredo wondered.

"That has always been the Calder way of doing things," she replied, her gaze turning to a quiet probing. "Where did you meet Chase?"

"In Texas."

"I don't recall him ever mentioning your name," she replied.

Laredo smiled easily. "I don't imagine there was ever a reason why he should." Something in her body language warned him that she was about to bring the conversation to an end. With every instinct telling him to trust her, he took a calculated risk. "Are you absolutely certain Chase is dead?"

"Why would you ask that?" she said, clearly surprised by his question.

"What if I told you he wants to talk to you?"

A cold anger flared in her eyes. Abruptly she swung away from him and struck out

115

for the barn. In two strides, Laredo caught her arm and turned her back to face him.

"Hear me out."

"Why should I?" she challenged hotly, showing a temper held under tight control. "If Chase Calder was alive, he would be here himself."

"Believe me, he has his reasons for staying away."

"I don't believe you." The muscles in her arm tensed as she made to pull away from him.

"Did you see his body? Did anybody?" Laredo demanded.

"No, it was . . ." She hesitated, the first flicker of doubt showing in her expression.

"Burned beyond recognition," he completed the sentence for her. "You, the police, everybody assumed the dead man was Chase."

"Why are you doing this?" Her gaze narrowed on him, turning hard and cold. "What's your game?"

"It's no game. Chase needs to talk to you. Alone. You pick the time and location, but it can't be a place where he might be seen."

A corner of her mouth quirked in cold contempt. "You are a total stranger. You don't really believe I would be foolish enough to meet you — alone — in some out-of-the-way spot, do you?"

Laredo smiled in approval and let his hand fall away from her arm. "You're wise to be cautious. Which tells me you'll also be wise enough to pick a place that will be secure for both you and Chase."

"Is this a setup for a ransom demand? Have you kidnapped Chase?" Jessy demanded.

"At least you are willing to concede Chase is alive." His eyes crinkled at the corners.

"Not yet, I haven't," she stated firmly. "I'm just trying to figure out your game."

"It's no game. And to answer your question, if I had kidnapped Chase, I would have sent a ransom note or called. I wouldn't show my face around here."

"Maybe not, but people have done stupid things before, Mr. Smith — if that's really your name."

"It's a little too common to be believable, isn't it," he agreed.

"Tell me why I should trust you," she challenged.

"You shouldn't. You should trust Chase. This is the way he wants it."

She studied him with a long, unwavering look while she mentally reviewed her options.

"What kind of vehicle are you driving?"

Jessy observed the sudden leap of wariness in his eyes. "A blue Ford pickup with Texas plates."

"I hope that's the truth," she said, "because tomorrow morning at exactly nine o'clock, I want to see a blue Ford pickup with Texas plates drive slowly past the east gate on the main highway. If I see Chase in the truck, ten minutes later I will leave a note on the gate telling you when and where I will meet you."

"Fair enough." He nodded in agreement. "We'll be there at nine o'clock sharp. Just one more thing: Chase is trusting that you will not mention this conversation to anyone. And he means *anyone*."

"Why?" Jessy asked, unable to make sense of any of this.

"I'll let Chase explain it himself when he sees you. 'Til tomorrow." Nodding, he touched his hat to her and moved away at an unhurried pace.

Still troubled and doubtful, Jessy watched him a moment, noting that he seemed to be headed toward the rows of parked vehicles that crowded the ranch yard. Briefly she toyed with the idea of having one of the men follow this Laredo Smith when he left, but she suspected he would be watching for that.

Approaching footsteps crunched across a section of gravel. Turning toward the sound, Jessy saw Monte coming toward her, a look of concern furrowing his forehead.

"Where is Trey? Haven't you found him yet?"

"Yes. He went up to the house to fetch his rope."

His expression cleared. "I am relieved to hear he is no longer among the missing. You appeared to be in such deep conversation with that cowboy, I though perhaps you were about to organize a search for Trey."

"Fortunately, no. He just wanted to talk to me about Chase," she answered truthfully. "I'd better go talk to the governor before he has to leave."

As she started for the barn, Jessy threw a last glance after the mysterious Laredo Smith. He had the look of a cowboy and the rolling gait of one, but she remembered the grip of his hand. It hadn't possessed the distinctive ridging of callus that went along with rope work. In her mind, a cowboy who couldn't handle a rope wasn't a cowboy.

Laredo Smith raised more questions than he answered. Chief among them was why would he insist Chase was alive if he wasn't?

Chapter Five

The two-lane highway was the only sign of civilization for miles in any direction. A lone pickup traveled over it while its shadow raced alongside. The morning sun's strong rays poured into the truck's passenger window, heating Chase's shoulder and arm.

But he was only distantly aware of the sun's building warmth as he gazed out the window at the surrounding plains. There was deception in the land's appearance of flatness, making it easy to overlook the lone buttes and wandering coulees. He waited to feel some tug of home, but other than experiencing an urge to ride across it, he felt no sense of belonging.

Vaguely disgruntled, he glanced at Laredo. "How much farther is it?"

"The gate is coming up on our left," Laredo replied then checked his watch. "It's five minutes till. We'll go a couple more miles and turn around. It should put us there right on time."

Chase spotted a pair of tall posts with a

sign suspended between them, marking the entrance. He was struck by the plainness of it.

"Not very pretentious, is it," Laredo remarked, as if reading his thoughts. "Nobody can accuse the Calders of being full of themselves."

"If the ranch is as big as you say, why shout about it? Everybody already knows it."

A wry smile tugged at Laredo's mouth. "Judging from some of the tales I heard about you at the funeral yesterday, that sounds like something Chase Calder would say."

As they drove by the gate, Chase craned his head to look out the rear window and scan the dirt road leading up to the entrance gate. "It doesn't look like anyone is there yet."

"Jessy Calder struck me as a cautious woman. My guess is she'll pick a vantage point and watch from there. I don't think she will show herself."

"The question is, how much can she be trusted? She could be on one of those hillocks looking through a rifle scope." His tone was dryly grim.

"If she is, that will make you literally a sitting target," Laredo replied with a touch of black humor. "But you are going to need somebody on the inside, and the list of choices was slim." He went over them again: "Your daughter is strong and a scrapper, but she tends to wear her emotions on her sleeve and, according to some, tends to be impulsive and hot-tempered. Her husband is the local sheriff and ex-treasury agent. As far as I'm concerned that is reason enough to eliminate him. He would want to turn it all into a legal investigation. From what I could gather, virtually all of your ranch hands were born on the place and are supposedly loyal to the core. But it seems you ran the ranch with a lone hand until your son died and you took Jessy into your confidence and began grooming her to take over. I think you made a good choice." The road ahead of them was empty of traffic. Laredo slowed the truck and made a U-turn in the middle of the highway. "She's savvy and coolheaded, able to think on her feet. She doesn't rattle easy, that's for sure. She definitely impressed me."

"Good-looking, is she?" Chase threw him a knowing look.

"Let's just say that your son had good taste." Laredo spotted the gate ahead of them and slowed the pickup again. "The entrance is coming up. Don't forget, she will want a good look at your face when we go past it."

Hunkered flat among the summer-brown grass, Jessy adjusted the focus on the binoculars, centering it on the man riding on the passenger side. Shock tingled through her. She lowered the glasses to look without the assistance of their magnification, then raised them again. It was impossible. Yet there was no mistaking those hard, angular features. It was definitely Chase in that truck.

She kept the binoculars trained on him until the pickup was well past her. For a stunned moment she simply lay there. Even though she had come this morning, Jessy had never given any real credence to Laredo Smith's claim that Chase was still alive. Logic had insisted that it was merely the opening gambit in some sort of scam.

But if that wasn't Chase in the pickup, then the man was a dead ringer for him.

She scooted backwards off the sloped side of the hillock, slipped the binoculars back into their leather case, and ran at a crouch back to where she had left the pickup and horse trailer parked. She scrambled into the cab and reached for the pen and notepad lying on the seat. She was surprised to discover her hands were shaking. She paused and took a deep, steadying breath, then scratched out the message, still dazed by the knowledge it wasn't the one she had expected to write.

Finished, Jessy tore off the sheet and started up the truck, mentally congratulating herself for having the presence of mind to advise Sally that she might not be back in time for lunch.

When she reached the highway, there was no sign of the blue pickup. Ten minutes, she had told him. Hurriedly she nailed the message to a gatepost and climbed back in the truck. After years of experience with towing trailers, she had no difficulty making the swing to reverse directions and head back down the ranch road with a good five minutes to spare.

The road she was on led straight to the Triple C headquarters, roughly forty miles distant. But Jessy didn't stay on it. Instead she turned north on the first intersecting road, part of the nearly two hundred miles of roads that connected the far-flung reaches of the ranch.

Almost exactly ten minutes after he had last gone past the gate, Laredo approached it again. This time he pulled into the entrance and stopped, his gaze fastening on the sheet of paper fluttering in the slight morning breeze. Leaving the motor running, he climbed out of the truck and retrieved the message from the gatepost, skimmed it, and swore softly. As he slid behind the steering wheel again, he passed the sheet to Chase.

"The bad news is she has agreed to meet you at the old cemetery north of Blue Moon," he said, shifting the transmission out of Park. "The good news is we have two hours to find it. You wouldn't, by chance, remember where it is, would you?"

"No. I thought you said you drove all around Blue Moon yesterday." Chase frowned at him.

"I did, but I don't remember seeing any cemetery. It must be off the highway on a side road somewhere. There's probably a way to reach it without going through town, but I don't know what it is," Laredo said grimly. "Now I wish Hattie was with us instead of back at the motel in Miles City washing up our clothes. If you can figure out a way to hunker down in the seat when we get to town, you'd better do it."

Chase chose instead to slump sideways against the door frame and cover his face with his hat, aware that no one was likely to pay any attention to Laredo's dozing passenger.

The cemetery didn't turn out to be all that difficult to find. The site suited all the privacy requirements. It was a secluded location along a seldom-traveled road with no residences close by.

Laredo parked the truck in the graveled turn-in and surveyed the weed-riddled, overgrown cemetery. A pair of lone trees stood watch over the faded tombstones.

"I wonder where she is this time," Laredo murmured, mainly to himself, then glanced at Chase. "The message said that she wants to see you alone. I guess she still thinks I might have kidnapped you."

"It's logical that the possibility would cross her mind." Chase pushed open the passenger door. "Where do you suppose the O'Rourke family plot is?"

"I'm betting it will be somewhere close to one of those trees. With all the brush growing up around them, it would be a good place to wait out of sight." He swung out of the truck. "I'd better give you a hand. You may be steadier on your feet, but this ground looks awful rough."

Just as they moved past the hood of the truck, Jessy stepped from behind a clump of brush, holding a rifle at the ready. "You didn't tell me he was hurt." Her gaze briefly bored into Laredo, then shifted its attention to Chase to inspect the bandage on the left side of his head.

"That's the first mistake you've made, Jessy," Laredo replied. "For all you know, I could be holding a gun on him."

"You could," she conceded. "But you would be a dead man if you used it. This rifle is already cocked, and I have shot more than my share of coyotes. One more wouldn't faze me."

His mouth quirked in a crooked smile. "You know what? I believe you."

During their exchange, Chase studied this tall, boy-slim woman in jeans and a well-worn straw Stetson, noting the high, strong cheekbones and sharp, angular jawline. Laredo's previous description of her hadn't conveyed the inner beauty that shone through her strong features. Not the rifle she gripped nor the manly clothes disguised the fact she was all woman.

"Do you still insist on talking to me alone?" Chase challenged smoothly. "Because I wouldn't be here at all without this man. Laredo saved my life. He is the only person I trust right now."

Jessy's hesitation was slight. "If you trust him, then I do." She engaged the safety on the rifle. "There isn't anyplace for you to sit out here. Maybe it would be better if we talked in the truck."

"Good idea." Chase promptly turned and started back to the pickup, with Laredo at his side.

"For safety's sake, you might want to leave the rifle outside," Laredo suggested as he kept a supporting hand on Chase while he climbed into the passenger side.

"I planned on it," Jessy replied and laid it in the open truck bed.

"And for your information, I do have a gun." Laredo stepped back from the door to allow Jessy to slide in next to Chase.

She skimmed a glance over his tapered shirt and snug-fitting jeans, identifying all his muscled contours for what they were. "But not on you," she concluded.

"Yup." He reached behind his back. When his hand reappeared, there was a thirty-eight in it. Her only show of surprise was a faint widening of her eyes. "Like you, Jessy, I play it cautious." Using both hands, he returned the gun to its hiding place.

"I won't be fooled by that a second time." She stepped onto the running board and pulled herself into the cab.

With the midday temperatures rising,

they left both doors open to keep the interior air circulating. Jessy ran a critical eye over Chase, concern clouding her eyes.

"How bad were you hurt?" she asked.

"Bad enough," Chase answered without elaboration.

"How did it happen? And why don't you want anyone to know you're alive?" She had come up with a dozen possible explanations en route to the cemetery, which made her anxious to hear the true one.

"It's a long story, one I'll let Laredo tell."

Privately it irritated her that he chose to defer to Laredo, but she kept her irritation to herself.

Sitting sideways, Laredo leaned forward, draping an arm over the top of the steering wheel, and gave her a bare-bones account of the events that had led up to this moment. When he finished, Jessy stared at Chase, making no attempt at all to mask her shock.

"You really don't remember who you are? Not even now?"

"My memory doesn't go back any further than that parking lot," Chase told her. "According to Hattie, in most cases like mine, it will return — maybe in a few days or a few months — in bits and pieces or full-blown. Or there may be parts I never remember, especially the time right before I was shot."

"And Hattie is some friend or relation of yours?" She looked to Laredo for confirmation.

"Something like that." He nodded.

"But how can you be sure of that when you haven't seen a doctor?" Jessy reasoned.

"Hattie is a registered nurse. And seeking a doctor is too risky. By law, gunshot wounds have to be reported. I don't need that kind of trouble." Chase's expression warned her that he was firm on that decision.

"But what are you going to do?" Jessy asked, conscious of the myriad of complications his amnesia created.

"That's where you come into it," Chase said. "I need a place close by the ranch where I can hole up — either until my memory returns or we figure out who tried to kill me. More importantly it needs to be a place where I don't have to worry about neighbors or a landlord stopping by. Laredo tells me the Triple C is big — managed in districts. Is there an old house or cabin sitting empty somewhere?"

"I can think of three off the top of my head, but it would be too easy for one of the hands to notice it was occupied. Other than those, there really isn't anyth— wait a minute." She stopped, a possibility dawning on her. "There used to be an old line shack up in the high foothills. To the best of my knowledge nobody has been there in years, probably not since my dad and I were up there hunting. I couldn't have been much more than twelve or thirteen at the time. We don't even run cattle up there anymore."

"It sounds perfect," Chase stated. "How do we get there?"

With the passing of that initial burst of excitement, Jessy turned hesitant. "I can't even swear that it's still standing, let alone whether the well still works, or how habitable it might be. There is definitely no running water or electricity."

"I've lived under rougher conditions," Laredo said with unconcern. "If you can supply me with the necessary tools, lumber, and maybe even a generator, I can make it livable."

"I'll figure out a way." Jessy knew it wouldn't be easy to do without arousing someone's suspicions. "I don't think directions will do you any good. Unless you know where it is, it would be sheer luck if you found it. I'll have to take you there.

Even then the old fire road will only get you within a half mile of it. I can't remember what the terrain is like to know whether you can drive any closer than that."

"In that case we'll find out when we get there." The whinny of a horse punctuated the end of Laredo's statement. In swift reaction, he came to full alertness, his gaze making a slashing survey of the area outside the pickup.

"That was my horse," Jessy said in quick assurance. "I picketed him in the hollow beyond the tree."

"You rode here?" Laredo questioned in surprise. "Why?"

"I didn't want to take the chance someone would drive by and see a Triple C pickup parked around here. Nothing would start the rumor mill buzzing quicker." That thought triggered another. "It will take me close to an hour to ride back to where I left the truck and trailer parked. If I try to take you to the line shack this afternoon, there won't be much daylight left by the time we get there. Do you have a place you can stay tonight?"

"We have a couple motel rooms in Miles City," Laredo answered. "We left Hattie there to do our laundry."

"That settles it then. We'll rendezvous back here tomorrow morning." Jessy paused to consider the drive they would have to make from Miles City. "Would nine o'clock be too early?"

"We can make it." Chase didn't hesitate.

A lazy smile curved Laredo's mouth. "I think he's tired of being snuck in and out of motel rooms."

"I don't blame him." There was empathy in the look Jessy gave Chase. Then the practical side of her surfaced. "If there is nothing else, I need to start back. We all have a lot to do before tomorrow morning."

She was halfway out of the truck when Chase stopped her. "Before you go, I have a question to ask you. What was I doing in Texas? Why did I go there?"

"You said you had a meeting with some-body named Brewster. Tom Brewster, I think it was." Her recollection of the man's first name was hazy.

"Who is Brewster? What does he do?"

"To be honest, I don't know," Jessy admitted. "To the best of my knowledge, the ranch has never had any dealings with him in the past. In some way he's involved with cattle, but I don't know if he's a buyer, a rancher, a broker or what."

"Didn't I tell you why I was going to see him?" Chase probed.

"Just that you wanted to talk to him about some cattle."

"Am I usually that vague?" Chase frowned in skepticism.

"No," Jessy admitted with a slight smile. "But you also told me that being away for a few days would give me an opportunity to run the ranch on my own. I thought that was probably your main reason for going to Texas. I know you didn't give me the impression the trip was of any great importance. I wish now I had asked more questions," she said with regret.

"Maybe the trip was an excuse to be gone." Chase was forced to concede that possibility. "But until we can be certain of that, see what you can find out about this man Brewster." The minute the words were out of his mouth, he withdrew them. "No, we don't want to tip our hand in case he is an important connection. So don't ask questions about him, but see if I wrote his address or phone number down somewhere. If I did, get that information to me. In the meantime I'll figure out the best way to handle it."

"It's logical that Chase would have called him from the hotel," Laredo inserted. "Look through the room charges and write down any phone numbers that you don't recognize."

"Logan took care of your bill while they were in Fort Worth. I'm almost positive he gave me the itemized receipt. I'll see what I can find," Jessy promised. "Anything else?"

"For now, only one. I'll need some cash," Chase told her. "I don't have a cent on me. I'm not sure exactly how much I owe Laredo and Hattie already, but it's adding up every day."

"I'll bring some money for you tomorrow." Jessy swung to the ground and retrieved her rifle, then turned back to them, unusually solemn. "I'll meet you here at nine tomorrow. Be careful."

"You can count on it." Chase pulled the passenger door shut. In silence, they swung out of the old cemetery. Not until they were on the road toward Blue Moon did Chase speak again. "You're right about Jessy. I would hate to learn she can't be trusted."

"Me too," Laredo said. "She's an easy woman to like."

"I just hope she doesn't give you reason to regret letting her know that you are armed."

"If she is as square as I think she is, she

needs to be alert for that." He slid a wry grin in Chase's direction. "Maybe you can teach her the ins and outs of cattle ranching, but I can teach her the skills to stay alive."

Absently amused and inwardly pleased, Chase ran his glance over the man's clean profile. "That sounds like you are signing on for the duration."

"Do you have a problem with that?" Laredo countered, a faint twinkle in his blue eyes.

"Not a one." Smiling, Chase settled back in the seat, making himself comfortable for the long ride back to Miles City.

The brown horse shuffled along at an easy trot, its rider in no hurry and bound for no particular destination. But Culley O'Rourke's wanderings rarely had a purpose. The sole exception to that rule involved his niece Cat Calder Echohawk. Ever since his sister had been killed in that plane crash when Cat was still a teenager he had made it his mission to watch over Maggie's daughter. But on this day Cat was at home, still enveloped in grief over her father's recent death.

But Calder's death was no cause for regret as far as Culley was concerned. There was a time when he had been consumed with hatred for the man. The hatred had burned itself out, though, and he had come to tolerate the man's existence, for Cat's sake.

Without a doubt, the years had wrought many changes in Culley O'Rourke, most notably in his appearance. His hair that had once been the glistening black of a crow had grayed to the color of a weathered barn board. His once wide shoulders had thinned and appeared permanently bowed in a protective hunch. The nervous, hair-trigger energy that had so often seemed poised on the edge of violence had faded to a constant restlessness.

It was that innate restlessness that pushed him to this endless wandering that knew no boundaries. Long ago the Triple C riders had grown used to seeing him ghosting over the ranch's vast holdings, invariably fighting shy of any contact.

If his presence drew any comment at all, it was generally something wry like, "Saw ole Crazy Culley today, sloping out of sight behind a hill." And it was always issued with an amused shake of the head.

Keeping to a swale in the plains and deliberately avoiding sky-lining himself on higher ground, Culley took a roundabout track toward a fence gate. He had yet to decide if he would make use of it or angle off in another direction. It would probably be the latter. Culley had never been one to travel along roads, and there was one on the other side of the fence gate.

The brown gelding pricked its ears, its nose lifting to scent the air. Culley had ridden the horse for too many years not to have learned to correctly read its body language. Something was nearby. By reading the horse's slight variations, Culley could tell if that thing was a cow, a coyote, or a horse. This time the gelding was reacting to one of its own kind. In this particular area of the Triple C, Culley knew that if there were a horse in the area, ninety percent of the time there would be a rider, too.

Obeying his initial impulse, Culley reined in his mount. It wasn't that he disliked other people. He simply wasn't comfortable around them. The small talk that came so easily to others was awkward for him, almost painful.

But to avoid such situations, he had to know the rider's location and destination so he could head in the opposite direction. It was that desire which prompted him to rein his horse up the sloping rise in the plains. He pulled up when he could see over the top of it.

A pickup and horse trailer were parked along the edge of the dirt ranch road a quarter mile distant. Near the rear of it, a rider swung out of the saddle. The sun's bright rays glinted on the blond lights in the long tail of hair that hung below the riderhat, making it easy for Culley to recognize Jessy Calder.

Culley watched as she unlatched the tailgate to load her horse into the trailer. The more he thought about it the more unusual it seemed for Jessy to be out here alone. There was a time before she married Ty when she had worked for the Triple C as an ordinary cowhand, but with Calder dead, she was running things now.

Knowing that, Culley couldn't help wondering what she was doing so far from headquarters. That curiosity coupled with the fact that Jessy was one of the few people he felt comfortable around, mostly because she didn't care whether he talked or not, pushed him forward.

By the time he reached the fence line, Jessy had loaded her horse and fastened the trailer gate. Moving with long, purposeful strides, she headed for the driver's side of the pickup, so wrapped up in her thoughts that she failed to notice him.

Loathe as he was to be the one making the opening gambit, Culley called out, "Sure didn't figure on seein' you out this way."

Jessy halted with an almost guilty start. An instant later her wide mouth curved in a smile. "Hello, Culley. As for being out here — you know how it goes. I got tired of being cooped up inside and decided I wanted to feel a horse under me again. Now it's back to work. See ya." She sketched him a wave and climbed into the truck.

Culley lifted a hand in return and watched the rig pull away. "Her reasons seem sound enough," he commented to his mount. "But they sure don't explain why she'd drive an hour from headquarters to go a-ridin'."

There were times when Culley couldn't help being nosy, although he never thought of it as snooping. He just wanted that old curiosity to stop nagging him.

As fresh as her tracks were, they were easy to follow. Reading sign, as the old-timers called the ability to identify a person or animal by the track it left, was a self-taught skill for Culley, something he had picked up over the years. One of the first things he had learned was how to tell whether a horse or a cow had left a trail through the grass. It was a difference that was easy to spot, since a cow left the grass stalks bent in the direction it had just come from and a horse laid it down in the direction it was going.

Culley didn't have to backtrail Jessy very far before he realized that she hadn't been out for an aimless ride. She'd had a destination, and she had taken the straight route to reach it.

The trail led him directly to the north boundary fence. His sharp eyes noticed a place where the top wire had been mended. He rode closer to it and bent sideways in the saddle to examine it. The bright marks on the metal told him that the wire had been first snipped, then twisted back together again — very recently.

The saddle leather creaked as he straightened to sit erect, puzzled by his discovery. "I gotta tell ya, Brownie," he muttered to the horse, "it's one thing to ride all the way out here to fix a break in the fence, an' it's a horse of a different color to ride all the way out here, cut the wire, an' then fix it. Why'd she want'a do that?"

The gelding snorted and swung its nose

at a pesky fly nibbling on its shoulder. Absorbed with solving this puzzle, Culley stared blankly at a tuft of brown thread hooked on a barb along the middle wire a long time before he actually noticed it.

"Well now, what's this?" He swung to the ground and picked it off the wire. There was another piece of thread snubbed on a barb next to the first. Only this one was more like a bit of lint. While Culley pondered the meaning of them, the gelding took advantage of the break to chomp on some grass.

"If I remember right," he said, thinking back, "there was a brown saddle blanket tied behind the cantle of her saddle." An answer began to form. "Now a horse ain't likely to jump what it can't see — like a single strand of wire. But if a body was to throw a blanket across it, he can see what he needs to clear. 'Course, why would she want'a jump that fence an' go traipsin' around the Dugan range?"

Before he concluded that was what Jessy had done, Cully studied the ground on the other side of the fence. As clear as the sky overhead, a pair of fresh gouge marks was visible, revealing the place where her horse had landed.

While he had never been one to respect a

boundary fence, Culley would have sworn that Jessy would. One thing was certain — he hadn't come this far to stop now.

After leading his horse well clear of the fence, he retrieved a pair of wire cutters from his saddlebag. "None of that fence jumpin' stuff for us," he said and proceeded to cut through all three wires, careful to avoid their back whip.

Again Jessy's trail led him in more or less a straight line. It struck him that only one place lay in this direction, and he couldn't figure out why Jessy would go there.

Short of the old cemetery, Culley found the place where Jessy had left her horse. A pile of horse droppings and short-cropped grass told him that the horse had been left for a time.

Dismounting, he dropped the reins, ground-tying his gelding. Following her foot trail wasn't as easy as following the horse tracks. But the occasional plain ones he found took him to some brush.

Well-flattened grass showed him where she had stood for a while. It was a place that would have concealed her from sight. It set him to wondering if she had been spying on somebody, or waiting for somebody. Which also made him wonder if Jessy was more of a Calder than he thought.

With no more to learn here, he started to retrace his steps. He was nearly to the thick clump of brush when his conscience prodded him.

Close by was the O'Rourke family plot. It had been such a long time since Culley had been there that he had trouble locating the slab headstones that marked the graves of his parents. Finally he found them, nearly hidden among the tall weeds. He tugged away the taller clumps in front of them and brushed away some of the dirt embedded in the carved lettering.

Straightening, he stepped back and removed his hat. There were no fancy sayings on his mother's marker, and nothing to identify her as either wife or mother. There was only her name, MARY FRANCES ELIZABETH O'ROURKE, followed by the date of her birth and death. Culley hadn't been much more than fourteen when she died, but he could still feel the gentle touch of her palm cupped to his cheek.

A smile touched his mouth in remembrance, but it faded when his attention shifted to the grave of his father. The stone was just as plain, with only the name spelled out: ANGUS O'ROURKE. As always, Culley's strongest memory of his father was that of his death. Some of the old bitterness resurfaced.

"Maybe you did rustle a bunch of Triple C cattle, Pa," he said. "But that didn't give old man Calder the right t' take the law in his own hands and hang ya."

Before the memory of those long ago days could upset him again, Culley turned away and shoved his hat back on his head. He hesitated, glancing back at the weed-choked plot.

"It ain't right the way they let this place go to seed," he said and experienced a twinge of guilt that he hadn't checked on it before. "I'll come back t'morrow an' tidy it up a bit."

Exploring further, he found some fresh tire tracks and more footprints, a set on either side of the vehicle. Judging from the depth of the impressions, Culley guessed they were made by men. Among them he found one of Jessy's boot prints. Which meant she must have met up with them.

Who or why, he still didn't know and wasn't likely to find out, either. But at least he had discovered the answers to some of his questions.

Chapter Six

⌘

The next morning it took Culley the better part of an hour to search through the barn and tool shed before he finally found the old hand scythe. After that he spent twenty minutes at the grindstone, sharpening its blade.

It was a few minutes past nine o'clock when he finally tossed the scythe into the back of his old pickup and climbed behind the wheel. He drove to the end of the lane and made the turn to head for the old cemetery.

The engine in the old pickup balked when he pushed down on the accelerator. The truck's top speed was usually between forty and fifty miles an hour. But this morning he had trouble getting it up to thirty-five.

When he saw another pickup traveling toward him, Culley glanced in the rearview mirror, relieved to see there was nobody behind him. He didn't want to find himself in an accident because some fool tried to pass him.

With his attention once more on the road ahead of him, Culley let his gaze wander to the oncoming pickup. He was quick to recognize the Triple C insignia on its door. He peered at the windshield, trying to identify the driver.

But he didn't get a good look until the truck went by him. The minute he saw Jessy Calder behind the wheel, he decided she was on her way to the Circle Six to visit Cat.

He wouldn't have given it another thought if he hadn't noticed a second pickup following close behind her. Culley saw right away that it had out-of-state license plates. It was rare enough for anyone to travel these roads, let alone a nonresident of Montana.

There appeared to be two, maybe three people traveling in it, but Culley had a good look at only the driver. Right away he felt there was something familiar about him. Then he remembered the cowboy who had talked with Jessy at the Triple C cemetery. It started him wondering if that cowboy might also be the same one she met yesterday.

"But," Culley said to himself with a frown, "why did she meet him on the sly?"

Located on the jutting shoulder of a rocky foothill, the old line shack was tucked against the slope to take advantage of its shelter from the cold winter winds. The terrain was more stone than soil, studded with brush, stunted pines, and patches of scrawny grass.

A deadfall had prevented them from driving closer than a hundred yards from the site. Jessy felt the tug and stretch of her leg muscles as she made the sloping climb.

When she topped the rise to the foothill's shoulder, she came to an abrupt stop and simply stared at the dilapidated structure. A sizable section of the roof had collapsed; all the windows were broken, and the door hung drunkenly on its hinges.

"Maybe this wasn't a good idea." Jessy glanced at Chase with a mixture of regret and concern. "It's in worse shape than I thought."

On the other side of him, Hattie murmured in dismay, "Lordy, this reminds me of where we stayed in Mexico —" She broke off the sentence and threw a worried glance at Laredo as if she had said something she shouldn't.

"Now, you aren't looking at it right." Laredo smiled lazily, hands on his hips, one leg cocked in a relaxed stance. "This place has a skylight, good air flow, and a quaintly rustic touch."

"Ramshackle, you mean," Hattie corrected with dry censure.

"You're forgetting that your house wasn't in much better shape when you and Ed bought the place. As long as the line shack doesn't fall over when you lean on it, it can be repaired." He laid a hand on her shoulder in quiet encouragement and urged her forward. "Let's go take a closer look."

"I'll go look," Hattie agreed with obvious reservations. "But I'm telling you right now that I'm glad we used the last of our cash to buy that tent. You can bet that's where I'll be sleeping tonight."

"Speaking of money," Jessy dug into her jeans pocket and pulled out a wad of bills. She handed it to Chase. "This is about all we had left in the petty cash fund. I haven't figured out how I'm going to account for it yet, but I will."

"That's easily handled." Chase glanced at the bills before stuffing them in his own pocket. "Do you have a slip of paper?"

"I have a tablet back at the truck. Why? What do you have in mind?"

"I'll write an IOU, sign it, and date it prior to my trip to Texas."

Jessy nodded in immediate understanding. "That way I won't have to explain anything."

When Hattie noticed they weren't behind her, she stopped and looked back. "Aren't you coming, Duke?"

"We'll be right there." He waved her on and started forward himself.

"Did she call you Duke?" Jessy eyed him curiously.

"They had to call me something when I couldn't supply them with my own name. Hattie came up with Duke." He didn't add that he was more comfortable with that name than he was with Chase Calder. Chase Calder was still a person he didn't know.

After an initial inspection of the old line cabin, Laredo concluded, "The damage looks worse than it is. Other than some rotten wood in the roof, the rest of the structure looks sound. Somebody built this to last."

"That's the only way Calders build things," Jessy said, echoing a statement her father had once made.

Hattie poked her head inside the door. "There's enough dirt in here to plant a garden. It will take a week to get it clean enough to live in — and evict all the creepy-crawly things." She turned away from the door with an expressive little shudder.

"Something tells me if anybody can turn a boar's nest into a home, it's you, Hattie," Chase declared in a voice dry with amusement.

Jessy swung toward him in surprise. "You remembered what we used to call this place."

"Did I?" Chase was skeptical. "It's possible, but in cowboy lingo, line cabins were often referred to as boar's nests."

"Maybe they were," Jessy conceded. "But we have two other old line shacks still standing, and this is the only one that went by the name Boar's Nest."

"You can do what you please, Duke," Hattie declared. "But I choose to believe you just recovered your first scrap of memory, even if it is an insignificant piece."

"While you two argue over who's right," Laredo inserted, "Jessy and I are going to unload the trucks so she can get back to the ranch. You might want to give some thought to where you want the tent pitched. Before I tackle fixing the cabin, I plan on clearing away that deadfall so we can drive all the way up here."

Jessy was impressed by his eminently practical decision. But she didn't say anything until they were on their way down the hill. "That's sensible to clear away the deadfall first."

"I'm glad you approve." Amusement gleamed in his blue eyes, faintly mocking her. Which annoyed her ever so slightly. "You understand, it's not that I object to the long walk, but I sure don't fancy dragging up all the plywood and lumber I'll need to fix the hole in the roof."

"That wasn't approval you heard," Jessy told him, a coolness in her voice. "It was relief that you seem to have some common sense. You have to remember you are a total stranger as far as I'm concerned."

"It bothers you that Hattie and I are looking after Chase, doesn't it," Laredo guessed.

"I know Chase trusts you," she replied, deliberately hedging.

"But you don't."

She reverted to her usual candor. "Not entirely."

"I imagine you are wondering if I'm in this for the money, that I might be hoping Chase will make a sizable contribution to my bank account when this is over." The mockery was there again in his lazy smile.

"It crossed my mind," she admitted and waited for Laredo to deny it was his motive.

"In the first place, I don't have a bank account, so any contribution he might offer would have to be in cash," he replied with a perfectly straight face.

Jessy halted in stunned surprise. "You are actually admitting that you are only here for money?"

"What's wrong with that?" he countered nonchalantly and kept walking. "The Old West is littered with stories of hired guns working for big outfits. In today's West, they still do, but they give them politically correct names like bodyguard and investigators." Laredo glanced back at her and grinned. "I disappointed you, didn't I? You wanted me to say something noble like, I'm here because Chase is a good man."

"I don't know what I expected." But it hadn't been what she'd heard. She resumed her descent of the hill. "I assume Chase knows this."

"The man has lost his memory, not his mind," he chided, and Jessy was irritated with herself for even asking the question. "The idea of me getting paid to look after Chase really bothers you, doesn't it? Maybe I need to put it in cowboy talk. When I take a rancher's money, I ride for the brand, and in my job, it usually means come hell or high water. This time it's more likely to be hell than high water."

He spoke in a jesting tone, but the hard steel of his eyes was all business. It was a quality Jessy had observed in Logan on rare occasions. But the similarities seemed to stop there.

"So you work as bodyguard for a living." She struggled to wrap her mind around this thought.

"There you go assuming things. I only said that's what I was doing now." Reaching the trucks, Laredo lifted a crate of canned goods from the back of his and hoisted it onto his shoulder, then hauled out the tent sack. He paused. "Any more questions? Because I'm likely to be puffing carrying this up the hill. I may not have enough air for talking."

"Just one. Is Laredo Smith your real name?"

He gave her a wry look and shook his head in mock amazement. "Do you really think any mother is going to name her son Laredo? I don't think so. But you keep asking questions. That's how you learn things." He started up the hill.

"I would learn more if I got straight answers," Jessy countered, lifting her voice to make certain he heard her. She was almost certain she detected a low chuckle from him.

After two trips, Laredo decided that they had carried up everything they would need that night. The rest of the items were loaded into the back of his truck to be hauled up later after he had cleared away the deadfall.

Preparing to leave, Jessy slid behind the wheel of her pickup. "Tell Chase I'll see him. I may not be able to make it back tomorrow, but I'll come as soon as I can slip away again."

"I'll do it," Laredo replied. "By the way, were you able to find anything on that Brewster fellow?"

"Not yet. I did check the hotel bill. There were several local calls on it and a few long-distance ones, but most of those were to the Triple C. I'll keep trying to find something," she promised and shifted the pickup into reverse, backing up and making a tight turn to make the bumpy trip back to the old fire road.

When Jessy arrived at the Triple C headquarters nearly two hours later, she was quick to notice Cat's vehicle parked in front of The Homestead. Trey was on the veranda, demonstrating his rope skills to Quint while Laura sat in one of the rockers, playing with her doll.

The minute Trey saw her pull up to the house, he abandoned his miniature lasso and ran to the steps to meet her. "Hi, Mom. Quint's here."

"I see that," Jessy said and playfully pushed the brim of Trey's cowboy hat down over his face, then glanced at Quint. "Where's your mom?"

"Inside with Sally."

With both arms wrapped tightly around her doll, Laura hopped out of the rocker and scampered to Jessy's side. "Sally's cryin'," Laura declared, attaching a high degree of importance to the news. "She misses Grampa a lot."

"Grampa's gonna buy me a horse," Trey stated and immediately galloped away, tossing his head and whinnying in his best imitation of the animal.

Jessy went straight to the kitchen to let Sally know she was home.

As expected, she found Sally seated in one of the kitchen chairs, a balled-up handkerchief pressed to her mouth in an attempt to smother the sobs that shook her shoulders. Cat was crouched beside the chair, a comforting hand resting on the housekeeper's arm while tears ran down her own cheeks.

When Sally caught sight of Jessy, she swallowed back her tears and mopped at the wetness on her face. "I'm sorry, Jessy," she sniffled. "I know I shouldn't carry on like this in front of the children, but" — her lip quivered — "I miss Chase so much."

"We all do, Sally." Cat's voice trembled with feeling. "But you know he would want us to be strong."

"I try. I really do," Sally insisted tearfully. "But when you said you wanted to —" She pressed the handkerchief to her mouth again as if the rest of the sentence was too painful to speak.

"Forget it," Cat told her. "We won't clean out his room today. Okay?" she said with quiet encouragement, and Sally nodded in mute agreement. "You look exhausted, Sally. Why don't you go lie down for a little while?"

"But the twins —" Sally began in protest.

"I'll watch them for Jessy. You go get some rest," Cat urged.

"I'll try." Sally pushed out of the chair and moved toward the doorway, a pronounced heaviness in her movements.

Jessy was grateful for Cat's silence as she waited for Sally to leave the kitchen. Jessy needed time to collect her wits. Cat's statement may have reassured Sally, but it had alarmed Jessy.

Right now the task of clearing Chase's room of all his clothes and personal belongings had merely been postponed. Jessy had to come up with a logical reason to keep it that way.

"I'm worried about Sally," Cat said the moment the woman was safely out of earshot. "Have you noticed the circles under her eyes and the weight she's lost?"

"I know. She admitted to me that she hasn't been able to sleep much," Jessy replied.

"She can't keep this up, not at her age, not without damaging her health," Cat murmured with concern. "Maybe she should make an appointment at the clinic. Perhaps Dr. Brown could prescribe a sedative to help her sleep."

"See if you can convince her of that," Jessy agreed. "In the meantime, it won't hurt to leave Chase's room as it is for a couple months, not only for Sally's sake but Trey's as well. He still goes in there a lot."

"You're right," Cat agreed and sighed heavily. "I just wanted to be useful. You and Sally have so much to do. This was something I could do to help."

"Then do me a favor: see if you can find someone to watch the twins during the day," Jessy suggested. "Sally doesn't need that responsibility right now. I'll leave it in your hands. Whoever you choose will be fine with me."

"I'll get on it right away," Cat promised. "By the way, Culley mentioned that he saw you this morning."

"Yes. I passed him on the road. I didn't notice him until I was all the way by." Jessy wasn't entirely comfortable with this new subject.

"He said he thought you were on your way to the Circle Six." Cat didn't come right out and ask where Jessy went, but the unspoken question was there.

"I thought about stopping by to see you, but I had too many things to do." Jessy smiled to herself, realizing that she had just taken a page out of Laredo's book with her evasion. "And I still have a lot to do, so I'd better get at it."

Using that as her exit line Jessy left the kitchen, and headed for the den to tackle the paperwork she had postponed.

The summer sun blazed hot and strong over the rough and rocky foothills. Perspiration rolled down Chase's neck as he hefted a bundle of shingles onto his shoulder, his muscles straining under the burden. But it was a kind of sweat and strain that felt good and vaguely familiar.

After adjusting his load for better balance, he moved to the ladder propped against the cabin. A shirtless Laredo was on the roof, nailing down the last batch of shingles. The rhythmic pounding of his hammer echoed in the stillness. With his free hand, Chase grabbed hold of a rung and started up.

He was halfway to the top when Hattie toted a pail of dirty water out of the cabin. The instant she saw Chase, she came to an abrupt stop.

"Would you mind telling me what you are doing on that ladder, Duke?" she challenged.

"Enjoying the view. What does it look like?" He smiled away her question.

"Then enjoy it from down here."

"I think I'll have to start calling you Harping Hattie," Chase replied, eyes twinkling. "A little honest work won't hurt me."

"It won't hurt you a bit," Hattie agreed, "as long as you do it on the ground. What would you do if you got a dizzy spell while you're on that ladder?"

"Count on you to catch me," he teased.

"You don't know me very well. I would let you fall just to teach you a lesson."

"Now that sounds like hard-hearted Hattie," Laredo said through the nails he held between his teeth.

"It's called tough love," she countered with her usual spunk and set the pail on the ground. "When you come down, you can empty this bucket and fill it with some clean water. When you get done with that, I have a mop waiting for you inside — or a scrub brush. You can take your pick." She turned on her heel and went back inside.

Laredo removed the last nail from between his teeth and glanced at Chase, dry amusement gleaming in his eyes. "If we aren't careful, she's going to turn into a slave driver."

"There is something about a dirty house that seems to get a woman's dander up." Chase slung the shingle bundle onto the tar-paper-covered roof not far from Laredo's feet, then paused and turned his face to the steady breeze. His idly roaming glance noticed a plume of dust in the distance.

"Better hold it, Laredo," he warned. "There is somebody on the road. They look to be a mile or so away yet, but sound can travel a considerable distance in this country."

Laredo immediately straightened from his task and slipped the hammer into the loop on his tool belt. Turning sideways, he scanned the long vista, zeroing in on the dust cloud. "Pass me those binoculars hanging from the ladder."

After removing the high-powered binoculars from their leather case Chase handed them to Laredo and waited in silence while the other man focused them on the source of the dust cloud. "Can you tell who it is?"

"A ranch pickup with the Triple C insignia on its door. I can't make out the driver. It might be Jessy. Then again, it might not be. We'd better play it safe. It's time to take a break anyway."

He waited until Chase had begun his descent, then moved to the ladder and swung a foot onto a rung. When he reached the bottom, he passed the binoculars to Chase and headed for the water jug. After guzzling down a large quantity of it, he poured some on his faded blue kerchief and used the wet cloth to wipe the sweat from his face and neck while Chase tracked the vehicle's progress through the binoculars.

Laredo cast a sideways glance at him.

"Which way is it headed?"

"If it turns west at the next intersection, probably here. Which should mean it's Jessy." He kept the binoculars trained on the pickup. "It's about time she showed up. It's been three days now. I expected her to come yesterday."

"I don't imagine it's easy for her to slip away." Laredo wandered over to stand beside Chase.

"Probably not." But the admission was a grudging one. A second later he announced, "She turned west." He lowered the glasses. "It's Jessy, all right, I just got a good look at her."

Fifteen minutes later, the pickup bounced onto the relative flatness of the hill's wide shoulder and rolled to a stop next to Laredo's truck. Jessy climbed out of the cab, stepped to the rear of the pickup, and lifted a duffel bag out of the back, then headed for the cabin where Chase stood with Laredo.

"Hi." Her smile of greeting was wide and warm as she ran her glance over Chase, noting the changes in him. "The bandage is off and your color is back. You must be feeling better." Without waiting for him to reply, she set the duffel bag on the ground. "I threw some clothes and a pair of everyday boots in here. I thought you would be needing them. Sorry I couldn't come any sooner, but I've been busy."

"With what?" Chase asked, faintly annoyed that he had no idea about what was going on.

"Actually it was 'with whom,'" Jessy replied. "I spent most of the last two days with lawyers and accountants, handling all legal loose ends that hadn't been tied up. Talk about something that was a total waste of time, that was it. I can't imagine what we'll have to go through to get you declared legally alive."

"That won't be for a while yet," Chase stated.

"You still don't remember anything." Jessy's gaze remained steady on him.

"No." Chase didn't mention the few disjointed items that rattled around in his mind, names that were either meaningless or made no sense.

Jessy shifted her attention to the cabin, taking note of the new windows, the rehung door, and new screen door before glancing at the partially repaired roof. "Why didn't you finish the roof before you installed new windows?" She turned a wondering look on Laredo.

"Hattie was tired of battling flies. Fixing

164

the roof was low on her list of priorities," he explained. "Getting the well pump fixed and running a water line into the cabin were first on her agenda, with the windows coming a close second."

As if on cue, Hattie appeared on the other side of the screen door. "Hello, Jessy. I don't mean to be rude, but I am up to my elbows in dirt. There is some lemonade in the ice chest. Tell Laredo to pour you some."

"I don't care for any right now, thanks anyway," Jessy said.

"It's there if you decide you want some. I'd love to visit, but it will take me the rest of the week to make this place habitable. Have Laredo show you the shower he put in out back. It's very ingenious. Of course I still have to heat the water for it, but it's a shower."

"A shower?" She glanced curiously at Laredo as Hattie moved away from the door to return to work.

"It's a little contraption I rigged up — a canvas bucket with a shower-head attachment. You pull the rope and water comes out. It stops when you let go of the rope."

"Sounds practical and efficient," Jessy remarked, impressed by his ingenuity.

"It is," Laredo agreed without any brag in his voice.

With a touch of impatience, Chase interrupted, "What have you been able to learn about the phone calls I made in Texas?"

"Not a lot, unfortunately," Jessy said with regret. "The man you went there to see was Tom Brewster. Some business came up and he had to postpone his appointment with you until the next day. When you didn't show up for that meeting, he said he was more than a little upset. It wasn't until the next day that he learned you had been killed in a traffic accident."

"What does he do? Did he know why I wanted to see him?" Chase felt certain that Tom Brewster was an important key.

"He's a vice president at the Blanchard Bank, and you didn't say why you wanted to see him, just that it was something you preferred to discuss in person. Since he's in the loan department, he assumed you had a project that you wanted to have financed."

"Do I?" Chase couldn't remember.

"Not that you ever mentioned to me," Jessy replied.

"And if you did, why would you go to a bank in Texas?" Laredo inserted. "I don't think you were after a loan."

"Not unless my regular bank had turned me down."

"After spending much of the last two days with accountants and bookkeepers, I can tell you with absolute certainty that the ranch has more than a sufficient amount of operating capital. There isn't any need for a business loan," Jessy told him. "There was one other thing Brewster said that might be important. You told him that you had obtained his name from a mutual friend, but you didn't identify the man by name." She paused, another possibility occurring to her. "Maybe it wasn't a man. Maybe it was Tara. It would be logical. After all, she's from Fort Worth. Should I ask her about it?"

"It might not be wise for you to start asking questions. The wrong person might find out that you are getting suspicious about what I was doing in Texas. He might decide you know whatever it is that I am supposed to know — assuming that's the reason someone tried to kill me." It was all a big, confusing puzzle to him.

Suddenly the horn in Jessy's pickup began honking incessantly, its stridency shattering the quietness. "That's the mobile phone." She ran to the pickup and picked up the telephone, silencing the horn.

"Yes, this is Jessy." She mentally braced

herself for news of an emergency somewhere on the ranch.

"Jessy. Monte here," came the cheerful reply. "At last I have succeeded in running you to ground."

"Hello, Monte." Jessy relaxed. "What do you need?"

"I planned to come by the ranch this afternoon, but no one at the house knew when you would be back."

"Probably around one or two this afternoon."

"Could you spare me an hour of your time?"

"Is it important?" she asked, thinking of the many and varied items on today's agenda.

"I have something special to deliver to you."

His statement aroused her curiosity. "What is it?"

"That is a surprise," he declared with a trace of smugness. "And I am confident you will be very pleased with it. I shall see you at two o'clock then."

"I'll be there," Jessy promised and hung up.

Observing her slightly bemused expression when she approached them, Laredo tipped his head to one side, studying her closely. "Is there a problem?"

"No," she said with a quick shake of her head, her mouth curving easily into a smile. "It was just Monte. He's coming over this afternoon and wanted to know what time I would be back. He has something to deliver — something special, he said — but he wouldn't say what. It's probably a calf from his herd of registered Highland cattle, although I can't imagine why he thinks I would be so pleased to get one."

"Who is Monte?" Chase questioned.

"Monte Markham, our newest neighbor," Jessy replied with a casualness that indicated her ease with the subject and the man. "He bought the Gilmore ranch last spring. But he's originally from England, and it shows."

"Just since spring, huh," Laredo murmured thoughtfully, "which means he's new to the area. That's interesting."

"You think it might mean something," Chase guessed.

"Like you once said, it's too soon to rule out anyone."

"You don't really think Monte might be involved in the attempt on Chase's life?" Jessy was more than a little skeptical.

"Is that so impossible?" Laredo's smile

made the question seem less of a challenge.

"Not impossible, but unlikely," Jessy replied. "I mean, what would be his reason? The man is practically a stranger. We barely know him at all."

"But I have the impression that he has become a frequent visitor. Am I right?" The smile stayed, but there was a watchful quality to his eyes.

"I don't know if I would call it frequent, but he has been over several times since he moved here. To me, it never seemed anything more than a desire for some company." She shrugged to emphasize her total lack of concern.

"Obviously he isn't married," Laredo concluded. "Just out of curiosity, how old is he?"

"Thirty or forty. I never asked." Quick to see where his thinking was leading, Jessy added crisply, "And if you're suggesting that he might be interested in me, you're wrong."

"Maybe." Laredo dipped his head in a gesture of concession, then held her gaze. "Then again, any man in his right mind is bound to spend a little time considering everything the widow Calder has to offer."

Annoyed, both with his implication and

his use of the phrase "widow Calder," Jessy spoke with a bit more force. "For your information, Monte has spent nearly all his time with Chase. He has never said or done anything to suggest he is interested in me."

"Yes," Laredo inserted. "He probably knows he needs to take it slow with you."

"I think it's more likely that he knows I am not interested," she said with some heat.

"Oh, you're interested all right," Laredo stated with utter certainty as he held up a hand to stave off her protest. "And by that, I'm not suggesting that you weren't very much in love with your late husband. I think you probably were. But you are flesh and blood, the same as the rest of us. It's as natural for a woman to want the company of a man as it is for a man to want that of a woman. It doesn't have anything to do with being unfaithful or disloyal. It only means you're human."

She had to work at it, but she managed to respond calmly. "I am well aware of that."

"I'm glad to hear it," Laredo said smoothly.

She turned to Chase. "If there isn't anything else, I really need to be getting back to the ranch."

"I have just one more question," Chase inserted.

"What's that?"

"Who is Captain?"

A smile lit Jessy's face. "You remembered him."

"Only the name. I don't know who he is."

"Captain is a longhorn steer, famous for leading the first trail herd from Texas to Montana, and all the subsequent herds that came after it. He has become something of a Triple C legend. When he died of old age, his horns were mounted above the fireplace mantel in the den."

"A longhorn." He was amused to learn the name that had nagged him belonged to a steer. At the same time, in some inner part of him, it rang true. "So the Calders moved here from Texas. Whereabouts in Texas?"

"Somewhere outside of Fort Worth. I know your great-grandfather, Seth Calder, is buried in an old cemetery in Fort Worth. Ty visited his grave site while he was attending college there."

"Do we still have any family ties in Texas?"

"None that I ever heard about," Jessy replied.

Later, as she drove away, Laredo remarked to Chase, "I would like to know more about this Monte fella. He seems to be the only new card in the deck. That may mean something — or nothing at all."

The brown horse moved at a lazy, shuffling trot, each stride marked by the swish of the summer-dry grass. Culley O'Rourke sat loose and relaxed in the saddle, his gaze making its idle comb of the broken country before him.

Earlier that morning he had ridden to the Circle Six and had a cup of coffee with Cat. Leaving there, he had swung south onto the Triple C range, skirting the rough foothills where it would be too easy for his horse to end up with a stone wedged under its shoe. That small section was the only part of the Triple C that wasn't fit for man or beast.

As usual, the direction he took was a whim of the moment, a decision sometimes made by his horse and sometimes by Culley. But always he maintained a natural alertness for his surroundings. Age may have stolen some of his strength, but it hadn't yet dulled his senses. He knew every sight, every sound, every smell that should be there, making him quick to catch any that were out of place.

The sudden, staccato bursts of a vehicle's horn somewhere in the far distance was an alien sound, one that instantly grabbed Culley's attention. He reined in the brown gelding, his head snapping up. The horn blasts didn't last long, just long enough for Culley to determine they were out of place.

The Triple C had a seldom used ranch road west of him that trailed off short of the north boundary line. He couldn't imagine why anybody would be traveling along that road unless they were checking fences. It was a question he had to answer for his own peace of mind.

Laying the reins alongside the gelding's neck, he swung the horse westward and lifted it into an ambling trot. It was a detour made to satisfy his curiosity but pushed by no sense of haste.

The road was almost a mile distant as the crow flies, but as Culley's trail wound, it was a little more than that. About the time he got within sight of it, he heard the steady hum of an engine. He rode to a vantage point, reaching it as a ranch pickup came into view. It was pure luck that Culley spotted long strands of tawny gold hair whipping out of the driver's side window.

"Has to be Jessy." Even as he muttered the words, a puzzled frown knitted the creases in his forehead. "What's she doin' way out here?" He snorted in skepticism, remembering. "The last time I asked her, she fed me a line 'bout fixin' fence. What d'ya want'a bet she was meetin' that cowboy again, Brownie? Wonder where their rendezvous was this time?"

No longer interested in the pickup, Culley aimed his horse toward the road and the slow-to-settle dust cloud the truck had left in its wake.

Chapter Seven

⌒⌒

Hot and tired after the dusty drive, Jessy entered The Homestead and automatically headed for the den. But her thoughts were still on the meeting with Chase. Since learning that Chase was alive, she had found it difficult to focus on the ranch and its operations. She kept getting sidetracked with thoughts of the dilemma his amnesia posed. She was heartened, though, that he had remembered Captain. Admittedly it wasn't much, but it was a beginning.

As she reached the doorway to the den, she caught a movement in her side vision and glanced toward the living room. When she saw twelve-year-old Beth Trumbo grab the newel post to start upstairs, for a split second Jessy couldn't think why the girl was in the house. Then it hit her that Beth was there to look after the twins. At almost the same instant, Jessy noticed the unusual silence in the house and realized the twins must be taking their nap.

"Are you going up to check on the

twins?" she asked Beth, feeling a twinge of guilt at how little time she managed to spend with them lately.

The red-haired, freckle-faced girl bobbed her head in acknowledgement. "They've been asleep a long time."

"I'll do it. You go ask Sally if she would fix me a sandwich. Anything will do. I'm starved."

"She said you would be when you missed lunch." Beth flashed her a shy smile and reversed her course to head for the kitchen.

Jessy crossed to the wide oak staircase and ran up the steps, her expression softening with a mother's affection at the thought of her sleeping children. When she reached the top of the stairs, there was a telltale turning of the doorknob to Chase's bedroom. When the door moved a fraction of an inch, Jessy knew immediately that Trey wasn't asleep — and he wasn't in the room he shared with Laura.

Altering her course, Jessy swung into the hallway and started toward Chase's room. As if sensing the jig was up, Trey opened the door.

"Hi, Mom." He gave her a look of straight-faced innocence. "I woked up."

"I see that." She also saw that he had on a pair of Chase's cowboy boots, the tops of them reaching above his knees. She fought down a smile at the comical picture he made. "What are you doing with Grampa's boots?"

"I was tryin' 'em on." He glanced down at them. "Grampa's got big feet."

"Definitely a lot bigger than yours." Jessy lifted him out of the boots, set him down, then picked up the boots and returned them to the closet.

Trey watched from the doorway. "Somebody took Grampa's razor."

"Is that right?" She pretended not to know what he was talking about. "You don't suppose somebody might have put it up so you wouldn't accidentally cut yourself with it, do you?"

"I looked in all the drawers."

"Don't you be snooping anymore in your grampa's things. It's very wrong to do that." She planted a hand on his head and turned him away from the door, pointing him down the hall while she pulled the door shut behind her.

A yawning Laura emerged from the bedroom, saw Jessy and broke into a run. "I'm glad you're home, Mom." She wrapped herself around Jessy's legs.

"So am I." Smiling, she smoothed a hand over Laura's blond curls.

Laura tipped her head way back to look up at her. "I want'a go see Aunt Tara, but Beth wouldn't take me." Her lower lip protruded in a sulky pout.

"That's because Beth isn't old enough to drive."

In a flash, Laura switched tactics and bestowed her most beguiling smile on Jessy. "But you are, Mommy."

"Sorry, I can't today. I have too many things to do."

Angrily Laura pulled away from her and buried her chin in her neck. "You always say that."

"We'll do something together real soon." It was a promise Jessy made as much to herself as to Laura. "In the meantime, let's go down to the kitchen. Sally is fixing me a sandwich and I'll bet we can rustle up some milk and cookies for you two. How does that sound?"

"Yippee!" Trey spun around in his stockinged feet, slipped on the hardwood floor and fell with a thud. Laura was considerably less enthusiastic, already aware of the value of emotional blackmail.

Jessy helped Trey to his feet, verified that the damage was mostly to his pride, and ordered, "You go get your boots on and meet us downstairs."

"Ah, Mom." With a disgruntled fling of the arms, he turned toward the bedroom. As usual, his despair didn't last long, and he broke into a run and slid the last few feet to the door.

With a mild shake of her head at Trey, Jessy started down the stairs. Truthfully, she was much more comfortable with Trey's sometimes wild antics than she was with the poise and dainty femininity of her daughter. She glanced back at Laura following her down the steps, looking like a little princess in training. Rather than out-distance Laura, Jessy slowed her own descent.

By the time they reached the bottom of the stairs, Trey was clumping down the steps at a reckless pace behind them. Two treads from the bottom, he jumped and landed at a run.

When the front door opened, Trey screeched to a halt and turned toward it with an air of expectancy that told Jessy he was expecting to see Chase walk through. But it was Monte Markham who stepped into the foyer.

"Ah, there you are," he said when he saw Jessy. His easy smile widened at the sight of the twins. "How perfect, the twins are here, too."

"We were on our way to the kitchen for a snack," Jessy explained. "Why don't you join us?"

"Later. First I want you all to come outside and see the surprise I brought." He motioned them toward the door, an enigmatic sparkle in his brown eyes.

"A surprise," Trey repeated with burgeoning interest. "What kind of surprise?"

"Come and see," Monte replied, deepening the mystery.

The possibility of a present was all it took to make Laura forget that she had been giving her mother the silent treatment. She looked up with bright-eyed eagerness. "Can we, Mommy?"

"Of course." She nodded her permission.

Both twins raced to the door that Monte held open for them, but he waited for Jessy. "I only hope my gift meets with your approval," he murmured to her. "I'm afraid I have been a bit presumptuous."

Jessy suspected he had been very presumptuous if he thought she would be excited to receive one of his registered Highland cows. For the time being she chose to say nothing at all.

Trey pounced on Monte the minute they stepped onto the veranda. "Where's the s'prise?" he demanded with suspicion.

"Down there." Monte gestured toward the Range Rover he had parked on a flat stretch of ground at the base of the knoll.

With a sinking heart, Jessy noticed the closed horse van that was hitched to it. It was all she needed to see to become convinced that his surprise was a shaggy-coated beast.

"Where?" Disappointment was already starting to cloud Laura's expression.

"I'll show you."

Monte took the lead, descending the steps and striking out toward the trailer. Trey trotted after him, followed by Laura, while Jessy lagged behind all of them.

He went directly to the rear of the horse van and paused with one hand on the gate. "All three of you stand over there and cover your eyes." He directed them to a spot near the trailer gate.

Obediently Trey and Laura stopped and reached up to cover their eyes. Laura stole a peek at Jessy. "You're supposed to hide your eyes, Mommy."

Complying, Jessy bowed her head and cupped a hand over her eyes, going through the motions for their sake. She heard the snick of the latch unbolting and the *thunk* of the gate ramp being lowered to the ground. She wasn't at all surprised to hear the clump of hooves on the ramp.

"Are you ready?" Monte called, dragging out the moment to Jessy's annoyance.

The twins shouted, "Ready!" in an excited chorus.

"Very well. You may look now," he told them.

Jessy lowered her hand and forced a smile onto her face, then froze at the sight of a pony, its chestnut coat brushed to a high gleam. Neck arched and ears pricked, the pony swung its head toward the trio of onlookers, showing off a snow white stripe that ran from nose to forelock.

Laura oohed and clasped her hands together in delight. Trey wasted no such time. He ran straight to the pony and held out his palm for the pony to nuzzle. Laura followed at a more composed pace.

"He's beautiful, Mommy," she proclaimed on closer inspection.

"Indeed he is," Jessy agreed and shot a glance at Monte, catching the hopeful way he was watching her.

"I warned you that I was being a bit presumptuous," he reminded her.

"So you did." Joining them, Jessy ran a hand over the pony's sleek neck.

"Does he have a name?" Laura wondered as the pony obligingly dropped its head to her level, allowing her to pet its cheek.

"He's called Sundance," Monte replied before bringing his attention back to Jessy. "He is a six-year-old registered Welsh, extremely well-trained, with an extraordinarily gentle disposition. The perfect mount for a child."

"And I thought you were bringing over one of your Highland cows," Jessy remembered with amusement.

"But it is a breed from another part of Britain," Monte said. Turning his attention to Trey, he said, "Would you like me to lift you aboard so you can ride him for a bit?"

Trey immediately stepped back from the pony and gave Monte a look that said he had lost his senses. "He's too little to ride yet."

For an instant, Jessy was too stunned to react. Then her mind flashed back to all the times she had said something similar to Trey when she had taken the twins to see a newborn foal. Trey had obviously taken her words to heart.

Monte responded to his assertion with a low chuckle. "Sundance may be on the small side at just under fourteen hands, but I promise you that he is full-grown."

When Trey remained skeptical, Jessy added her assurance. "It's okay to ride him, Trey. That is as big as he will get."

A frown puckered his forehead as Trey made another critical study of the pony. Finished with his assessment, he looked up at Jessy. "But Molly's bigger, Mom."

"I know," Jessy murmured and realized at once that, when compared with Quint's horse, the pony didn't measure up. "I'm sorry," she said to Monte in a voice full of apologetic regret. "I'm afraid Trey has his heart set on a horse like his cousin's."

"My grampa's gonna get me one," Trey asserted for the ump-teenth time.

"Well, this is an unexpected turn of events," Monte said, clearly at a loss over what to do next. "It would seem my grand surprise has turned out to be a bit of a flop."

Before Jessy could say anything, Laura spoke up, "Can I ride him, Mommy?"

"Of course you can." Jessy immediately picked her up and set her on the pony's back. Laura automatically grabbed a handful of the pony's flaxen mane, her expression alight with eager anticipation.

"It seems someone here appreciates you, Sundance," Monte murmured to the pony and led it away from the trailer.

Around and around the ranch yard they went, mostly at a walk but occasionally at a jogging trot that made Laura giggle. It was at times like this that Jessy was convinced a love of horses was the only thing her daughter had inherited from her.

An unusually subdued Trey watched his sister in silence. Glancing down, Jessy noticed the touch of envy in his expression.

"Are you sure you wouldn't like to go for a ride on the pony?"

It was obvious he was tempted to change his mind. Still he hesitated. "Would Tom or Jobe ride him?" he asked, referring to two of the ranch hands he particularly admired.

"I'm afraid they are too big to ride Sundance. But when they were your age, I'll bet they would have."

While Trey was mulling over her statement, Jessy's father, Stumpy Niles, drove into the ranch yard and pulled up near the trailer. Letting the pickup engine idle, he poked his head out of the driver's side window, an arm hooked over it.

"Hi. I didn't expect to see you this afternoon," Jessy said in greeting.

"Just came to pick up some things at the commissary for your mother," he replied, his attention shifting to Laura and a proud smile lifting his mouth. "Laura is sure a picture on that pint-sized horse. Look at that. Her hair's about the same color as that pony's mane."

"It is, isn't it." But Jessy was quick to notice the sudden glumness of Trey's expression. She suspected it was the phrase "pint-sized horse" that caused it — thus confirming his own opinion of the pony.

"I'm gonna get my rope, Mom," he said and took off for the house.

"What's wrong with him?" Stumpy frowned in surprise. "He didn't even say hello."

"I think he's disappointed. Monte bought the pony as a surprise for Trey, but Trey wants a real horse," Jessy explained. "I have been meaning to call and ask you to see if there was a horse gentle enough for him in our own string."

"Yeah, it breaks my heart the way he keeps sayin' how Chase is gonna get him one. I'll ask around and find out if the boys know of one," Stumpy promised. "Is everything else all right?"

"Fine," she assured him.

"Then I'd better get a-goin' before your mother has a fit." He sketched her a wave and drove off toward the ranch commissary.

His departure coincided with Monte's return with Laura and the pony in tow. "Did Poppy see me?" Laura asked, her brown eyes glittering with excitement.

"He certainly did." Jessy lifted the girl into her arms. "He told me that you and Sundance looked beautiful together."

"I know," Laura replied without a trace of modesty, then bestowed her sweetest smile on Monte. "Can you bring Sundance back tomorrow so I can ride him again?"

"Actually, Sundance is a present for . . . you and your brother." His hesitation was fractional, but Jessy caught it.

"He is?" Laura all but squealed the words then explained to Jessy, "He's a present. That means we can keep him, Mommy."

"It certainly does."

Laura wiggled to be put down. "I gotta go tell Trey." The instant Jessy set her on the ground, Laura ran for the house, any thought of decorum temporarily forgotten.

Monte watched, a wry amusement lacing his expression. "At least the pony is a hit with your daughter."

"I'm sorry about Trey," Jessy said in all sincerity. "He's at that age where he wants the exact thing that his older cousin has. He refuses to be satisfied with a smaller version of it. Calders can be single-minded that way. When they get a notion in heir heads, it's hard to get it out."

"Fortunately your daughter isn't so inclined."

"Laura likes anything beautiful, and Sundance is definitely a beautiful pony. It was very generous of you to buy him —" Jessy began.

Monte cut her off. "What good is money if you can't spend it to bring some joy into the life of a child?" He gave her no chance to reply. "Shall we get Sundance settled in his new home? You take the lead while I fetch his saddle and tack from the van."

But Jessy didn't find his beneficence so easy to dismiss. She tried again. "Still —"

"If you feel the need to repay me in some way, invite me to dinner." His smile was quick and teasing.

Giving up, Jessy smiled back. "Consider yourself invited."

"When?" he challenged lightly.

"Tonight if you're available."

"I am always available to dine at the Triple C. What time?"

"Around seven."

"I'll be here."

It wasn't until after he left that Jessy recalled the suspicions Chase and Laredo had voiced about Monte. It was a possibility that Jessy couldn't bring herself to dismiss out of hand. She remembered too well that once she would have regarded any suggestion that Dick Ballard might have had something to do with Ty's death to be completely preposterous. It made her much more hesitant to jump to conclusions about anyone's innocence again.

At the same time, she had no regrets about inviting Monte to dinner, convinced it was better to learn as much as she could about him, and certain it was what Chase would do.

As always, Monte was undemanding company, proving to be both entertaining and comfortable to be around. Any concern Jessy might have felt that he might read something into the fact that he was her sole guest for the first time turned out to be unfounded. Nothing in his manner indicated that he regarded it as anything more than two friends sharing a meal. In light of Laredo's insinuations that Monte might be interested in the "widow Calder," it was an observation that secretly pleased Jessy.

At dinner's conclusion, Jessy followed the Calder custom by asking Sally to serve their coffee in the den. She never thought twice about the request until she noticed a white-faced Sally standing frozen in the doorway, pain-filled eyes staring at the empty chair behind the desk. At that second Jessy realized it was the first time guests had been entertained in the den since Chase's supposed death.

"Sally." Jessy reached out a hand in instant apology for her thoughtlessness.

"Ah, the coffee has arrived." Monte immediately crossed to the doorway, eliminating any moment of awkwardness. "Let me carry that tray, Sally. I insist," he added when she attempted to protest. "It's much too heavy for you." Avoiding the desk, he carried it straight to the coffee table. Sally trailed after him, all flustered and upset. After placing the tray on the table, he turned back to her. "Forgive me for failing to compliment you on a delicious dinner. The Beef Wellington was magnificent."

"Thank you. I —" She stole a glance at the desk and immediately choked up.

Monte took her hand, clasping it warmly between both of his and then giving it a comforting pat. "I know. It's very hard for you, isn't it?" he murmured, all solicitous concern. Unable to speak, Sally merely nodded. Gently Monte slipped an arm around her shoulder and turned her away from the desk to walk her back to the door. "I won't tell you that it becomes easier with time, because it doesn't. It merely becomes bearable."

After Sally had left, he returned to the leather sofa. Jessy poured coffee for both of them and passed him a cup. "That was very kind of you, Monte," she said, touched by his sensitivity.

"It is rather obvious that she was very fond of him."

"They were friends for years." It took a conscious effort to refer to Chase in the past tense, and Jessy wasn't used to watching her words.

"I haven't met anyone who didn't think well of Chase." Monte stirred milk into his coffee and flashed her a quick smile. "But let's speak of other things. We can't escape sadness, but we don't have to dwell on it."

"I agree." Cup in hand, Jessy settled back against the sofa cushions.

"My brother phoned today," Monte began, then stopped, raising a forefinger to interrupt himself. "I just remembered something. I was told by . . . I don't know, someone . . . that the Triple C has a feedlot that isn't being used. Is that true?"

"There's one up on the north range, but we haven't run any cattle in it in years. It was an experiment we tried, but after the losses we suffered from a bad storm, we decided to stick to being a cow-calf operation. Why?"

"When I bought my ranch, it seems I stirred up a bit of envy back home. I think you would be surprised to learn the number of people from various walks of life who fancy getting into the cattle business," he said with amusement. "Several have been pestering me to put together something for them. My first thought was a feedlot operation, since I don't think they would want to commit to anything long term. I have been looking for a place to lease for the last two or three months. Then I heard about yours. Its proximity to my ranch makes it ideal." He paused, his mouth crooking with a rueful twist. "Although to be frank, I have been reluctant to even bring up the subject. I value our friendship very much. I wouldn't want any business arrangement to interfere with it."

"Neither would I."

"Think it over," he inserted before Jessy could say more. "In addition to paying a fair price to lease the feedlot, the investors would also contract with you to furnish the labor to run it. Financially you would have absolutely nothing to lose. According to

Ben Parker, arrangements such as this have become fairly common."

"True, although it would be a first for the Triple C." That alone was reason enough to make Jessy reluctant to give his proposal any consideration at all.

"No doubt it is." Monte nodded in understanding. "I wouldn't have suggested it at all except that I have complete trust that you will see that the cattle were properly fed and tended. Which makes it very easy to recommend you over some rancher I don't know as well."

"I can see that."

"As I said, think it over. If you should decide you aren't interested, I will simply look elsewhere." He smiled easily and took a small sip of his coffee, then abruptly lowered the cup. "It just occurred to me, though, an arrangement such as this wouldn't be all that different than when the Triple C leased drilling rights to that petroleum company."

"I had forgotten about that," Jessy murmured thoughtfully.

It was an argument that prompted her to decide to discuss the proposal with Chase rather than dismiss it out of hand.

The feedlot had been one of Ty's projects, built to diversify the ranching operation, and it had required considerable capital expenditure at a time when the Triple C had been strapped for cash. The losses caused by the storm, both in damage to the facility and cattle killed, had been crippling. It had been a personal blow to Ty at the time, shaking his confidence. Monte's proposal offered an opportunity to realize a return on the monies invested in the feedlot all those years ago. Jessy liked the thought of that, certain that Ty would be pleased with the idea.

But first she needed to see what kind of shape it was in. Other than being pressed into service as a holding pen during roundup, the facility hadn't been used in years.

Chapter Eight

That old devil curiosity had ahold of Culley O'Rourke and wouldn't let him go. Two days ago he had spent the better part of the afternoon attempting to backtrack Jessy without success.

Pestered by the questions of where she had gone and why, Culley had taken to haunting the area, mostly out of suspicion. He kept remembering Jessy's conversation with the cowboy at the funeral, her secret meeting with two men at the old cemetery, and the cowboy following her the next day in his truck. When Culley added it all up, it kept saying to him there was something funny going on. And just maybe it was going on here. If it was, Culley was convinced Jessy would show up in the area again. And he would be on hand when and if she did.

Culley was an old hand at waiting and watching. When there was a reason for it, it came as natural to him as all his restless wanderings. On the first day of his vigil, he had found a comfortable spot that offered some afternoon shade, graze for his horse, and a long view of the ranch road where he had seen her last.

Twice in the last couple days, Culley had sworn he heard the sound of a vehicle somewhere in the distance, but none had shown up on the road, which meant it was probably traveling on another one, making it of no interest to Culley.

Hunkered in the small shade of a grassy hill slope, he idly listened to the *clink* of the bridle chain as the brown horse chomped on some grass. Then he caught the faint hum of an engine and shifted his position to watch the road. The sound grew steadily in volume. Seconds later he spotted the dust cloud and the glint of sunlight on something shiny. Soon there wasn't any doubt a vehicle was headed in his direction.

Culley rolled to his feet and made his way down the slope to the brown horse. He gathered up the trailing reins and looped them over the horse's neck, then stepped into the stirrup and swung himself into the saddle. Wasting no time, he kicked the gelding into a lope and set a course to intercept the road well to the north, taking care to keep out of sight.

★ ★ ★

When Jessy pulled up to the line cabin, she first noticed the new shingles on the section of patched roof, then the general air of tidiness about the site. There were no tools or ladders about. Any weeds or tall grass growing next to the foundation had been cut short, and starched curtains hung at the windows.

As she climbed out of the cab, the screen door swung open, and Laredo's tall shape filled the frame. "Your ears must be burning. We were just talking about you."

"Nothing bad, I hope," she answered lightly.

"That depends. We were wondering what that English guy Markham delivered to you the other day." Stepping back inside, Laredo kept the screen door pushed open to admit her.

"A pony." Jessy moved past him into the cabin and paused to run an admiring eye over the many homey touches that had been added to the cabin's now spotless interior, everything from the seat cushions tied to the wooden chairs to the pair of rockers that flanked the old cast-iron stove. "You have been very busy," she said to Hattie.

"It's a beginning," the woman replied

absently and turned from the short stretch of cabinets, a serving dish in each hand. "We were just sitting down to lunch. There is plenty of food if you care to join us."

"Is it that late?" Jessy said in surprise, then belatedly noticed the place settings at the table where Chase sat. "I think I'll pass on lunch, but I'll take a cup of coffee if you have some made."

"It's in the pot." Hattie nodded in the direction of an old percolator-style coffeepot designed for use on a burner.

"Are you sure you don't want to join us? Hattie makes an excellent goulash." Laredo pulled out a chair and sat down at the table across from Chase.

"Don't listen to him," Hattie warned. "He's only saying that in hopes of convincing me that I don't need anything bigger than that Coleman stove to cook on."

"What's this about a pony?" Chase wanted to know.

"It wasn't for me. It was for Trey," Jessy explained while she filled a mug with coffee. "I happened to mention to Monte that Trey had decided you went to Texas to buy him a horse. Monte remembered that. Only he bought Trey a pony instead. I guess he thought Trey wouldn't mind the difference, but he did. Fortunately Laura fell in love with the pony. It was such a thoughtful thing for Monte to do that I would have hated it if he had to take the pony back."

"That would have been a real shame," Laredo said in dry mockery, "especially when you consider that the quickest way to a woman's heart is through her children."

Jessy bristled at his implication that Monte had his sights set on her. Certain he had said it merely to get a rise out of her, she focused her attention on Chase instead.

"Monte did have an interesting business proposition that I wanted to run past you," she said and proceeded to relate it to him.

Unable to remember anything about the feedlot or the reason it sat idle, Chase questioned Jessy about it. After she had given him the background on it, they went over Monte's proposal again.

"It sounds very similar to the deal I made," Hattie interjected. "I leased my pasture land to a company. They run their cattle on it and pay me to look after them."

"You have a ranch in Texas?" Jessy said with some surprise.

Hattie nodded. "Southwest of Fort Worth, but it's a small spread compared to the Triple C." She ran an idle glance around the cabin. "Actually the house on it was in worse shape than this cabin when my husband and I bought the place over thirty years ago. The previous owners had used it for hay storage. Fortunately the old house was still structurally sound, because we couldn't afford to build a new one, but it took a lot of work to make it habitable. One of our neighbors told us that it had been built prior to the War Between the States."

"Benteen Calder came from southwest of Fort Worth," Jessy recalled thoughtfully. "It's likely he visited that ranch at one time or another."

Uninterested in idle conjecture, Chase nodded an absent agreement and brought the discussion back to its original subject. "I know that Markham's proposal is financially a win-win situation for the ranch, but my instinct tells me to refuse it."

"On the other hand," Laredo inserted as he pushed back his now empty plate, "it might be wise to pick up the cards he's dealing. If he runs cattle in that lot, it sounds like he will be a more frequent visitor. Plus it gives Jessy a good reason to hire some extra help — namely me."

"But you are no cowboy." In Jessy's

mind, that presented a problem.

Laredo didn't deny it. "I know enough about cattle to pass for a feedlot cowboy. And none of your regular hands will think twice if a stranger asks a bunch of nosy questions. I might find out things you can't."

"That's true." But she doubted he would get many answers.

"Besides, it's going to become increasingly difficult for you to slip away and come out here. Since I would make the trip back and forth every day, I can bring Chase any information that you or I might have learned."

"That settles it as far as I'm concerned," Chase announced. "Tell Markham you'll do the deal. But I want to see any agreement before you sign it." Finished with his meal, Chase stood up, signaling an end to any further discussion.

Jessy rose as well. "I'll call Monte as soon as I get back to The Homestead."

Laredo reached the door ahead of them and stepped outside to hold the screen door open. Jessy was halfway through the opening when Laredo stepped into her path, blocking her exit, his head turned away, tensed and uplifted in a listening pose.

"I think I heard someone," he murmured in warning.

Just as Jessy was about to scoff at the notion anyone would be out here, she caught the creak of saddle leather, followed by the dull *clink* of an iron shoe on stone. She wasn't sure, but the sounds seemed to come from somewhere around the base of the hill.

"Get back inside. I'll see how close he is," Laredo ordered in a low but crisp undertone and slipped away from the door.

Jessy hesitated only a split second before following him, copying his hunched-over posture as he made his way to the edge of the slope. Well short of it, he sank to the ground and waited for her.

When she crouched beside him, he pulled her the rest of the way down. "I told you stay inside," he muttered, his eyes a hard blue.

"You wouldn't know if it was someone to worry about or not," she whispered back.

"And you would, I suppose," he taunted in disgust. "Make sure you keep flat. I'd like to see him before he sees us."

He slipped off his hat and laid it on the grass beside him, then crept forward on his belly. Copying his actions, Jessy inched up to his shoulder and lifted her head slightly to look below. Almost instantly Laredo's hand pushed her head down, but not before she had caught a glimpse of a horse and rider. Brief as it had been, it had been enough for Jessy to identify the man on horseback.

She signaled Laredo to follow and pushed backward, her thoughts weighted by a heavy certainty that this hiding place was about to be discovered. "It's O'Rourke," she whispered when he joined her. "I think he might be following my tire tracks. He must have seen me come this way."

It took Laredo a full second to remember where he had heard the name before. "Cat's uncle, the shy one in the trees?"

"I forgot to mention he can also be nosy."

"Come on." Laredo scooped up his hat and rolled to his feet in a low crouch. "We better warn Chase that we are about to have company."

They hurried back to the cabin. Laredo paused with one hand on the screen door and pinned his gaze on her. "O'Rourke — will he ride right up to the cabin or circle around it?"

"I don't know," Jessy admitted. "But he'll definitely come close enough to see where my truck is."

"Then go out by your truck and wait for him. Don't let him slip behind the cabin. And before he starts wondering what you are doing up here, make sure he knows you hired me to fix the place."

"But what reason would I have to do that?"

"Make up one," Laredo told her and went inside.

The scrape of hooves digging for purchase warned Jessy that Culley had started the climb. She moved quickly to the truck to watch for him. A few faint noises came from the cabin. Jessy could only guess at the source of them, but she suspected Laredo was spiriting Chase out of the cabin through one of the rear windows. All the while her mind raced to come up with a plausible story, but there simply wasn't a logical reason to repair the old line shack. Her only choice was to come up with a completely illogical story.

A half minute later, Jessy spotted the dusty top of Culley's hat. Within seconds more of it bobbed into view. The instant she could make out the brim, Jessy went through the motions of pretending to put something in the back of the truck, then made a natural swing around to make it appear that she'd caught sight of him at almost the same second that Culley saw her.

"Hi, Culley. I didn't expect to see you out this way." Her heart was hammering like that of a cornered rabbit, but she managed to sound unconcerned when she called to him, fully aware that her raised voice would alert Laredo. Culley immediately pulled up, and Jessy motioned him forward. "Come see the way we've been able to fix up this old line shack."

The instant the invitation was issued, Jessy set out for the cabin, confident that her offhand manner coupled with Culley's curiosity would impel him to follow her. The ploy worked as Culley rode his horse the rest of the way up the slope.

By then Laredo had already emerged from the cabin, communicating to Jessy with a small reassuring nod that Chase had made it safely out of the cabin. A second later, Laredo showed Culley a sunny smile and a fresh-faced innocence that was wholly deceptive.

Jessy threw a quick glance at Culley and saw the suspicious way he looked at Laredo. "Oh, Culley, I almost forgot — this is Laredo Smith. I hired him to do the repairs here. Laredo, this is Culley O'Rourke, the twins' great-uncle."

"Pleased to meet you, Mr. O'Rourke," Laredo drawled.

Culley stared back at him, unfazed by the big grin. "Saw you at the funeral."

"Oh, you mean Chase's. I was there sure enough, but I can't say I remember seeing you."

"You talk like you're from Texas." Culley's statement bordered on an accusation.

"It shows, don't it," Laredo replied easily.

Hattie picked that moment to step outside, drawing Culley's attention. "I thought I heard you talking to someone," she said, her smile pleasant but curious.

That's when Jessy realized that she still didn't know the exact relationship between Laredo and Hattie. She had no choice but to make up her own.

"This is Laredo's mother, Hattie. Culley O'Rourke."

"How do you do, Mr. O'Rourke? I'm sorry you didn't arrive sooner. You could have joined us for lunch. But the coffee is still hot if you would like a cup."

"No, thanks." Culley continued to sit on his horse, both hands resting on the saddle horn while he openly studied the woman. She was tall and firmly muscled, making her a little on the thick side. His glance kept going back to the cowboy boots she wore while he tried to figure out if they were big enough to have made the prints he saw at the cemetery. It seemed possible that they might have, even though it hadn't entered into his calculations that the second person there could have been a woman.

"Ty would really be pleased if he saw this place now," Jessy murmured, drawing Culley's glance to her. "We used to talk about someday fixing up the old Boar's Nest so we could have a place where we could get away by ourselves, without phones or interruptions."

Hearing Jessy spout such foolishness took her down another notch in Culley's estimation. One thing Culley knew for sure, if Chase were still alive he wouldn't have thrown good money away on repairs to this old shack. He wondered if Jessy knew that and whether that was part of the reason she had hired an outsider to do the work.

All of which raised the question of how Jessy had become acquainted with the Texan. But it wasn't part of Culley's nature to come right out and ask. His approach was more roundabout.

"Guess you'll be goin' back t' Texas now that you're done," he said to Laredo.

"Not for a while," he answered.

"Laredo just agreed to come to work for the Triple C," Jessy explained. "I'm making a deal to lease the old feedlot to Monte Markham, and he'll pay the ranch to feed the cattle, which means I'll need some extra hands."

Her announcement was another surprise to Culley. He couldn't help thinking that Chase hadn't been in his grave a month yet and already the face of the Triple C was changing. And not for the better.

"Guess you ain't got nothin' to draw ya back to Texas," Culley remarked, trying to figure out how much this Laredo fellow might have influenced Jessy's decisions.

"Not anymore," Jessy answered for him. "They recently sold the ranch they had down there. That's how they knew Chase."

"Good friend, was he?" Culley said in a voice thick with skepticism.

"Obviously we never saw him all that often," Hattie admitted smoothly, "but we counted him as a friend."

Culley decided at once that Hattie had probably set her cap for Chase. She certainly wouldn't have been the first woman who did. His own opinion of Chase Calder had never been all that high, but Culley had never been able to fault him when it came to the love he had shown for Maggie.

Satisfied that he had learned as much as he would, Culley ran a last glance over the three of them standing in a loose bunch and reined his horse away. It never crossed his mind to tell them he was going. He just went.

"Come back any time, Mr. O'Rourke," Hattie called after him, but received no response.

"How about some of that coffee, *Mom?*" Laredo asked, putting laughing emphasis on her new title.

"I'll bring it right out. You'll stay long enough to have a cup with us, won't you, Jessy?" Hattie asked over her shoulder as she moved toward the cabin door.

"Of course she will," Laredo answered for her as he glanced at the departing rider. His lips barely moved at all as he murmured to Jessy, "What do you think?"

"I think I've lied more in the last few days than I have in my whole life," she replied in an equally low voice. "Sooner or later, I will get caught in one."

"You can worry about that when and if it happens. Right now he's the one that has me worried," he said with a faint nod in Culley's direction. "Will he leave or hang around?"

"It all depends on whether he believed anything we said. My guess is he will leave. But you probably should play it safe and get Chase back inside the cabin. Culley has been known to stake out a place and keep watch for hours at a time."

Laredo thought about that a moment, then nodded in abrupt decision. "I'll go find Chase. There's a brush-choked draw south of here that he mentioned he was going to head for. Meanwhile, go mess around your truck and keep an eye on O'Rourke. If it looks like he's going to circle around, honk the horn once — accidental-like."

The two split up, with Jessy crossing to her pickup and Laredo heading into the cabin. He made sure the screen door made a loud bang when it swung shut behind him.

"Forget the coffee, Hattie. I'm going after Chase," Laredo said and climbed out the back window.

Using as much cover as he could, Laredo worked his way around the rough slope and descended into the twisting draw. Silence was difficult to achieve as stones rolled under his feet and his shoulders brushed against branches.

The minute he rounded a corner, he saw Chase on his knees right in the middle of an open stretch. He seemed to be looking at something on the ground, but Laredo couldn't see anything there.

"Chase," he called to him in a hushed voice, but there was no response at all. Laredo moved swiftly to the man's side and laid a hand on his shoulder. "What are you doing out here in plain sight? Don't you —" He broke off the demand the instant he saw the ashen color of Chase's skin and the sightless stare of his eyes. "Snap out of it, Chase." He gave his shoulder a hard shake. When that failed to have the desired effect, Laredo crouched in front of him and caught hold of Chase's jaw to force the man to focus on him. He was stunned by the clammy feel of his skin. "What the hell is wrong, Chase?"

At last Chase seemed to register his presence. Raw pain flickered in his expression. "So much blood." He closed his eyes as if trying to shut out some image.

Laredo guessed at once that he had remembered something. "Come on. Let's get out of here." He hooked an arm around Chase and pulled him to his feet.

For much of the way back to the cabin, Laredo had to help him. Chase offered no further hints about what he had remembered, but it was obvious it had shaken him. By the time they reached the cabin, the memory seemed to have lost its grip on him. He no longer had that dazed look and his color was back. Just the same, Laredo opted not to have him crawl back through the window.

"Wait here." He left him by the side of the cabin and ducked around to the front, immediately locating Jessy. "Where's O'Rourke?"

"He just left the fire road and turned east. Did you find Chase?"

"He's right here," Laredo answered and went back for him.

Laredo's watchful attitude toward Chase when he walked alongside him to the cabin door alerted Jessy that something was wrong. She forgot all about Culley and hurried into the cabin after them.

"What happened?" she demanded.

"He remembered something." Laredo's glance stayed on Chase, watching as he sat down at the table.

"What?"

Laredo shook his head. "He mumbled something about so much blood, and that was all he said. I found him kneeling in the middle of the draw, right out in the open."

"Ty," Jessy murmured in realization and moved to the table, lowering herself into a chair facing Chase. "You saw Ty lying there, didn't you?"

"I saw a man. There was blood all over the front of him, and on the ground, too. God, I can still smell it," Chase muttered through clenched teeth, the image obviously still there on the edges of his mind.

"You were the one who found Ty's body after he was killed," Jessy explained in a pained voice. "It was in a coulee over in the Three Fingers area. He'd been stabbed."

"And Ty was my son," Chase recalled. "That must be why I felt such a sick, awful fear." He dug his fingers into his palms, balling his hands into fists of unconscious anger.

Conscious of the sudden sting of tears in her eyes, Jessy stood up. "I'd better be going," she mumbled and moved away from the table.

Laredo's hand gripped her shoulder, stopping her before she reached the door and turning her back to face him. "This is the first time he described what he found to you, isn't it?" His blue eyes made a close examination of her face.

Jessy nodded and swallowed away the knot in her throat. "After Ty's horse was found with blood all over the saddle,

Chase ordered me back to camp."

"I wish Chase had remembered something that was less painful to you," Laredo said, the tightness of regret in his voice. "Some memories shouldn't be shared. It's better to remember the way he lived than the way he died."

Just for an instant the image that Chase had impressed on her mind was replaced by one of Ty hoisting Trey into the air and laughing at his happily gurgling son.

A small smile touched the corners of her wide lips. "I do." And the shine of love in her eyes had Laredo wishing it was meant for him.

Chapter Nine

Sitting high in the vast sweep of Montana sky, an indifferent sun blazed down on the confused young steers milling together in the feedlot. The idling rumble of the semi's diesel engine could barely be heard above the bewildered lowing of cattle and the clatter of cloven hooves on the chute's wooden ramp. Shouts and curses from the cowboys added to the noise as they kept the young stock moving out of the trailer and into the feedlot. Another semi loaded with cattle waited to take the place of the first.

Jessy watched the proceedings from the top rail. Trey straddled the fence next to her, totally absorbed by the action before him. When a big crossbred calf burst out of the chute and plowed into the milling mass, sending them scattering in all directions, Trey gave her a sage look.

"He's a wild one," he observed soberly.

"He was probably tired of being cooped up in that trailer."

"If I had my rope, I'd catch 'im."

"I don't think you have to worry about that. He isn't going anywhere." Her glance strayed to the rider working with quiet calm to drift the newly unloaded stock away from the chute gate.

There was nothing about the way Laredo went about the task with which she could find fault. Jessy smiled to herself, realizing he had been right — he could pass for a feedlot cowboy. Officially this was his third day on the payroll, listed on the books as Samuel Smith. Despite the Social Security card he presented, Jessy still had doubts that it was really his name.

The last animal in the load trotted out of the chute and headed straight for its traveling companions. The semi's diesel engine growled to life, spurting dark smoke from its exhaust stack. As the semi rumbled away from the chute to make room for the next truck, Laredo swung his horse toward Jessy and walked it to the fence.

"Morning, Trey, Jessy." He nodded in greeting then let his glance stay on the boy, observing, "I see you left your rope at home."

"Mom said I should." The glumness in his expression revealed his disagreement with her decision.

"Your mom was right," Laredo told him.

His glance shifted from them, making a brief and idle sweep of the parked vehicles. "I thought Markham would be here."

"He's probably on his way. Somebody from the bank was flying in, and Monte had to pick him up." Jessy was quick to notice the sudden sharpening of his gaze as he focused on something beyond her. "What is it?" She looked back.

"Isn't that O'Rourke just beyond that semi?"

"Looks like it," Jessy confirmed when she spotted the stoop-shouldered rider. Culley had one leg hooked over the saddle horn, a sure indication that he had no intention of leaving any time soon. "Sometimes he watches from a distance and sometimes he takes a closer look." She was soon distracted by an approaching vehicle that she quickly identified as Monte's Range Rover. "Here comes Monte now." She swung off the fence and reached up for Trey. "Come on, let's go meet Monte and the banker."

But Trey drew back from her outstretched arms and emphatically shook his head. " 'Redo's gonna give me a ride on his horse."

"Laredo is working."

"No, he's not. He's just sittin' there."

Laredo spoke. "It'll take the driver a couple minutes to get his rig backed up to the chute. Time enough to take him on a short ride around the lot," he said as a smile spread across his face. "Besides, any boy who figures out at such an early age that bankers are boring deserves a ride."

Amused by his droll observation, Jessy relented. "All right, you can go for a *short* ride," she said.

Jessy lingered long enough to see Laredo lift Trey onto the saddle in front of him. To her son's utter joy, Laredo let him handle the reins. The sudden realization that this was only Trey's second meeting with Laredo gave Jessy a moment of pause. Although exuberant and outgoing by nature, her young son had always been leery of people he didn't know. She had never known Trey to actually back away from someone new, but she had always had the impression that he tolerated rather than trusted new acquaintances. That was definitely the attitude Trey took toward Monte. Yet he appeared to be completely comfortable with Laredo. Recalling how much his grandfather trusted Laredo, Jessy couldn't help wondering if Trey somehow sensed that.

Jessy turned to meet the new arrivals.

Despite the black cowboy hat and boots, pearl-snap white shirt and boot-cut pants, Adam Weatherford of Denver looked exactly like what he was — a banker. Jessy wondered if it was the wire-rimmed glasses that gave him away.

"Welcome to the Triple C, Mr. Weatherford." She shook his hand with a man's firm grip. This was one part of her new position that she didn't like, but, then, she had never cared much for social niceties.

"It's good to be here, Mrs. Calder. I had the pleasure of meeting your late father-in-law a few years back. Such a tragic loss that was," he added in a brief aside. "I always hoped I would have an occasion to visit your famed ranch. Then Monte was good enough to provide me with one."

"I do believe the truth is out," Monte declared with light amusement. "He made the loan so he would have an excuse to visit the Triple C at the bank's expense. Would you like to take a look at the cattle your money bought, Adam?" With a grand sweep of his arm, he gestured to the feedlot.

"Since I'm expected to confirm we do have collateral on the hoof, that would be a good idea." Weatherford spoke the literal truth but in a jesting manner that made light of it. "And it's always best to get business out of the way first."

"My thought exactly," Monte agreed.

The two men moved to the fence and stepped onto the lower rail for a better view of the animals in the lot. Dressed as they were — the banker in cowboy duds and Monte in khaki-colored jodhpurs, a white polo shirt, and an Aussie hat straight out of the Outback — the two men looked as out of place as a pair of pelicans in the desert. Jessy joined them.

"Starting them a bit young, aren't you, Mrs. Calder?" Smiling, the banker nodded in the direction of the small boy proudly reining the horse toward them with no assistance from the adult rider seated behind him.

"You can never start them too young, Mr. Weatherford." Her smile took nothing away from the sincerity of her words.

"That's Trey, isn't it?" Monte said.

"Yes. He insisted on coming with me this morning." And Jessy had spent too little time with the children lately to refuse him.

"Is that your son?" the banker asked with more than passing interest.

"It is indeed," Monte answered for her and climbed to the top of the fence to greet the boy. "Hello there, young Trey."

"Hi." Trey waved back.

Laredo took over the reins and maneuvered the horse close to the fence where the three waited. "Sorry, buddy. This is where you get off and I go back to work."

"I have him." Monte lifted Trey off the saddle and onto the fence as the first steer scrambled out of the next trailer. "Adam, I would like you to meet Master Chase Benteen Calder the Third, better known as Trey. Trey, this is Mr. Weatherford from Denver."

"How'd ya do." Unprompted, Trey stuck out his hand.

"How do you do, Trey." Hiding a smile, the banker gravely shook hands with him. "I see you had a good, close look at the cattle. What do you think of them?"

"They ain't the ropin' kind," Trey replied. " 'Redo says they're the stand-around-and-get-fat kind."

Monte threw back his head, releasing a rich laugh. "Well, he is absolutely correct."

"I know." Trey turned to Jessy, once again all bright-eyed with excitement. "Did you see me, Mom?"

"I certainly did."

"I did good, huh?" He worked his way down the fence to her.

"Very good."

He heaved a big sigh. "Ridin' is real thirsty work, Mom."

"Why don't you go get yourself a drink," Jessy suggested. "There's a jug of water in the truck."

"Okay." Trey wasted little time scrambling off the fence and racing for the pickup.

From his watching post by the trailers, Culley observed the Calder kid's dash to the ranch pickup, but he was more interested in how cozy the boy had been with that Laredo character. Ever since Jessy mentioned she was going to let the Englishman run fat cattle in the lot and planned to hire the cowboy to help tend them, Culley had been making a regular swing past the feedlot. Two days ago he had spotted a cowboy making repairs to the fencing. This morning he had heard the rumble of the arriving cattle trucks long before they came into view.

Until he saw them with his own eyes, Culley had been having a hard time believing Jessy intended to let somebody else's cattle on the place. It made no more sense to him than fixing up that old line shack had. And it made him wonder if that cowboy and his ma had something on her.

It seemed possible when Culley remembered how rigidly furious Jessy had looked when she talked to the cowboy after the funeral. Somehow or other the cowboy had persuaded her to meet him the next morning at the old cemetery. Culley was willing to bet that it was after that meeting that Jessy decided to stash the pair at the old line shack.

He shifted his attention to the Englishman. Maybe it was just coincidence that shortly after the cowboy showed up, the Englishman began hauling cattle into the Triple C. Or maybe the cowboy and the Englishman were in cahoots. Whatever the case, something about this whole business smelled funny to Culley.

The brown horse snorted and turned a wary eye on the semi that pulled into the unloading area with another batch of cattle. Swinging his leg back over the saddle, Culley tucked his foot in the stirrup and gathered up the reins to ride over to get a closer look at them.

Just like the previous loads, the cattle were a mixed lot, mostly young and mostly all crossbreds. And, same as all the others, they were slick, a cowboy term for an animal without a brand, sporting only ear tags.

As Culley approached the semi's tractor,

the driver climbed down from the cab. He shot a look at Culley. "How long a wait am I gonna have before I can unload?"

"Not long." Culley fastened his black eyes on the man. "Mark-ham buy all these cattle?"

"Got me." The driver shrugged his ignorance. "The manifest says they belong to the High Plains Corporation. That's all I know."

The name wasn't a familiar one. Making no comment, Culley simply nodded and rode closer to the chute area where there was a bit of commotion going on.

The culprit was a big black calf that had decided it preferred the trailer over the feedlot. Its attempt to reverse directions had jammed up the ones behind it, much to the exasperation of the cursing cowboys attempting to prod the animal in the opposite direction. Personally Culley admired the animal for bucking the flow. In the end, the young steer lost its battle and trotted into the feedlot with the rest.

Even though the outcome was a foregone conclusion, Culley felt oddly saddened by it. He reined his horse away from the feedlot and threw a last glance, catching a glimpse of Jessy and the Englishman, but not the other man.

"Something's not right," he murmured to his horse. The trouble was he couldn't put his finger on exactly what it was.

Ordinarily he wouldn't have given a damn about what Jessy did or why. But he couldn't help wondering what Cat knew about this. With Calder in his grave, the Triple C now belonged to her as much, if not more, than it did to Jessy.

Monte leaned both arms on the top rail and surveyed the livestock in the yard with something of a proprietary air, then glanced at the banker standing some distance from them verifying the health certificates on the delivered cattle. He switched his attention to Jessy, flashing her an appreciative smile.

"It was very kind of you to invite Weatherford to lunch before he flies back to Denver. Thank you."

Jessy shrugged off his thanks. "It would have been rude to let him leave on an empty stomach. That isn't the way we do things on the Triple C."

"And the ranch is, without question, famous for its hospitality," Monte agreed and once again faced the feedlot. "The man on the chestnut, is he new? I don't recall seeing him before."

Her pulse skittered, making it obvious to Jessy that she would never get comfortable with this lying business. "You mean Laredo," she said with forced evenness. "He's going to be working here at the lot. You probably should meet him."

When she issued a shrill, two-fingered whistle, heads turned in her direction, but she motioned to Laredo, summoning him to the fence. Only after he had turned his horse toward her did Jessy notice the way Monte stared at her in a marveling fashion.

"Astonishing," he declared. "One day you must teach me how to whistle like that."

"It isn't all that difficult." She shrugged off his comment, a little surprised that he would be impressed by something so insignificant.

Trey raced back to her side and scrambled to the top rail in time to greet Laredo when he rode up. "Hi, 'Redo. Can I ride your horse again?"

"Sorry, not this time," Laredo replied. Although disappointed, Trey accepted his answer without protest. "What did you need?" he asked Jessy, a boyish openness to his expression.

"Laredo Smith, Monte Markham." Jessy

made the introduction without ceremony. "I thought the two of you should meet since the feedlot is your assignment," she explained to Laredo.

"I guess that makes you the owner of this bunch." Laredo flashed Monte a totally artless smile.

"Technically speaking, I only represent the owners," Monte corrected.

"Brokered the deal for 'em, did ya?" Laredo observed and cast an assessing glance over the stock in the lot. He pushed the brim of his hat off his forehead, and said, "You'll be turning a quick profit on this lot. They're in good shape. I reckon they'll fatten up easy."

"There will be a profit as long as grain prices don't rise." But Monte showed no concern that they would. "Your name is Laredo. I expect you are from Texas?"

"Nope. I was born in New Mexico. Laredo is a handle I got stuck with a long time ago. I always figured it brightened up the Smith end of my name. It beats being called Smitty like my dad was, that's for sure." He paused a beat, then asked, "You ever been to Texas?"

"Texas, Arizona, Colorado Wyoming — I have even been to your state of New Mexico to sample a bit of Santa Fe. Then I came to Montana and knew this big land under a big sky was the place for me."

"Yup, it's the kind of place that can give a man big ideas." There was nothing in Laredo's voice to suggest his observation was any more than an idle comment.

"I expect the first Calder would agree with you," Monte replied.

"I'll bet he would." Laredo grinned. "I guess I'd better get back to my work." He lifted his hat and set it back square on his head before gathering up the reins. "If you got any questions about these fellas, just look me up, Mr. Markham."

"Thank you, I will," Monte replied and watched him ride away. "Talkative chap, isn't he?" he remarked to Jessy.

"No one has ever called Laredo a Silent Sam." It seemed the safest reply to make considering that Jessy knew Laredo would be doing a lot more nosing around.

Morning's dawn found Culley camped next to a rocky outcropping that provided both concealment and an unobstructed view of the Circle Six ranch yard. The kitchen light had come on about ten minutes ago. Culley figured it was likely Logan in there, making a pot of coffee.

Some mornings Logan had a cup first,

and on others he went straight out to do the morning chores. Sometimes he left by the front door, and sometimes by the back. In Echohawk's profession, routines could be a dangerous habit, and he was careful not to follow any.

Knowing this about the man, Culley settled back to wait. Within minutes the big draft horses in the corral nickered a greeting and trotted to the barn door. Cully hadn't seen Logan cross the yard, which meant that he must have exited the house through the back door.

Most mornings Culley would have ridden down and given Logan a hand with the chores, but this wasn't one of them. This morning he didn't budge from his spot until Logan drove off in his patrol car nearly an hour later. Even then Culley didn't ride directly to the house, but circled around to the rear, left his horse among some trees, and slipped quietly through the back door.

Cat was busy clearing the breakfast dishes from the table. Not at all surprised by his sudden appearance, she threw him a quick smile. "You just missed Logan. He left less than five minutes ago."

"I heard him." Culley lingered by the door, making a searching scan of the living room. "Isn't Quint up yet?"

"He stayed up late last night so I decided to let him sleep in this morning." She placed the dirty dishes in the sink and took a clean cup out of the cupboard. "Want some coffee?"

After a small hesitation, he nodded. "Sure." He crossed to the counter and took the filled cup of coffee from her.

"I'll bet you haven't eaten this morning. How about some bacon and eggs?" Without waiting for an answer, Cat collected the items from the refrigerator and set about preparing them. Hovering close by, Culley watched in silence. "I haven't seen much of you these last couple days." Her sideways glance swept over him in idle curiosity. "What have you been up to?"

"Not much."

But Cat noticed the way he avoided meeting her eyes. She turned the bacon in the skillet and stole another glance at him. Her uncle was a man who was never entirely comfortable within the confines of four walls, yet she had the impression that he was more on edge than usual.

"Is anything wrong?" she asked in a deliberately idle tone.

"Nope."

Cat felt certain there was something on

his mind, but she didn't press the issue. He was a secretive man by nature, but she was the one person he trusted. Sooner or later he would tell her, but his approach to the subject was likely to be indirect.

"You been over to the Triple C lately?" he asked.

"No." Everything inside her tightened up at the mere mention of the ranch. It was impossible for Cat to think of the ranch without thinking of her father. Everything about it reminded her of him.

"I didn't figure you had," Culley replied. "I guess it still hurts too much."

"Every time I drive up to The Homestead, there is a part of me that still believes I'll find Dad in the den sitting behind his desk. But here, I'm not reminded every single minute that he's gone, not like Sally is." Just talking about it brought all the pain back.

For a long minute, Culley said nothing, then he remarked, "Do you remember anything about a rancher from Texas by the name of Smith?"

"I don't think so. Why?" She darted him a quick smile, grateful for the change of subject.

"No reason in particular." His slim shoulders lifted in an indifferent shrug. "I heard Calder was supposed to be a friend of the family."

"He could have been. But I don't recall them." She cracked an egg on the edge of the skillet and emptied it into the hot grease, then picked up the second egg. "That doesn't mean anything, though. Dad knew a lot of people that I didn't."

"Jessy knows 'em."

"Then the Smiths were probably somebody Dad met at a cattleman's function. Ty and Jessy went to a lot of them with Dad."

"I saw Jessy talkin' to 'im at the funeral."

"Did you?" Cat replied without any real interest.

"The next day she slipped off an' met 'im at the old cemetery."

"The old cemetery?" Cat frowned in confusion. "You mean where your parents are buried?"

"That one." He nodded.

"Why would she meet him there?" She used the spatula to baste his eggs.

"Don't know," Culley replied.

"How curious," Cat murmured and removed the bacon strips from the skillet, laying them on a paper towel to drain.

"They moved here."

"Really." A quick check confirmed that

his eggs were done. She dished them up, retrieved the toast from the toaster, added the drained bacon and carried his plate to the table. "I guess they sold their place in Texas."

"I reckon." Culley pulled out a chair and sat down. "The old man must'a died. It's just the mother and the son. He's a man grown, though, about Jessy's age."

Cat poured herself a fresh cup of coffee and sat down at the table with him. "Where are they living? In Blue Moon?" It was only Culley's interest in them that made Cat curious about a family she didn't know.

"Nope. They've set up house in that old line shack up in the foothills."

"You're kidding," she said in disbelief. "That old cabin has been empty for years."

"Jessy paid 'im to fix it up," Culley replied between bites of food.

"The family must have fallen on hard times," Cat concluded, before her thoughts jumped to another track. "But if they needed a place to live, why would Jessy stick them way out there? The old Stanton place is empty, and so is the house at East camp. Good heavens, there isn't even a road to that old shack. Although, I suppose she could have hired them to fix it up so it wouldn't look like charity. They might have been too proud to accept otherwise. And goodness knows, the ranch doesn't need extra hands at this time of year."

"Well, the son's on the Triple C payroll."

"Naturally. You said Jessy hired him to fix the cabin." Cat raised her cup to take a sip.

"Oh, he finished that." Culley scooped the last bite of egg onto his fork. "Now he's workin' at the feedlot."

"The feedlot?" Cat lowered her cup. "What is there for him to do at the lot? We haven't fed cattle since — why, since Ty and Tara were still married."

"He's lookin' after that English fella's cows."

"You mean Monte Markham? You must be mistaken." Cat shook her head, convinced that Culley's age was beginning to show.

"Nope. Saw the semis unloadin' 'em with my own eyes two days ago. An' it was Jessy herself who tole me she was leasin' the lot to that Monte character, an' he was going to pay her to look after 'em. It seemed peculiar to me. I can't remember a time when a cow that didn't carry the Triple C brand was allowed on the place. Now there's a whole lot full of 'em. If Calder knew about it, he'd turn over in his grave." He leaned back in his chair and patted his stomach. "Mighty good breakfast, Cat. But you always did know how to fix my eggs just the way I like 'em."

Cat was too stunned by his previous statements for the compliment to register. She looked at him with dawning knowledge. "This is what you came here to tell me, isn't it?"

Culley didn't deny it. "That ranch is yours, too. Figured you ought'a know what's goin' on over there."

"You're right. Dad would never have agreed to it." The longer she thought about it the more convinced Cat became.

"I figure somebody talked her into it." He stood up and moved away from the table.

"Who?" The instant she asked the question, she guessed the answer. "The Smiths."

"Could be," he replied with a small restless movement of his narrow shoulders.

"Why, I wonder?" she murmured.

"Could be they got somethin' to gain outa it."

"But what?"

"I ain't figured that out yet," Culley admitted. "But it smells funny, don't it?"

After giving it a moment of thought, Cat was forced to agree. "Yes." She nodded. "Yes, it does."

But Culley wasn't there to hear her response. He had already slipped out the back door, only a faint snick of the latch marking his exit.

Chapter Ten

Flies buzzed around him, drawn by the salty smell of sweat, while Laredo worked to tighten the water pipe's connection and stop its slow leak. The ground at his feet was slick with mud, making for poor traction. Unable to tighten the connection another centimeter, he disengaged the wrench and straightened to watch for any telltale beading of moisture. Seeing none, he stowed the wrench in the tool chest, flipped it shut, and wiped the sweat from his face on his shirtsleeve.

He idly threw a glance at the cattle in the lot. They were a contented bunch, their bellies full with their morning rations. The sun's rays streamed over their backs, creating a mottle of highlights. But it was the interested lift and turn of their heads that caught Laredo's attention.

When he looked beyond them, he noticed the fast-spreading boil of dust on the road, signaling the approach of a vehicle. Satisfied that it wasn't some critter that might spook the herd, he checked the pipe connection one last time. It was still dry, so he walked over to the faucet. The day was young, but already he was hot and sweaty. Desiring nothing more than to cool off, Laredo gave the handle a turn, and a steady gush of water flowed from the tap. Pulling off his hat, he didn't bother to look around when a vehicle crunched to a stop somewhere close by. A door slammed as he stuck his head under the water and let its coolness stream over him, then pulled away from it, shaking off the excess water.

He had a hand on the tap, ready to turn it off when he caught a movement in his side vision. Glancing toward it, he saw a petite brunette striding toward him with fire in her eyes. He knew at once who she was — Chase's daughter, Cat.

"Exactly what do you think you are doing?" she demanded hotly.

A bit taken aback by the hostility emanating from her, Laredo was a split second slow with his answer. "Just cooling off, ma'am."

"You've done it. Now turn that water off."

"Yes, ma'am." He didn't bother to tell her that he was about to do that very thing. He simply gave the handle a turn. Metal squeaked against metal, cutting off the flow.

"I don't have to ask who you are." Green eyes raked him with a look of contempt and disgust. "You're the new man Uncle Culley told me about. The one called Smith from Texas."

"That's right, ma'am. Laredo Smith." Using his fingers he combed his wet hair into order and settled the hat back on his head. "And you are Chase's daughter, Cathleen. I saw you at the funeral."

But Cat didn't warm to his smile. "Water is a precious commodity in this part of Montana, Mr. Smith. I don't know what you do down in Texas, but up here we don't waste it by letting it run on the ground."

"Actually, ma'am, neither do we."

Her hands snapped to her hips as she adopted a challenging stance. "Really? Then how do you explain all this mud?"

Laredo glanced at the tool chest, then decided against telling her about the leaky pipe he had just fixed. "Something tells me you didn't drive all the way out here to lecture me about wasting water." But it was possible she had come just to get a look at him. Laredo wished he knew what O'Rourke had told Cat about him.

240

She seemed momentarily thrown that he had offered no argument in his own defense. Recovering quickly, she fired back an answer. "As a matter of fact, I didn't." With that, she turned on her heel and started back to her truck.

"What was it you needed?"

She jerked open the driver's door, glanced at the cattle in the lot, and threw a glare in his direction. "I have already seen what I wanted."

The pickup's engine roared to life almost before she had the door shut. An instant later she drove off, fast-spinning tires kicking up another dust cloud.

Amidst all the swirling dust, Laredo smelled trouble, but he wasn't sure what form it would take. One thing was certain, though — Chase's daughter didn't seem to like him very much. That in itself didn't worry him. But knowing she was married to a lawman made him a tad bit uneasy.

Pen in hand, Jessy scratched her signature across the bottom of the check, picked it up with its attached invoice, and passed them both to the Triple C's bookkeeper, who hovered next to her chair. She remembered all the times in the past when Ty and Chase had complained about the seemingly endless stream of paperwork involved in running the ranch. It was a sentiment she totally echoed now.

When she caught the sound of Laura's happy squeal coming from outside, Jessy looked up, welcoming even this momentary distraction. But she wasn't exactly thrilled when she recognized the cause for her daughter's excitement, although Tara had always made a habit of showing up unannounced.

"It looks like we have company," she told the bookkeeper and laid the pen aside. "I'll sign the rest of the checks later. You go ahead and take these."

Leaving him to collect the stack of signed checks, Jessy rose from the desk and made her way to the entry hall. She arrived as Tara walked through the door, carrying Laura. Laura had both hands fastened on a brightly wrapped gift.

"Look, Mom. Aunt Tara got me something." Laura's dark brown eyes shone with pleasure.

"I hope you thanked her for it."

"I gotta open it first," Laura declared as Tara set her down. Immediately she dashed into the living room.

"I wish you wouldn't bring her presents all the time." Jessy didn't attempt to hide her irritation. "You are spoiling her."

"I know. That's what aunts do." There was a suggestion of taunt in the smile Tara flashed her before she followed Laura, moving with her usual gliding grace.

"Sit here, Aunt Tara." Laura patted the sofa cushion next to her.

Obediently Tara sat down beside Laura while Jessy reluctantly joined them in the living room, her temper at a low simmer.

"Go ahead and open it, sweetie," Tara urged while Jessy looked on from her post by the living room's overstuffed armchair.

Eager fingers tore into the package, making short work of discarding its pretty bow and ribbon. Laura ripped off the bright paper to expose a slender white box. With barely contained excitement, she pried it open and pushed aside the tissue.

Deflated by what she saw, Laura turned her disappointment on Tara. "It's panties."

"Very, very fancy ones." Tara picked up the top one, a silky looking pink-flowered pair with fussy lace edging. "You're too old to still be wearing those plain old white ones." She tipped her head closer to Laura's blond curls in a confiding attitude. "We girls should always have beautiful underthings like this to wear."

"Do you wear them?" Laura asked, still

not sure how thrilled she was with the present.

Nodding that she did, Tara whispered, "Today I'm wearing ones that are mint green. See?" Delicately she pulled aside the collar of her blouse just enough to give Laura a glimpse of her bra strap, then took another item from the box. "And you have a little undershirt to match your panties, too."

Laura's mouth rounded in a little "o" as she began to embrace this new fashion idea. "I'm gonna put 'em on now."

When she started to grab for them, Tara held them just out of her reach. "But you must remember that after you put them on, you must never show them to anyone. Pretty undies like these are a secret just between us girls."

"I promise." All in one motion, Laura took the underclothes from Tara, pushed the box off her lap, and scrambled off the couch.

"You forgot something, Laura," Jessy prompted, to remind Laura of her manners.

After a brief hesitation, Laura swung back to Tara and flung her arms around her. "Thank you, Aunt Tara."

"You are welcome, darling." She kissed

the child lightly on the cheek, then gave her a push toward the stairs. "Go put them on."

Needing no second urging, Laura raced upstairs to change. Jessy waited until she was out of earshot, then let some of her temper boil over.

"I could throttle you for this, Tara," she said, her voice thick with contained anger. "Every morning she argues with me over what she's going to wear. Now I'll have to fight with her over underclothes."

"Laura has a natural sense of fashion, doesn't she," Tara remarked with a feline smile that seemed to take delight in Jessy's anger.

"No more presents," Jessy stated, determined to lay down the law. "You are not to bring Laura one more thing unless it's her birthday or Christmas. If you do, I swear I will take it from her and burn it. I don't care how big a fit she throws. Is that clear?"

"Don't you think you are overreacting just a bit?" Tara chided ever so mockingly.

"Probably. But that seems to be the only way I can get my point across to you," Jessy replied, gripped by a steely calm now. "If you should choose to ignore me and attempt to give Laura something behind my back, then understand that you have set foot on Triple C for the last time. And I hope you know that isn't an idle threat."

Tara's lips thinned in a tight line of displeasure. "You would be just mean enough to do it even though you know if would break my heart not to see Ty's children."

"There are times when I have serious doubts whether you have a heart." Remembering all the misery she had created for Ty, Jessy grew angry all over again.

As if sensing this was not the time to push Jessy, Tara rose from the couch. "But even you can't question that Sally has one. And she is the real reason I'm here. The present was merely an afterthought. I never dreamed you would be this offended by me giving Laura something so trifling as matching underwear."

"It wasn't the underclothes; it was the fashion lessons that came with them."

"You wish that she would wear jeans all the time and be a little tomboy, just like you probably were. If that were Laura's nature, nothing I might say would influence her. But that isn't the case, and that is what really galls you, isn't it," Tara stated with infuriating certainty.

Jessy wasn't about to give Tara the opportunity to point out her lack of fashion knowledge. "What about Sally? You said she was the reason for your visit."

Tara's smug smile said she knew exactly why Jessy had changed the subject. "When I spoke to Cat yesterday, she mentioned that Sally seemed on the verge of collapse. Cat felt that Sally is finding it much too difficult to cope with being surrounded by constant reminders of Chase. Cat thought that Sally should go away for a while."

"I agree, but Sally won't hear of it."

"I understand that better than anyone," Tara said and let her gaze roam familiarly about the room. "It is impossible to be in this house without feeling their presence. There is pain in knowing they're gone. At the same time, you feel oddly close to them here. And more than anything you want to feel close to them again." She leveled her gaze once more at Jessy, a faint sparkle of challenge in her dark eyes. "Whatever else you might think about me, Jessy, I did love Ty very much."

Jessy didn't give an inch. "I'm sure you loved him as deeply as you can love someone other than yourself."

For an instant she thought Tara was going to unleash her claws. "You have to believe that, don't you," Tara purred instead. "It makes it easier for you to justify stealing him from me."

"You walked out on him," Jessy reminded her. "You were the one who insisted that he choose between you and the Triple C. Only a fool issues an ultimatum like that to a Calder. Don't blame me because you misjudged him."

"I never said I didn't make mistakes."

"But you made one too many."

"And you didn't make any at all, did you?" Bitterness coated the challenge Tara hurled.

"I guess I always knew if Ty was the man I thought he was, sooner or later he would see beyond your blinding beauty." Even now Jessy suspected that Tara's interest in Laura was based mainly in a desire to steal something of Ty's from her.

"You are always so sure of yourself, aren't you?" Tara all but spat the words.

"No," Jessy replied calmly. "I was always sure of Ty."

"How disgustingly noble you sound," Tara murmured with contempt. "None of this has anything to do with Sally except in the most indirect way. And she is my main concern at the moment."

"We're all concerned about her." But

Jessy knew of nothing that would help the woman except time.

"Sally needs to openly grieve for Chase. Loving someone without being loved in return makes that difficult. It somehow forces you to hold in your grief. I know this from my own experience," Tara stated. Jessy couldn't recall Tara ever holding anything back, but she was too tired of trading barbs with the woman to point it out. "Sally understands this, I'm sure," Tara continued.

"I think all of us are aware that Sally loved Chase. And we have made it known that we understand his death is a deeply personal loss to her."

"No doubt you have, but coming from his family that can be embarrassing," Tara said. "In its own way, it is a reminder that she doesn't truly have the right to grieve. But I thought if I could persuade her to come to Dunshill and stay with me for a while, she would finally be able to speak freely about her feelings for Chase. I know her regrets must be enormous. Mine were. But she wouldn't feel comfortable talking about them to you."

"I'm not the one you need to convince that it might be good for her to go away. It's Sally. I don't know how successful you'll be, but you are welcome to try. You'll probably find her in the kitchen."

"Not right now, I won't," Tara said with utter certainty. "When I drove in, Sally was on her way to the cemetery. I don't know whether you are aware that she spends a great deal of time at Chase's grave."

"I know she makes sure there are always fresh flowers on his grave." Jessy didn't pretend to know more than that. "Obviously I have been busy."

"Obviously," Tara echoed in a voice dry with criticism.

"Aunt Tara!" Laura hollered as she peeked out the door of her upstairs bedroom. "Come see."

Tara arched a jet black eyebrow in Jessy's direction. "Is it allowed?"

In answer, Jessy called up to her daughter, "She'll be right there."

"Thank you," Tara murmured. "I didn't want to overstep my bounds."

Jessy held her tongue with an effort and glared at Tara's back when she crossed to the staircase. Every time she was around the woman she swore that she wouldn't allow Tara to rile her. It was no use. The woman's all-knowing, superior attitude rubbed her the wrong way.

Sighing, she turned toward the den. Before she had taken a step, Trey burst into the house. "Mom, Quint's here! I'm gonna take him to the barn an' show him Laura's pony!"

Out he went, giving Jessy no chance to reply. But his exuberance was like a tonic that banished the bad taste Tara had left with her.

There was nothing forced or false in the smile she gave Cat when she walked in. "Hi —" she began but got no further before Cat attacked.

"Why did you do it?"

Jessy drew back in surprise. "Do what?"

"Did you think I wouldn't find out?" Cat challenged in full temper. "For your information, I just came from the feedlot. It happens to be full of cattle, but not a single one of them carries the Triple C brand."

"I leased it to a group that Monte represents —"

"What right do you have to take it upon yourself to make a decision like that without first consulting me?"

"It was business. We agreed —"

"We agreed that you would have full say in running the ranch." Cat impatiently waved off the words. "But this goes considerably beyond that and you know it."

"That's ridiculous," Jessy protested,

struggling to understand why Cat objected so strongly. "Financially you have to see that it's a wise move. This will be the first time the ranch will see a return on the money it invested since the lot was built."

"The Triple C has always been a cow-calf operation. It was a mistake to build the feedlot in the first place. Dad realized that. That's why it has stood empty all this time. He would never have agreed to this, and neither do I." Cat paused, green eyes narrowing with suspicion. "Something tells me you knew that. That's why you were careful not to say anything to me about it."

"That isn't true. It simply never occurred to me that you might object." Jessy felt trapped, unable to explain that Chase was the one who had made the decision to go ahead with the lease agreement.

"Well, I do object." Cat was emphatic.

"Object to what?" Tara inquired from the staircase landing, her glance running between the two women with intensifying interest.

Cat never took her eyes off Jessy. "She leased the feedlot without my permission."

"How could she do that when, technically speaking, you own half the ranch?" There was something in Tara's voice that hinted at a delight in the news.

"That is exactly what I would like to know," Cat stated.

"I didn't do it deliberately. I simply didn't regard it as anything major —"

"Not major?" Cat jumped on that. "How could you not think it was major when it changed the policy of this ranch?"

"I wasn't looking at it that way." Everything Jessy said sounded weak.

"But that is precisely what happened. Not for long, though," Cat added. "I want those cattle gone, Jessy."

She was flabbergasted that Cat would make such a demand. "That's impossible. The agreement has been signed. It's a legal document. Until Monte decides to ship those cattle to market, he has possession of the lot. Even if I could break it, I wouldn't. I gave Monte my word."

"But I didn't give mine," Cat reminded her. All the while Tara stood to one side, a very interested spectator. "I don't care how you do it, but you get those trucks back here and ship those cows someplace else."

"Cat, you're not being reasonable. I admit I made a mistake in not discussing it with you first, and I'm sorry for that. But this last couple weeks haven't exactly been easy for me."

"I suppose you expect me to overlook this."

"I wish you would."

For a long second Cat didn't say anything and simply stared at her. "I might be inclined to do that if it was the only thing I found out you had done."

Jessy knew immediately what was coming. Culley had told her about fixing up the old line shack as well as about Laredo and Hattie.

"There is something else?" Tara asked, nearly smiling with pleasure over the prospect.

"Jessy decided to fix that abandoned line shack up in the foothills. So far she hasn't run electricity to it, but I understand it now has running water."

"It was something Ty and I often talked about doing," Jessy repeated the lie she had told Culley.

"I wonder why you never did anything about it until after my father died," Cat murmured coolly.

Put that way, it didn't look right. Jessy scrambled to come up with an explanation. "Mostly because there wasn't a reason to do it. But the Smiths needed work and a place to live. There weren't any openings here at the ranch. Then I remembered the

254

Boar's Nest. I knew Laredo was handy at such things so I hired him to fix it up and make it habitable again."

"Laredo, what an odd name," Tara remarked. "Who is he?"

"The Smiths are presumably friends of my father. Supposedly they have a ranch in Texas. What happened to that?" Cat asked Jessy.

"They ran into some financial difficulties after" — for the life of her, Jessy couldn't remember the first name of Hattie's late husband, or if she had even heard it — "John passed away. They were forced to sell it. There wasn't much left after the debts were paid."

"So you took pity on them and came up with this scheme to repair the cabin so you could help them out."

"They're good people." She found she could say that with conviction. "And the ranch isn't paying for the repairs. The moneys are coming out of my personal account." Mentally she crossed her fingers, vowing to do just that. "I know Chase would approve of my decision to help them even if you don't."

"Maybe he would, but I don't think my father would slip off to the old cemetery to meet them."

Alarm shot through Jessy that Cat should know about that. She managed to push out a surprised laugh. "What on earth are you talking about?"

"Are you saying you didn't?" Cat challenged.

Suddenly Jessy remembered seeing Culley that morning, but it had been after she'd met Laredo at the cemetery. Had Culley back-trailed her? Even if he had, it was only his word against hers. He had no proof she had been there — or that she had met anyone. Considering there was no rational explanation for her to be there, Jessy felt she had no choice but to bluff it out.

"That is exactly what I'm saying," she insisted in denial. "Why would I meet Laredo or anyone else at the old cemetery? It doesn't make sense."

"Uncle Culley claims that you did. Are you suggesting he lied about that?"

"No, only that he was mistaken. If he saw me over there at all, it must have been when Laredo and his mother followed me out to the Boar's Nest. The easiest way to get there is along that road past the cemetery." Jessy could tell by the small flicker of uncertainty in Cat's expression that she had succeeded in planting a seed of doubt.

"If you hired this Laredo Smith to repair

the cabin, what is he doing at the feedlot? I saw him there this morning, carelessly letting water run on the ground."

"I needed some extra help to run the feedlot, so I hired Laredo. He had already finished the bulk of the repairs to the cabin."

"How convenient," Tara murmured. "When he first shows up, you don't have any ranch work for him, so you make work by deciding to fix up an old shack. Then you rush out and make a deal to lease the feedlot. And all of a sudden, you need extra help on the ranch. You seem to have gone to a great deal of trouble to make certain this Laredo Smith has a job."

"It's purely a coincidence," Jessy insisted, growing more and more uncomfortable.

"Naturally." Tara smiled. "Still, he must be a very close friend."

"He is," Jessy replied, then saw the trap in that and rushed to add, "They both are."

"Isn't it odd that I have never heard of them." Cat hadn't let go of her anger. It was still there, close to the surface.

"I don't think it's odd." Jessy continued to convey calmness despite her chaotic jumble inside. "I imagine there are a lot of people Chase knew that you didn't."

"Smith, with a ranch in Texas." Head down, Tara made a show of searching her memory. "Ty and I were in Texas dozens of times and I can't recall a single time when he mentioned anything about wanting to visit a rancher named Smith. You would think if the Smiths were such close friends to Chase, Ty would have felt obliged to at least phone them."

Jessy was quick to answer that. "Back then you cared so little about ranching, Ty wouldn't have told you about them. He would have known that you couldn't be bothered with such ordinary people."

"I still find it hard to believe he never mentioned them at all. On the other hand, maybe they never were his friends. Maybe they were yours."

"How would I have met them except through Chase or Ty?" Jessy reasoned.

"How should I know?" Tara dismissed her questions with an elegant shrug of her shoulders. "I don't keep track of who you see or when. Perhaps someone should." Holding her gaze on Jessy, she said to Cat, "If I were you, Cathleen, I would look into this."

"I intend to."

Jessy knew immediately that she would only weaken her position by arguing with

Cat. Her only choice was to take a firm stand and bluff this through the whole way. "Look into it all you want. You won't find anything different from what I have told you."

"That remains to be seen, doesn't it," Tara murmured, clearly enjoying Jessy's predicament. "Of course, there is a simple way to prove Cat's suspicions are ill-founded."

Jessy was instantly wary. "What's that?"

"Get rid of the Smiths. Let them find a place to live in Blue Moon. I know for a fact the mine has several openings. If he needs work, he can get a job there. It would certainly eliminate the necessity of you supporting them."

"I could do that," Jessy agreed. "But I won't. Because I don't feel that I need to prove anything — to you or anyone else."

"I think it's rather obvious where her loyalties lie. Don't you, Cathleen?" Tara cast a smug glance at Cat.

"My loyalty is to the Triple C. It always has been, and it always will be," Jessy stated somewhat fiercely, angered that Tara would suggest otherwise.

"You have a funny way of showing it," said Cat. Then she erupted in a mixture of anger and frustration. "How could you do this, Jessy? After my father fought his whole life to keep the Triple C intact, less than a month after he's gone you sign a lease giving someone else possession of part of it. How could you betray him like that?"

"I didn't," Jessy insisted. Chase had made the decision, yet she was honor bound to keep that a secret.

"You certainly had no right to do it without Cat's permission," Tara inserted.

Jessy turned to her. "You're wrong. I had every right. Chase named me to take over the ranch in the event anything happened to him. He made it clear that Cat was to have no say in the running of the Triple C. The decisions are mine to make, not hers."

"As long as you make the right ones," Tara added with false sweetness. "Otherwise there is such a thing as malfeasance. If the actions you take are deemed not to be in the best interests of the ranch, as owner, Cathleen has a legal right to step in and take over."

"None of this is really any of your business, Tara," Jessy snapped, her patience exhausted. "Why don't you just stay out of it?"

"You would like that, wouldn't you," Tara countered smoothly. "Without me around, you think you have a better chance of talking Cat into accepting your decision."

"Cat knows I would never do anything to jeopardize the Triple C. It represents my children's future. I would do whatever it takes to protect both."

"I always thought you would," Cat said. "But I also thought I knew you, Jessy. Now I wonder if I ever did at all."

Fighting back tears, Cat whipped around and headed for the door. Tara lingered a moment, a pleased look in her eyes. Then she hurried after Cat. Jessy's first impulse was to go after Cat, but she sensed she would just be giving Tara another chance to fan Cat's distrust.

Chapter Eleven

In the den, Jessy went through the motions of comparing the invoice total against the check amount before adding her signature, but the numbers didn't register. Just outside the window, Cat and Tara had their heads together. Jessy could imagine the sympathetic noises Tara was making while adding a few sly insinuations.

As if the present situation wasn't complicated enough, now Cat had put this new twist on it. Something had to be done before this rift between them became any wider. But what that could be Jessy didn't know.

Not until both women had climbed into their cars and left did Jessy lay the pen aside and reach for the ranch phone directory. With a finger on the number for the feedlot, she dialed it and waited. After a dozen rings, Laredo answered.

"It's Jessy. We have trouble."

"I thought we might. She was in a temper when she came by here." He didn't bother to refer to Cat by name, confident she was the source. "I figured she would unload on somebody, and it seemed very likely you would be that person. What's the problem?"

On the off chance someone might walk in, Jessy kept her voice pitched low and gave him a bare-bones answer. When she mentioned Tara's role, Laredo responded with a soft whistle.

"I didn't figure on the ex sticking her nose in," he admitted thoughtfully. "She doesn't like you, you know."

"It's mutual," Jessy replied grimly, then suddenly wondered, "How do you know that?"

"I talked to her once."

"When?" She felt more uneasy than before.

"Down south."

She heard the front door open, followed by the sound of boots. Speaking at a normal level, Jessy said, "It's impossible for me to get away right now. Explain it to Duke for me," she added, using Hattie's name for Chase. "Let me know what he says."

"Got company, do you?" Laredo guessed. "In that case, why don't we meet tonight at the old barn. Is ten o'clock too early?"

"That will be fine." She looked up as Jobe Garvey walked into the den. "I'll talk to you then."

All the windows at the Boar's Nest were propped open, allowing a welcome breeze to flow through the interior. Chase sat in a wooden chair, a towel draped around his shoulders, his fingers clutching it tightly together at his throat. Hattie stood behind him, a pair of scissors in one hand and a comb in the other.

"I can't believe how fast your hair has grown." She ran the comb down the back of it and held the ends flat with its teeth. "Do you know it's almost long enough to cover your scar? Which, by the way, is healing nicely."

When she made the first snip, Chase asked warily, "Are you sure you know how to cut hair?"

"I did my husband's for years."

"I saw a picture of him at your place. He was bald."

"Only on top. He still had to have the sides trimmed."

As the scissors made steady progress along the nape of his neck, Chase warned, "Watch my ear."

"Look on the bright side," Hattie told

him. "If it should accidentally get nicked, you have a nurse right here. Now keep your head down."

Chase tucked his chin lower and grumbled, "Something tells me you are a better nurse than a barber."

"Are you always such a grump?" she chided.

That sobered him. "I don't know. I don't remember."

"Now, that isn't entirely true," Hattie admonished while deftly switching from comb to scissors, snipping, and switching back again. "You've remembered a few more things."

"Yeah, from when I was child," he admitted, unimpressed. "It's not exactly important to remember that one time I caught a fish with my bare hands when Buck and I were skinny-dipping in the river."

In his mind's eye, he could see again the dappling of sunlight on the water, feel the fish's firm but slippery sides, hear Buck's gleeful shouts, and smell the odor of the river. It was a happy memory, but one that didn't bring him any closer to knowing who tried to kill him or why.

Caught up in the past, Chase almost missed the faint humming noise carried by the breeze. The instant he became aware of it, his head came up, his body stiffening.

"Will you hold still," Hattie said in exasperation.

"Wait a minute." He held up a hand. "I hear something."

Hattie paused to listen. "It's a vehicle."

"Coming this way." He let go of the towel and stood up.

"Maybe it's Jessy." Hattie darted him an anxious glance.

"Maybe." But it was that uncertainty that had him moving toward the corner of the cabin where they had rigged up a hiding place for him, under a bunk bed, disguising it to look like a set of storage drawers.

Before he had taken three steps, a horn honked twice. After a short pause, it sounded again.

"That's Laredo," Hattie said with surprise, recognizing their prearranged signal. "What's he doing back here in the middle of the day?"

"I doubt if he's coming to bring good news," Chase replied, his mind already racing to anticipate what it might be.

Of all the potential problems he had considered, none of them were even close to what Laredo told him. The set of his jaw hardened when he heard about Tara's part in the confrontation between Cat and Jessy.

"Good God," Chase muttered in disgust. "And my son was once married to a woman like that."

"She is a looker, Chase," Laredo said in Ty's defense.

"She is a divisive bitch," Chase declared and shot a skeptical glance at Laredo. "Would you have been taken in by her?"

"I don't know." Laredo thought about it. "When I was younger, if she had turned those dark eyes on me . . . maybe. But I'm older now, and a little wiser. I expect that's what happened with your son."

"That's beside the point. Right now our problem is with Cat," Chase stated as his thoughts turned inward to examine his options. "The last thing we need right now is a battle for control of the ranch."

"Jessy gave me the impression that's exactly what she thinks will happen if she can't get Cat settled down soon."

"Who would have thought leasing the feedlot would cause such an uproar?" Chase muttered to himself.

"I didn't understand myself why your daughter would consider it a betrayal," Laredo admitted. "But on the way here, I remembered some gossip I picked up at your funeral. From what I gathered, you spent most of your life fighting to gain title to ten thousand acres of rangeland within the ranch boundaries. Tara was mixed up in it somehow, but I never got the straight of that. I do know that shortly after your son was killed, she deeded the land over to you, but kept the right to live in the house she built there."

"Wolf Meadow. Dy-Corps had leased the mineral rights to it from the government so they could strip-mine the coal on it," Chase recalled in a sudden flash of memory. "I can remember Ty telling me about it." He had an image of a hospital room, of being surrounded by tubes and monitors, and of a tall, broad-shouldered man with a dark mustache standing by the bed — the same man he had seen lying dead in the coulee. His son. He felt a deep swell of tenderness and pride and a sudden tightening ache in his chest.

Hattie laid a hand on his shoulder. "You see, it is coming back, Duke."

"I wish you could remember your daughter." Laredo helped himself to some coffee. "She seems to be the passionate kind. Everything is black and white — you're either for me or against me. Proud was the word people kept using at the funeral." Cup in hand, he returned to the table, swung a chair around and straddled it. "Jessy didn't give me a blow-by-blow account of all that was said, so I'm just guessing. But most daughters think their dads can't do any wrong. In your case, it's probably more true than in others. Cat wants everything to stay the way it was. Suddenly Jessy isn't doing the things Cat is convinced you would. On top of that, it's happening too fast after your funeral. More than likely she believes being in charge has gone to Jessy's head. I'd be willing to bet that's what Tara is telling her."

"I can't fault Cat for fighting for what she believes is best for the Triple C." While he could admire her reason, Chase was still irritated by her actions.

"It will take some tall convincing to make her back down," Laredo warned. "Personally I don't think it can be done short of you stepping forward."

"There might be another way." He turned to Hattie. "Do you have a paper and pencil?"

"I'll get it." She moved away from the table.

"You said you were meeting Jessy tonight?" Chase glanced at Laredo.

"Ten o'clock."

"Good. I'll have a note for you to give her — one that she can show Cat. Hopefully I can word it in such a way that Cat will be convinced Jessy has acted as I would." His mouth curved in a dry smile. "Presumably my daughter will recognize my handwriting."

Laredo lifted his cup, speaking against its rim. "Our luck, she'll think it's a forgery. Especially if Tara hears about it."

"If nothing else, it should gain us some time," Chase said as Hattie returned with a writing tablet and ballpoint pen.

With agonizing slowness, the minute hand ticked its way closer to ten o'clock. Five minutes before the hour, Jessy rose from the big desk, a high tension running through her nerves. Leaving the den, she made her way to the living room. As expected, she found Sally sitting in Chase's favorite chair, watching television.

"I'm going for a walk and to get some air, Sally," Jessy said, trotting out her carefully rehearsed excuse. "Will you listen for the twins just in case they wake up while I'm gone?"

"Of course." Sally managed a wan smile of assurance that didn't even come close to reaching her pain-filled eyes.

"Thanks. I won't be long." Jessy's glance touched briefly on the wadded-up tissue in Sally's hand, a sure indication she had been crying again.

She was almost sorry that Tara hadn't followed through with her plan and spoken to Sally about staying with her. The woman was breaking her heart over Chase.

Outside The Homestead, Jessy paused at the top of the steps and skimmed her glance over the ranch yard. Ten minutes earlier she had heard a vehicle and assumed it was Laredo. But there was no sign of his pickup.

She descended the steps and struck out for the old timbered barn, adopting what she hoped would be perceived as a strolling pace by anyone who might see her. Tall yard lights cast wide pools of light at intervals, their brightness dimming the twinkle of stars in the night sky.

When she reached the barn, Jessy had to force herself not to glance guiltily over her shoulder. She didn't think anyone was about, but she couldn't be certain of that.

Striving to make every action appear normal, she stepped into the barn and immediately flipped the wall switch, turning on the lights that ran the length of the barn's wide alley. Her heightened senses immediately registered the rustling of straw and the slightly musty odors of hay and horse. Pausing, she scanned the interior, paying special attention to the many shadowy areas made even darker by the overhead lights. The Welsh pony thrust its nose over the top of its stall and blew softly. It was the only movement she detected.

Nerves taut and at a loss as to how to kill time until Laredo arrived, Jessy walked over to the pony's stall. "How are you tonight, Sundance?" The pony lipped at the hand she extended to it. "Sorry, no carrots. I'll make sure Laura brings you some tomorrow."

"Down here." The low-voiced call came from her left.

Her pulse instantly rocketed, an indication of the jumpy state of her nerves. She gave the pony a parting scratch and wandered down to the next stall. It was empty, the door open, a bed of fresh straw on the floor. When she glanced inside, she saw Laredo perched on the feed bunk, chewing on a stalk of straw.

"Right on time." He pushed off the bunk, coming soundlessly erect. His lips parted in a grin that showed the whiteness of his teeth and the straw clenched between them. He removed it, a devilish twinkle in his blue eyes. "I like a woman who doesn't keep a man waiting." He observed the flicker of annoyance in her expression that told him she was not amused by his trite remark. "Smile, Jessy," he admonished lightly. "You don't do it enough."

"Find me something to smile about." The line of her mouth thinned in grimness.

He reached into his shirt pocket and pulled out a slip of paper. "I may have an answer for your problem right here."

"What is it?" she asked with a sudden lift of interest.

"Duke wrote it." He passed it to her and watched the eager way she shifted into the stall opening to allow the light to fall on it. "Basically it indicates he intended to explore the possibility of leasing the feedlot. The idea is that you show it to Cat, tell her you came across it in one of the desk drawers. With any luck it will go a long way in convincing her that her father was thinking along the same lines."

Propping her back against the stall's door frame, Jessy studied the note. It looked like idle jottings, listing the pros and cons of leasing the feedlot. "It doesn't really say he planned to lease it."

"No. It might have looked a tad too convenient that you found it if it did. We don't want Cat to become even more suspicious. We just want her to concede that he could have been considering it. It should make it harder for her to be against it."

"I suppose I should wait a day or two before I *find* this."

"I think so," Laredo agreed.

She folded the paper and slipped it inside her jeans pocket. "That's one problem solved," she murmured.

Laredo cocked his head, sensing a heaviness in her. "Are there more?"

"You."

"I've been called many things, but never a problem." He felt a need to lighten her mood, lift some of the trouble from her.

"Tara doesn't remember a Texas rancher named Smith. She finds it hard to believe that Ty never contacted you on any of the trips they took to Fort Worth." Jessy pulled in a deep breath and let it out in a rush. "And if that isn't bad enough, she didn't buy the story I gave O'Rourke about fixing up the Boar's Nest. If it was a job you needed, Tara couldn't understand why you didn't apply for one at Dy-Corps. Apparently they have several openings. She made it sound like I rushed out and leased the feedlot so I could keep you at the ranch."

"Are you saying that Tara thinks you are interested in me — woman to man?"

Jessy gave him a startled look that made him just a little bit angry. Then she appeared to consider his question. "Probably," she concluded. "Either that or she thinks you've got something on me. What, I don't know, but it planted a seed in Cat's mind. To make matters worse, O'Rourke told Cat about me meeting you at the old cemetery."

Laredo stiffened. "He was there?"

"I don't think so." Jessy shook her head. "I did see him shortly afterwards. It's possible he might have backtracked me there."

"How did you explain that?"

"I didn't. Basically I denied it and insisted he was mistaken. I didn't really have any choice." She leveled a look at him. "I can explain away a lot of things, but you aren't one of them."

"Which means I will likely be the weapon Tara will try to use against you," he murmured thoughtfully. "We'll have to see what we can do about that."

"On the phone, you mentioned that you had talked to her in Fort Worth," Jessy remembered. "What was that about?"

"I bought her a drink in the hotel bar

where Chase had stayed. By then I was fairly certain who Chase was, and I wanted to pick up information to fill in some of the blanks for him. It didn't take me long to figure out I wouldn't get anything out of Logan, not without answering a lot of questions from him first. But I had no problem getting Tara to talk. Needless to say, your name came up."

"I don't need to ask what she had to say. I know it wouldn't have been anything complimentary." Jessy tilted her head back, letting it rest against the frame.

"It wasn't so much what she said as the way she said it when she told me Chase's death had left you in charge of the ranch. She seemed to think your only qualification for the position was that you were born and raised on the ranch. The envy in her voice made it easy to read between the lines and guess that she felt she was better suited for the position."

"God help us all if she ever got her hands on the Triple C." Her face was half in light and half in shadow, a study in strength and composure softened by the honey-dark hair lying loose about her shoulders; but it was the long, full line of her lips that Laredo found himself watching. "In a way, I'm surprised that

Tara didn't play the wronged woman and accuse me of stealing Ty from her."

"Did you?"

"No. Ty had stopped seeing me well before they parted."

"Then the two of you had an affair while he was still married to Tara," Laredo realized and marveled again at her frankness, knowing it was something most women wouldn't admit.

"You mean you hadn't heard." The laugh lines around her almond brown eyes crinkled in a smile. "It's common knowledge on the ranch. Nothing ever stays secret for long on the Triple C. The range telegraph sees to that."

"Funny, I never would have thought you were the type to get involved with a married man. It's notoriously a dead-end relationship."

"My eyes were wide open when I went into it. I knew Ty would never leave Tara for me. A Calder doesn't do that, and Ty was a Calder. Life is nothing but a series of good times and bad times. I seized my chance for one of those good ones."

"You loved him for a long time, didn't you," Laredo guessed.

"Since I was a kid." Her mouth lifted in a smile of remembrance. "Ty even gave me my first kiss. He did it as a joke, right in front of Buzz Taylor and Bill Summers. It was so embarrassing I was furious with him."

"But you never forgot how it felt."

She touched her fingertips to her lips in a remembering fashion and shook her head. "No, I never did."

He sensed a loosening in her. This mental trip back to happier times had relaxed her, lessened some of the strain and tension of the current situation.

"If it wasn't over you, why did he split with Tara?" Laredo couldn't help being curious.

"She made the mistake of siding with her father against Ty. Calders put a high value on loyalty, and she didn't show any. Even then Ty might have overlooked it if the future of the Triple C hadn't been an issue."

"So he walked from her straight to you."

"Something like that."

"At least he finally wised up."

She released a soft breath of laughter. "Thank you. That sounded distinctly like a compliment."

"It was."

"Thanks. You're good for my ego. But we both know Tara is an incredibly beautiful woman."

"That's what most men probably see when they look at her, but I'm not most men."

"No, you're cut from a different cloth," Jessy agreed. "I just haven't figure out what kind."

"It's nice to know you've wondered about me. After the way you reacted when I suggested Tara thought we were having an affair, I had just about decided you didn't think I was human, let alone a man."

Something had changed. One minute Jessy was relaxed and at ease for the first time in days. Then suddenly she was full of a tingling awareness. She felt uncertain of her footing, a sensation that made her uneasy and hesitant.

"It didn't have anything to do with you. I was surprised that anyone would think I might be interested in someone else," she explained.

"Because of Ty." Laredo stood much closer than she remembered.

"That's right. He's the only man I ever loved."

Laredo nodded as if he had anticipated that's what her answer would be. "Gave you your first kiss, and probably was your first lover, too. That makes for some tough competition."

Worried that she might be misinterpreting this shift in the conversation, Jessy blurted, "Are you flirting with me?"

Amusement gleamed in his blue eyes. "I am. Any objections?"

Her throat felt strangely tight. She had to swallow to get the words out. "I think so."

"That's encouraging." He grinned crookedly, a kind of sexiness in his smile. "You aren't sure. You just think so."

She gave him a long, level look. "You know what I really think?"

"What?" The corners of his mouth deepened in a near smile.

"I think you've spent too many nights alone at the Boar's Nest. What you really need is a trip into town, a few beers, and an easy woman."

He threw back his head and laughed. It was a rich and hearty sound, genuine and impossible to resist. Jessy found herself chuckling softly along with him. At last his laughter subsided, ending with a mild shaking of the head.

"You might as well admit I'm right," she said, feeling comfortable and sure of her footing again. "I spent too many years working side by side with men not to know when one gets randy from spending too many nights out on roundup."

"Ah, Jessy, that's what I like about you. You just cut through all the trimmings and get right to the meat of things. It's a very effective weapon. I'm surprised more women haven't discovered it."

"Weapon?" His choice of words puzzled her.

"Sure, it's just like that calm composure of yours that somehow pushes a man back. Your blunt talk cuts a man's legs right out from under him. Here I am, working things around to where I can steal a kiss, and you" — he made a slicing motion with his hand — "completely destroy the romantic mood I was trying to create by declaring I must be horny."

"Aren't you?" Jessy challenged.

"Sorry, that won't work this time," he informed her. "I'm gettin' my kiss."

For a split second she was too dumbfounded to react. In the next breath it seemed, his face was inches from hers, the incredible blue of his eyes briefly mesmerizing her. He hooked a finger under her chin and tilted it up. Then his mouth came down and she felt the warm, lightly exploring pressure of it on her lips, more curious than demanding.

If he had been a bit more forceful, she

would have been quicker to object. As it was, he was lifting his head and stepping back before she had a chance to end it. Eyes sparkling, he thrust out his chin and turned it slightly to one side.

"Go ahead," he said.

She deliberately pretended not to understand. "Go ahead and what?

"I thought you might want to hit me."

"If I did, my target would be much lower. And I wouldn't be using my hand," Jessy replied, angry without being sure why. "Which proves you don't know me as well as you think."

"I guess you didn't notice that I was careful to keep my legs together when I kissed you. I wasn't about to give your knee easy access to its target. I guess that means you were a bit distracted by my kiss." His smile widened a little. "Now do you want to hit me?"

"Believe me, it's a tempting thought — for no other reason than just to find out how you would go about explaining a black eye to Chase."

"You're right. That could prove awkward, couldn't it?"

"You are really a cocky bastard, aren't you?"

"Look on the bright side, Jessy. At least I

took your mind off your problems for a while.

"You certainly did that," she agreed in an ultra-dry voice. "Pardon me if I don't thank you for it." She straightened away from the stall and made no effort to avoid bumping against his shoulder as she pushed her way past him into the alleyway.

"You're thinking this is a complication you don't need right now," Laredo said to her back, making no attempt to follow her.

"You are wrong. It doesn't complicate anything for me," Jessy retorted.

"You are getting awfully good at this lying business, Jessy," he remarked. "Maybe you don't see this as a problem, but it complicates things for me. When I came here, I didn't figure on being attracted to the widow Calder."

"You'll get over it," she replied over her shoulder and struggled to dismiss an unexpected sense of depression.

"Maybe," Laredo conceded, his voice following her as Jessy made her way to the door. "I only know I always figured I would spend my declining years alone, the same way I have always lived. And now that prospect doesn't appeal to me at all."

She stopped at the door and turned back to look at him. He stood in the stall opening, arms raised, a hand braced on each side of the entrance. "Go have a few beers. Maybe things will look a little brighter."

"That idea is sounding better and better all the time. I think I may just do that. Don't forget about that note in your pocket."

The reminder jolted her thoughts back to her current troubles with Cat. She touched her pocket as if to verify the folded slip of paper was still there. "I won't." She turned and walked out the door, hitting the light switch on her way out.

Laredo stood in the barn's pitch-darkness and cursed himself for being fifty kinds of fool. When he looked back, all he saw behind him was one mistake after another. He had made the first one when he rescued Chase, and the second one when he hadn't made tracks for Mexico and left Chase in Hattie's care. The third one came when he volunteered to bring Chase to Montana. And the fourth one had been a jim-dandy one when he had given in to the attraction he felt toward Jessy. He was a fool to even think in that direction. He was a man without a future, with nothing to offer her or any woman, not even his name.

Trouble, that's all he knew. Very likely it was all he would ever know.

In the past, darkness had always been a friend. Tonight it pressed in on him, intensifying that empty, lonely feeling that gripped him. Made restless by it, he pushed away from the stall's opening.

He left the barn the way he had entered it, through the stall's rear door that opened into the corral. After the blackness of the closed-up barn, the night held the illusion of brightness for him. Pausing, he closed the stall door without allowing so much as a click of the latch to betray his presence.

Keeping to the shadows, he moved along the barn wall to the corral fence, ducked between the rails, and followed it away from the barn, letting it lead him to the pickup he had left parked behind the ranch commissary. As he slid behind the wheel, he decided to take Jessy's advice, head into Blue Moon and have himself a beer.

The blare of the television greeted Jessy when she walked into The Homestead. After pausing a moment, she headed for the living room to let Sally know she was back. She found Sally still ensconced in Chase's old chair, sound asleep, her snow white head lolling to one side, her mouth open and her eyes closed.

A faint smile of empathy curved Jessy's mouth at the picture of exhaustion the woman made. Knowing the difficulty Sally had had sleeping lately, Jessy hated to wake her. At the same time, she didn't want Sally to wake up later and start worrying whether she had returned or not.

"I'm back, Sally," she called, but the woman didn't stir. Jessy walked over and shut off the television so she wouldn't have to compete with it. "Sally," she repeated her name. When the woman still didn't respond, Jessy gave her shoulder a gentle shake. But with the first push of her hand, Sally slumped sideways. Alarmed now, Jessy felt for a pulse and found none.

"Sally. Dear God, no."

Chapter Twelve

A heavy dusting of stars glittered in the night sky. No yard light gleamed near the house or outbuildings of the Circle Six to dim their brilliance. With the night's mystery before him, Logan Echohawk tilted the rocker back and propped his booted feet on the porch railing. He raised a pipe to his mouth and took a puff on it, but it had gone out, and he had no inclination to relight it.

The broken country beyond the ranch yard was a tangle of shadows in varying degrees of darkness. A lazy breeze carried the scent of the land's wildness to him, touching some answering spark within him.

As was his habit, he sat in the deep shadows of the long porch, well away from the light that poured through the open screen door. Light footsteps approached. A smile of welcome automatically lifted the corners of his mouth as he glanced sideways.

The screen door swung open under the push of Cat's hand, its movement accompanied by a faint squeak of its hinges. "Quint asleep?" he guessed.

"Finally." Cat walked straight to the railing and leaned both hands on it to gaze at the night. She rocked there a moment, then pushed away and wandered toward his chair. She was restless and tense. The feelings emanated from her in waves, disturbing the night's peace.

Logan didn't have to ask what was troubling her. He already knew it was Jessy. Cat had barely given him a chance to walk through the door that evening before she'd launched into an account of all that had transpired.

"Have you decided what you're going to do yet?" He knew she wanted to talk about it, so he gave her the opening.

"No." Her voice was riddled with impatience and confusion. "I hate thinking these things about Jessy." She walked back to the railing and braced her hands on it again. "But there is something wrong over there, Logan. I can feel it."

"It's one thing to feel something in your gut, and another thing to prove it." He had relied on his own instincts too many times to discount hers. At the same time he knew instinct wasn't enough, especially not in this case.

Cat swung around to face him, tension in every line of her body. "I wish you had been there today. At first, when I confronted her about leasing the feedlot, Jessy seemed genuinely surprised and contrite that she hadn't discussed it with me first. I was ready to believe her. I still thought it was wrong, but I believed she had acted out of what she perceived was best. But the minute I challenged her about the Smiths, she changed. I don't know how to explain it exactly, but" — Cat paused to search for the words — "something about her hardened. It was as if she suddenly threw up a wall."

"Tara might have had something to do with that," Logan pointed out.

"I know," she admitted and released a heavy sigh. "Part of me wishes Tara hadn't been there. But if she hadn't, then I might never have known that Ty never mentioned any family named Smith while they were married. Yet Jessy keeps insisting they were close friends. It doesn't make sense."

"It could be the age difference. Maybe it was Chase they were close to," Logan suggested.

Cat pivoted away from the railing to face him. "But the son is about the same age as Ty would be. You should have seen him," she recalled with disgust. "It was all ma'am this and ma'am that, but there was something about his attitude that I didn't like. The whole time I had the feeling that he knew something I didn't. But Jessy refuses to hear one word against him."

"That doesn't surprise me," Logan replied in a reasonable voice. "Jessy is the type of person who would stand by her friends."

"Still . . ." Cat let the sentence trail off unfinished and folded her arms tightly across her middle

The harsh jangle of the telephone came from inside the house. Logan pulled his feet off the railing and rocked out of the chair. "I'll get it," he said. "At this hour of the night, it's bound to be for me."

When he reached the door, Cat remembered. "It could be Tara. She said she would call to give me the name and phone number of a lawyer she thinks I should consult."

"Do you want to talk to her?" Logan asked as the phone rang again.

Cat shook her head. "Tell her I'm tied up and ask her to give it to you."

"No problem." He stepped into the house and eased the screen door shut behind him.

Alone on the long porch of their single-story ranch house, Cat was soon distracted by her own troubled thoughts. Long ago, she had found that there was little to be learned from listening to only Logan's side of a telephone conversation.

Her glance skimmed him when he rejoined her on the porch. "Was it dispatch?"

"I'm afraid so."

"Don't tell me you have to go," she murmured, wavering between disappointment and concern for his safety.

"No. This time it was more or less a courtesy call." The steadiness of his gray eyes seemed to warn her to be ready for some unpleasant news. "Jenna thought she should let us know that they received a call from the Triple C. Sally Brogan passed away a short time ago."

Shock held Cat motionless for a long moment. "She's been so distraught ever since Dad was killed. You only had to look at her to see how hard she was taking it, but I never —" She broke off the sentence with a dazed shake of her head and abruptly moved toward the door. "We need to go over there."

Logan stepped into her path. "There is nothing that can be done now. Besides, it would mean waking up Quint. He had a hard enough time dealing with your father's death. He doesn't need to be exposed to this."

"I didn't think about Quint," Cat admitted. "It wouldn't be the best place for him. You stay here with him and I'll go by myself."

"Why?" His challenge was quiet but firm. "What would you accomplish?"

"It isn't a question of accomplishing anything, Logan. It's my place to be there, especially now that Dad is gone. It's simply something that is expected of me," Cat explained, a flash of determination in her eyes.

"Maybe it is," Logan conceded. "But given your present differences with Jessy, we both know that if you go there now, you would end up quarreling with Jessy before the night was over. And it wouldn't be the time or the place for that."

She knew he was right, and it made her furious. "All right, then, you go," she snapped in ill temper. "It certainly won't look right if neither one of us shows up, especially when they learn we were notified of her passing. And you can bet word will get around that I knew and didn't care enough to show up. I won't have people saying that about me. Maybe they will understand that I had to stay here with Quint — although I'm sure they will have something to say about that, too."

Logan chuckled softly and drew her rigid body into his arms. "No wonder Jessy clammed up on you today. Sometimes silence is the best way to handle a spitfire when she's on a tear."

"Sometimes I just can't help it," Cat stated, her voice tight with impatience. "I worked hard to earn the respect of everybody on the Triple C. I hate the thought they might think less of me for not being there tonight."

"Personally I don't give a damn what they think. As far as I'm concerned, our son is more important than their good opinions."

The tension flowed out of her. Smiling, she relaxed against his chest. "That is the absolute truth. Thank you for reminding me."

She tipped her head back and Logan obligingly bent his down to kiss the softness of her curved lips. The warmth of his kiss reminded her that the only home she would ever truly care about was right here in his arms.

"Still want me to go?" he teased and nuzzled the corner of her mouth.

"Not really," Cat admitted. "But I still think one of us should be there. I mean, it is Sally. I've known her my entire life."

This time Logan didn't argue.

With his mind blank of conscious thought, Laredo stared at the ranch road ahead of him. The pickup's headlight beams revealed its approaching dips and swells before he reached them. The overhead sign that marked the Triple C's east entrance made a black slash against the night sky.

Slowing the truck to make the turn onto the highway, Laredo automatically scanned the highway and immediately spotted the flashing blue-and-white lights to the north. The vehicle's boxy silhouette made it instantly recognizable as an ambulance. Laredo braked the pickup to a stop at the intersection and waited for the ambulance to pass. Instead it slowed and made the swing into the ranch entrance.

Surprise held him motionless for a split second. He hesitated a moment longer, then made a tire-spinning U-turn and took off after it. There were a dozen possible explanations for an ambulance to be summoned at this hour of the night, everything from an illness of one of the workers to an accident on one of the ranch roads. But there was always the possibility Chase's would-be killer had shifted his focus to Jessy, and Laredo knew he wouldn't have any peace of mind until he assured himself that Jessy was all right.

It was a long forty miles back to the Triple C headquarters. When he pulled into the ranch yard behind the ambulance, lights blazed from the first-floor windows of The Homestead. Three vehicles were parked in front of it, vehicles that weren't there when Laredo left over an hour ago.

The ambulance pulled up to the veranda steps and stopped. Laredo parked his pickup next to the house, partially hidden in the shadows and out of the way.

Wasting no time, he piled out of the cab and headed straight for the veranda. By the time he reached the steps, the paramedics were letting themselves in the front door.

Laredo followed them inside, his own tension mounting at their lack of haste. Quick to note that all the activity seemed to be centered in the living room, he headed in that direction, unconsciously scenting the air for that distinctively tinny odor of blood.

Before he reached the living room, he was stopped in the wide hall by a short, squatly built man somewhere in his sixties. "Are you with the ambulance?" he asked with wary skepticism.

"No, I —" Laredo caught a glimpse of Jessy in the living room, alive and unhurt. He felt an instant loosening of his muscles. "I was checking to make sure Jessy was okay. What happened?"

But the man didn't immediately answer. "Who are you?"

His attitude was one of aloof distrust toward a man he regarded as an outsider. Before Laredo could answer, Jessy noticed him and quickly excused herself, leaving an older woman to talk to the paramedics.

"It's all right, Dad," she said to the man planted in Laredo's path. "I know him. It's the new man I hired to work the feedlot, Laredo Smith." Her glance bounced off Laredo. "I don't believe you've met my father, Stumpy Niles."

"Mr. Niles." Laredo nodded in acknowledgement, but no hand was thrust forward for him to shake. His only response was a brief bob of the head and a level stare that seemed to demand an explanation. "I passed the ambulance and saw it was headed this way," Laredo began, forced to watch his words. "Naturally I started wondering what the problem was."

Jessy came to his rescue. "It was good of you to stop in case you could be of help."

"I don't mean to be nosy, but what happened?" Laredo worded the question for her father's benefit.

"It's our housekeeper, Sally Brogan. I went out for a short walk before turning in." This time Jessy looked him square in the eye, providing him with the excuse she had used to cover her absence from the house. "When I came back, I found her. She must have had a heart attack. I called Amy Trumbo right away. She's a nurse," she added in quick explanation. "We tried, but — we couldn't revive her."

"I'm sorry," he said, and meant it.

"We all are," she said and shrugged. "But there really isn't anything we can do now except wait for the coroner to arrive."

"I can see that." Laredo took the hint. "I guess I'll be going then."

When he turned to leave, Jessy moved to his side and fell in step with him. "Thanks again for stopping," she said, loud enough for her father to hear.

"Thanks aren't necessary."

"Probably not," she agreed. When they reached the front entry, she pushed Laredo out the door and stepped out after him, darting a furtive and slightly anxious look behind her. "Be sure to tell Chase about Sally," she said in a hurried undertone. "He probably doesn't remember, but Sally's been in love with him for years, even before he and Maggie were married."

"Was he fond of her?" Laredo asked curiously.

"*Fond* is probably the right word. I don't think Chase ever felt anything more than that for her," Jessy admitted, turning thoughtful. "After Maggie died, I really thought the day would come when he would turn to Sally. But he never did. Instead Sally grieved herself to death over him. Do you see the irony in that? She died without ever finding out he is still alive."

It wasn't a question that required a verbal answer, and Laredo didn't make one. There was little in Jessy's expression that revealed the sorrow and regret he sensed in her. But he understood the stoicism she used to contain her feelings. She saw nothing to be gained from giving rise to them.

"I'll make sure he knows about Sally," he promised and turned as a set of headlight beams sliced an arc across the ranch yard, taking aim on The Homestead.

Jessy noticed them as well and swore softly, "Damn. It's Logan. You had better go. Quick. Cat is bound to have said something to him about you."

But Laredo knew that undue haste was the surest way to arouse a lawman's suspicions. That knowledge prompted him to first touch his hat to Jessy and amble across the veranda to the steps. Halfway down them, he met Echohawk on his way up.

"Evenin'," Laredo nodded to him as if he had nothing in the world to hide. But he felt the touch of those gray eyes on his back when he passed him.

Projecting every ounce of calm she could muster, Jessy waited for Logan to reach her. "I guess you heard about Sally," she said in lieu of a greeting.

"Jenna called me at the ranch," he said with a nod, then glanced in Laredo's direction as he disappeared around the side of the house. "Is that the new man Cat was telling me about?"

"Laredo Smith, yes," Jessy confirmed. She released an audible sigh. "I guess I don't have to ask what Cat said about him."

"I guess you don't." There was something gentle about the brief curve to his mouth. "I didn't expect to see him here tonight." Logan also hadn't expected to see the bulge in the cowboy's boot when he went down the steps.

"An ambulance parked in front of The Homestead tends to attract attention," Jessy replied. "I would have thought less of him if he hadn't stopped to find out what was wrong."

"You're right, of course," Logan acknowledged.

"Does Cat know about Sally?"

He nodded. "She wanted to come, but Quint was already in bed asleep."

"It's just as well. There wouldn't have been anything she could do."

"That's what I told her." The growl of the pickup's engine turning over drew Logan's attention to the side of the house. It stayed there to watch Laredo's pickup back into the ranch yard. When Jessy turned to go back inside, Logan asked, "Does he always carry a hideaway?"

Jessy swung back, frowning in genuine puzzlement. "A what?"

"A hideaway," Logan repeated the term, then clarified, "That's another word for a concealed weapon."

"What are you talking about?" She let her frown deepen and mask the sudden shaft of unease.

"I noticed the thickness in his right boot

when he was coming down the steps. I worked with a Texan once who always carried a hideaway in an ankle holster. His boot looked just like that. It's something you remember if you want to stay alive in my business." His tone had an offhand quality to it, but Jessy wasn't fooled by its casualness. "I hope he has a license to carry that."

She feigned an indifferent shrug. "You should have asked him."

"I'm here as family tonight. But there will be another time." Logan copied her shrug while his gray eyes continued to study her with close attention. "Just how well do you know him, Jessy?"

"Don't you start on me about him, Logan," she said in exasperation. "Not tonight. I received enough grief about Laredo from Cat. I don't need more right now."

"She told me this Laredo character was a touchy subject," he remarked with seeming idleness.

But it put Jessy on guard. "Logan, do you have any idea how difficult it is to defend your friends when the accusations against them have no basis in fact? It's impossible. And Tara didn't help the situation — as usual."

"An excellent point." A wry smile tugged at a corner of his mouth. "Tara would love to see you fail. Mostly because she envies you and wishes she were in your shoes."

"Tara in charge of the Triple C — now that is a scary thought," Jessy declared with feeling.

The front door opened behind her. "Jessy, what on earth are you doing out here?" At the familiar sound of her mother's voice, Jessy turned to face the slender woman she favored. "Logan," Judy Niles said in surprise when she finally noticed him. "I didn't know you were here."

"I just drove up a couple minutes ago."

"Isn't it just terrible about Sally?" Judy Niles declared, doing everything but clicking her tongue. "It seems like it's just one tragedy after another. My mother always told me death comes in threes. I can't help but wonder who might be next."

"That is nothing but an old wives' tale, Mom."

"I know. Still . . ." she murmured, unconvinced, then appeared to realize she was standing with the door open. "Good heavens, what is the matter with me? Come inside, you two." She stepped back to admit them and kept talking. "Amy and I were just discussing whether Sally should be buried next to her late husband. What's your opinion, Jessy? Do you think it would be appropriate?"

"I didn't realize she had been married," Logan said.

"Years and years ago," Judy declared. "To an ex-rodeo rider. He had been working at the Triple C less than a year when he was killed in a car accident. Stumpy said he was next to worthless. Naturally he didn't have any insurance. What cowboy does? So Chase paid for the funeral and buried him here on the ranch. Ike says the plot next to him is available. But they were married so long ago — and not very happily. I just don't know if Sally would want that."

"It isn't something we have to decide to-night." Jessy paused in the entryway while her mother closed the door.

"I know, but the decision has to be made soon," Judy Niles remarked, then quickly raised a finger as something else occurred to her. "Before I forget, I thought of someone you might want to consider hiring to cook and look after the house. DeeDee Rains. She did nearly all the cooking for Sally when she had the restaurant in town. I don't know what she's doing now, but I know she isn't working at Harry's."

"I forgot about DeeDee," Jessy admitted. "I'll talk to her and see if she is interested in working here."

"I hope she will be, because we wives can fill in for a while, but you will need someone permanent." Judy stopped, a look of contrition claiming her expression. "Isn't this awful? Here we are, talking about such things and Sally is still lying in there."

"It's reality, Mom. Sally would be making her own suggestions right now if she were still alive." The conversation with her mother claimed only half of Jessy's attention. The rest of it was on Logan as he wandered into the living room where the others were gathered. Somehow she needed to alert Laredo to the comments Logan had made. And soon.

Night cloaked the cabin's interior in darkness. The only light came from the starshine that grayed the windowpanes. Restless, Chase rolled onto his side and stared into the darkness. He had no idea of the time, but knew it had to be somewhere around midnight. Sleep had eluded him. The best he had managed was a fitful doze that fell somewhere between sleep and wakefulness.

He shut his eyes and tried again. After a few seconds, he gave up the effort, threw back the summer-weight blanket, and swung his legs out of the bunk. He had no difficulty locating the clothes he had taken off only hours ago. He put them on and stepped into his boots. After a glance at the twin bed along the opposite wall where Hattie slept, he quietly crossed the cabin and walked outside into the star-studded night.

The breeze's cool breath touched him, prompting Chase to button the front of his shirt that he had let hang open. Shadows blanketed the landscape, deepening to black in the low places and lightening to charcoal along the higher areas. There was a stillness and calm out here that soothed some of his edginess.

It was a big and empty land that stretched before him, a land that would still be here, changed yet unchanging, long after he was gone and forgotten. It wasn't a thought that bothered him; instead he found some comfort in it, a sense of right-ness.

The stretching of the screen door's spring made a faint sound, but in the still-ness of the night, it was loud to his ears. Swiveling at the hips, Chase looked behind him as Hattie stepped outside, her hands tying the sash to her cotton robe.

"Is any thing wrong?" Her dark eyes were thorough in their quick inspection of him.

"Couldn't sleep." He squared around to run his gaze over the broad sweep of land beyond them.

"It's almost too stuffy in there to get any rest." She moved to his side, standing tall next to him, the dramatic streaking of gray in her hair silvered by the starlight.

Chase located the North Star and calculated the time by the position of the stars around it. "It's well after midnight."

"Twelve thirty-six, to be exact," Hattie replied. "I looked at the alarm clock when I got up."

"I wonder what's keeping Laredo. I thought he would be back by now."

"Over the years I have learned not to worry about him. He always shows up when I least expect him."

Chase picked up on the affection in her voice. "You are very fond of him, aren't you?"

"In a way, he's like the son I never had. It hurts to know that a bad mistake made long ago has taken away his future. It could have been a good one."

"He has a home on the Triple C as long as he wants it," Chase stated, but the minute he mentioned the word "home," he was reminded that this wasn't hers. "I guess you'll be heading back to your ranch soon."

"I guess," she agreed and gave him a sideways smile. "It's for sure you don't need anyone to look after you anymore."

"After being gone so long, you're probably eager to get back."

"Not as much as I thought I would be," Hattie replied. "I don't know — coming here to a brand-new place, all the work it took to whip the cabin into shape. I enjoyed it. It made me feel young again. Sounds crazy, doesn't it?"

"Not to me." And he couldn't explain why. "It's for sure I'll miss you when you go." He found he wasn't looking forward to that. Hattie had been the one constant in his new life without a memory.

"Well, you'll have to wait, because I haven't left yet," she retorted.

Chase chuckled. "That's what I like about you, Hattie. You are never at a loss for a comeback."

"With a man like you, a woman doesn't have a choice. She either stands toe to toe with you or gets walked over. And you aren't walking over me, Duke."

The smile stayed. "I wouldn't try."

"Yes, you would — if I let you."

"You don't have a very high opinion of me, do you?" He couldn't say exactly why that bothered him, but it did.

"That wasn't a criticism, Duke," Hattie admonished lightly. "It isn't even something you would do knowingly. It would simply happen, because you would be too busy to notice. Heaven knows, there are worse faults a man could have."

"I'll take your word for it." Seeking to change the subject, Chase went back to the previous one. "How much longer will your neighbor look after your place?"

"He'll probably start squawking in another week."

Chase found himself thinking back to the time he had spent there, the comfort of its old kitchen and the old wooden rocker on the porch. Those thoughts prompted him to recall the old branding iron. Suddenly another memory clicked into place.

Abruptly he swung around and grabbed her by the upper arms. "That old branding iron was a C Bar. That was the brand of Seth Calder's ranch in Texas. You own his old place." The certainty of it flashed through him. "My God, I may have slept and ate in the same house he did — and Benteen, too." A stunned laugh came from him at the incredible coincidence of that.

Hattie looked at him as if he had taken leave of his sense. "What are you talking about, Duke? Who is Seth Calder?"

"My great-grandfather, I think." He smiled with the realization that he remembered that. "He was Benteen's father." In a burst of exuberance, Chase lifted her off her feet and swung her around, ignoring her gasp of surprise.

"You idiot," Hattie protested laughingly.

But she had no chance to say more. The minute her feet touched the ground, his head swooped down, and he claimed her mouth in a silencing kiss. It wasn't something he had planned, but the instant he made contact with the soft, giving warmth of her lips, it not only felt right, it felt good, awakening desires that had been long dormant.

What had likely begun as a smack on the lips turned into something more as he explored their rounded curves. His arms wound around her, molding her against him while her hands spread themselves across his back and her body arched, seeking a greater closeness. His blood heated, old needs surfacing with young vigor. He took satisfaction in the discovery that her breathing was as rough as his own.

He was slow to untangle himself from her lips and lift his head to look at her, just for the pure pleasure of it. Her eyes remained closed, her lips slightly swollen from the demands of his kiss.

"Whew." Hattie released a shaky breath and opened her eyes to look up at him with a slightly dazed and dazzled look. "You pack quite a punch, Duke," she declared, the huskiness of her voice telling him that she was still feeling the same disturbances he was. "I'm not surprised, though. I somehow knew you would."

"Are you saying this is something you have been thinking about?" The possibility pleased him.

"How modest you sound." A soft laugh bubbled from her. "That was unexpected. Only an immature female would fail to find you attractive and wonder what it would be like to be kissed by you." She absently straightened the collar of his shirt, a gesture that conveyed a comfortable intimacy. "And I have definitely wondered." Her gaze lingered a moment on the masculine line of his mouth, then lifted to his eyes. "Or is that something you think I shouldn't admit? You seem to live by an old code. Maybe you don't believe a woman should admit she sometimes feels desire, too."

"You know something, Hattie." A smile crinkled the lines around his brown eyes. "You talk too much."

"And you don't talk enough," she countered. "For instance, I don't know if it bothers you that I am a widow. Do you think I'm being unfaithful to Ed's memory by wanting to kiss you?"

"Shut up," Chase growled and took steps to make certain she did.

The kiss was a long and deep one, each giving free rein to their passions. Each had felt this heated rush of feeling before, but being new to each other gave it a heady twist.

Their lips parted a second time, and again they stayed in the embrace, each breathing hard and smiling a little at this oddly giddy feeling they had. His hands roamed over her back. Chase was vaguely irritated by the enveloping nightrobe when he wanted nothing between them.

This time Hattie didn't say a word, leaving it to Chase to speak first. "I can't promise you anything, Hattie." He felt honor-bound to say that. "Not even tomorrow."

She placed a shushing finger on his mouth. "I wouldn't hold you to it even if you did. It wouldn't be fair, not when you haven't fully recovered your memory. As a woman, I've learned not to count too much on tomorrow. It's much wiser to make the most of tonight. It may be all there is." She paused a breath, then swore softly and ruefully, "Oh, hell."

Chase drew back. "What's wrong?"

"Laredo's coming." She nodded in the direction of the road.

Turning his head, Chase spotted the pickup's headlights before he heard the steady hum of its engine. Hattie pulled out of his arms and hurriedly straightened the front of her robe and re-knotted the sash that had worked loose. When she began to pat and smooth her hair into order, he chuckled.

"Such old-fashioned modesty. That's unexpected," he said with a grin, turning her words back on her.

She slapped at his arm in playful retaliation. "Be quiet."

"It's not many women your age that need to make those kind of repairs to their appearance," he teased, quick to notice she was a little bit flustered.

"And whose fault is that?" Hattie retorted, then cupped her hands to her cheeks. "Oh, my goodness, I'm actually blushing. I didn't think I still knew how."

She laughed softly at herself, and Chase joined in, wrapping an arm around her shoulders to nestle her against his side. That's the way they stood when Laredo drove up to the line shack.

But Laredo was too preoccupied with his own thoughts to notice.

"You're up late." His glance bounced off them as he slipped the truck keys into his pocket. "You weren't waiting up for me, were you?"

"As a matter of fact, we weren't," Chase replied. "But considering how late it is, what took you so long?"

Laredo pulled in a deep breath and let it out. "Sally Brogan, the housekeeper, is dead. It looks like a heart attack. The coroner hadn't got there yet when I left, but Echohawk had arrived."

"Did he talk to you?"

"No." He studied Chase for a moment. "You don't remember Sally, do you?"

After a short pause, Chase replied with a small negative movement of his head.

"Jessy said she's been in love with you for years. I guess your 'death' really tore her up. Now it's her death that's weighing on Jessy." There was no emotion in Laredo's voice.

But Hattie knew him too well, and understood the things he had left unsaid. Instinct had her moving from Chase's side and laying a comforting hand on Laredo's arm.

"It must be awful for Jessy," she said. "I don't even know Sally, and it hurts that she went through all that anguish without ever knowing Chase was still alive. I can imagine the sense of guilt Jessy must be feeling."

"Yeah." Laredo's voice was flat, almost clipped. "It can't be helped, though."

"And Jessy knows that, too."

"Yeah. She'll get over it." A muscle worked in his jaw, a clamping down of feeling.

With a sudden flash of intuition, Hattie realized it was another emotion entirely he was masking. Soft as a whisper, she murmured, "It's Jessy, isn't it?"

He slid her a downward glance, a sardonic wryness twisting his mouth. "I'll get over it."

"Duke and I were talking before you came." She spoke in a normal voice, glancing at Chase to include him. "He said you have a home here as long as you want it."

"That's generous," he said with an acknowledging nod in Chase's direction. "But it's not likely to be up to me. Now if you'll excuse me, I think I'll turn in. It's been a long day." Head down, he headed for the cabin.

Her heart went out to him as Hattie watched him disappear inside the cabin's darkened interior. Chase moved to her side.

"Is something wrong?"

She felt the curious probe of his gaze. Earlier she would have hesitated before sharing Laredo's secret with him. But kissing him had changed all that.

"It's the hell of loving someone when you feel you don't have the right," she confided.

"And we are talking about whom?" Chase questioned.

"Laredo and Jessy."

His head lifted in sudden understanding. "The wind is blowing that way, is it?"

"If you have a problem with that, tell him now, Duke." It wasn't a request. The firmness of her voice had it bordering on a threat.

"It's not my decision to make," Chase replied. "For either one of them."

Hattie smiled, the worry easing from her.

"You are smarter than I thought."

"I'm glad you realize that." There was an unspoken longing in the way his gaze moved possessively over her face. "I guess we might as well turn in, too. If I have trouble getting to sleep this time, at least it will be for a different reason."

She laughed, feeling that exhilaration of a new love found, and hooked her arm in his. Side by side, they walked to the cabin.

Chapter Thirteen

The afternoon sun blazed hot and strong on The Homestead's towering facade. Inside, the hum of the air conditioner kept a steady flow of cool air circulating through the den. After a chaotic morning full of phone calls and endless comings and goings, the house was blessedly quiet.

Taking advantage of the lull in activity, Jessy retreated to the den to see if there was any ranch business that needed her attention. She had barely sat down when the front door opened. Mentally crossing her fingers that it wasn't someone who wanted to talk to her, she continued going through the stack of telephone messages. But the quiet footsteps in the hall came straight toward the den.

Jessy looked up when they stopped at the doorway. Monte Markham stood in the opening, dressed in a pair of chinos and a plain white shirt rather than his usual jodhpurs and boots. His finely drawn features wore a look of concern.

"The house was so quiet, I had almost decided no one was home," he said and hesitated. "Have I come at a bad time for you?"

"Of course not. Come in." She rose from the chair and came around the desk to greet him. "I was going through my messages to see if there was anything urgent that needed to be handled. There wasn't. You heard about Sally," she guessed.

"Yes. This sorrow doesn't seem to end for you. I am so sorry, Jessy." There was a mixture of compassion and understanding in his expression.

"Thank you," Jessy murmured automatically.

His mouth curved ever so slightly. "How many times today have you heard the same words and answered the same way? Quite a few I would imagine."

Her smile was wide in admission. "After a while, it becomes a something of a reflex."

Monte nodded. "I understand."

"I think you do." That surprised her a little. Yet, on reflection, she realized he was sensitive that way.

"Dare I ask where everybody is? I expected to see more vehicles parked outside when I drove up."

"There were quite a few people here earlier." But nowhere near the numbers that had descended on The Homestead when news of Chase's death had spread. Nearly all of them were ranch women, come to offer their help in whatever way they could. Sally had been well-liked, but she wasn't Chase Calder.

"Have you decided when the funeral will be?"

"Day after tomorrow," Jessy replied. "Cat is handling all the details. As a matter of fact, she and Amy Trumbo are down at the cemetery selecting a burial site now."

The mere mention of Cat's name made Jessy feel uncomfortable. Cat had been cool to her when she'd arrived that morning. Fortunately there were others around, so nothing was said. And no one appeared to notice there was any strain between them.

"I am glad you don't have to handle that responsibility. You have strong shoulders, but you are already carrying a heavy load running this ranch," Monte observed. "I wish there was something I could do to help, but I know there is nothing."

"The thought counts for something," Jessy replied, feeling suddenly mentally weary.

As if sensing it, Monte reached out and gathered her into the loose circle of his arms. "You have been through so much, Jessy." He nestled her head against his shoulder and rested his chin atop it. The embrace was too reminiscent of one of her brothers wrapping her in their arms in a gesture of comfort for Jessy to raise any objection to it. "I don't know how you keep your head up sometimes."

"I guess it's knowing that this too shall pass." When she drew back, Monte made no attempt to hold her.

Just then something registered in her side vision — something that shouldn't be there. She glanced past Monte's shoulder and saw Laredo standing motionless in the doorway, steel-blue eyes regarding her without expression.

Shock held her motionless for no more than an instant, but it was long enough for Monte to realize something had distracted her. As his arms fell away from her, he made a half-turn and glanced toward the hall.

"Sorry to interrupt," Laredo said in a bland voice. "You left a message that you wanted to see me."

"I did, yes," Jessy confirmed, quick to adopt a brisk, businesslike pose. "Would you mind excusing us, Monte?"

"Not at all." He was quick to agree, but the glance he darted between them was clearly curious. "No problems at the feedlot, I hope?"

"No sir," Laredo replied. "Your cattle are fed and fit."

"My mother is in the kitchen, Monte," Jessy told him. "Why don't you see if you can persuade her to brew you some tea?"

"I'll do that." With a parting nod to Jessy, Monte exited the den with a jaunty stride.

Laredo was slow to enter, letting his gaze wander over the room's interior, taking note of the old map on the wall and the set of sweeping horns mounted above the fireplace. He came to a stop a few feet from her, his roaming glance finally pausing on her.

"What's the problem?" He didn't say a word about seeing Monte's arms around her, but, innocent though the gesture had been, she sensed his disapproval.

It made her angry. Jessy didn't feel she owed him any explanation and she refused to offer one. "I thought you should know that Logan asked me last night if you always carried a hideaway in your boot."

His eyebrows went up slightly. "The man has sharp eyes."

"I thought I should warn you about that, and I knew it would be easier for you to get away than it would be for me."

Laredo nodded in understanding, turning thoughtful. "I guess I'll have to go around naked for awhile. Maybe it will make him wonder if he really saw what he thought he did." He paused, his glance tunneling into her. "Has Cat said anything more?"

"No."

From the front entryway came the chatter of voices. Jessy recognized Cat's voice among them. "You'd better get back to work," she said, wishing he had left before Cat returned.

"I'll do that." He crossed to the door, paused, and turned back, showing a marked unconcern for Cat's presence. "By the way, you were right. Duke didn't remember Sally."

With that he disappeared into the hall, but his place was almost immediately taken by Cat.

"Who is Duke? Another family friend?" Cat inquired. Her green eyes glittered with challenge.

"Personally I don't know him. I think Chase did." Constant practice had allowed the lies to come easily. "Did you choose a plot for Sally?"

★ ★ ★

In the end it was decided to bury Sally next to her late husband, thus avoiding any future questions as to why she wasn't. The only townspeople to make the long drive to the Triple C for the funeral were those who were long-time residents of Blue Moon. All the rest of the mourners were from the ranch except for Monte Markham and Tara.

To Jessy's relief, Laredo stayed away. Still fewer mourners chose to attend the reception at The Homestead following the graveside service.

As always at such gatherings, small or large, the men gravitated to one area and the women to another, with the children running about to claim all. Jessy stood on the outer fringes of one group of women and feigned an interest in their discussion. In truth, she had no idea what they were talking about. She was too distracted by the sight of Cat and Tara with their heads together.

Ever since she arrived for the funeral, Tara had barely left Cat's side. Judging from the glances the two women kept sliding in her direction, Jessy guessed that she was the topic of their conversation. And she had no difficulty imagining that it was in connection with her position as head of the Triple C. She wouldn't have been surprised if Tara had twisted things around to insinuate that she hadn't done enough to prevent Sally's death, even though it was obvious to everyone else that Sally's health had seriously deteriorated.

Jessy thought again about the note Chase had written for Cat's benefit. There simply hadn't been any opportunity for Jessy to show it to Cat these last couple of days. Jessy decided it was time to make that opportunity. Immediately a calm settled over her.

With no hesitation, Jessy left the small group and crossed the living room to Cat and Tara. They stopped talking the instant she was within earshot.

"Excuse me, Cat," Jessy began smoothly. "Would you mind stepping into the den with me for a few minutes? I have something I want to show you."

"What is it?" Cat asked, coolly indifferent.

"Something I found in the desk," Jessy replied.

Confident that Cat's natural curiosity would force her to follow, Jessy moved toward the den. She walked directly to the desk, opened a side drawer and removed the handwritten note from its keeping place. She wasn't at all surprised to see Tara had come along with Cat. She had expected it.

"Here." She held out the note to Cat. "I ran across this the other day when I was looking through one of the drawers. It may not change your opinion, but it reassured me about the decision I made to lease the feedlot."

Clearly skeptical and a little wary, Cat took the paper from her and unfolded it. Tara inched in closer to peer over her shoulder.

"I think you'll agree that is your father's handwriting," Jessy added for good measure.

After skimming the note, Tara moved a step away from Cat. "Exactly what are you trying to suggest, Jessy?" she challenged, clearly unimpressed by what she had read. "It's nothing but disjointed scribblings."

Jessy waited a beat, but Cat made no comment and continued to study the notations. "I'm not attempting to suggest anything. It's what the note suggests — that Chase appeared to be considering operating the feedlot. It looks like he might even have been thinking about leasing it, thus enabling him to receive a return and eliminate any risk. Which is the same decision I made."

"And you managed to interpret all that from those few scratchings," Tara mocked. "Isn't it possible someone was trying to sell him on the idea, and he idly made notes of the conversation with no intention of doing anything at all?"

"Of course, it's possible." The suggestion immediately prompted Jessy to think about Monte and the vague suspicions both Chase and Laredo had voiced about him. It made her wonder if Monte had raised the possibility to Chase of leasing the lot and been turned down flat.

She felt sure that Chase would have said something to her at the time if Monte had. But it was also possible he wouldn't.

"I wouldn't pay any attention to that note if I were you, Cat," Tara declared, positively gloating over the concession she had obtained from Jessy. "It means absolutely nothing. You might as well tear it up and throw it away."

"No, I think I'll keep it." Cat refolded the note, still deep in thought, then glanced at Jessy. "Do you mind?"

"No, you can have it." Jessy knew she hadn't convinced Cat of anything, but she had made her wonder. That, in itself, was a victory of sorts. "Tara is right, though. It only means what we want it to mean. I know how I read it. You made me doubt the other day that I had made the best decision for the Triple C. I'm convinced now that my reasoning was sound. I know you see it as a betrayal, but to me, it was strictly a business decision. And this is a business, Cat. Your father taught me that."

"So you told me," Cat replied.

The coolness was still there, but it didn't seem to have that combative edge. Jessy thought there was a distinct possibility they had arrived at an undeclared cease-fire. Time, that was all she hoped to gain, sufficient time for Chase to recover his memory, identify his killer, and take over the reins of the Triple C once more.

"Here you are, Jessy. I should have known you would be in the den." Monte halted a foot inside the room, hesitating at the sight of Cat and Tara. "Am I interrupting something?"

"Not at all," Tara declared with a regal lift of her head. "We were just leaving, weren't we, Cat?"

Cat's only response was a nod and an exiting turn. Tara walked with her, then paused to lay a hand on Monte's arm. "We must get together sometime soon. Perhaps for dinner at Dunshill one evening next week?"

"Perhaps," Monte replied, committing himself to nothing.

Tara didn't press for a more definite answer, threw a brief look at Jessy that was full of veiled warning, and went after Cat.

"Am I wrong, or are you having some in-law problems?" Monte ventured then hastened to add, "I wouldn't have said anything, but the atmosphere in here was electric. It stopped me the moment I walked in."

"It usually is, whenever Tara and I are in the same room." Jessy could have let the subject drop with that, but there was still that question in her mind as to whether Monte had talked to Chase about leasing the feedlot. "In this case, Cat was questioning whether we should have signed the lease agreement with you. Needless to say, Tara took an opposing view."

"What a surprise," Monte murmured in a dry voice.

"Exactly." Her smile was wide with amusement. Then she cocked her head questioningly. "By any chance, did you ever talk to Chase about leasing the feedlot?"

"No, of course not." He reacted with

surprise. "I intended to, but I never quite got around to it. Why would you ask?" he added with a slightly puzzled frown.

"I ran across some notations Chase had made." She gestured toward the desk. "It looked like he might have been weighing the pros and cons of either leasing it or starting it up himself."

"Really." His expression was one of curious interest.

"Naturally I thought you had been talking to him."

"Of course you would." Monte was quick to agree. "It's the logical assumption. But, on my oath" — he automatically raised his right hand — "I never said a word to him about it."

"I'm sure you didn't. It's probably nothing more than an odd coincidence."

"Now I'm curious. You don't still have his notes, do you? I would be interested to see what he wrote."

Jessy shook her head. "No, I gave the paper to Cat. There was no reason for me to keep it, and it meant something to her since it was in her father's handwriting."

"It's amazing, isn't it," he murmured with a tinge of sadness, "how trivial items suddenly become treasured mementoes after the loss of a loved one."

"It always seems to happen that way," Jessy agreed.

"Speaking of trivial things," Monte began, "how are you progressing in your search for a horse for Trey? I think I may have found a suitable mount for him if you are still looking."

"As a matter of fact, Dad mentioned yesterday that he had one he wanted me to see."

"It's a good thing I asked, and saved myself a bit of embarrassment later. I shall never forget the shock I felt that day when Trey announced that the pony wasn't big enough to ride."

They shared their separate recollections about the incident. The passage of time allowed them both to have a good laugh over it. Privately Jessy marveled at how much more relaxed she felt now that she had delivered Chase's note to Cat. She felt confident that it had achieved the desired result. Tara could do all the lobbying she wanted, but Cat had a mind of her own, one that Tara wouldn't find easy to sway.

With that complication out of the way, Jessy hoped things might go more smoothly now. But it was a hope that turned out to be short-lived.

After the last of the guests had left The

Homestead, her parents and two other ranch wives stayed behind to help with the cleanup. While making a sweep through the rooms, Jessy spotted a coffee cup that had been left on a windowsill in the dining room. She picked it up and glanced around for any other stray item. Her father came through the room on his way to the kitchen, a stack of sandwich plates in his hand.

He stopped when he saw her. "I've been meaning to ask you, Jessy, how come Logan was asking so many questions today about that new man you hired, Laredo Smith?"

"What kind of questions?" she asked, her stomach suddenly churning.

"General things . . . where he worked before — stuff like that. 'Course nobody could tell him much because Smith hasn't been here long enough for anybody to know much about him." He gave her a half-worried look. "What do you know about him, Jess?"

"I know he's a good man and a good worker. We've never asked any more than that at the Triple C." It was another one of those old codes that was still followed on the ranch; nobody delved too deeply into a man's background.

Stumpy Niles nodded in agreement. "Logan sure is, questioning though," he said.

"Maybe, but I know Chase . . . thought highly of him." Jessy almost forgot to put it in the past tense. "That's all the recommendation I need."

"You're right there," he said and headed for the kitchen.

Jessy knew that one of these times she would get tripped up by a little slip of the tongue. She also knew that if her father had noticed all the questions Logan was asking, other ranch hands had as well. Which meant they would be watching Laredo more closely than they might otherwise have.

She sighed, convinced that this entire situation had more knots in it than a green bronc on a frosty morning. It was going to require skillful riding to not get bucked off.

Dust motes danced in the shaft of morning sunlight that poured through the kitchen window. Culley observed their erratic movements, aware as he always was of all things around him no matter how small and insignificant. Cat belonged in neither category. Most mornings she gabbed away like a magpie, but this wasn't one of them.

She stood at the counter, methodically spooning cookie dough onto a baking sheet. Culley poured himself another cup of coffee and lingered by the pot to watch her.

"Not many folks showed up fer Sally's funeral the other day," he remarked.

"No." The single syllable answer did little to encourage conversation.

"I kinda thought that Laredo fella might be there, but he didn't show."

"No." The flat pitch of her voice never changed, but there was something slightly savage in the way Cat dipped out the next spoon of dough.

"What's Logan got t'say about him?"

After a vague movement of her shoulders, Cat replied, "He's going to call someone in Texas he knows and see what he can find out about the Smith family."

With the cookie sheet filled, she stuck the spoon in the remaining dough and checked on the batch baking in the oven. The opening of the oven door released a fresh bloom of vanilla and chocolate scents into the kitchen, but it was the edgy briskness of her movements that Culley noticed. Leaving the cookies to bake a little longer, Cat turned away from the stove, paused, and exhaled a troubled sigh.

"I don't know, Uncle Culley. Maybe I was too quick to find fault with Jessy. It's for sure Dad would hate it if he knew Jessy and I were at odds over the ranch. I've heard that anger is often a manifestation of grief."

"Maybe," Culley conceded, unconvinced, "but it don't explain the Smiths."

"No, it doesn't, does it," she said, a new awareness of that dawning in her green eyes. An instant later both heard the sound of a vehicle pulling into the ranch yard. Cat immediately groaned. "It's probably Tara. When I talked to her yesterday, she said she might stop by this morning." But when she looked out the window, it wasn't Tara she saw coming up the walk. "It's Monte," she said in surprise and hurriedly brushed at the dusting of white flour on her blouse. "I wonder what he wants." The rhetorical question was addressed to Culley, but when she turned to look, he had already slipped out the back door.

It was so typical of him to avoid casual contact with people he didn't know well that Cat simply shook her head in amusement and went to the front door to welcome her unexpected visitor. Monte rapped lightly on the screen door just as she reached it.

"It's a surprise to see you out and about this morning, Monte." Cat pushed the door open. "Please come in."

He hesitated. "I haven't come at an inconvenient time, have I?"

"Not at all."

With an idle lift of his hand, he motioned in the direction of the barn before entering. "Is that Quint I see at the corral?"

"Yes. He's doing some groundwork with our Appaloosa colt. It's his summer project."

"Isn't he a bit young to do that by himself?" A slight frown creased Monte's high forehead.

"Usually I supervise, although he doesn't really need anyone. Besides, my father would tell you a child is never too young to assume responsibility." Her nose told her the cookies were done. Cat moved toward the kitchen, saying over her shoulder, "Excuse me a minute. I have a batch of cookies in the oven that need to come out."

Monte sniffed the air. "Ah, that's what that delectable aroma is." He trailed after her into the typically large and roomy ranch kitchen. "It reminds me of my schoolboy days when I used to snitch biscuits from the cook's larder."

"Biscuits are what you Brits call cookies, aren't they? I almost forgot that." Cat went directly to the stove and slipped on the insulated mitt she had left on the counter.

"Indeed they are." Monte bypassed the long wooden table with its ladder-backed chairs and wandered over to the old rolltop desk in the alcove off the dining area. "What a marvelous old desk. Is it a family heirloom?"

"No. As a matter of fact, I think Logan told me he found it at a used-furniture store in Miles City." Cat removed the baking sheet from the oven and set it atop the stove. She smiled when she noticed Monte examining the desk's many pigeon-holes. "When Quint was younger, he was fascinated by all its little nooks and drawers."

"Does it have any hidden compartments?" he wondered. "I know many of these old desks do."

"None that I know about." With a spatula, Cat removed the hot cookies from the sheet, one by one, and placed them on a wire rack to cool. "I have some coffee made if you would like a cup. Or I can brew you some tea."

"Regrettably I can't stay that long. I have an appointment in town. I only stopped to see if you have any plans for this coming Sunday. So many things have happened lately that forced the postponement of the dinner I planned to host for all of you. Perhaps it isn't appropriate now, so soon after Sally's funeral, but I concluded there may never be a proper time so I have decided to have it Sunday — assuming everyone is available, of course."

Tensing a little, Cat kept her back to him. The prospect of spending a social afternoon in Jessy's company still wasn't a comfortable one. She had said some harsh things to her, and Cat hadn't yet decided that she wanted to retract them.

"I don't think we have anything on the calendar, but I probably should check with Logan before I commit to coming." She bounced a glance off Monte as she slipped another sheet of cookies into the oven. "Is it all right if I call you tomorrow and let you know?"

"Tomorrow will be fine." He drifted away from the desk. "I have yet to speak to Jessy, but I plan to phone her this afternoon. Therefore, nothing is definite yet."

"I understand." Privately Cat hoped Jessy wouldn't be available.

"Your . . . uh . . . cookies . . . smell delicious." His hesitation over the word choice was deliberate, edged with a smile. "As much as I would like to stay and indulge in such a treat, I really must be going."

"I hope you stop by again when you can stay longer." In preparation for walking him to the door, Cat slipped off the mitt and laid it on the counter.

But when she started toward him, Monte lifted a detaining hand. "There's no need for you to accompany me. I can find my way out."

"I'll call you tomorrow and let you know about the dinner," Cat promised.

He inclined his head in acknowledgement and exited the kitchen. Listening to his footsteps make their way to the front door, Cat swung back to the counter, slipped the mitt on again and picked up the still-warm cookie sheet to spoon more dough onto it. By the time she had the next batch ready for the oven, Monte's vehicle had pulled out of the yard.

When she turned to check on the ones in the oven, she was startled to see Culley standing there. "Good Lord, you scared me," she said with a half-laugh. "I thought you had left."

"I didn't go far." The hardness in his eyes was a little disconcerting.

In that instant Cat realized he had stayed

close to protect her, unwilling to leave her alone with a man he didn't know. "You were in the utility room, weren't you?" she guessed.

In former days it had been a small back porch that had since been closed in to house the washer and dryer. The door that opened from the kitchen into it was still the old door, the top half of it a glass window.

"Thought I should stick close by in case he took a notion t'try somethin' with you," Culley said in an indirect admission.

Warmed by his deep-caring gesture, Cat smiled. "It wasn't necessary, but I'm glad you did."

"He didn't stay long."

"No. He only stopped to invite us to his place on Sunday." After checking the cookies on the rack, Cat decided they were cool enough to stack, and provide room for the new batch from the oven.

"You goin'?"

"I haven't decided. I told him I would call tomorrow and let him know."

"What was he doin' snoopin' around that old desk?"

"He was just admiring it."

"He poked around it like he was figurin' on buyin' it," Culley observed.

A small smile deepened the corners of her mouth. Cat couldn't help being a little amused by the proprietary attitude Culley took toward anything he regarded as hers. "Some people are fascinated by old furniture, Uncle Culley."

He responded with a disdainful snort. "He probably likes paintings an' statues, too. He looks like the type."

This time Cat laughed out loud. "Coming from most people, that would be a compliment. But something tells me you just insulted him."

Culley didn't deny it. "To my way of thinkin', he strikes me as bein' a bit too dandified."

Cat suspected that Culley based his opinion on the patrician fineness of Monte's features and upper-crust British accent, but she didn't say so. "The cookies are still warm from the oven. Would you like a couple with your coffee?"

"No, thanks." Culley had never been one for sweets, although he always kept a box of something on hand at his ranch, the Shamrock. Cat was the one who craved them, especially anything chocolate. "He bought the old Gilmore place, didn't he?"

"That's right." Cat located her empty cup and filled it with coffee.

"Ain't been by there in a spell. Reckon it's changed some."

"I know he's done a lot of work there."

Culley toyed with the idea of riding over that way and taking a look-see one of these days.

Chapter Fourteen

Church bells rang joyously over the quiet town of Blue Moon while a playful wind danced among the parishioners exiting the sanctuary, tugging at shirts and skirt hems and any loose item it could find. With her hands occupied holding on to the twins, Jessy simply nodded to Reverend Pattersby as she filed past him, eschewing the customary handshake.

They were halfway down the steps when the wind snatched Trey's Sunday-school drawing from his fingers and sent it fluttering across the lawn. Trey immediately jerked free of her hand and raced after it. Laura was much too worried about scuffing her white patent-leather Mary Janes to speed up even a little. Anxious that Trey might run into the street in his haste to retrieve his paper, Jessy glanced back at her parents. "Watch Laura for me," she said and went after Trey.

To Jessy's relief, the wind slapped the paper against the leg of a fellow rancher,

George Seymour. When Trey pounced on it, startling the rancher, the barrel-chested man looked down, identified the cause, and retrieved the paper for Trey. Jessy arrived on the scene just as the rancher returned the drawing to its owner.

"Tell Mr. Seymour thank you, Trey." She gave Trey a little nudge.

But Trey was too intent on smoothing out the creases to do more than mumble his gratitude. When Jessy looked up to add her voice to Trey's barely intelligible words, the wide smile was gone from the rancher's face.

His sudden look of cool reserve caused Jessy to temper the friendliness in her manner. "Thank you. I had visions of Trey barreling in front of a car trying to get his paper."

"You need to keep a tighter check on him. But I guess a Calder figures they can do whatever they like."

Jessy was quick to challenge his statement. "You aren't talking about my son when you say that. Out with it. What's got your back up, Mr. Seymour?"

"As if you didn't know," he snorted.

"As a matter of fact, I don't."

The hardened contempt in his expression never wavered. "I suppose you're gonna tell me that you don't know Markham came to me first with his lease deal," he countered. "My mistake was in calling Chase to check this English guy out. Chase said he'd look into it for me. He did that all right. He snatched the deal for himself. It shouldn't surprise me. The big ones always gotta get bigger — and to hell with the little guys."

There was a touch of sarcasm in the polite way he touched his hat to her before walking away. Stunned, Jessy stood motionless, letting the full implication of his words wash over her.

The expression of resentment wasn't new. No ranch could be as big as the Triple C without sowing seeds of envy among smaller spreads. What made it unusual this time was Monte's involvement. It seemed to be almost too much of a coincidence.

Trey tugged at her hand. "Can we go, Mom?"

After a brief hesitation, Jessy nodded. "First, though, we have to find Gramma and Poppy."

"How come?" Trey wanted to know.

"Because we are riding with them." But when she glanced toward the church, it was Monte she saw in her line of vision, gliding straight toward her. For the first time Jessy felt a new wariness of him.

"Good morning." His greeting was typically warm and friendly. "Lovely sermon today, wasn't it?"

"I enjoyed it." Curious, she tilted her head to one side. "You must have been sitting in front. I don't remembering seeing you."

"Indeed I was," Monte confirmed. "A habit from home, I expect. Our family always occupies the front pew at Sunday service." Just when Jessy had nearly convinced herself a simple coincidence was no basis for suspicion, Monte glanced in the direction of the Seymour sedan as it pulled out of the church parking lot. "Isn't that George . . . George . . ." With an impatient snap of his fingers, he attempted to recall the rancher's surname.

"George Seymour." Jess supplied it. "Yes, I was talking to him only a minute ago. The wind blew away Trey's paper and George was kind enough to snare it for him."

Jessy didn't volunteer more than that. Monte seemed to wait a beat to see whether she had anything else to add.

Before the silence became too long, he offered wryly, "I always remember names and faces, but not always together."

Jessy chose not to comment on that. "I'm sorry we weren't able to come to your place for dinner today."

He waved off her apology. "I understand, although it seems circumstances are conspiring to prevent me from returning your hospitality. Just the same" — Monte paused, glancing at Trey, a touch of fondness in the curve of his mouth — "I agree that Trey has waited long enough for his surprise."

"I gotta s'prise?" Trey asked, suddenly all ears. "Where? What is it?" Instantly he was cautious. "It's not another pony, is it?"

Monte chuckled. "I have it on good authority that it is definitely not a pony."

Her parents joined them. After the customary exchange of greetings with Monte, Stumpy turned to Trey. "I see you caught up with your drawin'. Did it get hurt any?"

"Naw." Trey smoothed the paper again, then darted a look at Monte. "He says I gotta s'prise, Poppy. Do you know about it?"

A smile twitched Stumpy's mouth. "I reckon I know a little about it."

"What is it?" Laura chimed in. "Do I have one?"

"Not this time, pet," he told her.

Laura thought about it a minute, then

346

decided. "That's okay. Trey can have one this time."

"I'm glad you feel that way," Stumpy declared, still fighting not to smile.

"Where is my s'prise, Poppy?" Trey wanted to know.

"At my place," he replied. "Are you ready to head in that direction? I think we should. Your grandma left dinner in the oven, and we don't want it to burn up before we get there."

"Will I get my s'prise before or after dinner?" Convinced now that his grandfather was the source of his surprise, Trey was more eager to have it.

"After."

Trey's surprise was a ten-year-old quarter horse gelding, red roan in color and named Strawberry Joe. Trey couldn't have been happier if he had been presented with the moon.

Confident that it would be a long afternoon spent with horse and rider getting to know one another, Jessy knew it wasn't likely she would be missed. As always, her parents were eager for any opportunity to look after their grandchildren. Her mother was especially happy to have, at last, a little girl who loved dolls and tea parties — unlike the tomboy daughter she had raised.

Stumpy readily accepted Jessy's excuse that she needed to drive around and get a feel of range conditions for herself. But when she left the South Branch camp, Jessy drove straight to the Boar's Nest. It was close to mid-afternoon when she arrived, the heat of the day. But high up in the foothills, a cooling wind lessened the effect of a blazing sun.

Stepping out of the pickup, Jessy looked around. There was no sign of Laredo's truck anywhere. The whole place had a deserted feel to it.

"Hello?" Her seeking call seemed harsh in the stillness. "It's me, Jessy!"

Faint noises came from inside the line cabin. Immediately she approached it. A tanned and fit-looking Chase pushed open the screen door to admit her.

"I wondered when you would be able to slip away again." There was a smile of welcome in his brown eyes.

"It wasn't easy." Stepping inside, Jessy glanced around. "Where is everybody?"

"Hattie and Laredo went to town for groceries. They should be back anytime." Chase crossed to the sink and set about brewing some coffee. "Have you had a chance to show Cat my note?"

Vaguely restless, Jessy wandered over

to watch him. "I did — at the reception following Sally's funeral." She had barely begun to fill him in on the details when she heard the distant honking of a horn. She immediately stiffened in alarm.

Noting her reaction, Chase explained, "That's Laredo. He always signals from the road so I know it's him and not someone else."

"That's another thing," Jessy recalled. "At the reception, Logan was asking questions about Laredo."

"I was afraid of that." A grimness thinned the line of his mouth. "Maybe we can get Cat settled down before he gets any answers that might start him looking into Laredo's past on his own." Chase lit the fire under the range-top coffee percolator and turned away. "We might as well give them a hand unloading those groceries. The coffee should be ready by the time we're through."

Jessy followed him outside, conscious of an odd tension tingling through her at the prospect of seeing Laredo. She knew it was that teasing kiss he stole in the barn that was responsible for the vague discomfort she felt. Mostly because she hadn't found it offensive. After Ty, she hadn't expected to be physically attracted to another man.

It was disconcerting to discover that a part of her was.

Hattie bounded out of the cab seconds after the pickup rolled to a stop. Laredo was slower to emerge. "Hi, Jessy." She waved to her and went directly to the truck's tailgate. "Am I ever glad we took the cooler with us. If we hadn't, half of what we bought would be spoiled from the long drive in this heat."

Hattie lowered the tailgate and dragged the heavy cooler onto it. As she maneuvered it around to lift it out of the truck bed, Chase moved to take it from her.

"I'll get that for you," he said.

"Are you sure it isn't too heavy for you?" But the sidelong glance she gave him was teasing, rather than concerned.

Chase smiled down at her, eyes twinkling. "It shouldn't be. You aren't."

Stunned by the intimate exchange, Jessy stared at the pair. She couldn't recall hearing Chase saying anything remotely like that to Sally.

She was too distracted to notice when Laredo came up behind her. Jessy was unaware of his presence until he murmured near her ear, "Better close your mouth unless you plan on catching flies."

Her mouth happened to be closed, but it

snapped open when she swung around to deliver a sharp answer. But Laredo was already moving away. Jessy clamped her mouth shut and moved to the truck to help with the groceries.

Hattie hurried ahead to hold the screen door for Chase while he manhandled the bulky cooler through the opening. Jessy curled her arm around the second sack of groceries and started for the cabin. Laredo slowed his steps, allowing her to catch up with him.

His side glance was lazy but cool. "Aren't you going to ask how long that's been going on?" he asked with a nod in Chase and Hattie's direction.

"It's none of my business."

"I'm glad you realize that," he replied. "When you think about it, it's natural. A man and a woman, alone in a cabin, hour after hour, day after day, no radio, no television. Nothing but each other."

"I could figure that out for myself," Jessy replied tightly. "I don't need you to draw me pictures."

"I don't imagine there is much that you *do* need me for," he stated with a faintly sardonic smile. "But Chase does need me."

When they reached the cabin, Laredo waited, letting her enter ahead of him.

Jessy found she didn't like the touch of acid coolness in his attitude toward her. She much preferred his lazy mockery and laughing eyes. She was careful not to examine too closely the reason for that.

Later Jessy couldn't help noticing the way Laredo lounged by the cabinets, not joining them at the table. After she brought Chase up to date on Cat's reaction to the note, Jessy switched to the incident after church that continued to nag at her.

"Do you remember George Seymour?" she asked Chase.

"Seymour," he thoughtfully repeated the name. "A rancher, on the heavyset side," he said with a slow nod. "He has a small spread southeast of Blue Moon, doesn't he?"

"Yes, the Rafter J," she said, supplying the ranch's brand.

"What about him?"

Jessy told him about her brief meeting with the rancher after church, and the comments Seymour had made. "Maybe it doesn't mean anything," she admitted. "But it sounds like you might have done some discreet checking into Monte's business practices. Maybe that's the connection with the banker in Fort Worth. I wish now that I had thought to ask George if he had given you Brewster's name. Maybe I should call George and ask." Jessy hesitated, recalling, "Although Monte did see me talking to Seymour."

"Did Markham ask about him?" The question came from Laredo.

"No, not a thing. As a matter of fact, other than making an offhand comment — wasn't that George Seymour — he never really said anything." An absent frown clouded her expression. "You would think that if he was worried about whether George had said something to me he would have tried to find out."

"You would think so," Chase agreed. "But he also might be smarter than that. Questions might arouse your suspicions, while a lack of interest in what was said wouldn't."

"Do you realize how devious that sounds, Duke?" Hattie declared.

"I'm only trying to think the way Markham might," Chase countered, matter-of-fact in his pronouncement.

"But you don't know that Markham has done anything wrong," Hattie said in a kind of protest, then went still for a split second. "Or do you?"

Jessy immediately picked up on the thought. "Do you remember something about Monte?"

"I know there is something. I get flickers of it, but nothing definite enough that I can actually say I remember anything specific. Yet I have this certainty in my gut that Markham is involved."

"How frustrating," Hattie murmured in empathy.

Jessy felt it, too. "So," she said, releasing a sighing breath, "what do you think? Should I call Seymour and see if I can find out what information he gave you?"

"I don't think so." Chase was slow in his answer, mulling over their options. "There's always a chance George might mention your call to someone else and word of it would get back to Markham. I don't want Markham to start wondering whether you are a threat to him. Call Brewster and run Markham's name past him, find out if he has had any dealings with him."

"But Brewster will want to know why. What do I tell him?" Jessy frowned, uncertain of her approach.

"Make up something," Chase replied. "Or use the feedlot lease as a reason."

Laredo straightened from the cabinet. "Maybe I should make the call. Making up convincing stories isn't exactly Jessy's forte. And Brewster might be more forthcoming talking to another man. No offense,

Jessy, but it can work that way."

"None taken," she replied. "You are more than welcome to talk to him."

"Better make the call from The Homestead," Chase instructed. "There will be less chance of a bystander catching part of your conversation."

Laredo nodded and glanced at Jessy. "Is there a problem if I come by tomorrow morning, say, between nine and ten?"

"Make it closer to nine. I told Jaspar I would swing by the east camp tomorrow morning."

"I'll be there right at nine," Laredo stated.

"In the meantime, Jessy," Chase began, "I think you need to have a private talk with Cat and make peace with her. Explain that there is nothing you can do about the current lease, but if she still feels strongly about it, you won't renew it under any circumstances. If she challenges you about Laredo, simply tell her that without cattle in the feedlot, you won't have any work for him so you'll have to lay him off. With any luck Cat will be satisfied with that — and hopefully she'll call Logan off."

Nodding in agreement, Jessy said, "I'll run by the Circle Six and talk to her before I pick up the twins. Anything else?"

"I don't think so," Chase said. "If there is, Laredo can tell you about it tomorrow."

"If I'm going to stop at Cat's I'd better be going, then." She pushed out of the chair.

"Let Laredo know what she says," Chase told her.

"I will," Jessy promised.

"I'll walk you to your truck." Unhurried, Laredo set his empty coffee cup down before following her outside.

Jessy headed straight for her pickup without pausing, yet all the while conscious of Laredo ranging alongside of her. She tried to ignore the faint sizzle of tension she felt.

"Did you want something?" she asked when Laredo failed to break the silence.

"Not really." He kept his gaze to the front. "Although I am curious about something — am I wrong, or has Markham spent more time at the Triple C than usual?"

"Between the feedlot and Sally's funeral, he probably has," Jessy admitted. "Why?"

"Because I think he's leading up to something."

Jessy suspected she knew exactly what he thought. "Are you back to that crazy notion that Monte is interested in me?"

"Maybe not you in particular, but in a rich widow with a ranch almost as big as some eastern states. It's bound to be a tempting package for a man with ambition."

"What makes you think he's ambitious?" Reaching the truck, she opened the door and planted a foot on the running board.

Laredo caught hold of the door. "The cattle in the feedlot. He indicated to you that some of his English friends wanted to get into the cattle business. But he brought a man by the feedlot the other day who was supposedly one of the investors. The man was a Texan."

Jessy didn't see what that proved. "So?"

"So, I don't think he put the deal together as a favor. He did it to make money."

"And we leased the feedlot to make money. That isn't a crime. It's business." Jessy maintained her own grip on the door, her hand inches from his.

"But you are up front about your reason. Markham likes to pass himself off as a gentleman rancher, someone who isn't in it for the money. It makes me wonder if he isn't hard up for cash. How is he at paying his bills? Have you heard any talk?"

"No, but I probably wouldn't, though. It

isn't something people would talk about to a Calder. If somebody's slow about paying their bills, word would go through Blue Moon pretty fast. One of the hands might have heard something. I'll ask around."

"Better not. They would wonder why you're asking. Let me nose around Blue Moon instead."

"You're a stranger. They may not tell you."

Laredo grinned crookedly. "It depends on how convincing my story is."

"You are good at feeding people stories, aren't you?" The thought made Jessy oddly angry.

Suddenly he was no longer smiling as his gaze pinned her with a new intensity. "I haven't fed you any. Or Chase."

She flashed back to his statement in the barn when he admitted he was attracted to her. She felt a mixed rush of heat and uneasiness.

His expression hardened with a kind of anger. "Don't worry, Jessy. I have no intention of pursuing it."

It never occurred to her to be coy and pretend she didn't know what he was talking about. She told herself she was glad there would be no repeat of that scene in the barn, but she had trouble believing it.

As fleeting as the kiss had been, she remembered how alive she had felt inside after so many months of feeling dead and empty.

"Good," Jessy lied and turned to slide behind the wheel.

But she got no farther than that as Laredo grabbed her and hauled her against him, blue eyes blazing. "Just what the hell is so good about it," he challenged, then gave her no opportunity to answer. "There isn't one damn thing about it that's good. But it's necessary. Do you know why?"

Jessy shook her head, made mute by the ferocity of the emotion she saw in his face, a staggering combination of raw yearning and need.

Jaws clenched, he ground out the answer to his question. "Because the hell of having you and walking away would be worse than the hell of never having you at all." He held her an instant longer, fingers digging into the flesh of her upper arms. Then he was shoving her away from him. "Now get going."

It wasn't fear but wisdom that kept Jessy silent. She knew that if she was going to say anything to him at all, she had better know exactly what it was she wanted from him — whether it was to be left alone or to feel the heat of the passion he had let her see. It wasn't a decision she was ready to make yet.

Without a word, she climbed into the pickup and pulled the door shut. She was careful not to look in his direction as she started the truck and reversed away from the cabin. When she drove away, the reflection of him standing by the track, watching her leave, was there in her rearview mirror.

Indecision had never been a problem of Jessy's. From the time she was old enough to know her own mind, she had known what she wanted. As a child it had been to cowboy for the Triple C. After that, it had been Ty she wanted. After he had been killed, she hadn't expected to want anything else except the health and happiness of her children.

Then Laredo had come along and disrupted the calm and settled path of her life. By the same token, Jessy knew that no man could do that unless she allowed it. But this didn't feel like something she could control.

Promptly at nine o'clock the next morning Laredo's truck pulled up to The Homestead. Jessy had been watching for it, expecting it, but everything inside her quickened just the same. She listened to the even tread of his footsteps across the front veranda and into the house. The instant Laredo walked into the den, her tension went up another notch. But she was too skilled at hiding her feelings behind a mask of calmness to let it show.

Conscious of the searching probe of his glance, Jessy offered no greeting. "Good, you're right on time. Brewster's phone number is right here." She touched a slip of paper on the desk and rose from the chair. "You can use this phone."

"Thanks." But he hesitated before approaching the desk, waiting to see which way she went so he could move in the opposite direction.

His action somehow reassured Jessy that Laredo shared the same wariness of any close contact. Bypassing the wing-backed chairs that faced the desk, Jessy headed toward the door.

Laredo's voice stopped her before she reached it. "You better stay while I make this call. If someone walks in and sees me here alone behind the desk, it won't look right, especially with all the questions Echohawk has asked about me."

"I'm only going to the kitchen to get us both some coffee. I'll be back," she told him and continued on her way.

By the time Jessy returned with an insulated carafe of coffee and two cups, Laredo was on the phone with Brewster. She poured a cup for each of them, set his on the desk, and carried hers to one of the wing-backed chairs.

There was little Jessy could glean from Laredo's side of the conversation. He did more listening than talking, and the few questions he asked weren't particularly informative. Twice he jotted something on the paper with Brewster's phone number.

When he hung up, an absent frown cut a single furrow of concentration across his forehead. He waited a second or two, then gave her a thought-filled glance.

"Does the name Ben Parker mean anything to you?" he asked.

"He has a big ranch in Wyoming. Chase has known him for years," Jessy replied without hesitation. "In fact," she recalled, "he was the one who brought Monte to our registered stock sale. Why?"

"His name came up in my conversation with Brewster."

"Did Brewster know Monte?" Given the mention of Ben Parker, Jessy didn't expect Laredo's answer to be anything other than an affirmative one.

As she expected, he nodded. "He knows

him — and spoke very highly of him."

"Now what?"

"I think I'll call Parker. Do you have his number somewhere?"

"I believe so."

Rising, Jessy set her cup aside and stepped to the desk, turned the Rolodex around, flipped through the cards, and removed the one bearing Ben Parker's address and telephone numbers. She passed it across the desk to Laredo and sat back down. He punched out the numbers and waited through several rings.

Trey galloped into the den just as she heard Laredo identify himself as a lawyer and rattle off the name of a fictitious firm. Jessy quickly pressed a forefinger to her lips, asking her son for silence. For once Trey didn't announce his arrival and simply threw himself against her legs.

"Hi, Mom," he whispered.

"Hi." She rumpled the top of his hair.

Catching sight of someone behind the desk, he turned to look. " 'Redo's here."

I know," Jessy replied softly. "He's making an important call. That's why we have to be quiet. What did you need?"

"Can I go to Timmy's house and play? Becky said I had to ask you."

"Where's Becky?" She glanced toward the hall.

"Her an' Laura are colorin'." He wrinkled up his nose, making a face to show his opinion of that pastime. "That's boring, Mom."

"I know." Jessy smiled. "You can only sit still so long, can't you?"

"Can I go to Timmy's?"

"I think we should ask Timmy's mother whether it's all right first."

"She won't mind," Trey hastened to assure her.

"Just the same, I think we should call and ask. We'll use the phone in the living room. Come on."

Taking him by the hand, Jessy led him into the living room and dialed the number for the Rasmussens who lived in one of the houses at headquarters that were provided for married ranch hands. She stood by while Trey made his request.

Still holding the receiver, he looked up at her. "She said I could come. I told you it would be okay."

Taking the phone, Jessy confirmed the answer and made sure Connie Rasmussen understood that Trey was to come back to The Homestead for lunch. Instead of bolting for the door to race to his playmate's house, Trey waited until she had hung up.

"Has 'Redo seen my new horse?" he asked with undisguised eagerness.

"I don't believe he has."

"Should I take 'Redo to see Joe when he's finished talkin'?" It was a prospect that clearly appealed to Trey.

"Maybe another time."

"But we could go ridin'. This time he wouldn't have to share his horse."

"I'm afraid he has to go back to work at the feedlot when he's done with his call."

"Me and Joe could help him," Trey suggested.

Jessy frowned in surprise. "I thought you wanted to play with Timmy."

"But if 'Redo wanted me to help him, I could do that instead."

It didn't seem to matter to Trey that Laredo was essentially a stranger. He still wanted to spend time with him. She blamed it on the absence of any other male figure in his life. But it still didn't explain why he had picked Laredo when there were so many other ranch hands, most of whom he had known his entire, albeit short, life.

"Timmy is expecting you. I think you should go there this morning," Jessy told him.

He accepted her decision without argument. "Okay. See ya, Mom." He took off at a run.

When Jessy returned to the den, Laredo had vacated the chair behind the desk. He stood next to the coffee tray, the carafe poised above his cup.

"Did you learn anything from Ben Parker?"

"Quite a lot, but I don't know how useful it is." Finished refilling his cup, Laredo tightened the lid on the carafe and set it back on the serving tray, then hooked a leg over the corner of the desk and reclined against it. "This isn't the first cattle deal Markham has put together. As near as I can tell, he's acted as a cattle broker for the last five, maybe six years. Parker invested in several and has nothing but good things to say about Markham's reliability and honesty. And the banker echoed just about everything Ben Parker said."

"That's a relief," Jessy declared, once again taking a seat in one of the wing-backed chairs. "It was uncomfortable not knowing whether I should trust Monte."

"There doesn't seem to be any blots on his reputation," Laredo admitted, showing no pleasure in it. "According to Parker,

Markham has investors waiting in line. I can see why, though. It's a helluva deal he offers them, too."

"What do you mean?" Observing his troubled expression, Jessy guessed it came from Laredo's unwillingness to let go of Monte as a suspect.

"I mean it's one of those sweet deals without any risk to the investor," Laredo replied. "The purchase price of the cattle is established. Markham guarantees to fatten them for market for a set amount per hundred weight. The cattle are sold on the futures market to be delivered in four or six months, establishing their sale price. Which means the investor knows exactly what his profit will be. If there is any increase in grain costs during that time period, Markham has to absorb it, not the investor. Maybe he's had to absorb a few too many losses lately."

"Even if he had, what would that have to do with Chase?" Jessy reasoned.

"Maybe he knew Markham was financially in hot water."

"I don't think that's a motive to kill someone."

"I know." Laredo sighed in frustration. "There's a reason, though. We just haven't discovered it yet."

"Maybe it isn't Monte at all." The minute the statement was out of her mouth, Jessy knew why Laredo was convinced it was. "But the banker in Fort Worth knows him."

"Chase must know something specific," Laredo concluded. "Something that he either didn't want to discuss over the phone with Brewster or something that he couldn't, something that required a face-to-face meeting. Whatever Chase knew, it had to be very damning."

"He seems to remember more every time I see him."

"But nothing so far about why he went to Texas," Laredo reminded her.

"He will, in time," Jessy stated with confidence.

"Let's hope time stays on our side," he declared and downed a swallow of coffee.

"Were you able to find out anything in Blue Moon about Markham?" she wondered.

"Not really. He doesn't seem to do much business there." Laredo eyed her with quiet speculation. "There's a lot of talk, though, about the amount of time he's been spending at the Triple C. Quite a few people are convinced it's the beginnings of a romance."

Jessy shrugged off the gossip. "Well, they're wrong."

"It makes for a good story, though — wealthy Englishman from a noble family woos rich and beautiful widow of a cattle dynasty. I guess the surprise would be if they didn't try to marry you off to him." His mouth crooked in a brief smile, something Jessy had seen little of lately. "What about Cat?" he asked. "How did your meeting go with her?"

"It didn't. She wasn't home when I stopped by the Circle Six yesterday," Jessy explained. "I left a note asking her to call. We have been playing phone tag ever since. Unfortunately I'll be in and out most of today. I probably won't be able to talk to her until tonight or tomorrow."

"Let me know when you do so I can pass on the results to Duke." He drained the last of the coffee and set the empty cup on the tray. Through it all, his expression had been one of heavy thought. "I'd better head down the road," he said absently and straightened from the desk. But he stood there, still pondering something.

"What's wrong?" Jessy sensed his concern.

"I think I may have made a mistake

calling Parker," he stated, staring into the middle distance. "If he talks to Markham, he's likely to mention getting a call from a lawyer. Markham will wonder who my supposed client is. It depends on how paranoid he is as to what he'll do about it."

"What do you mean?" She felt a mounting uneasiness.

"I mean, if he does any checking at all, he'll find there is no such law firm of Cummins, Fitch and Stillwater in the Denver metropolis." His gaze locked with hers. "The next time you see him, Jessy, be very careful what you say. One slip, no matter how small, might make him start wondering what you know. That could be dangerous, Jess."

"I know." She nodded, feeling the first faint lick of fear.

"Be on the lookout for any questions from him about Chase, regardless of how casual or innocent they might sound," Laredo warned.

"I will." She showed him the stony calm that had long been her protection against questions that probed in closed areas.

"Let me know if there is any change in his attitude toward you. Any at all," he stressed. "If there is, you may have to find some work for me to do here at headquarters. Because it's for damn sure I can't protect you from the feedlot."

"You just worry about protecting Chase," Jessy replied, finding the prospect of seeing Laredo a dozen times or more a day to be too unsettling.

"You can count on it," he told her and left.

PART THREE

A shifting wind,
It sees him die,
And Calder knows
The time is nigh.

Chapter Fifteen

A big yellow sun sank closer to the western horizon, its golden color bleeding into the sky and adding a touch of amber to the late afternoon light. Slowing the Suburban, Cat made the turn into the Circle Six ranch lane. The distinctive scent of fresh-cut hay invaded the vehicle long before she came within sight of the forty acres of ridge-top planted in alfalfa.

As she approached the field gate, she noticed Logan standing just inside the opening. Culley was there as well, slouched atop his brown horse with one leg hooked over the saddle-horn. Both men had their attention focused on something in the field. Looking beyond them, Cat saw the pair of big bay draft horses pulling the mower hitched behind them. Quint held the reins, perched on the mower seat.

Pulling onto the shoulder, Cat stopped the Suburban and joined Logan at the gate to witness this major event in her young son's life — his first time mowing with the horse team. Logan slipped a welcoming arm around her shoulders, drawing her close to his side.

"How's he doing?" Cat asked anxiously. "Has he had any problems?"

"How could he have any when Jake and Angel know the routine better than he does," he said, referring to the two Clydesdales. "How did your meeting go with Jessy?"

"It couldn't have gone better," Cat admitted. "In fact, I wish now that I hadn't kept putting off getting together with her, but I dreaded the thought of arguing with her again."

As the team neared the end of the field, Logan called, "Set them up to make the turn, Quint. And don't forget to raise the blade."

"I won't," Quint called back and beamed at Cat. "Hi, Mom."

"Good job, Quint." She smiled, pride swelling within her. "Keep it up." The turn was made without incident, due, in no small part, to the well-trained horse team. "He's doing really well, isn't he?" she murmured to Logan.

"He is." His gray eyes echoed the pride she felt in their son's accomplishment.

"So what did Jessy have t' tell you?" Culley asked.

Cat related Jessy's decision not to renew the feedlot lease, which would ultimately result in laying off Laredo. "She more than met me halfway," she concluded. "How could I continue to object under those circumstances?"

"Assumin' she does what she says she'll do," Culley said, remaining skeptical.

"I have to give her the benefit of the doubt, Uncle Culley," Cat insisted. "It's what Dad would want me to do."

"It's fer sure nothin's been the same at the Triple C since he got himself killed. An' I don't see that changin', neither," he concluded. "If she ain't slippin' off to see that Laredo character, then she's hangin' around with that English guy."

Cat had never known her uncle to say anything without a reason. "Have you seen Jessy with Laredo again?"

"I saw her drivin' away from that old line shack where he's been livin' on Sunday afternoon. It musta been before she swung by here an' left that note fer you. It could be just a coincidence that she talked t'that Laredo fella' afore she came here. An' it could be they're both mighty anxious to keep you from raisin' a bigger fuss."

"I think you are making something out of nothing, Uncle Culley." But his doubts made her wonder.

"Maybe. But there's somethin' about this whole business with that Laredo guy that ain' right. I just haven't figured out what it is," he concluded and glanced down the lane, catching the sound of an approaching vehicle. "Sounds like ya got company a-comin'."

The minute Culley recognized the Land Rover he knew it was Tara. Unhurried, he swung his leg back over the saddle and slipped a boot into the stirrup. A turn of the reins aimed the brown horse in the opposite direction. He rode off, leaving Logan and Cat to greet their arriving guest. As usual, he didn't travel any farther than his usual watching post.

Drawing level with the gate, Tara stopped and rolled the window down. "Is that Quint in the field?"

"Yes. It's his first time to drive the team without Logan riding with him," Cat explained with considerable pride.

"He seems to be doing well."

"He's doing very well," Cat stressed.

"Isn't that wonderful," Tara declared with a show of enthusiasm.

"Yes, it is." Knowing Tara, Cat doubted that this was a social visit. "So what brings you here?"

"I'll tell you all about it at the house," Tara replied and sent the Land Rover rolling forward.

"I think you are supposed to follow her," Logan murmured dryly.

"I know." Cat sighed in annoyance. "For two cents I'd stay right here, but she would simply wait until I showed up. So I might as well find out what she wants."

"Quint has only one more sweep of the field to make to finish the mowing. I'll stay here until he's done . . ." He paused, shooting her a questioning look. "Unless you think you'll need me."

"No. More than likely she wants me to talk to her lawyer about Jessy. And there is no reason to do that now," Cat told him.

She turned out to be only partially right about the purpose of Tara's visit. It was indirectly about Jessy. But Tara chose a different approach.

"Do you still have that note Jessy gave you? The one that was supposedly written by your father?" Tara asked the minute they walked into the house.

"Yes. Why?"

"Because I just spent most of the last two hours talking to a handwriting expert —" Tara began.

Cat came to an abrupt halt in the middle

of the living room and swung around to face Tara. "How many times do I have to tell you that I want to drop this for now? I talked to Jessy today and we have worked out everything. I have no more problems with her."

Unfazed, Tara countered, "Do you really believe Chase scribbled those things on that paper?"

"I think it's very possible he did, yes."

"But what if he didn't? Or what if Jessy manufactured it for your benefit?" Tara challenged.

"She didn't."

"Are you positive of that? According to Allen Thornton, the expert I spoke with, it would be relatively easy to fake something like that. All a person would need to do is take various examples of someone's handwriting, select pertinent words or numbers, and trace over them to create a new example that looks authentic. Heaven knows, Jessy would have had plenty of opportunity to do just that, not to mention access to who knows how many notes or memos Chase might have written over the years."

"Of course it's possible," Cat admitted with growing impatience.

"It certainly is. That's why I want to see the note. Thortnon explained that amateurs often make rudimentary mistakes. He mentioned two very obvious things and suggested I look for those before going to the expense of having him examine it."

"Tara, I told you I am not going to hire a handwriting expert or talk to a lawyer. End of discussion." Cat held up both hands in a gesture of finality.

"If that's your decision, naturally I will accept it." Tara lifted one shoulder in an elegant shrug. "Although I don't see what harm there would be in letting me look at the note. Aren't you a little bit curious to know if it's real or something Jessy created to fool you? If it turns out that she lied about the note, chances are she is lying about other things."

The comment was too close to the one Culley had made. If it was only Tara who had said it, Cat would have ignored it. But she trusted Culley.

"All right, you can look at it. But you aren't going to find anything," she added in an attempt to convince herself of it.

Leaving the living room, she entered the kitchen and walked straight to the rolltop desk in the alcove. But the note wasn't lying next to the phone book. She checked beneath a few more papers on the desktop.

"Can't you find it?" Tara stood by, watching her search.

"Logan was doing some bookwork the other night. He probably moved it." She looked in the desk's many cubbyholes, then moved to the drawers.

"Don't tell me it's missing, Cat," Tara stated on a critical note. "Do you realize how valuable it could be to you?"

"It isn't missing," Cat insisted, but she was beginning to feel a bit panicky. "I simply haven't found it yet." She shifted her attention back to the desktop, intending to methodically check every piece of paper on it.

"Tell me one thing, Cat: has Jessy been over here?" Tara's voice was rife with suspicion.

Cat felt the pressure of it and broke off her search. "I don't have time for this right now. Quint and Logan will be coming in any minute, and I haven't started supper."

When she moved toward the kitchen proper, Tara blocked her path. "You didn't answer me. Was Jessy here?"

"I haven't seen her. Are you satisfied?" It wasn't actually a lie. Cat hadn't seen Jessy when she stopped on Sunday.

Disappointed didn't begin to describe Tara's reaction to her answer. She looked positively annoyed. "That doesn't mean she might not have slipped over here and taken it."

Rather than admit the same thought had occurred to her, Cat simply shook her head in feigned exasperation. "I'll look for it after supper. As soon as I find it, I'll call you," she promised. "Now, unless you want to peel some potatoes, I suggest you move out of the way so I can. I would ask you to stay for dinner, but I'm sure Brownsmith is busy seeing to the preparations for your evening meal."

She brushed past Tara, crossed to a cupboard, took out a three-quart pan, carried it to the sink, and proceeded to fill it with water, conscious of the silence behind her. After interminable moments, she heard the sharp click of Tara's footsteps exiting the kitchen. Cat waited until she saw Tara's vehicle leave the ranch yard, then returned to the desk and resumed her search.

She was still at it when Logan and Quint came in. She was so engrossed in looking for the note that their presence in the house barely registered on her.

Logan walked into the kitchen. "I hope we have time for a shower before supper. We could both use it."

Quint charged in behind him. "Dad said

the team handled real good for me, Mom."

But it was the word *supper* that did it as Cat suddenly realized that she had forgotten about it. A little rattled, she rose from the desk.

"You have plenty of time. I . . ." She paused. "I thought we would have spaghetti, so I haven't even started supper yet."

"Sounds good. I called to Culley and told him to join us." Logan lingered in the kitchen, watching while Cat set the pot of water on the stove and turned on the burner beneath it. "What did Tara want?"

"Nothing really." She added salt to the water, a distracted frown purling her forehead. "Do you remember that note Jessy gave me? The one where Dad had jotted some things down about the feedlot? I could have sworn I laid it on top of the desk. Now I can't find it."

"I remember you showing it to me when we came home after Sally's funeral. But I don't recall seeing it since then." He wandered over to the desk. "Are you sure you didn't put it in one of the drawers?"

"I'm positive." Joining him, Cat again began sifting through the papers on the desk. "I was about to go through the wastebasket when you came in, just in case it was accidentally wadded up and thrown away."

"I haven't thrown away anything except some junk mail," Logan replied as Culley slipped into the house through the rear.

He paused, eyeing them curiously. "What'cha huntin' for?"

"I mislaid a paper, something Dad wrote." She didn't look up from her task. "It was here on the desk last week, and now I can't find it."

"Important, was it?" Culley guessed.

"Mostly to me." She shot Logan a dry look. "Right away Tara accused Jessy of taking it."

"Why am I not surprised at that?" Logan countered with a droll smile.

"It coulda been that English fella," Culley pointed out. "He was pokin' around the desk, remember?"

"Monte?" Cat dismissed the notion as preposterous. "He didn't even know I had it. Besides, it wouldn't have meant anything to him."

Offended by her rejection, Culley clammed up. To him it was as obvious as a willow tree in a desert that if Jessy didn't want suspicion falling on her, she would likely put Markham up to getting it. In Culley's mind, Jessy, Markham, and

Laredo were entwined in some way.

First, that Laredo character showed up at the funeral; then Jessy secreted him up in the foothills. Not long afterward the Englishman has his cattle in the feedlot. Such strange happenings back to back made Culley wonder if Laredo and Markham were in cahoots. And it was for sure Jessy was awful friendly with both of them, which had to mean something.

Culley would have told Cat and Logan all of that if they had bothered to ask what he thought. But they didn't, and he didn't volunteer it.

The quiet of midmorning claimed the town of Blue Moon. It was an hour when its streets were empty of traffic. Those with jobs were already at their place of work, and the old-timers were gathered around their customary table at Harry's, drinking coffee and swapping stories of the past.

Culley was as familiar with the town's ebb and flow of activity as he was with the big land that surrounded it. He had deliberately picked this hour of the day to make a trip into town, fully aware it was a time when he would encounter few people.

The gas gauge on his old pickup had stopped working years ago, but he knew its tank had to be close to empty. No other vehicles were at the pumps when he pulled off the highway into Fedderson's combination gas station and grocery store.

Stopping next to the regular pump, he switched off the engine and listened to its dying cough and sputter. As he climbed out of the pickup, he cast a furtive glance around, but saw no one about. He pulled out the wadded-up rag that served as a lid for the gas tank and stuck the nozzle in. He let five dollars' worth flow into the tank before shutting off the pump.

There were no customers about when he walked into the store. Culley sidled up to the counter and pushed five crumpled one-dollar bills toward the bored-looking woman behind the counter. It used to be that it was always Emmett Fedderson himself who took his money, but Culley rarely saw the owner nowadays.

"Want a receipt?" the woman asked while managing to keep her jaw working, cracking the wad of chewing gum in her mouth.

Culley answered with a shake of his head and turned away, moving quickly to escape the store's confines. As he stepped into the sun-warmed air, a powerfully built Range Rover drove up to the pump island, stopping on the opposite side from Culley's rusty pickup. A powdering of dust dulled the vehicle's sleek sides, evidence of the dirt roads it had recently traveled.

Culley's black eyes narrowed thoughtfully when the tall, lean Englishman stepped out of the vehicle. The memory of Cat's fruitless search for the missing paper was still fresh in his mind. And his opinion hadn't changed that the Englishman had taken it. Those two things worked together in his mind to embolden him.

Instead of hurriedly sliding behind the wheel of his pickup and driving off, Culley dawdled outside it until he managed to catch the Englishman's eyes.

There was a moment when he thought the haughty foreigner was going to look right through him as if he wasn't there. Then recognition flickered. Instantly the man's expression took on a look of hearty welcome.

"Good morning, O'Rourke. I must say I didn't expect to see you in town," Markham declared while the pump meter spun, ticking off the gallons his vehicle guzzled.

"Needed gas," Culley replied in clipped explanation, then added slyly, "Did Jessy put ya up t' stealin' that paper from Cat's desk?"

Open-mouthed, Markham stared at him for a split second. "Paper?" he echoed with a great show of blankness. "I don't believe I know what you are talking about."

"You know," Culley pronounced. "And I know, too. I saw ya pokin' around her desk that day."

"I was merely admiring it," Monte chided lightly. "It's a fine example of workmanship, and I have always had an appreciation of old things. I suspect it comes with being British."

Culley hadn't expected the man to fess up. At the same time it galled him that Markham would think he was gullible enough to believe such malarkey. It pushed Culley to take a step beyond the truth.

"Was it the desk you were admirin' or that paper you slipped in your pocket? I may be old, but my eyes are as sharp as they ever was."

Markham forced out a brief laugh. "My good man, I have no idea what you think you saw, but I took nothing from that desk."

Culley ignored the denial. "I'm curious — did ya give the paper to Jessy or that Laredo fella?"

"Are you referring to Laredo Smith?" Monte frowned in surprise. "The cowboy

Jessy hired to work at the feedlot?"

"Yeah. He's your partner, ain't he?"

"Wherever did you get that idea? You have the most extraordinary imagination, Mr. O'Rourke," Markham declared with amusement.

"It jus' makes sense," Culley replied, undeterred. "He shows up outa the blue. Jessy hides him away up in that old abandoned line shack in the foothills, then keeps slippin' off to see him. Then, boom, after years of never allowin' a cow on the place that don't wear a Calder brand, you're fillin' the feedlot with your cattle. I figger you an' that Laredo guy got somethin' on Jessy."

"Obviously I cannot speak for Mr. Smith, but you are wrong about my involvement. It was a straightforward business arrangement I made with Jessy concerning the feedlot. There was absolutely no one else involved in it."

"So you say." Culley retained his skepticism. "You make all the deals ya want, but you keep Cat outa it. You mess with her an' you'll mess with me."

"I have no desire to *mess* with either of you, as you put it," Markham assured him, then cocked his head at a curious angle. "But what was that you said earlier about a

— what did you call it? — a line shack? I am not familiar with that term. Is it a building?"

"It's a cabin they built in the old days, on the outskirts of the ranch so's a cowboy wouldn't have so far t'ride at day's end." The sudden shift to answering questions instead of asking them made Culley uncomfortable. He edged closer to his truck.

"And this one is located in the foothills, you say. Sounds like an ideal location for a hunting lodge. Where is it, exactly?" Immediately Monte smiled and held up a detaining hand. "It would be pointless to tell me. The sort of directions people give here, I have found impossible to follow. Perhaps you could show me where it is. Not today, though. I have several appointments. Perhaps tomorrow morning we could meet. Say, around nine o'clock?"

"Have Jessy take ya." Culley turned toward his pickup.

"I would much rather that you took me. I can make it worth your while."

Culley hesitated. But curiosity got the better of him and he turned back to listen.

Chapter Sixteen

A stiff breeze swirled around the Boar's Nest, searching for an opening. A raised window provided an entrance, and it swept in, riffling through the notepad on the table in front of Chase. Hattie sat opposite him, holding two playing cards in her hand. Positioned between them was a cribbage board.

Chase removed a ten of hearts from his playing hand and placed it on the table. "Ten."

Hattie laid down an eight of clubs. "Eighteen."

"Nine for twenty-seven," Chase said as he put a nine of hearts on his stack.

A trifle smugly, Hattie played her last card, a four of diamonds. "And four for thirty-one, and two," she said, moving her white peg two positions on the board.

"You are on a hot streak this morning," Chase accused in mild complaint and began counting up the score in his hand. "Fifteen two, fifteen four, fifteen six . . ." He paused, tuning in to the distant sound of a vehicle. "Somebody's on the road," he remarked idly.

Hattie paused to listen. "Sounds like it stopped. Should I go look?"

Chase shook his head. "There's no need. It isn't that close to us." He moved his peg the necessary number of holes. "What do you have in your crib?"

"Enough to beat you again," she declared, eyes sparkling when she showed him the cards. "Do you want to try for three out of five?"

"With your luck at cards, I'll pass, thank you." He gathered up the playing cards and returned them to the packet while Hattie put away the cribbage board.

"Want some coffee?"

"No, thanks. I've had enough this morning." With too little to do and too much time on his hands, Chase rose from his chair and wandered restlessly to the window. "It's going to be another hot one today."

"Not as hot as it would be in Texas. Why don't I cut up that leftover chicken and make a cold salad for lunch? Does that sound good to you?"

Chase turned from the window, arching an eyebrow in her direction. "You aren't already thinking about lunch, are you? It wasn't that long ago that we finished breakfast."

"Do I detect a testy note?" she countered lightly. "It wouldn't surprise me if you came down with a touch of cabin fever considering how long you have been cooped up here. If that vehicle is gone, why don't you take a walk?"

The breeze carried the faint rumble of an engine turning over. "Sounds like it's leaving now. And as for the walk, as much as I would like to get out and move around, I better not. O'Rourke hasn't been around in a while, but that doesn't mean he isn't hunkered down somewhere watching the place."

"He's always snooping around, isn't he," Hattie said with disapproval and set a container of leftover chicken on the countertop.

"He doesn't have anything else to do. Even if he did, he's too much like his father to get too friendly with hard work."

"You remember a lot more, don't you?" Hattie remarked as she set about deboning and cutting up the chicken.

"Maybe, but I still can't remember why I needed to see the banker in person. There was a reason, and it had to do with Markham and something about cattle."

Chase frowned, straining to recall the exact details. "I was puzzled about something."

"It will come to you," she said confidently.

"There is another name whirling around in my brain, too. Pauley or Monte, something like that."

She gave him a startled look. "You aren't thinking about Carlo Ponti, the Italian movie director — Sophia Loren's husband."

Chase drew his head back in surprise. "I don't think so."

"You're beginning to worry me, Duke." Hattie glanced at him with narrowed eyes. "It's one thing to stand around and daydream about Sophia Loren. And quite another to be thinking about her husband."

Chase laughed in genuine amusement and slipped up behind her, sliding his arms around her waist. "If I was thinking about him, it was probably with envy," he murmured near her ear and bent his head to nibble at her neck.

"Stop that," Hattie said in false protest while a pleased smile curved her lips. "If that isn't just like a man. Here I am, trying to fix something for lunch and you start feeling frisky."

"Is that bad?" he teased.

Turning in his arms, she looped her hands around his neck, still holding the knife. "Now, I never said that," she said, tilting back her head to invite his kiss.

Cat stood in the barn's lengthening shadow and anxiously scanned the broken country to the south and east. With the lowering of the sun, the afternoon breeze had died, leaving a sultry quality in the air that added to the tension she felt.

"What are you looking at, Mom?" Joining her, Quint glanced in the direction she was looking.

"I thought I might catch a glimpse of your uncle Culley," she admitted, careful not to voice the uneasiness she felt at his continued absence. "Have you finished haying the horses?"

"All done," he announced. "Dad will be surprised when he gets home and finds out we already did the evening chores for him, won't he?"

"He certainly will." Cat managed a smile and stole another look at the empty land. She knew Culley wasn't anywhere out there; it was a feeling she had. "Let's go to the house and get out of this heat," she said to Quint.

Side by side, they set off for the house. "Dad said the hay should be ready to bale this weekend," Quint announced in a businesslike tone. "It looks like we'll have a good crop this year."

Cat was too used to his adultlike ways to take much notice of it. "Let's hope it will be enough to carry us through the winter and we won't have to buy more." As they drew close to the house, Cat automatically looked toward the stand of trees beyond it.

"He's not there, Mom," Quint said.

With a guilty start, she jerked her gaze away from it then smiled ruefully at her son. "You see too much."

"Why don't you call Dad and have him swing by Shamrock on his way home?" he suggested. "Uncle Culley might be there."

"That's a good idea. I'll do it. And you can go take a shower. You are covered with hay chaff." She brushed at the bits clinging to the sleeve of his T-shirt.

"Yeah." He nodded in agreement. "I'm already starting to itch."

Once inside the house, Cat waited until Quint turned the shower on before she went to the phone and called Logan. "Hi, it's me," she said when he came on the line.

"What's up? Need me to pick up something at the store?"

"No. If you don't mind, would you stop at Uncle Culley's place and see whether he's around?" She added in a rush, "There's probably nothing to worry, but he didn't come by this morning and he wasn't here last night. Knowing Uncle Culley, he probably camped out somewhere overnight and —"

"You think something has happened to him." Logan's statement carried no trace of disagreement.

Cat was relieved that he didn't make light of her concern. "It's not like him to stay away this long, Logan. Uncle Culley is an old man. Heaven knows where he might be or what might have happened." She heard the frantic note in her voice and didn't care. don't even know where to start looking for him. He roams all over the place."

"You're right. He could be anywhere. Just to be on the safe side, give Jessy a call and have her spread the word to keep an eye out for him," Logan suggested. "It's better to look foolish when he turns up than to let more time go by and live with the regret of that."

"I'll call her as soon as I hang up," Cat promised as the screen door's hinge creaked nosily. "Wait. Somebody just walked in. Maybe —" She turned, but the loudness of the footsteps crossing the living room already told her they weren't made by her soft-footed uncle. "Never mind," she said into the phone. "It's Tara. I'll talk to you when you get home."

"Honestly, Cat, you promised you would call," Tara began with impatience the instant she hung up the phone. "And I have yet to hear from you. Which can only mean that you haven't found the note. Have you?"

"No, I haven't. And I don't have time to discuss it with you, either," Cat retorted with equal sharpness and rapidly punched the numbers for the Triple C.

"Who are you calling now?" Tara demanded with dramatic exasperation.

"Jessy, if it's any of your business," she replied and listened to the ringing on the other end of the line.

"It's about time." Tara took a seat and gracefully crossed her legs. "At least you finally realize that she was the one who took it."

There was a heaviness to the air that seemed to warn of an approaching storm, but the sky over the Triple C headquarters held only a few puffy clouds. Jessy sighed with regret, even though she knew there was too much hay down for rain to be a welcome event right now. Later, after it was dry and baled and stored, it could rain all it wanted. She also knew Mother Nature didn't always pay attention to whether it was the right time for something or not.

As she neared the steps to The Homestead, the front door opened and Trey tumbled out of the house to race across the veranda to meet her. "You been gone a long time, Mom," he declared in a backhanded welcome.

"I know I have. So what did you do all day?"

"Nothin'." He waited at the top of the steps.

"You must have done something," Jessy chided.

"Nothin' fun. Next time can I go with you?"

"We'll see. Where is Laura?"

He fell in beside her as she crossed to the door. "Her an' Becky are havin' a tea party." The derisive stress he placed on the last two words made it clear what he thought of it.

The air-conditioned coolness of the house greeted Jessy when she walked inside. It washed over her like a balm. She could almost feel her tiredness sliding away.

"Jessy," Becky called to her from the living room. "Cat's on the phone. She wants to talk to you. She says it's important."

"I'll take it in the den," Jessy called back and made a slight alteration in her course, aiming for the room. "You can go home anytime you like, Becky. I'm back for the rest of the evening."

She didn't bother to ask the girl if there had been any problems. Jessy knew she would get a blow-by-blow account of the day's activities from Laura, especially any mischief Trey might have caused.

"Are you sure you don't want me to wait until you've talked to Cat, just in case?" Becky said, rising from the living-room sofa where Laura was holding her tea party.

"No, you run along. I'll manage," Jessy assured her and made the swing into the den.

Trey stayed right on her heels. "What're we gonna have for supper, Mom? I'm hungry."

"You are always hungry." But his question served as a reminder that she had yet to find someone to prepare their meals.

"So what're we gonna eat?" he repeated.

"We'll discuss it after I talk to your aunt." She crossed to the desk and picked up the phone. "Hi, Cat. It's Jessy. What did you need?"

"It's Uncle Culley," Cat said in reply. "I haven't seen him in — it's been more than a day and a half now. He's probably fine, but I'm worried about him. I was wondering if you could —"

Guessing at the request, Jessy said, "I'll pass the word to keep a lookout for him."

"Thanks. He'll probably show up, but . . ." Cat left the sentence unfinished.

"I know."

"That's all I wanted," Cat said. "I'll let you go ahead and start making your calls."

In the background came Tara's voice, "Aren't you going to ask her about the note?" she demanded. "For heaven's sake, Cat, you know she took it."

Tension raced along her nerve ends. "Was that Tara?" Jessy asked, certain of the answer.

"Yes." But there was a hesitancy in Cat's reply.

"She mentioned a note. What was that about?" Unconsciously she held her breath, little alarms going off in her mind.

"That note you found, the one Dad had

written, I've misplaced it," Cat explained. "But that's the least of my worries right now. Make your calls, and let me know if anyone has seen him."

"I will," Jessy promised and held down the cradle's disconnect button.

"How 'bout s'ghetti, Mom?" Trey suggested.

"Let Mom make a couple calls first. Then we'll talk about it."

Ignoring Trey's exaggerated sigh and roll of the eyes, Jessy phoned her father first and passed on Cat's request. "Will you start spreading the word?" After receiving an affirmative response, she hung up.

"One more call," she told Trey and dialed the feedlot. One of the ranch hands answered. "Kirby. It's Jessy Calder."

"Yeah, Jessy. What do you need?"

"I spoke to Cat a few minutes ago. O'Rourke has come up missing."

"Are you putting together a search party? Finding him could be a tall order. There's no telling where his wanderings might have taken him."

"She doesn't plan to organize a search yet. For the time being she just wants everyone to keep an eye out."

"We can do that."

"Thanks. Is Laredo still there."

"He's getting ready to leave. I'll see if he's gone yet."

Seconds after he laid the phone down, Jessy heard a piercing whistle, followed by a shout telling Laredo he was wanted on the phone. There was a brief mumble of voices. Then Laredo came on the line.

"Did Kirby tell you about Culley?" she asked.

"Yes."

"Good. There's more. It may not mean anything." Yet Jessy had an uneasy feeling that it did. "The note with all those jottings about the feedlot that Chase wrote — I just found out it's missing. Right now Cat says she misplaced it, but Tara is trying to convince her I took it."

"Wonderful," he murmured dryly as Trey scrambled over to the window.

"Somebody's here, Mom," he announced.

"I wanted to let you know about that," she said into the phone. "Trey tells me we have company, so I'd better go." She glanced out the window to identify the caller and tensed a little at the sight of Monte's vehicle parked in front of The Homestead. "It's Markham."

"Watch yourself," Laredo warned.

"I will."

When she placed the receiver back on its

cradle, Trey pushed away from the window. "He's carrying something real big, Mom," he declared with big-eyed excitement.

"Maybe we should go see what it is."

Needing no second urging, Trey galloped ahead of her to the entry hall. Jessy arrived as Monte walked in, toting a mammoth picnic hamper.

Trey stared at it. "Whatcha got in there?"

"As I understand," he addressed his reply to Trey, but his sparkling glance kept sliding to Jessy, "your mother has yet to hire any kitchen help. So I thought I might treat you all to a special feast my cook prepared specially for you. Do you think I could persuade you to join me for a picnic supper?"

"Supper." At last Trey heard a word that he understood. "Whatcha gonna have?"

"Fried chicken, potato salad, corn, a relish tray, and for dessert, I believe the cook said he included a chocolate cake."

"Yum!" Trey proclaimed.

Monte laughed. "Is that a 'yes'?" he asked Jessy.

"A very definite one," she replied, aware that her son's reaction had left no room for refusal. She wondered if Monte had counted on that, then realized he couldn't have known Trey would be on hand when he issued the invitation.

"I understand there is a picnic area down along the river," he began.

"Yeah, it's down where we go swimmin'. Is that where we gonna eat?" Trey asked, enthused by the idea.

"That was my plan, yes," Monte told him, then said to Jessy, "In my opinion, a leisurely meal is best enjoyed far from the reach of telephones and the pressures of business. As beautiful as this home is, it has both."

She wasn't given a chance to reply as Trey pulled at her hand. "Let's go, Mom. I'm hungry."

"We need to get your sister first."

"Do we have to?"

"Yes, we do. Why don't you take Mr. Markham to the river while I get Laura."

"Okay." Quick to agree, Trey motioned to Monte. "Come on."

As Jessy expected, the prospect of eating outside didn't appeal to Laura. But she changed her mind when they reached the river and she saw the snow white cloth that covered the picnic table near the gazebo. On top of it, china plates gleamed, reflecting the sparkle from the crystal tumblers. When Monte set out a half dozen votive candles, Laura was completely enthralled.

Trey's mind ran along much more practical lines. "Why'd ya bring them? It won't be dark for a long time."

"I was told they would help keep the mosquitoes away." Monte began lighting the votives one by one.

"They'll bite ya anyway," Trey declared and made like a mosquito, buzzing around Laura and reaching out to sneak little pinches.

As far as Jessy was concerned, the children were a godsend. For the first time she found herself unable to relax in Monte's company. But the children's lively presence eliminated any awkward lulls in the conversation.

She watched constantly for any change in Monte's attitude toward her but he seemed exactly the same — friendly, considerate, and totally undemanding.

All too soon, Trey excused himself from the table and went off to look for frogs. Without her brother to torment her, Laura's attention shifted to her doll. Suddenly it was left to Jessy to keep the conversation going. And she had never been adept at social chitchat.

Fortunately Monte took the lead. "Your children are a joy."

"You haven't seen them at their worst."

"I suppose I haven't," he agreed. "Still, being around them makes me realize how much I have missed by not having a family of my own."

Jessy recalled Laredo's insinuations that Markham was interested in her. "Coming from a bachelor, it sounds like it's time you started looking for a wife," she remarked.

"That is much easier said than done," Monte declared, turning thoughtful. "It is amazing how much we change as we grow older. When I was younger, a woman's looks — the physical attraction aspect — counted for a great deal. Now I find it's more important to actually like her — to enjoy her company. I would much rather have the warmth of that relationship than the fire of some grand passion. Yet I have discovered it is easier to find someone you love than it is to find someone you like." A rueful smile tugged at his mouth. "I expect I sound very dull."

"Not at all." But Jessy couldn't help thinking that no more than a couple weeks ago she would have said that it described their relationship perfectly. She had liked being with him. More importantly, he had been good with the children, showing un-bounded patience with their endless ques-tions. Now she wondered if that patience had been sincere or merely an attempt to ingratiate himself.

"You would be surprised by the number of women who have their feelings hurt by such talk. But you are different, Jessy." He gave her a long, deep look that was meant to say so much more than words could.

She suddenly felt chilled. "No, I'm not," Jessy replied, determined to deflect his attention. "You just haven't met the right woman. I'll see what I can do to change that. Here," — she stood up and began gathering the dishes — "I'll help you put all this away."

"There's no rush, surely," Monte said in mild protest.

"I wish there weren't, but I have some phone calls to make. Right before you came, I talked to Cat. She's worried that she hasn't seen her uncle in nearly two days."

"Is that unusual?"

"A little. Enough that Cat's worried. I promised I would alert everyone on the Triple C to watch for him. Now I've passed the word to you, too."

"Actually I did see O'Rourke. Yesterday morning, it was."

"Where?" Jessy instantly gave him her full attention.

"In Blue Moon. I stopped at Fedderson's for some petrol and he was there. He seemed fine," Monte added. "Although with a gentlemen of his years, I expect health is always an issue."

"Yes, but Culley is a tough old guy." Jessy went back to scraping any remaining bits of food from the plates into an empty container. "People have tried to kill him off before, and he survived."

Monte reacted with surprise. "You surely don't suspect there is foul play involved in his disappearance, do you? I assumed you thought he might have had a heart attack. I can't imagine why anyone would want to hurt a harmless old man like that."

"Neither do I. Actually it never crossed my mind that someone would," she admitted. "I suppose I mentioned it simply to point out his resilience."

"Sorry, I seemed to have placed a literal interpretation on your previous remark." Monte set the hamper out. "I should think it's much more likely that he had a heart attack or took a fall."

"Probably. But I can't imagine that old brown horse he rides ever trying to throw him."

"As rough as some of this country is, it

may have been the horse that took the fall and pitched him. Or his horse may have gone lame, and that is the cause for his delay in returning home."

"It's possible," Jessy agreed.

A breeze sprang up, rustling through the leaves of the cottonwoods and whipping at the ends of the tablecloth. A corner flipped dangerously close to one of the votive candles.

When Jessy leaned over to blow it out, Laura said, "Put the candle by me so I can see my dolly better."

Jessy suddenly noticed the premature darkness that had nothing to do with the cool shade of trees. To the west, black clouds had blocked out the setting sun. From within them came flashes of lightning. She studied the clouds for a moment, watching them build and expand.

"We have a storm coming. And it's traveling fast by the looks of it." When she turned back to the picnic table, she caught sight of Laredo's pickup parked by the barn. In that instant she knew he was somewhere close by, watching, but she didn't attempt to locate him.

Chapter Seventeen

Despite the dusty film on the barn window's glass, Laredo had a good view of the picnic site by the river. Taking no chances that he might be seen, he stood to one side of the frame and watched the familylike scene.

He couldn't honestly say that he was there because he anticipated Markham would make some move against Jessy. While there was a remote possibility of it, he told himself that he merely wanted to learn what Markham had to say. But the twistings of resentment and envy he felt inside seemed to make a mockery of that idea. It did no good to remind himself he had no claim on Jessy. The building tension within him remained rough and raw.

There was a slight lessening of it when he observed them stowing the picnic items back in the hamper. Laredo stayed by the window until he was certain they were bound for The Homestead. Then he made his way out of the barn to his truck. He raised the hood and pretended to tinker with the motor, all the while watching to see if Markham went inside. But Jessy said her good-byes on the steps, surrounded by the twins.

The breeze stiffened, bringing the smell of rain to him. A distant rumble of thunder was lost in the growl of the Range Rover's powerful engine turning over. Laredo left the pickup's hood up until Markham drove out on the ranch lane. He lowered the hood, checked the latch, and took a step toward The Homestead. But then he thought better of it. He wanted to talk to Jessy alone, without any interruptions from the twins, which meant waiting until they were in bed.

Briefly Laredo considered making the trip to the line shack and returning later in the evening. But if he did that, he would be driving into the teeth of the approaching storm. Common sense told him to wait until after the storm had passed.

Instead he drove to the cookshack, where evening meals were provided for unmarried ranch hands. The first fat raindrops plopped on his windshield as he pulled up to the building.

Halfway through Jessy's third reading of Trey's favorite bedtime story, she stole a glance at her son. His eyes were closed and his mouth was open, drawing in slow, even breaths. A sharp clap of thunder rattled windowpanes. Trey shifted slightly and snuggled deeper under the covers.

Satisfied that he was asleep, Jessy closed the book and laid it on the nightstand. After tucking the blanket around him and making a final check on Laura, she tiptoed from the room. The steady drum of the rain masked any sound she made.

As she descended the wide oak staircase, the brilliance of a lightning flash reached into the house. Jessy couldn't help wondering if Culley was out there somewhere in the storm. On the off chance he might have shown up at the Circle Six, Jessy crossed the living room and picked up the phone to call Cat.

"No. She would have let me know," she murmured absently to herself and replaced the receiver. A phone call now would only add to Cat's concern.

Jessy headed for the kitchen. Earlier in the evening, Trey had informed her that they were out of cookies, something Sally had never allowed to happen. Jessy knew that a single phone call to her mother would correct the deficiency. But stirring up a batch of cookies appealed to her, much more than the paperwork that waited for her in the den.

She pushed through the door into the kitchen and froze at the sight of the back door opening. The breath of alarm she had caught back sailed out of her when Laredo stepped inside, drenched to the skin, water pouring from the rolled brim of his hat.

"That door was locked," Jessy remembered. "How did you get in?"

"It's an old lock. Those kind are easily opened." He took off his hat and gave himself a shake. "If you want to make it hard for somebody to break in, you need to install a dead bolt."

"I will." But it was the sight of his shirt plastered against his muscled torso that sent Jessy to the laundry basket. She came back with a clean towel and pushed it into his hands with the admonition, "You're soaked."

"It's raining," Laredo replied in a wry statement of the obvious.

"No kidding."

"I thought you might not have noticed," Laredo mocked, a mischievous sparkle in his blue eyes.

It was a look that warmed her. "I noticed earlier that your pickup was gone. I thought you had gone to the Boar's Nest."

"I went over to the cookshack for supper." He used the towel to absorb the excess moisture, slowing down the drips. "I wanted to give you time to put the twins to bed before I stopped to find out what Markham had to say."

"He didn't really have anything to say — at least nothing important." She crossed to the sink. "I'll put on some coffee."

"You don't have anything stronger, do you?"

Jessy hesitated. "There's whiskey in the den."

But one look at the slim, woman's shape of her warned Laredo that whiskey wasn't a wise choice, not when there were too many raw needs tumbling inside him.

"Coffee is good enough," he told her. "So Markham only came over to take you on a picnic?"

"He didn't ask any questions, if that's what you're wondering." She scooped fresh grounds into the coffeemaker's basket. "He did mention that he saw O'Rourke in town yesterday morning, but that's about it."

But O'Rourke was the least of Laredo's interests. "Have you talked to Cat again?"

"No. I thought about calling to let her know Monte had seen Culley. But there didn't seem much point since it was yesterday he saw him. Why?"

"I thought she might have said something more about the missing note." A troubled frown dug a line between his sandy eyebrows as Laredo continued to absently move the towel over his wet clothes. "Who else knows of the note's existence?" he wondered aloud.

"Tara, of course. And I imagine Cat showed it to Logan, but that's —" Jessy stopped, recalling with a touch of guilt, "Monte knows about it."

"Markham!" Laredo exploded. "How the hell did he find out about it?"

"I told him."

"You what? Dammit, Jessy, you were supposed to watch what you said around him." His voice was tight and ominously low.

"For your information, I told him about the note *before* you warned me to be careful of what I said," she fired back just as hotly. "Monte came into the den shortly after I had given it to Cat. When he asked me about it, I told him exactly what I had said to Cat. It isn't like the note was something I actually found. Chase made it all up for Cat's benefit."

"But Markham didn't know that!"

Laredo was in her face, temper blazing.

"Of course not! No one did, except us. At the time, we didn't have any more than a suspicion against him, with absolutely nothing to back it up!"

Laredo was untouched by her argument. "I wish to God I had never told you Chase was alive. I had the ridiculous idea you knew how to keep your mouth shut." He spun away from her, muttering, "God only knows what else you've blabbed."

He hurled the towel aside and grabbed his hat off the counter on the way to the door. It took Jessy a full second to realize he actually intended to leave. Furious, she went after him and jerked the door out of his hand when he tried to close it behind him.

"I never told anybody anything," she stated, her voice flat and hard.

Laredo paused on the steps, standing sideways to look back at her, the rain pelting him. "Yeah, just like you didn't say anything to Markham," he mocked.

"What difference does that make?" She stood in the doorway, indifferent to the wind-driven drops that reached her. "I didn't tell him anything he couldn't have found out by asking Cat."

"But he wouldn't have asked Cat if you

had made up some story to throw him off the track. You could have told him that note was anything, and he would have believed you. Stop being so damned proud, and admit it, Jessy: you blew it, big time!" Laredo swung away and walked down the last two steps.

Jessy hesitated and glanced at the curtain of rain, then ran down the steps after him. She caught him by the arm and turned him back to face her.

"Explain what you meant. How did I blow it?" she demanded.

He stared at her for a long second, moisture glistening on the tautly ridged line of his jaw. "When Markham found out about that note, he must have started worrying that Chase might have written down whatever it was he knew about him. Five will get you ten that Markham took that note. I don't know how or when, but it doesn't matter. For all we know Chase could have unknowingly scribbled something damning in it. Even if he didn't, I'm betting Markham is wondering if there are any more lying around. And he knows that if there are, *you* would be the one who would know about them."

"But there isn't," Jessy protested. "I looked and couldn't find anything. Oh my

God." She bowed her head with the sudden stirring of a memory.

"What!" Laredo grabbed her arms, giving her a stiffening shake.

"Before the funeral, someone sat with the coffin around the clock. Monte took one of the predawn shifts. He would have been in the den by himself for two or three hours. He could have easily gone through the desk and destroyed anything damning." The wetness of the rain lost any meaning in the face of this new realization.

Laredo took her thought a step further. "Then you produce a note that Markham knows he never saw in the desk." His fingers tightened their grip on her arms. "Are you certain he hasn't asked . . . No, he wouldn't do that," he said, answering his own question. "He wouldn't want you to start wondering why he wanted to know where Chase kept his personal papers. Markham is too smart for that. I have a feeling that you are going to see a whole lot more of him from now on, Jessy," he warned.

"Why?"

"For starters, he'll be wondering if there are more notes like the one you supposedly found. And he'll be watching you, looking for any change in your attitude toward him. Hell, he may not do that at all. He may have already decided you are too big a risk."

"Don't be ridiculous." Jessy brought her arms up to break free of his hold.

"This isn't a man who takes chances." Thunder rolled under Laredo's words. "Look at how quickly he acted to get Chase out of the picture. He didn't give any warning. If he had, Chase would have told you what he knew — or suspected." His fingers dug into her flesh. "From now on, you stick close to the house, Jessy."

"That's impossible," she retorted. "I have a ranch to run. I can't hole up like Chase."

"You'd better, if you want to stay alive."

"I can take care of myself," Jessy insisted impatiently.

"Like hell you can. This guy doesn't work close up, Jessy. He does his killing from long distance — with a rifle and a scope. Unless you have some dumb luck like Chase, you won't even know what hit you."

The near savagery of his expression chilled her. "If you're trying to scare me, you succeeded. Satisfied?"

"Yes, I want you scared," Laredo snapped as lightning lit the sky behind him. "If you're scared, you might stay alive. If anything happened to you, Jessy —" He clamped off the rest of the sentence and brought his hand up, flattening it against the side of her wet cheek, his thumb sliding to her chin.

It was the only warning he gave her before his mouth drove against hers. The suddenness, the heat of it was a shock. One moment there was space between them and in the next, she was pressed against the length of him, thigh to thigh, hip to hip, stomach to stomach, while his mouth tunneled against her lips with hungry insistence, awakening a rush of unexpected sensations.

Struggling to surface from them, Jessy started to turn her face away, but Laredo abruptly broke off the kiss and raised his head scant inches from hers, rain funneling off the brim of his hat onto her head.

"Don't give me some damned lecture about me needing a woman," he growled while his gaze devoured her upturned face. "If any woman would do, that's where I'd be. But it's you I need."

"You don't understand." But Jessy wasn't sure she did, either. She wanted to tell him it was happening too fast, except she had felt it coming. But she hadn't decided if it was what she wanted.

"What! That you loved your husband?" The warmth of his breath fanned her cheek. "I understand that. But he's gone and I'm here. If that's wrong, then I don't know what's right. I just know God didn't make flesh and blood to live alone."

In that moment Jessy understood the issue wasn't one of loyalty, but one of life and living. Love always wore many faces in a person's life. She would never know another Ty Calder, but that didn't mean there wasn't room in her life for a man who called himself Laredo Smith.

She gave him an answer that needed no words, pushing his hat off and pulling his head down, giving herself to his kiss — and to him — without reservation. His low, inarticulate moan of need said it at all as he claimed her lips.

In an act that was never new and never old, they made love in the storm and the rain. Their clothes lay in a sodden heap on the grass. Lightning lit up the sky, reflecting off their wet bodies, one slender, one muscled, giving them a silvery sheen. It was difficult for either of them to tell where the rolling thunder ended and the pounding of their hearts began. The storm within built in intensity, the heat and pressure mounting until they both strained for a release. It came in a shuddering, blinding crash of light.

For a long moment they lay there, washed by the rain, all loose and drained of tension, still caught in the tingling afterglow. Laredo was the first to break the spell, his hand sliding up her cheek to turn her face to him.

"My God, what have I been missing all this time," he murmured thickly.

Moved by the depth of feeling in his look, Jessy felt suddenly and oddly shy. "Clothes, for starters. And a dry towel."

He burst out laughing and rolled Jessy onto her back, leaning over her, his wide shoulders shielding her from the rain. "You're always so damned blunt and practical."

His laughter made the difference. That calm confidence returned, warmed by new feelings. "One of us needs to be." The corners of her mouth deepened with an impish smile. "In case you haven't noticed, it's raining."

"So it is." Laredo combed the wet hair away from her face. "Do you suppose we should get out of it?"

"Probably." She linked her hands behind his neck and admired again the lean, strong lines of his face.

"This is one of those moments you don't want to end," he admitted, "even though you know it must."

"It's called life, I guess." But inwardly she agreed with him.

"This is the first time I can recall hoping that mine would be a long one," Laredo told her.

"In that case, you'd better start hoping that you don't catch pneumonia, because you have a long drive ahead of you — in some very wet clothes." The slickness of his skin made it easy for Jessy to slide out from under him, and Laredo did little to stop her.

He remained on the ground, lying on his side, propped up by an elbow, watching while she scooped up her wet clothes. "And you only have to go inside to get warm and dry."

She held the wet bundle in front of her, but not out of any sense of modesty. "You could come in for a while," she suggested with a touch of hesitancy. "I could throw your clothes in the dryer."

"No, thanks." He rolled to his feet and gathered up his jeans.

Jessy watched the struggle he had to pull them up. "Are you sure? It won't take long to dry them."

"I'm positive. If I went in there, I might not come out." Laredo dragged his shirt on, but didn't bother to button it. "Besides, it's late, and Chase will be wondering where I am." Barefoot with boots in hand, he moved to her side. "I'll walk you to the door, though."

Jessy couldn't help smiling. "My, but that sounds old-fashioned."

"That's the kind of feeling I have."

When he paused at the bottom of the steps, she turned to face him, still holding her clothes. A breath later, his mouth moved onto hers, claiming it with an evocative tenderness that had more power in it than passion could possess. Jessy felt it course through her, filling all the empty places with something warm and enduring.

Words seemed unnecessary. She went inside without uttering a single one, conscious of Laredo watching every step she took.

Up at daybreak, Laredo whistled softly while he shaved. He caught himself and smiled, certain he had never been so damned happy in his life.

It was as if the world had taken on a fresh flavor. Everything seemed to taste better to him, from coffee to the plate of bacon and eggs Hattie set before him. He lingered over a final cup long enough to fill Chase in on the previous day's happenings — all except the way it ended.

As serious as those subjects were, it didn't take the slight bounce from his step when he walked outside. He paused, filling his lungs with a deep draught of invigorating rain-washed air. It was a crystal-clear morning that gave a sharp definition to the sprawling landscape before him. Smiling again, Lared headed for his truck, convinced he had never felt this eager for a new day to begin. There was only one reason for it, and her name was Jessy.

When he turned onto the dirt ranch road, he unconsciously started whistling again. A shadow drifted across the road in front of him. Leaning over the steering wheel, he peered skyward. His searching gaze finally located the buzzard floating on a morning thermal. An instant later, he noticed a second one, then a third and a fourth, all on a descending spiral, intent on something west of the road. Which likely meant they had spotted breakfast.

Laredo stopped whistling and slowed the truck, telling himself it could be anything from a dead rabbit or pronghorn to a steer. But with O'Rourke missing, he knew he needed to check it out. He parked the truck on the shoulder and headed off on foot.

In short order, he was back, piling into the pickup and making a sharp U-turn. He gave the horn two long blasts and drove back to the line shack.

Chase was outside waiting for him when he arrived. "What's up?"

"We've got trouble," Laredo stated. "O'Rourke's down there. He's dead. A bullet hole in the back."

Humming softly to herself, Jessy stood next to Trey's chair and cut his pancake into bite-sized portions. He sat slumped in his chair and absently rubbed the sleep from his eyes.

"I need more syrup, Mom," Laura announced after taking the first bite of pancake.

"Are you sure? I think you're sweet enough," Jessy teased.

"I know, but the pancakes aren't," Laura explained patiently.

"Sorry." Jessy bit back a smile and reached for the syrup bottle just as the phone rang. She stopped moving for a second, then went ahead and drizzled more syrup over Laura's pancake. On the fourth ring, she picked up the receiver. "Calder Ranch."

"Hi, Jessy. It's Cat," came the reply, issued in a voice riddled with tension.

Unconsciously Jessy tightened her grip on the phone, concern banishing some of that good mood she had felt. "What's wrong?"

"Uncle Culley. That brown horse he always rides — when Logan stopped by the Shamrock this morning, the horse was at the barn. It was still wearing its saddle and bridle." The disjointed phrasing as much as Cat's voice indicated the elevated level of her concern. "Logan asked me to call. He wants to start a search."

"I'll call everybody in," Jessy promised and reached for a pen and notepad. "Just tell me when to meet Logan and where."

O'Rourke's Shamrock Ranch was to be the starting point. The rendezvous time was nine-thirty, nearly two hours away. Logan planned to enlist Tara's helicopter and pilot in an aerial search and asked that the Triple C plane take part in it as well.

By the time Jessy concluded her conversation with Cat, she had made a mental list of the contacts she needed to make, and their order. But she had no chance to make the first one as Laredo walked into the kitchen.

"There's coffee in the pot. Help yourself." Jessy waved a hand in the direction of the coffeepot, still holding the telephone receiver in the other.

"Whoever you are talking to, hang up. I have to make a call."

Jessy was too distracted to notice the no-nonsense tone Laredo used. "You'll have to wait. This is important."

"Not as important as this." He took the phone from her and pressed the disconnect button.

Recovering from her initial shock at his high-handed action, Jessy reached to take the phone back, demanding, "What are you doing?"

He easily checked her attempt and held her gaze. "It's O'Rourke, Jess." The gravity of his tone held a wealth of meaning.

Jessy drew back, stunned into an instant of silence. "Where? How?"

Laura's petulant voice interrupted them. "Mommy, I need more syrup."

Laredo threw the young pair at the table a grim look and hung up the phone. "I'll make the call in the other room. They don't need to hear this." He moved off in the direction of the living room.

Jessy tarried long enough to dump more syrup on Laura's pancakes and sit Trey up to his plate, admonishing him to eat. Then she joined Laredo in the living room.

He was already on the phone. "I'm calling from the Triple C. A body's been found. It's Culley O'Rourke." He paused, his glance sliding to Jessy. "It looks like the cause of death will turn out to be a bullet hole. The buzzards have been at him, so it's hard to say for certain." After a second longer pause, Laredo replied, "After I determined he was dead, I left everything the way I found it." More questions followed. "It's in a remote area northwest of the Triple C headquarters. Have your men meet me here at the main house, and I'll take them to the site."

When he hung up, Jessy had trouble meeting his gaze. She felt sick inside, her muscles knotting up with disbelief and denial.

The necessity to remove any shred of doubt made her ask, "You are absolutely certain it was Culley. There isn't any question at all in your mind?"

"None."

"He was always such a tough old coot," she murmured. "I thought the only way he would ever die was when his heart gave out. I didn't think anything else could kill him." She looked up. "You think Markham did it, don't you?"

"I think it's likely, especially if it turns out O'Rourke wasn't shot at close range."

"But why?" Jessy searched for a motive and came up with none. "What could Culley possibly know that would be harmful to Monte?"

"Maybe something. Maybe nothing. If Markham only suspected O'Rourke knew something, that could be all it took." Laredo's hands closed on her upper arms in a demand for her full attention. "Get it through your head, Jessy. This man is as ruthless as they come. Markham doesn't wait for a threat to surface. The minute he thinks there is one, he eliminates it."

The cold-bloodedness of it sparked her anger. "What makes him think he can get away with it?"

"Why would anyone suspect him?" Laredo countered. "If Chase hadn't survived, would you?"

She didn't have to answer. He already knew no one would have suspected Monte, not in a million years.

Laredo stood at the head of the hollow, his hand tucked in the hip pockets of his jeans, one leg cocked in a relaxed pose. His back was to the sun, his shadow stretching away from him. On either side of it were

432

two shorter shadows cast by the uniformed deputies who flanked him.

With the heat of the sun's rays penetrating his shirt to warm his skin, Laredo watched in silence while Logan Echohawk slowly worked his way to the body that lay facedown in the hollow, carefully studying every inch of the ground as he went. A light breeze curled into the area, whispering through the sparse stalks of grass and ruffling O'Rourke's wiry gray hair.

At last, Echohawk crouched next to the body, looking but not touching. "Did you move him at all?"

"No," Laredo replied. "The minute I took hold of his wrist to check for a pulse, I could tell rigor had set in."

"And you didn't see any other tracks?"

"No. If there were any, the rain probably washed them out."

Logan straightened, coming erect and leveling a measuring look at Laredo. "So you think the body was here before the storm broke?"

Hard amusement lifted one corner of Laredo's mouth. "Don't you?"

Echohawk smiled without humor. "As a matter of fact, I do." He backed away from the body, turned and retraced his route to the head of the hollow. He halted a few feet from Laredo and looked back at the scene. Then he lifted his gaze to the rough and rocky slopes west of them. "You say you live around here."

"I fixed up the old line shack up there in the foothills." Laredo indicated its direction with a nod of his head.

"What time did you get back last night?"

This was old ground. They had been over it already during the drive to the site. At Echohawk's suggestion, Laredo had ridden with him to the spot. But they both knew it hadn't been a suggestion Laredo could refuse to accept.

Familiar with the routine, Laredo repeated his previous answer. "It must have been somewhere around ten o'clock."

"And before that?"

"I left the feedlot around five o'clock, drove to headquarters and had supper at the cookshack, waited around for the storm to let up, and left around nine o'clock or thereabouts."

"Is that where you usually eat?"

"No. It was the first time," Laredo admitted, volunteering information he knew Echohawk would have quickly discovered on his own.

"Too bad you didn't come back before the storm hit," Echo-hawk remarked in a voice that pointed out the convenient change in Laredo's routine. "You might have found the body before the rain did its work."

"That thought has crossed my mind more than once," Laredo replied.

"I understand your mother lives up there with you. Did she mention seeing or hearing anything unusual yesterday?"

"No. But I'll ask her."

"I think I'll do that," Echohawk replied, a dry humor in the look that said he knew this was a game they were playing.

"Suit yourself."

"In fact, I think we'll take a ride up there now while we're waiting for the coroner to arrive," he announced.

The deputy on Laredo's right stirred. "Want me to ride along with you?"

Echohawk's pause was slight. During it, Laredo felt the probe of those gray eyes, gauging the degree of threat Laredo represented. "No, you and Garcia stay here. We shouldn't be long."

The walk back to the patrol vehicle was made in silence. Laredo slid into the passenger side and waited while Echohawk fastened his seat belt. Not a word was said until they were heading toward the old fire road.

"I had an interesting phone call yesterday morning." The comment by Echohawk was made casually, with no change in the expression on his chiseled features. "It was from a friend of mine at Treasury." Laredo mentally braced himself for the worst. "It seems the Mexican government is very interested in a man who sometimes uses the name Laredo."

"Did they say why?" Laredo asked as if Echohawk hadn't said anything out of the ordinary.

"He's wanted in the murder of a prison guard. As I understand it, this Laredo was part of a small group that broke two Americans out of a Mexican prison, killing a guard in the process."

"It's a good thing I'm not that Laredo," he stated smoothly. "A Mexican prison is the last place I would want to spend the rest of my life." Laredo focused his attention on the road ahead of them. "Your turn is just ahead."

"You fit his general description — blue eyes, light brown hair, somewhere between six-one and six-two."

"So do a lot of other men."

"It will be interesting to find out if there are any fingerprints on file."

Laredo swore inwardly. "Hopefully there

will be," he lied smoothly. "It's the quickest way to prove you're talking about two separate people."

"I agree."

Laredo's many trips up and down the slope to the line shack had worn a set of parallel tracks across the rough ground to point the way. Seconds after the patrol vehicle crested the foothill's shoulder, Hattie stepped out of the cabin, wearing an expression of mild curiosity.

She smiled pleasantly when Echohawk introduced himself. "It's a pleasure to meet you." She gave his hand a firm shake. "Although I have been expecting you."

"Really?" He managed to inject a request for an explanation in his single-word response.

"Not you in particular, but — after Laredo told me about finding the body, I expected someone in authority would come to find out what I might have seen or heard," Hattie explained.

"And what was that, Mrs. Smith?"

"Not much, I'm afraid. I do remember hearing a vehicle on the road sometime yesterday. It did stop for a while, then start up again and drive away. It didn't seem all that unusual at the time," she told him. "I assumed it was one of the ranch hands fixing fence or checking on livestock."

"What kind of vehicle was it?"

She shook her head. "I don't have any idea. I wasn't curious enough to look. And, as you can tell, the view of the road from here is somewhat limited."

"Yes, I noticed. Do you remember hearing anything else?"

"Like what?"

Laredo supplied the answer. "I think he wants to know if you heard a gunshot."

Hattie released a laughing breath of denial. "Definitely not. I would have mentioned that first thing. It isn't something as common as hearing a truck on the road."

"Do you keep any weapons here?"

She darted a quick glance at Laredo. "We have a .30/.30 Winchester."

"Would you mind showing it to me?" Echohawk watched her closely.

"Not at all. I'll get it for you."

When she turned toward the cabin, a voice came from inside. "Ask Logan to come in, Hattie."

Logan's reaction to the discovery of a third person was small but significant — a sudden tensing of muscle and a quick movement of his right hand to the holstered weapon at his waist. But it was the flicker of confusion and doubt in his expression that brought a slight curve to Laredo's mouth.

"I guess we sprang a little surprise on you, didn't we? Then again, maybe it isn't so little," Laredo said and moved past him toward the door.

"Please come in, Sheriff." Hattie paused in the doorway, holding the screen door open for him.

"No. Tell whoever your friend is to come out." Logan shifted a little closer to the cabin wall, ready to seek its protection and make himself a less easy target.

Slipping past Hattie, Laredo went inside, his gaze sliding to Chase. "I told you he was a careful man."

Chase took Hattie's place in the opening, making himself fully visible without setting foot outside. "I can't do that, Logan. It's better if I'm not seen here."

"Chase?" Logan still questioned what he was seeing. "You're alive?"

"Yes, and I plan on staying that way awhile longer. Come in." Chase moved away from the door.

Logan followed him into the line shack. "What are you doing here?" he demanded, anger showing at the way he and everyone had been tricked, both then and now.

"Why did you let us all believe you were dead?"

"At the time it suited my purpose." Chase crossed to the table and pulled out a chair.

"I always knew you were a hard man, Calder, but I don't think you realize what you put your daughter and grandchildren through, not to mention —" Logan stopped, eyes narrowing. "Jessy knows you're alive, doesn't she." It was a statement, not a question. "All the times Culley saw her slipping up here, it was to see you."

"She knows," Chase confirmed. "But she is the only one who knows outside of those here in this cabin."

"Why?" His gray glance flicked to the red welt that reached into the hairline above Chase's temple. "And what happened to your head?"

"You might as well sit down. This could take a few minutes." Chase gestured to one of the other chairs and sat down. "Hattie, will you pour some coffee for us?"

Keeping to the facts, Chase told Logan as much as he knew about the attempt on his life and its aftermath. On occasions, he deferred to Laredo, letting him fill in any blanks he could. Logan listened without interruption until he was finished.

"I have trouble believing Markham is behind this." Logan continued to mull that one over. "There are a few circumstances that appear to point in his direction, but you haven't built any case against him — or given me a good reason to pin my suspicions on him."

"I remember something, but . . . I can't quite remember what it is." The frustration of that slipped into Chase's voice, giving an edge to it.

"So, why did you decide to make yourself known now?" Logan lifted his coffee cup.

"O'Rourke's murder."

Logan nodded in understanding. "As close as the body was found, it was only a matter of time before you would be discovered."

Laredo disagreed. "If Chase didn't want you to know he was here, it would have taken dogs to find him."

"Laredo's right," Chase confirmed. "My decision to come forward has nothing to do with fear of discovery. O'Rourke's death changed things because I'm certain Markham killed him."

"Now you really are reaching, Chase," Logan said with a mildly amused shake of his head. "Markham had even less reason to kill O'Rourke than he did you."

Chase replied with a question of his own. "What can you tell me about the note that came up missing? The one Jessy gave to Cat. I understand that Tara is convinced that Jessy took it."

"You think Markham is behind that," Logan guessed.

"Why not?" Chase countered. "He wouldn't have known what was written on it. For all Markham knew, it could have been something that would have pointed to him."

Logan thoughtfully rubbed a hand across his mouth, then glanced at Chase, a stony hardness in his gray eyes. "You may have just convinced me, Chase. I remember now that after the note came up missing, Culley made a point to remind Cat that he had seen Markham poking around the desk."

"And Markham mentioned to Jessy that he had seen O'Rourke at Fedderson's the other morning. My guess is that's when Culley accused Markham of taking it — and ultimately sealed his fate," Chase stated. "I don't know when or where Markham did the killing, but I think he probably dumped the body around here in an attempt to throw suspicion on Laredo, especially if he had somehow learned that you were checking on him."

"And finding some answers, too." Logan pushed his cup away, glancing up when Hattie breathed in sharply. "Just what do you know about him, Chase?"

"I know he saved my life. And if you are referring to that business in Mexico, that happened a good many years ago," Chase replied. "I'm not going to tell you to ignore it. Neither one of us would have much respect for the other if I did. But I am going to ask that you forget it for a while. Whatever else you might say against him, Laredo is the kind of man you want watching your back when things get hot. And they *will* get hot very soon. That note has Markham running scared right now, but it's a smart scared. Laredo and I agree that he has probably picked out his next target. But we don't know if it's Jessy or Cat."

"Now I get it." Logan nodded. "That's why you decided to come back from the dead — to make Markham readjust his sights. You plan on becoming a decoy."

"It's the quickest way that I know to flush him out," Chase stated. "O'Rourke's death made me realize that I don't have the luxury of waiting until I completely re-cover my memory."

Logan turned to Laredo. "So why didn't you tell me any of this on the way here? You could have saved us both a lot of time."

Laredo nodded toward Chase. "It was his play to make. Not mine. I just follow orders. He said to bring you here alone, and that's what I did."

In order to do that, Logan realized that Laredo had made himself a suspect in O'Rourke's death. It spoke loudly of the loyalty and trust Laredo had in Chase. And it had Logan looking at him with a new respect.

He brought his attention back to Chase. "So what's your next move?"

"You are going to help me stage my re-turn to the Triple C," Chase replied calmly. "No one else must know that I've been staying here at the Boar's Nest, and that includes Cat. We can't afford to have anyone think that Laredo was a part of this. Will you do it?"

"Count me in," Logan agreed without hesitation.

Laredo spoke up, "I hope that means you won't object if I start carrying again."

Logan's pause was a deliberate one. "I

didn't hear you say that."

Laredo's smile was slow and lazy. "Thanks."

"So, when do you want to return, Chase?"

"The sooner the better," he replied. "Later on today you can tell Cat that I called you and that I will be flying into Miles City tomorrow. Explain as much of the truth as she needs to know — that I was mugged, suffered from amnesia, and finally remembered who I was. Laredo can drop me off at the airport in the morning, and I'll wait there until you come to pick me up."

"Sounds simple enough." Logan nodded. After a pause, he added, "Although, to be honest, Chase, it's not clear in my mind why I'm sitting here now. You don't really need my help to stage your return. You could have done it on your own and kept me in the dark."

"I considered it," Chase admitted. "But you wouldn't have known there was a possibility Cat was in danger. That wasn't a risk I was willing to take."

"I should have guessed," Logan murmured.

"Laredo will call you sometime late this afternoon. The two of you can decide what time would be best. That will be the alleged call from me. Whatever you do, don't keep the call a secret. The sooner Markham gets word that I am still alive, the less likely he'll be to look at anyone else until he deals with me."

Chapter Eighteen

All over the Triple C there was a kind of electricity in the air. The range telegraph buzzed with it. People everywhere seemed to walk with a lighter step. The name that had rarely been mentioned since the day of his premature burial was on everyone's lips.

Chase Calder was alive.

Rumor and fact spread from one end of the ranch to the other. And no one seemed to care if one masqueraded as the other. They welcomed any excuse to call someone else and pass on the latest.

By midmorning Jessy had fielded dozens of calls. Regardless of their initial content, each ended with the same question: when would Chase arrive? All were frustrated by her inability to be more specific than somewhere around noon or one o'clock.

Even her own mother found it hard to believe she couldn't be more exact. Judy Niles had arrived at The Homestead shortly before nine o'clock in the morning, ostensibly to give the house a thorough cleaning so everything would be neat and tidy when Chase arrived. She spent almost as much time chattering at Jessy as she did cleaning.

Finding it difficult to maintain the pretext that she knew little more about Chase than anyone else, Jessy left her mother to answer the phone while she made her escape from the house. With no particular destination, Jessy struck out toward the corrals.

She was halfway across the ranch yard when she recognized Laredo's pickup coming down the lane. She stopped and waited for him to arrive. He pulled up alongside her, an arm draped over the open driver's side window.

"Good morning." His smile was warm and faintly intimate.

"Good morning." Jessy stepped closer and casually laid a hand on the pickup's sun-warmed metal skin. "Did you drop him off at the airport?" she asked, referring to Chase.

"Delivered him safe and sound," Laredo confirmed.

"The telephone hasn't stopped ringing all morning. Did you know that Chase has been in a coma until a few days ago?" she asked, passing on one of the many rumors making the circuit.

"I didn't know that." Laredo grinned.

"Somebody else told me that they had heard he had been in Mexico all this time."

"Amazing. What about Markham? Has he called?"

"No. It makes me wonder if he's heard."

"He has. You can bet on it."

The mere mention of his name altered the tenor of their conversation, adding a tension to it. "Cat called before they left for the airport," Jessy said. "O'Rourke's funeral is set for eleven o'clock Saturday morning. Graveside services will be held at the old cemetery."

For the most part, Culley's death had become lost in the excitement of Chase's imminent return. When anyone bothered to remember it, it was usually in connection with Cat, invariably framed in a remark that noted the irony of losing her uncle on the same day she found out her father was alive. Not even the fact that O'Rourke had died of a gunshot wound seemed to arouse much interest. Most people seemed willing to believe someone had been shooting at a coyote or prairie dog and the bullet went astray — one of those tragic freak accidents. Considering the way O'Rourke ghosted over the countryside, they doubted that the shooter had known anyone was in the area.

"I hear there is a big barbecue planned for Sunday to welcome Chase back," Laredo remarked.

Jessy nodded. "My mom told me about it. There seemed to be a groundswell to do something to mark the occasion." She paused, her thoughts turning to another concern that was never far from her mind. "I still think Chase should have laid low awhile longer. I know Culley's death made that difficult. Just the same, though, I don't think it's wise for him to come forward now."

"It was his decision. Whether it's wise or not doesn't matter anymore. It's done." It was a statement that pointed out the futility of second-guessing now.

Jessy understood the reasoning behind the decision — to force Monte to make another attempt at Chase, hopefully panicking him into a rash one. There was always the possibility Monte would wait to see how much of his memory Chase had regained, but somehow Jessy knew that wasn't likely.

"At least there shouldn't be any problems at the barbecue. Monte isn't apt to try anything with so many people around." She found some relief in that thought.

"Don't count on it," Laredo warned. "Markham has to know he will have trouble luring Chase away from the ranch. And there aren't many places he can lie in wait for Chase around here without running the risk of being seen. The crowd and confusion of a barbecue might just be the kind of setup he wants."

She felt a chill of foreboding. "You'll be here at headquarters from now on, won't you?"

"Don't worry," he reassured her. "I plan to stick as close to Chase as his shadow."

"Where are you headed now?"

"Back up to the Boar's Nest. If I'm going to be staying around here, Hattie will need the truck. If Markham shows up while I'm gone, let me know his reaction."

"Will do," Jessy promised and stepped back from the truck, watching as he drove away.

The highway cut a long gray line through the plains of eastern Montana. The traffic thickened, signaling the nearness of a city. Spotting a signpost ahead, Cat leaned forward in the passenger seat, her expression a mix of anxiety and excitement.

"Seven more miles," she announced. "Thank heavens. This is the longest drive

451

to Miles City I ever remember making. I wish now we had flown here in the ranch plane."

"It wouldn't have been any different. The flight would have seemed twice as long." Logan took his gaze from the highway long enough to run a glance over Cat. Throughout the trip she had been a bundle of restless energy, rarely still, all edgy nerves with emotions running the gamut.

She turned her face toward the side window for a moment. Swinging back toward him, she asked for at least the tenth time, "Are you absolutely certain it was Dad you talked to?"

"Positive. His voice is unmistakable. The minute I heard it I knew it was Chase even though my mind told me it was impossible," Logan replied. "It was an eerie moment."

"But what if it's an imposter? You told me yourself that the man claimed to have amnesia. He could remember some things, but not others. There wasn't any way he could prove to you he was Chase Calder."

"We'll know soon enough whether or not he's an imposter." Logan made the turn onto the road that led to the airport. "But I'm positive he'll turn out to be the genuine article."

"I hope you are right." Cat propped an elbow on the window ledge and closed her hand, holding it against her chin. "I'm just afraid to believe it, though."

Reaching over, Logan covered her hand, aware of the emotional roller coaster she had ridden during the last twenty-four hours, first learning of her uncle's death, then receiving the stunning news that her father was alive.

From the backseat, Quint asked, "Do you think he will remember us, Dad?"

Logan glanced at his son's reflection in the rearview mirror, observing the troubled light in his eyes. "I think he will."

"What time did you say his flight is supposed to land?" Cat focused all her attention on the terminal building. It was a small one by big-city standards.

"In about fifteen minutes," Logan replied. "I'll let you two out and go park."

"Mom, look!" Quint hurriedly unbuckled his seat belt and leaned over the back of the front seat to point. "Isn't that Grampa?"

Cat stared at the tall, thick-chested man standing close to the building's entrance, his dark hair shot with silver, a duffel bag sitting at his feet. She breathed in sharply in recognition.

"It's him, Quint." The emotion of the moment made her voice small and thin. She fumbled frantically with the clasp of her own seat belt. She barely gave Logan a chance to pull up to the curb before she was out the passenger door and running to greet him. Quint wasn't far behind her. Logan took his time, content to observe the moment of reunion. The unbridled joy in the faces of his wife and son moved him, but he knew too many things that they didn't for him to share in it.

Childlike, Cat threw herself into Chase's arms and hugged him tight. "You're alive. You're really alive," she murmured, reassured by his solidness. "I was so afraid it wasn't true."

Chase smoothed a big hand over her sleek black hair and tilted her head up. His dark gaze moved over her face and halted on the sheen of tears in her green eyes.

"I had forgotten how much you look like your mother." There was a note of wonder in his voice.

Closing her eyes, Cat caught hold of his hand and pressed a kiss into his palm, a deeply felt joy and gratitude all mixing together to steal her voice. She felt the light touch of his hand on her shoulder and opened her eyes to again drink in the sight of his familiar craggy features.

"Logan told me about O'Rourke. I'm sorry, Cat."

She nodded in response. The loss of her uncle was still too fresh. Culley had been a constant presence in her life for too many years, not always seen but always there, her own personal guardian angel. Cat doubted that few people understood just how much she would miss that so-called crazy old man.

"Hi, Grampa." Quint's quiet voice reminded her that this reunion wasn't hers alone.

Cat turned in her father's arms, letting a hand slide behind his back while she directed his attention to her son. Uncertain of how much memory he had recovered, she said, "I don't know if you remember, but this is your grandson, Dad."

A smile gentled his hard features. "Are you sure this is Quint? This young man is about an inch taller than the boy I remember."

"I am not, Grampa." Quint managed to smile at the half-teasing remark and gazed at the man with his heart in his eyes.

Chase crouched down to eye level. "Maybe not a full inch," he revised his earlier opinion. "I'm glad about that. It means you aren't too big to give me a hug."

Quint was in his arms almost before he opened them. Chase had only a glimpse of the tears that sprang into Quint's eyes before the boy buried his face in the crook of Chase's neck, wrapping his arms fiercely around him.

"I missed you, Grampa." His voice was choked to a throaty whisper.

The sun was nearing its zenith when Jessy returned to The Hometead for lunch. The twins barely gave her time to close the door before they planted themselves in front of her and assaulted her with questions.

"Where's my grampa?" Trey demanded with an impatient scowl.

"You said he was coming home this morning," Laura added in quick reminder.

"Yeah," Trey echoed the thought. "Morning's over. How come he's not here?"

"He's on his way. I promise," Jessy assured them as the phone rang. Judy Niles answered it, her voice coming from the living room.

Laura sighed with great annoyance. "That's what Gramma said, too."

"How come it's taking him so long?" Trey put his hands on his hips, adopting a challenging stance.

"Because your aunt Cat had to drive all the way to Miles City to pick him up, then drive all the way back again," Jessy explained.

Trey's dark eyes narrowed with suspicion. "Did Quint go with her?"

"Probably," Jessy admitted and mentally braced herself for the uproar the news was sure to cause.

"How come he gets to see Grampa first?" Trey protested.

"That's not fair." Laura's lower lip jutted out. "He's our grampa, too."

"I know." She tried a change of subject. "What did Grandma fix for lunch today? Shall we go see?"

Trey wasn't about to be steered into the dining room. "I don't want lunch. I want my grampa."

"I'm gonna see if he's here yet." Laura dashed to the door.

Trey raced after her. Turning, Jessy started to call them back then sighed in defeat and let them go. Two sets of hands fought briefly to pull the heavy door open.

Before she even crossed the threshold, Laura squealed with excitement, "I see him! He's here, Momma! He's here!"

At almost the same instant Jessy caught the crunching sound of tires rolling across gravel. She moved quickly toward the door as her mother hurried out of the living room.

"You're so stupid, Laura," Trey accused with contempt. "That's not Grampa. That's Mr. Markham."

The announcement tingled through Jessy's nerve ends like an electrical charge, halting her in midstride for a fraction of a second. Head up, Jessy continued to the door, reaching it as Trey came back inside, shoulders slumped in disappointment.

Halfway into the hallway, Judy Niles changed direction. "I'll go set another place for lunch," she said to Jessy.

Offering no response, Jessy walked onto the veranda, cognizant that she couldn't let her new wariness of Markham show. Laura's presence made it easy. Ever the social butterfly, Laura ran to the top of the steps to welcome their arriving guest.

"Hello, Mr. Markham," Laura issued her breezy greeting as he approached the front steps. "I thought you were my grampa. He's coming home today."

The vaguely preoccupied look vanished from his expression as Monte paused with one foot on the steps, his hazel eyes locking on Jessy. "Then it is true," he said with a slightly incredulous frown. "Chase is alive."

"Amazing, isn't it." The rejoinder came easily to Jessy, thanks to all the practice she'd had fielding phone calls from others seeking confirmation.

"Amazing hardly describes it," he declared, mounting the steps. "It rightly should be called a miracle. How did it happen? Where has he been all this time?"

"In Texas, I guess. We don't have many details," Jessy told him. "I'm not sure Chase does, either. He has amnesia. From what Logan told me, not all of his memory is back yet. There are still parts that are missing for him."

"What a frightening experience it must be not to know who you are or where you live." An eyebrow arched in idle contemplation of it.

"It had to have been awful," Jessy agreed. "We were about to sit down to lunch. Why don't you join us?"

"It seems I always arrive at mealtimes," Monte replied with a touch of rueful amusement.

"You can't refuse. Mother has already set a place for you at the table," Jessy told him.

"Yeah, if you stay, you can see Grampa

when he comes," Laura inserted.

"I wouldn't want to intrude at such a personal time," Monte began, then sharply turned his head to stare at the Suburban pulling into the yard.

"That's Aunt Cat." The words were barely out of Laura's mouth before the significance of them registered on her. She breathed in sharply, her mouth rounding in a silent "o" of excitement as she looked up at Jessy. "Grampa's here," she murmured. "I gotta tell Trey." She scampered across the veranda, pushed the door open, and stuck her head inside, issuing a very unladylike yell, "This time it really is Grampa!"

"I think she's excited," Jessy said to Monte, using the comment as an excuse to observe him, alert for any hint of apprehension.

"She should be," he declared and turned to face the drive with a look of avid interest.

Trey tore out of the house, nearly knocking Laura down in his haste. He launched himself down the steps and reached the passenger door when it opened. Chase swung his legs out. But Trey didn't give him a chance to get out as he scrambled onto his lap.

"I knew you'd come back, Grampa,"

Trey stated as Laura crowded close, seeking to claim her grandfather's attention. "I knew it all the time."

Jessy was content to observe the touching reunion between her children and their grandfather. Not until her mother emerged from the house, hastily wiping her hands on her apron, did Jessy remember that she should be showing some eagerness to welcome Chase home as well.

"My, but he looks wonderful, doesn't he?" her mother remarked with a mixture of surprise and relief.

"He certainly does." Jessy crossed to the steps, conscious that Monte remained behind.

"Oh dear, do you see that awful scar above his temple?" Judy Niles murmured.

Jessy made an affirmative sound, but she was too busy looking at Laredo as he crossed the ranch yard with long, unhurried strides. Even from this distance, she could tell it was Monte he was watching.

Almost as quickly as Trey climbed onto Chase's lap, he scooted off it and grabbed hold of his hand to pull him out of the Suburban. "Come on, Grampa. Ya gotta see my new horse. His name's Joe."

"Joe. That's a good name." Chase stood up, a little stiff after the long ride.

"You can show him your horse later." Jessy briefly placed a detaining hand on Trey's head, then stepped forward to give Chase a light kiss on the cheek. "Welcome home, Chase."

"It's good to be back," he told her, but each knew it was part of an act they were going through and only they knew it.

"Grampa's not sick, Momma," Laura informed her and tipped her blond head way back to look up at Chase. "Momma said you got 'nesia, but you remembered me."

Jessy experienced a moment of unease, aware that Monte had to be listening to every word. But Chase simply chuckled.

"I can remember a few things, and I am very glad you are one of them," he told Laura.

With that settled, Laura moved on to more important matters. "Did you bring me a present, Grampa? You were in Texas an awfully long time."

Chase didn't immediately answer and glanced at Jessy instead. "Do I usually bring presents for them?"

Jessy couldn't tell if he genuinely didn't remember or was merely pretending. "No, you don't. And you shouldn't be asking," she admonished Laura and drew her aside, making room for her mother.

Taking no chances, she introduced herself, "I'm Judy Niles, Chase. Jessy's mother." She fairly beamed at the sight of him. "It's so good to have you back with us."

"I remember you, Judy." Chase's smile was wide. His glance went past her. "Is Stumpy here, too?"

"No, but I expect he will be," Judy declared. "He's just like all of us at the Triple C. It's such a miracle to have you back with us that we're half afraid to believe it until we see you with our own eyes."

While her mother chattered away to Chase, Jessy stole a glance at Monte. He stood near the pillar at the top of the steps, looking perfectly at ease, but his gaze was locked on Chase.

"Doesn't he look good, Jessy?" Cat murmured near her elbow, pulling Jessy's attention away from Markham.

"He certainly does." She smiled at Cat's glow of happiness.

"He told me on the way here that one of the first things he remembered was Captain. A longhorn steer, for heaven's sake." Cat shook her head in amusement. "Isn't that just like a Calder?"

Catching a movement in her side vision,

Jessy turned her head. Monte was coming down the steps at a casual pace. She knew at once that he intended to approach Chase.

He waited until Judy Niles finished her sentence before he stepped forward. "I don't mean to intrude," he interrupted with a smoothness that was completely natural to him. "But I wanted to add my welcome to all the others. I'm Monte Markham." He extended a hand in formal greeting. "I am glad that, like Lazarus, you have come back to walk among us."

"Mr. Markham." Chase took his hand and stared intently at him. The impression he gave was that of someone straining to recall something important.

"Monte is the Triple C's newest neighbor, Dad," Cat inserted in an attempt to help him identify Monte. "He bought the old Gil-more place."

Chase responded with a slow and thoughtful nod. "It was good of you to be on hand today, Markham."

"Sheer coincidence," Monte assured him with a bluff heartiness.

There was a faint narrowing of Chase's eyes. "You are in cattle."

"Indeed, sir, I am. In fact, you were to be my guest when you returned from

Texas. An invitation I extend to you again. I am very eager for you to see the herd of Highland cattle I recently imported."

"Highland cattle," Chase repeated.

"The finest, I assure you," Monte insisted, then added dismissively, "But don't let me get started extolling the many attributes of the breed. We'll save that for another occasion. I am certain you are anxious to go inside and relax after your long flight. I won't keep you."

When Monte retreated toward his vehicle, Judy Niles protested, "Aren't you joining us for lunch? I set a place for you at the table."

"Another time," Monte said and glanced at Chase. "Your first hours at home should be spent with family."

"If you won't stay for lunch, then you must come to the barbecue we are having for Chase on Sunday," Judy insisted. "It will start at one and last until the cows come home."

"I would enjoy that. Thank you." Monte nodded his acceptance and continued to the Range Rover.

Laredo arrived just as Monte started up the engine. "Hello, Chase. Remember me?" A twinkle of impish humor was in his blue eyes.

Chase stared at him for a full second before he murmured with amazement, "What are you doing here?" His surprise looked so genuine that Jessy wanted to applaud.

"Working," Laredo replied and gestured in Jessy's direction. "Your daughter-in-law put me on the payroll."

Chase pumped his arm with a two-handed shake. "Where is your mother? Did she come with you?"

"She did."

"Wonderful. It will be good to see her." Chase turned to Cat. "I may have just found the solution to the trouble you mentioned Jessy was having finding someone to take charge of the house and cooking chores. Laredo's mother is an excellent cook, as I recall. Have you met her?"

"No." A flicker of discomfort crossed Cat's expression. Jessy suspected Cat was recalling her skepticism that Chase knew these people. It was a well-founded skepticism, but that wasn't something they could tell her yet. "I haven't had the pleasure."

"We'll soon correct that," Chase said with an easy smile and glanced at Jessy. "In the meantime, you might want to talk to Hattie and see if she would be interested in taking on the responsibility."

"That's a good idea," Jessy agreed. "I'll talk to her."

"Speaking of food, what are we doing standing around out here. Lunch is ready." Judy Niles shooed them toward the door.

Jessy lagged behind to have a quick word with Laredo. "Chase deserves an Oscar," she said in a low undertone.

"It was quite a performance, wasn't it?" Laredo said with a grin. "Just about the equal of Markham's."

"He said he was coming to the barbecue," she told him.

"I expected that."

"I'm half surprised he didn't stay for lunch." Her glance strayed to the thinning dust cloud that lingered over the ranch lane, left by Monte's departure.

"Right now I imagine he's worried, not so much about what Chase might remember, but when. This is one time when Monte has to be hoping that out of sight really will mean out of mind."

"So why would he come on Sunday?"

"I don't know. But in the meantime, you can bet he'll be making some plans. Stay alert." It was more of a reminder than a warning.

"I will." She paused, angling toward the steps. "I'd better go in. There is bound to be a fight over who gets to sit next to Grampa at the table."

Laredo nodded his understanding. "I'll talk to you later. And don't worry. I'll be sticking close by."

As Jessy climbed the veranda steps, she couldn't help thinking that a man with a rifle wouldn't have to get close.

Chapter Nineteen

T-bone steaks as large as dinner plates sizzled side by side with thick rib eyes on the massive grill. Three cowboys-turned-chefs kept watch over the meat. One was armed with a spray bottle to douse the grease fires that frequently erupted.

Smoke and heat rolled from the grill area, but nobody minded. The gathering was a celebratory one, and the mood was festive. Pennants were strung about the large gazebo near the river's edge, their bright colors fluttering in the light breeze, while a huge homemade banner hung above its entrance. Written across it in big bold letters were the words WELCOME HOME, BOSS!

A few of the cowboys who were musically inclined had taken over the gazebo, turning it into a country-western bandstand.

Mixing in with the laughter and constant hum of voices were rhythmic guitar strummings and lively fiddle licks, underscored by the thump of an upright bass with a harmonica occasionally taking a ride.

Most of the cowboys lounged in their lawn chairs, nursing a cold beer, alternately swapping stories and listening to the music. A couple of the older ranch hands stood guard at the beer kegs to make certain no youngsters snitched a taste. Which made a few of them more determined to do so.

As always, the women were in charge of setting out the food. Everybody brought something, usually two or three different dishes. In all, three banquet tables were set up to hold the array of salads, vegetables, breads, and desserts. The arrival of each new guest required a rearranging of the bowls and platters already on the tables.

Jessy paused to chase a fly away from the edge of a cellophane-covered dish. Out of the corner of her eye, she noticed a small hand reaching into the potato-chip bowl.

"No snacking before mealtime," she admonished, quick to intervene. At gatherings the size of this one, everybody parented everybody else's child.

"But I'm hungry." The Simmons boy scowled in protest.

"Have a carrot." She took a stick from

one of the many relish trays and handed it to him.

He took it, mumbled a disgruntled "thanks" and walked off, none too happy with a carrot but resigned that it was the best he could do. Automatically Jessy scanned the crowd for a glimpse of the twins. She quickly spotted Trey twirling his rope a few yards from Chase. Since Chase had returned, Trey had rarely let him out of his sight.

Jessy's gaze made another sweep over the area, but failed to locate Laura among the scattering of blond heads. If Trey had come up missing, she wouldn't have been surprised, but she had never known Laura to wander off.

Deciding that she must be somewhere around the gazebo, Jessy started in that direction and met Amy Trumbo making her way back to the food tables. "By any chance, have you seen Laura?" she asked.

"No, I haven't." But the question prompted Amy to start looking for her. "Here she comes." She pointed toward the area east of the barn that had been transformed into a parking lot.

Jessy turned, her glance instantly lighting on Laura's familiar blond curls as she happily skipped alongside Tara. Buck Haskell trailed both of them, toting a large basket and an insulated jug. Other men had trailed their wives, laden with dishes. Yet there was something in the way Tara carried herself that made it clear this man worked for her, thus turning a simple arrival into an entrance.

As usual, Tara looked the picture of high fashion in designer sunglasses and a halter-style sundress, her black hair sleeked away from her face and secured at the nape of her neck with a filmy chiffon scarf. And there was Laura, taking it all in.

Jessy wondered how the woman had the gall to show up at the barbecue after all she had done to undermine her position. But gall was something Tara had in abundance.

"What a marvelous party, Jessy." Tara made a regal survey of the scene. "It has been ages since this place was so decorative and festive. This reminds me of all the parties Ty and I used to throw here."

"You'll find this one is much more simple. We didn't import a chef or hire a catering staff for it." The jibe was smoothly delivered, but effective just the same.

"What a pity," said Tara with acid sweetness. "I would have thought Chase's return would warrant such a special effort."

"In this case, the ranch hands are the ones who are giving the party. And they are doing it from their hearts, not their wallets. It makes it that much more special," Jessy informed her. "Which is something you never quite understood."

"Whereas you always have, haven't you? After all, you were born and raised here." Tara's smile was all saccharine.

But Jessy took little notice of it. Laredo had moved into her line of vision. With a lifting tilt of his head, he signaled that Markham had arrived. Jessy glanced toward the barn and ranch yard, seeking to locate him.

She was quick to spot him. Never one to blend in, Monte sported a crisp white polo shirt, khaki-colored Bermuda shorts, matching socks, loafers, and aviator glasses, attire that guaranteed he would stand out in the sea of cowboy hats, blue jeans, and boots. Again Monte carried the same oversized hamper that he had brought to their picnic a few days earlier.

"What is it?" Curious to learn what had caught Jessy's attention, Tara turned to look. "It's Monte." Raising her hand, she gave him a cheery wave. When he altered his course toward them, Tara murmured to Jessy, "How nice that you also invited some civilized guests."

Tired of trading insults with the woman, Jessy ignored the remark and concentrated on Monte. A new tension strung her nerves.

After the usual exchange of greetings, which Tara managed to monopolize, Monte scanned the crowd. "Where is our guest of honor?"

"The last time I saw him he was over by the cottonwoods talking to the Garveys." Jessy nodded in that general direction.

"I see him," Monte confirmed.

"Isn't it amazing to have him with us again?" Tara said. "I know everyone is greatly relieved that he's once more in charge of the ranch." She glanced pointedly at Jessy. "Well, perhaps not everyone. After all, Jessy did lose her job. But I'm sure she will adjust to taking orders again, instead of being the one to give them."

"Knowing Jessy, I am certain it will be an easy adjustment," Monte stated with total unconcern.

"Of course," Tara murmured, making it clear she retained her skepticism. Chin high, she turned to Jessy. "Buck has a few items I had my chef prepare. I'll have him leave them with you. But I see these tables seem to be strictly for food. Where are the drinks?"

"Over there." Jessy gestured to the beer kegs. "There is beer on tap, and the stock tank is filled with a variety of sodas on ice."

"Is that all?" Tara managed to inject a wealth of criticism in the phrase. In an exaggerated Texas drawl, she added, "Honey, don't you know that a barbecue isn't complete without a jug of margaritas? How fortunate that I brought one." She made a graceful turn to the patiently waiting Buck Haskell. "Let me have the jug so I can personally deliver this much needed addition to the bar." He surrendered it into her care without a word. "I'll see you in a bit, Monte," Tara promised and swept away while Amy Trumbo relieved Buck of the other items he carried.

"Tara is in fine form today, isn't she," Monte remarked dryly. "But jealousy rarely allows a person to hold their tongue."

"I don't think I'll comment on that," Jessy replied, aware that his observation was much too true, and focused on the picnic hamper. "Obviously you brought more food for us."

"I did, indeed." He set the hamper on the ground and began to unload it, passing the dishes to Jessy. "This time I decided to bring a sampling of traditional British fare, including shepherd's pie and some bangers."

"Bangers? What on earth is that?"

"I imagine the American equivalent would be a frankfurter."

"They should be a hit with the children," Jessy murmured absently, momentarily distracted by the sight of Chase and Hattie drifting toward the grill area.

"The man with Jessy, the one in shorts" — Hattie stole a glance at the pair, being careful not to stare — "is that Markham?"

"That's him," Chase confirmed without bothering to look.

"Laredo definitely won't have any trouble keeping track of him in that outfit. He stands out like a stalk of corn in a cotton patch," Hattie observed.

Chase laughed low in his throat. "He does that."

She sighed heavily. "I'll be glad when this is over."

He saw the worry in her eyes. He started to tell her that everything would work out fine, but Hattie wasn't a woman to be taken in by empty assurances. She knew as well as he did that life came with no guarantees.

Instead Chase took her arm and steered her toward the grill, keeping upwind of the smoke. "The steaks smell good, don't they?"

Catching his remark, Stumpy Niles turned. "Better pick yourself one, boss. We haven't got ear tags to mark it, but we can burn your brand on it with a running iron."

Chase froze, not hearing anything after "ear tags." There was an almost audible click in his head, unlocking the door to a whole roomful of memories.

"Are you all right, boss?" Stumpy asked, worried by Chase's sightless stare.

Chase blinked, and waited, but all of it was still there. "I'm fine, Stumpy." His smile was as cool as the determined gleam in his eyes.

"Did you want to pick out a steak?"

"No need. It's Calder beef. There isn't a bad one in the bunch." The remark drew grins of pride from the cowboys manning the grill, but Chase didn't stick around to chat with them. Instead he moved away, his gaze scanning the throng until he located Laredo.

"You remembered something, didn't you?" Hattie guessed.

"The one damned thing that has eluded

me all this time." Raising a hand, he motioned for Laredo to join him.

"Do you see Logan?"

"No." But Hattie started looking for him.

"What did you need, Chase?" Laredo halted beside him and kept his eye on Markham, who was still by the food tables talking to Jessy.

"I think I just remembered what this is all about," Chase told him. "When I was checking on Markham for George Seymour, I had two different people tell me they owned the same pen of cattle. Markham had brokered the deal for both of them. There was a folder in the rental car that had a list of ear tags. The banker in Texas had made the loan on one of the deals. I wanted to check my list against the one he had been given as proof of collateral to see if they matched. I wanted to be certain of my facts before I confronted Markham."

"And he caught wind of it somehow," Laredo surmised. "Sounds like a helluva scam — selling the same cattle to two different parties."

"My guess is this wasn't the first time," Chase said. "More than likely it's some sort of pyramid deal. A Ponzi scheme, I think they call it."

"Ponzi." A laugh gurgled from Hattie's throat. "That's the word you were trying to remember. Not Carlo Ponti."

Laredo frowned. "What are you talking about?"

Still smiling, Hattie shook her head, dismissing the subject. "Nothing important, just a private conversation between Duke and me."

He took her word for it. "Better track down Logan and tell him what you remember," he said to Chase, his attention once again directed at Markham. "There he goes," he observed, already shifting into action. "Looks like he's headed back to his Range Rover. I'll tag along to be sure. Go find Logan," he said again and moved off.

Careful to stay well behind Markham, Laredo set a course that angled in a slightly different direction yet kept Markham in his range of vision. He made a quick scan of the vehicles, trying to spot where Markham had parked. As late as Markham had arrived, Laredo doubted he had found a place close to the barbecue site. More than likely it was somewhere in the ranch yard.

Laredo slipped into the maze of parked trucks, satisfied to merely catch glimpses of Markham. He never caught Markham looking around to see if he was being watched. The man simply kept walking, lugging that oversized hamper, in no apparent hurry at all to reach his vehicle.

As Laredo suspected, Markham turned into the row of pickups parked in front of the barn. Within seconds he lost sight of him. Only then did Laredo quicken his pace, but it was an automatic thing, not done with any sense of urgency.

When he drew level with the spot, he glanced down the row. There was Markham's Range Rover, the fourth vehicle from the end. Laredo headed in the general direction of a blue pickup parked beyond it close to the corral. He kept stealing glances at the narrow walkway on the driver's side of the Range Rover, trying to spot Markham. The closer he got, the more uneasy he became.

Markham wasn't there, not in the vehicle or anywhere near it.

Laredo grimly scanned the entire area. There was no one around except for two boys carrying fishing poles and a tackle box. Which left only one place where Markham could be — in the barn.

That uneasy feeling turned into a fullfledged fear that manifested as a kind of anger. Laredo swore bitterly under his breath, torn between wanting to warn Chase and needing to stop Markham. Instinct told him there wasn't enough time to reach Chase. Knowing he only had one choice, he reached inside his boot and pulled out his pistol.

He yelled to the two boys, "Get Logan — and get him quick! Tell him we've got trouble." Halting, they stared wide-eyed at the gun in his hand. "Run!"

Laredo heard the tackle box hit the ground, but he didn't hang around to watch them take off. He moved to the side door and slipped inside. No lights were on, giving a shadowy darkness to the interior. He took a step to the side and listened to the eerie stillness. Markham had to be somewhere toward the back, but where?

Hugging close to the stalls, Laredo began moving along the alleyway, constantly scanning the shadows and upper reaches of the barn. His heightened senses magnified every sound from the whisper of his clothing to the hammering of his pulse.

There were too many places for Markham to hide in the massive old barn. Laredo knew he was running out of time to find him.

"I know you're in here, Markham!" He lifted his voice, letting it echo through the timbered rafters. He strained to catch some sound that would betray Markham's location, but all he caught was a faint scrape, coming from somewhere off to his left. "Give it up, Markham! Even if you get Chase, you'll have to get past me!"

There was a faint *thump* mixed in with a muted *chink*. The tack room. Laredo remembered there was a window in it that overlooked the river and the barbecue site.

Laredo worked his way toward it, sinking deeper into the concealing shadows of the opposite wall. Markham had to be sweating now.

Determined to increase the pressure, Laredo called again, "Even if you get lucky and get past me, Logan will be waiting for you. Chase remembered everything. By now Logan's already heard the whole story. And we both know ballistics will match the slug they took out of O'Rourke to your rifle. You're finished, Mar —"

He was still in midword when the tackroom door flew open. Simultaneous with a muzzle flash was the reverberating *boom* of a high-powered rifle. At almost the same instant that Laredo squeezed the trigger, a board not three inches from his head exploded in a shower of splinters. The rifle clattered across the concrete alleyway.

The sudden silence was deafening. Wisps of gunsmoke hung in the air, its acrid odor mingling with the hay smell. Laredo kept his gun pointed at the bare-legged man lying motionless across the tack room's threshold. Sweat ran down Laredo's face, and his ears still rang with the thunderous clap from the rifle while his breathing ran shallow and fast. He worked to even it out.

The barn's side door burst open, letting in a long flood of light. Laredo wheeled as Logan ducked inside, gun at the ready.

"It's okay, Logan." Laredo raised his weapon skyward. "It's over."

Still cautious, Logan moved out of the shadows and slowly approached the body. He kicked the rifle well out of reach, crouched next to Markham, and checked for a pulse.

He straightened. "He's dead."

"I can't say I'm sorry." Laredo joined him as Logan glanced into the tack room.

On top of the picnic hamper sat a wooden case that had held the rifle's disassembled parts. Seeing it, Laredo remarked, "Want to bet that hamper has a false bottom?"

"No, thanks. I don't like the odds." Logan stepped back from the doorway and glanced at the gun in Laredo's hand.

After an instant's hesitation, Laredo offered it to him, butt first. "I imagine you'll need this. That stall board over there will tell you it was a clear-cut case of self-defense."

"I know. I heard you shouting to draw Markham's fire." Logan held the gun for an indecisive moment, then leveled his gaze at Laredo. "I assume this isn't registered."

"Not hardly," he replied dryly.

"That's what I thought." Logan tucked it inside the waistband of his jeans. "It may be a bit easier for me to explain what I was doing with an unregistered firearm than it would be for you . . . considering you weren't here when the shooting took place. Right?"

"There are two boys who might say differently," Laredo reminded him, "although I'm grateful for the gesture."

They both knew his past wouldn't hold up to close scrutiny. Even if the shooting were ruled to be justifiable, there would likely be extradition papers waiting for him.

"Those are Triple C boys. They aren't going to say a word," Logan told him. He nodded toward the door. "Go on. Get out of here, and let Chase know what went down."

PART FOUR

A shifting wind
Blows soft and cool,
And once again
A Calder rules.

Epilogue

The horse herd swept over a rise in the plains, their summer-sleek coats rippling with muscle in the morning sunshine. With Hattie at his side, Chase sat atop the fence, the heels of his boots hooked on a lower rail. On either side of them was a twin.

"Here they come, Grampa!" Too excited to be satisfied straddling the top rail, Trey stood up to point at the approaching herd.

"I see them." It was something Chase had witnessed endless times in his life, but it was new to these three, allowing him to enjoy the spectacle through their eyes.

"Look at all the colors, Grampa," Laura marveled, staring wide-eyed at the glistening mix of sorrels, bays, grays, and buckskins.

"What a sight," Hattie exclaimed as the drumbeat of their hooves reached them, the sound of it like a low roll of thunder. "I'm glad you insisted I come watch."

His side glance moved over her with intimate warmth. "I never intended for you to spend all your time in the kitchen when I suggested that you do the cooking at The Homestead."

"What are you gonna do with all them horses, Grampa?" Laura frowned curiously as the herd swept toward the open gates to the big pen, accompanied by a quartet of riders.

"Roundup time is just around the corner. We'll need the extra horses to fill out each rider's string." But his answer sailed over her head, requiring a further explanation.

By the time he finished, the last of the horses had trotted into the pen and the gates were swung shut. Two of the out-riders peeled away from the gates and rode over to join them.

"Hi, Mom. Hi, 'Redo." Trey rushed the greeting. "Next time can I help get the horses? Me an' Joe, we could do it."

"We'll see," Jessy replied.

Trey took it as a "yes." "Yippee!" he shouted and launched himself off the fence. "Come on, Laura. Let's go look at the horses."

Hattie watched the pair race to the big pen. "Oh, to have that much energy again."

"Getting to be a dim memory, is it?"

Laredo teased, but his expression was much more serious when he directed his attention to Chase. "I saw Logan pull in earlier. What did he want?"

"He stopped by to give me an update on what they have learned so far about the scope of Markham's operation." The news of Monte's death had caused an initial flurry of headlines that had died within a few days. The ongoing investigation into his activities had garnered little media attention, but the ramifications of it were proving to be far-reaching. "The numbers they have right now indicate that Markham supposedly sold close to one hundred and fifty thousand head of cattle. So far they have located about thirty thousand. Which leaves over a hundred thousand head missing, at a value of roughly fifty million dollars. And that might be just the tip of the horn."

Laredo whistled softly when he heard the dollar figure. "No wonder he was so anxious to shut you up."

"What made him think he could get away with it?" That was the part Jessy didn't understand.

"He's been at it for at least the last seven years without anyone getting suspicious," Chase replied. "Maybe even longer than that."

"What about the shooting? Has anyone questioned it?" Laredo asked with a certain wariness.

Only three people knew the exact circumstances — Logan, Chase, and Laredo. And that is the way Chase wanted it to stay. "Anytime an officer is involved in a shooting there is always an investigation. Logan explained what happened and the evidence bears him out."

"I'm glad to hear it."

Jessy was too wise in the ways of a Calder not to read between the lines and guess at the real story. But she was also wise enough not to ask. She understood that it wasn't necessary for her to know the true facts.

"Then it's finally over, isn't it?" Jessy said.

"It's over," Chase confirmed. "You always told me you were going to stay for the duration, Laredo. I hope you know that you have a home here as long as you want it. But that's for you to decide."

When Laredo didn't immediately respond, Jessy felt a tightness in her chest. She wanted to speak up and insist that he stay. But she wasn't foolish enough to believe she could hold him if he wanted to leave. So she waited for his answer, tense, and braced for the worst.

Laredo tipped his head into the cool breeze that came out of the north. "If I get on it right away, I should be able to get the cabin insulated before winter sets in."

Relief soared through Jessy. She covered it with a surprised laugh. "You don't have to stay there," she protested.

"It suits a bachelor like me, peaceful and quiet, far from prying eyes." There was a twinkle in his blue eyes when Laredo looked at her, the kind that had her heart skipping a little faster. He added, almost as a warning, "It's for sure I don't belong up there." He nodded toward the big white house that overlooked the whole of the Triple C headquarters.

It was his way of making sure Jessy had no false expectations of what the future might hold for them. She understood that it wouldn't likely ever include marriage — not because of his pride, but because of his past.

Jessy directed her reply to Chase. "We better plan on getting a road built to the Boar's Nest as soon as we can get a crew on it."

"Good idea," Chase agreed. "In the meantime, you need to join us at dinner tonight for a little celebration, Laredo. Earlier this morning I received a call from my attorney —"

"Don't tell me," Jessy interrupted. "The courts have declared you are legally alive."

"Actually, they did, but he was calling to let me know they completed the title search and confirmed that Seth Calder was a former owner of Hattie's ranch in Texas," Chase explained. "She has agreed to sell it to me and bring it under the Calder brand again. That way she can't accuse me later on of marrying her to get my hands on it."

Jessy was too stunned by his decision to buy the ranch for the significance of his latter comment to register with her. "Are you serious? Are you really going to buy it? I didn't think the day would ever come when a Calder would go back to Texas."

"Then maybe it's time. He glanced sideways at Hattie, his smile alive with warmth and shared amusement.

About the Author

Janet Dailey has written over 100 novels and become one of the most popular female authors in the world, with 325 million copies of her books sold in nineteen languages in ninety-eight countries. She lives with her husband, Bill, in Branson, Missouri.